THE MONITOR

CATHY VASAS-BROWN

First Print Edition: January 2014
ISBN 13: 978-1493697496
ISBN 10: 1493697498 (10)

Visit: www.cathyvasasbrown.com
Cover and Formatting: Streetlight Graphics

In loving memory of John Storie Brown and (Sarah) May Brown, the two best in-laws I could ever have hoped for. The bid euchre games, the laughter, the stories and the cherry pie are greatly missed.

"We get so much in the habit of wearing disguises before others that we finally appear disguised before ourselves."
François de la Rochefoucauld

PROLOGUE

August 25, 2009
North Cascades National Park
Washington State
2 p.m.

He refocused his binoculars and smiled. The five were all in place now, the eldest and stoutest of the group having made several granddaddy stops along the mountain trail before finally joining the others on the wide ledge. The climb was steep but nothing they couldn't manage. He had made sure of that.

It was a marvelous day for a celebration. The sky was a vivid ultramarine, teased with spun wisps of clouds. Tufts of yellowed grass jutting from the side of the rock face barely moved in the still, cool air. Earlier in the month, when he was searching for the perfect location, he had flicked pebbles, like so many marbles, over the side of the cliff and swore he could hear each one as it bounced its way into the valley below. In the distance loomed the twin peaks of Mount Triumph and Mount Despair, and to the east, the ripsawed crags of the Pickett Range. He had heard that the first climbers of Triumph had ascended the peak by following five mountain goats to the top, enduring a volley of falling rock loosened by the animals from the path above. An amusing picture, he'd always thought, expending all that effort only to be conked on the head by a hailstorm of stones. A perfect Wile E. Coyote image.

The five were faring much better. They had been well prepared and well educated. They drank plenty of bottled water en route, having learned that giardia, a naturally occurring organism, could contaminate the most pristine-looking stream, river or lake. Though symptoms of the parasitic infection wouldn't appear for days, no one was risking a sudden attack of diarrhea while trekking to the summit.

Once again, he looked across the chasm at the group. They would be feeling the sun against their faces as they congratulated each other. One of the two women, barely out of a training bra and still battling acne, laid out a blanket on the smoothest section of rock; the other female, decades older, poured red wine into five plastic glasses, then arranged a mix of flowers into a crystal vase. They had each brought their favorites—white roses and lilies, yellow daisies, irises, and cushion mums. The older woman had brought elegant stationery as well—nothing too feminine, she had promised—and a clipboard.

There was plenty of food, too. Baguettes, cheese, fresh fruit, and—why the hell not?—a bag of Lays potato chips and a dozen Krispy Kreme donuts, which they devoured. And they had music. Some Bessie Smith, a little bluegrass, Pink Floyd's "Comfortably Numb"—this from the heavyset man—and a selection of tunes by The Cure provided by the bearded man wearing the torn denim, the one who least appeared to be in a partying mood. "No offense," he wrote last week when they'd all chatted online, "but I've gotta get into my own zone."

No offense taken, they'd posted back. They would respect what he needed to do.

They settled on the blanket, circling around a fat scented candle the young girl had removed from her backpack. The final male in the group—well-built, ruggedly attractive, and HIV positive—fished a joint from his shirt pocket and lit up. They all smoked. They finished the wine, played more music, talked. The girl, looking nervous, leaned toward the stout man then they both stood up and executed a passable waltz along the ledge, treading carefully. At the end of their dance, the man gave his partner a courtly bow. She raised her hand to her mouth. A shy giggle.

Some wrote. They wedged their completed pages beneath the candle that was much shorter now. The man in denim looked briefly at the others then reached forward, pinched out the flame. The party was breaking up. A fastidious group, each of them began to repack belongings into knapsacks, but the candle remained, the papers and flowers, too. And there was a framed photograph, added to the still life by the older woman.

The sun eased around the valley. Now it shone directly on the spot where they gathered. The group was on its feet. The women embraced, then the men. Except the one in denim who waited in silence.

They lined up, shoulder to shoulder. Boy-girl-boy-girl-boy. They joined hands. They faced Mount Despair. Seconds later, they stepped over the side in a perfectly choreographed swan dive, the sun not on their faces now, but on their backs as they plummeted to the rocky valley below. Exactly as instructed.

CHAPTER 1

November 25, 2009
Cypress Village, Oregon

Carolyn Latham, who dropped the Holt part of her surname when her husband dropped her, had been enjoying the first decent sleep she'd had in months when her bedside phone rang. Groggy, her mouth filled with what felt like duck feathers, she rolled over onto the stuffed animal that had become her constant bedmate. With the mini-halo of a four-watt nightlight to guide her, she groped for the receiver. "Whosit?"

"Who else would call you at this hour?" came the voice from the other end. "It's your favorite gypsy."

Sergeant Zygmunt Takacs. 2:30 a.m. This couldn't be good.

"You gotta come, C.L.," he said. "It's ugly. Worse than ugly."

Ziggy's next comment made Carolyn jolt upright. It couldn't be. "Where did you say?"

"You heard right," he said. "I'll be waiting for ya."

Carolyn went to her closet, felt around for denim, grabbed her jeans and stepped into them, the waistband inches too big now. Then she went to her dresser, flicked on the lamp and grabbed thick socks and the warmest sweater she could find. Maybe then she could stop shaking.

The Aerie. That's what Ziggy had said. Four teenagers, no ID, and a rented Neon filled with charcoal fumes parked in the driveway of a millionaire's getaway home. Carolyn shivered again. The place was cursed.

Minutes later she had located her hiking boots and started up her Explorer, pointing it in the direction of Signal Hill.

There were days when she still had to baby her arm. She favored the left one for mundane tasks: carrying groceries, pushing a vacuum cleaner, washing windows. She saved the right one for bigger things: writing out police schedules and shooting practice. Even an act as simple as waving to someone across the street could evoke that now familiar twinge, that constant reminder that she wasn't the same, not since a Smith & Wesson had ripped a hole in her shoulder, just about a year ago. At the Aerie. There were times too, usually in the middle of the night, when Carolyn would take shallow breaths, afraid that a full inhalation would elicit a searing chest pain, even though her doctor had assured her that her punctured lung had completely healed.

So that was good news. Better news? The bastard who'd shot her was in jail.

The road at the base of Signal Hill was lined with cars by the time Carolyn arrived. Now, to add to her already flesh-crawling shivers was a core-deep rage that threatened to explode when she spotted reporter Fallon McBride's white Ford Escape among the vehicles. Yellow tape stretched across the entry to the estate's driveway, but it would take more than the words CRIME SCENE DO NOT CROSS to deter Fallon. A croc-filled moat might slow her down, but not for long. Carolyn hoped some well-muscled cop was ushering McBride away from the scene now, hopefully with a Taser aimed at her ass.

Partway up the hill, Carolyn was met by a sweet-faced patrol officer. He introduced himself as Ben Mitchell, first on the scene, and despite the chilled November air, he wiped sweat from his brow. "It's bad, C.L.," he said using her initials too familiarly, since he was brand new to the force and they'd hardly spoken. C.L., she reasoned, was a much better moniker than her previous handle, Rambette.

"One of 'em's no more than fifteen." The officer talked a nervous streak the rest of the way up the hill, filling every silence. "Two guys. Two girls. And something else? They're all dressed up. I mean really dressed up. Guys wearing suits. Girls in long gowns with their hair done. Like a prom night gone wrong, you know?"

Keep talking, Carolyn thought. Keep talking so you won't see me shake. Won't see that I'd rather be anywhere than here.

"Serious about dying, too. Had enough charcoal on that hibachi to cook sausage for an entire Eye-talian family reunion. Put electrical tape around the inside of the doors. Taped over the vents, too. Car was sealed airtight. Pretty effective gas chamber, but you'll see for yourself."

Carolyn didn't want to see it, didn't want to believe that not one but four teenagers had decided that life wasn't worth the trouble. She didn't want to face the long night ahead, knowing that eventually she would be knocking on doors, telling worried parents their child wouldn't be coming home. Carolyn, so preoccupied with her ex-husband's impending marriage, and especially his new baby, had trouble enough finishing sentences these days, frequently halting in midstream, even mid-word, her thoughts fragmented, jumbled. How would she ever find the right words when she looked into those parents' eyes?

"I'm sorry to have to tell you that ..."

"There's no easy way ..."

"I'm Sergeant Latham, and I'm afraid I have some terrible news ..."

Lame, lamer, lamest.

The long gravel driveway curved and the Aerie came into view, a custom-built river rock and shingle house, the same five thousand square-foot hellhole where she'd been ambushed by a lunatic. She quelled a series of shudders that scudded up her spine and wondered how many aftershocks she would have to endure. She had pulled through. She was in one piece. Wasn't she?

"No wallets, no ID," Ben Mitchell continued, nudging Carolyn back to the present. From one hellhole to the next. "It's like they wanted to disappear."

"No," Carolyn said, finding her voice. "If that were true, they wouldn't have come here. Wouldn't have dressed up."

She took the flashlight Mitchell offered. Even before she approached the car, saw the bodies, she knew. "This is about punishment. These kids are sending a message."

"Ah, shit. Son of a bitch. Goddammit."

"You disagree?"

He was looking over her shoulder. "How did that parasite get up here? I stopped her at the bottom of the hill, told her we were securing the scene."

Carolyn whirled around to face the object of Ben Mitchell's grimace. Fallon McBride, looking too well groomed, too trim, too exuberant for this hour, was trying to coax a statement from Sergeant Zygmunt Takacs and a grey-haired couple standing next to him.

"I've got nothing for you at this time, Ms. McBride," Carolyn heard Ziggy tell the reporter as she drew nearer. "And if you continue to get in our way and disrespect both this crime scene and the job of the police, I promise you'll be writing the recipe column for a paper somewhere in the bleakest, most godforsaken corner of Alaska."

"And Sergeant Takacs will have the full support of his department, Ms. McBride," Carolyn said, now close enough to see Fallon's sooty eyelashes, long and thick enough to look good without mascara, damn her hide. "What we can tell you right now is that you will accompany Officer Mitchell here back to your car and you will leave this area." She ushered McBride a good distance away from Ziggy and the couple.

"You know I always cooperate with the police, Sergeant," McBride said, smiling too widely, her teeth perfect. "But you have something I can print?"

"Oh, sure. It goes like this. You'll write that four unidentified youths have been found in an isolated area north of the village. Police are investigating and trying to determine the identity of the teenagers—" Carolyn squinted through the darkness to peer inside the car, her throat tightening as she beheld the four still figures before looking away again "—two males and two females. What I do not want is a headline on the pages of the *Examiner* with the word 'suicide' in it. And nowhere in your article will I see a description of the method by which these young people died."

"Oh, really, Sergeant. Why don't you just write the article for me?"

"If I had the time, I would. What I'm asking you to do is accept a degree of responsibility. I know what you've seen here, Ms. McBride, and I'm pissed that you've seen it. But what I don't want is to be awakened from a sound sleep on another night and have to do this all over again. Exposure to suicide methods in the media can do a lot of damage, and copycats we do not need. There's a vast difference between reporting the news and providing some depressed reader with a formula for dying. Do I make myself clear?"

"Looks like we've all got our work cut out for us," was Fallon's only reply then she obediently followed Ben Mitchell back down the long driveway, her sculpted behind proof that the money for her gym membership had been well spent.

Carolyn felt a sickening thud in her already hollow stomach. If Fallon put her mind to it, she could be trouble.

"Sergeant Latham," Ziggy said when Carolyn turned toward them, "this is Gary and Noelle Lynch. They live on the adjacent property, about a half mile down the road. They called this in."

The Lynches had their backs to the vehicle. Mrs. Lynch looked ready to heave. Her husband kept his arm protectively around her waist. They told Carolyn the same thing they'd told Ziggy. They were returning from seeing a movie around midnight when they spotted a red Neon turning into the Aerie's driveway. They didn't think too much about it at first, figuring that the absentee owner must have been paying someone to watch his property. But about an hour later, when they let their dog out for a pee, they noticed the car was still parked near the house and none of the Aerie's lights were on. They wondered if they should do anything about it, thought maybe it was a couple of teenagers up there making out, just like in the days before the owner had built on the land. Ignoring it didn't sit well with Mrs. Lynch, so they decided to check things out and found the car, with its four occupants dead.

"We didn't touch anything," Gary Lynch said. "I had my cell with me and we called right away."

Ziggy had been thorough. Carolyn had little else to ask the couple, so she thanked them for their time and helpfulness, assured them they had done the right thing and could not have known when the Neon made that turn into the driveway that the intent of its passengers was something so dreadful. They felt guilty nonetheless.

"We should have checked it out sooner. Should have been better neighbors."

Carolyn told Ziggy she would walk the couple back home, though the Lynches insisted they were fine. Carolyn's wishes overrode their insistence; she wanted them to follow the same path down the gravel drive that Officer Mitchell and Fallon McBride had just taken. It wouldn't do to have the Lynches take a short cut through the brush and wooded area, attaching scraps of wool from sweaters and hats to bare branches which the officers might misconstrue as evidence.

They had barely turned to go back down the drive when Carolyn stopped dead. She had almost missed it. If she'd been talking, distracted, she would have. To the right of the driveway was a stand of Douglas fir, their needles still glistening from the early evening rain. But among the evergreens the ground had been disturbed, the wet grass trampled into a rectangle. She tried to suppress a shiver. Could not.

Carolyn remained rooted to the gravel, about six feet from the spot. She spun around and looked toward the house as another seismic ripple traveled up her back. Her mind was clear now. If she stood on the flattened spot she realized that Ziggy, standing beside the Neon, wouldn't be able to see her. She would have been protected by the dense fir branches.

Had someone else been protected, too? Earlier tonight, had someone stood—or perhaps even sat, on this very spot?

At once she crouched and swung the flashlight's beam in a slow arc beneath the trees. About twenty feet ahead, near the trunk of one of the evergreens, she saw it. Cautioning the Lynches to remain where they were, Carolyn ducked under the low branches. She crouched at the base of the tree and with gloved hands, picked up a fat cork from a champagne bottle. The cork was clean, not muddied by the elements, not wet. And it had been a rainy week.

Someone had sat here, celebrating. Recently. With a bottle of Dom Perignon.

One of the four in the car? Police would check for muddy shoes, grass-stained clothes. If they found neither, another possibility existed.

Someone had watched those four young people die.

CHAPTER 2

busridersforum.com
November 22, 2009 03:15
Join date: March 16, 2009
Location: Nevada
Posts: 33
Jackpot
Suicidal Tendencies
My mind is a hurricane, with constant chaos swirling within me. I used to worry about my family, what they would feel, how they would manage without me, but I don't think about that anymore. Now I just want to shut everything off. I want to sleep. I want to die.

November 22, 2009 03:32
Join Date: October 20, 2009
Location: Utah
Posts: 15
Pilgrim
Suicidal Tendencies
I hear you, Jackpot, and I understand. I pray constantly that I'll fall asleep and not wake up, but every day, the world shows up, and I fear my secret will be exposed. I can't go on much longer. I'm ready to CTB, but I'm so afraid. I've always been afraid. I don't want to die alone. Are you really ready?

Jackpot's response was brief. *I am ready.*

The Monitor had been privy to Jackpot's whining for months and had followed his threats to jump from the balcony of a casino penthouse. Wah wah wah. So you want to die, Jackpot? And Pilgrim? At your service. He read on with glee.

November 22, 2009 03:49
Join Date: September 20, 2009
Location: Oregon
Posts: 30
Nightshade
Suicidal Tendencies
Glad Pilgrim spoke up. Makes what I have to say easier. These last two months, I've been telling you about my dysfunctional family, how they've been driving me crazy, how rotten it is to have parents and step-parents. You've all been trying to help, but I've been wasting your time, and I'm sorry. The truth is, my parents are terrific. They're not divorced; they've been married for twenty years. Everything I've told you about them is a lie. In fact, my life is a lie, and if anybody knew who I really am, *what* I really am, it would kill them. So I'll take my secret to the grave, maybe sooner than you think.

November 22, 2009 04:07
Join Date: November 2, 2009
Location: British Columbia
Posts: 10
Geezer
Suicidal Tendencies
Nightshade, don't take this the wrong way, but you sound young. I know life really can suck, and problems always look worse around

Christmas, when all the jolly people try to turn everything into a Norman Rockwell card.

You said your parents are terrific. Won't they love you no matter what your secret is? I'm trying to tell you to give yourself more time. Catching the bus is a one-way ticket. Would you still feel like ending it if you hadn't found us? Think about it. Please.

Me, I'm fifty-five and in a different kind of hell, in chronic physical pain since a drunk driver sideswiped my car the day I turned thirty. Ever slam the car door on your hand? My entire body feels like that all the time. I've drunk, I've drugged, I've done everything to try and get rid of the agony. After only three days on Effexor, my depression was so bad I wanted to ram my car into a concrete wall. I've had procaine injected into my trigger points—more agony. I can't sleep, can't even cover myself with a sheet at night. Can't stand wearing a wristwatch. Can't bear to be touched. My ex-wife said it was like being married to a walking, breathing corpse. So now I'm alone, stuck in a body that's declared war on me. But not for much longer. I'll be buying my ticket soon. Spare my kids having that discussion about 'what to do with pop.'

Nightshade, I've suffered for twelve years, and I've run out of choices. I know the decision I've made is right. Do you think you can wait? At least a little while? Maybe things will work out for you. I hope so. You hang in there.

It didn't take long for the site moderator, Bella Donna, to respond to Geezer's post.

Nightshade is communicating on this forum because she's in pain too—maybe not the same way you are, but it's just as real to her. She needs affirmation, not condemnation. We're all about choices here, not browbeating someone into changing his/her mind, no matter how well-intentioned. Consider yourself warned—remember the rules of this message board.

Thou shalt not deter someone from killing himself. That Bella Donna was a good sport. The Monitor grinned and added his own post to the mix.

Nightshade, you'll know when the time is right, just as I will. As an elderly woman suffering from terminal cancer, I've come to the end, except my body doesn't know it. I'm making final preparations now. Anyone looking for someone to travel with can PM me. It will be nice to ride the bus with caring friends.

P.S. Jim Stark, where are you?

The Monitor continued to read the postings on the Suicidal Tendencies thread until well past midnight, but the elusive Jim Stark didn't materialize. A freelancer? Impossible. Stark was too much of a coward to check out on his own.

In the Monitor's mind, magnificent wheels turned in perfect synchronicity. He tapped a pen against his temple. So Pilgrim had secrets, did she? And little Nightshade too. They all did, he suspected. Deep, dark, terrible secrets. But not for long.

And poor Pilgrim didn't want to die alone.

He would see that she didn't have to. For those troubled members of the flock—Nightshade, Pilgrim, Jackpot, Geezer and Jim Stark—he would plan something extraordinary. Something excruciating.

They were ripe for the picking.

CHAPTER 3

Carolyn yawned. "Tell me, Zig, how bad is it?" She added milk to her fourth cup of coffee. She must have looked like hell, judging from the collection of Styrofoam cups lined up on her desk.

"Java for you, C.L.," one of the officers had said earlier, depositing a cup. "Pick you right up," said another cup bearer, half an hour later. As yet, the caffeine had done little except distend her bladder.

"Eyes are toting some serious baggage," Ziggy admitted. "But on you it looks good. Me, I'd prescribe a good long nap, preferably under a palm tree someplace."

"Not an option. But a shower would sure feel good."

"Breakfast first," Ziggy said, grabbing his jacket from the back of a chair. "Croissant or danish?"

"Neither. Thanks. You go ahead."

They had worked through the night, getting decent photographs of the four deceased teens, as much as photos of dead people could be decent. These, along with thorough descriptions of their clothing, identifying scars, piercings, bunions and warts, had been sent to the state's Missing and Unidentified Persons unit as well as the National Crime Information Center. By the next afternoon they had learned the identity of three of the teens, all from out of state. Each had been reported missing within the past few days. Local police had the ugly job of telling the parents, sparing Carolyn that agony.

Heavy-duty liaising with investigators in Idaho, Massachusetts, and California provided Carolyn with abridged biographies of the known victims. Kevin Randolph, 18, lived in Marblehead. He arrived in Cypress Village on Sunday, having booked a flight from Boston to San Francisco the day before. There was no shortage of money in the Randolph household—Leland Randolph was an investment banker; his wife June ran a successful decorating business with her sister. Kevin, the Randolph's only child, had been raised with tennis lessons, sailing lessons, riding lessons. An empty bottle of single malt scotch had been found on the floor of the rental car the four had died in, courtesy of the Randolphs' liquor cabinet. The suit Kevin had been found in bore a Zegna label. That he had chosen to die was incomprehensible. The Randolphs were devastated. And why so far from home, they wanted to know.

The second boy, fifteen-year-old Tim Schultz, was from Eureka. Though he didn't have Kevin Randolph's pedigree, Schultz was no slouch. He was a solid student, a dedicated athlete, and popular with his classmates—this according to his mother. His younger sisters adored him. Signs of depression? Weren't all teenagers subject to dark moods once in awhile? Mrs. Schultz responded when questioned.

Heather Conklin had taken a bus from Boise, Idaho, on the 23rd. The ticket taker remembered the seventeen-year-old clearly. He wondered why such a pretty young girl was traveling alone, and why she wasn't in school. Boise police said Heather was a rising star on the local arts scene, an accomplished ballerina who still found time to volunteer at a seniors' center.

All good kids. At least, that's how they appeared on the surface.

The fourth victim was still a mystery. She was a mousy brunette—butt ugly, as one of the officers said before Carolyn froze him with a stare—with the belly flab that spoke of too many fast-food meals. Even in her best dress, a pale mauve, floor-length with an empire waist, and with her hair carefully styled, the girl hadn't quite pulled off a dance-with-me look. Her fingernails, painted mauve to match her dress, were chewed to nubs, and the make-up she'd applied didn't fully conceal her flaming case of acne. Not the type of girl that Kevin Randolph would look twice at, or Tim Schultz, for that matter.

I hope they had the class to tell you that you looked beautiful, Carolyn remembered thinking. I hope you felt like a princess, just once before you died.

Carolyn needed to find out who this girl was, how long she had been missing and why no one seemed to know she was gone. She also needed to learn how the teens had met and how they had come to choose dying in Oregon. At the Aerie.

She thought about the girls' hair. They were elegantly coiffed, the nameless girl with sparkles throughout her updo. Carolyn glanced at her watch. 4:00. Salons were still open for business, and in Cypress Village, population 5500, there weren't many places to go for a cut-and-blow-dry. Hetty's catered to the blue-rinse set, and Mister Jack was a men-only establishment. Minutes after Ziggy's exit, Carolyn reached for her own jacket and headed straight for Swan, a trendy day spa in the center of the village.

Inside the spa, the sounds of sea birds and rushing water wafted from speakers. A woman, clad in a white terry robe and slippers, padded by on her way to one of the treatment rooms. A burning candle emitted a pleasing mix of almond and vanilla.

Carolyn's stylist, Angie, greeted her.

"You were just in two weeks ago. Problem with your cut?"

Carolyn shook her head. "Business this time, I'm afraid. Do you recognize either of these girls?" She held out a pair of photographs.

Angie's face fell. "Oh God, no." Angie told Carolyn a client had come in earlier, sputtering horrific news about the fate of four teens on Signal Hill.

In the village, word spread like a grease fire.

Carolyn's notepad came out. "Tell me what you remember."

Angie swallowed hard, unable to look away from the photos. "They were both here yesterday. Three o'clock. Hair, make-up, manicures. This one was my client." She carefully touched the face of the victim as yet unnamed. "Wendy looked after the other girl."

Carolyn waited, avoiding the temptation to fill the silence with badgering questions. She allowed Angie to collect her emotions and her thoughts.

"They were sweet kids," she said eventually. "Very kind to each other, you know, telling each other how nice they looked. But not gushing or overly excited. None of that giggly stuff we sometimes get from young clients. I remember thinking it odd that they were getting so gussied up. It's not prom season. I figured they must have been going to a family wedding or something, but who gets married on a Wednesday?"

"Did you ask where they were going?"

Angie nodded. "They just said it was a very special night. They're the ones, aren't they, Carolyn. The ones you found up on the hill."

Carolyn simply closed her eyes a good long moment, answer enough.

"It just can't be," Angie said. "People with plans for the future don't kill themselves. Isn't that what they say? Those appointments were made nearly a month ago."

"What?"

Angie flipped back in the appointment book, lying open on top of the reception desk. "Yes, look. Here are their names. They booked online."

"How do you know that?"

Angie turned the book around to face Carolyn. "See? We always enter the code OL, meaning 'online,' whenever someone books from their computer. It's a way for us to track how effective our website is."

"The names. Jill Munroe and Susie Cox. That's how they booked?"

"Yes—wait a minute. That can't be right."

Carolyn kept her mouth shut, bit her lip.

Angie cast her gaze to the ceiling, winced, as if the pained expression would force the appropriate memory forward. "No, no, no. Not right at all. When the girls were finished, Wendy's client turned to mine and said, 'Oh, Brenda, you look terrific!'"

Carolyn's pen scratched across the page. "How did they pay? Did you see who picked them up?"

"Cash," Angie replied. "And a nice tip, too, which I felt funny about taking because of their age, but they insisted. I thought their parents must have given them the money. I told them to have a good time and that was it. I had another client, so I didn't see if anyone was waiting for them at the curb or anything. I'm sorry. So very sorry. They were really nice girls."

Another robed woman emerged from the back of the spa and sat in a black swivel chair before a long mirror. Angie's next client. Carolyn thanked the visibly shaken stylist, told her to take care and call her if she remembered anything else.

In her car, Carolyn made sure the radio was turned off. No distractions, not now. The girls had planned their deaths, at least a month in advance. Had made appointments for a specific day. A special day, they'd said. An anniversary? A birthday? What was so special about November 25th? And when did Kevin and Tim enter the picture?

Four teenagers. From at least three different states. Carolyn wasn't even a full twenty-four hours into the case and already the investigation was leaving a rancid, metallic taste in her mouth. Perhaps the 25th was special only because that was the day they had all chosen to die. Kevin, Tim, Heather, and ... Brenda.

A good hair stylist was worth her weight in precious stones. Angie had always been a good listener. Attentive to her clients' needs. And bright. She had remembered immediately that Jill and Susie weren't Jill and Susie. Heather Conklin had let her friend's real name slip. For some reason, Heather's pseudonym bothered her, too. Jill Munroe. Where had she heard that before? At least now Carolyn had one more scrap of information she hadn't had twenty minutes ago.

A first name. And a bone to toss at Fallon McBride.

CHAPTER 4

"TOWN'S GONE TO RATSHIT," STAN Gardner said.

Joshua poured juice for his neighbor and didn't disagree. Over breakfast, both men had read Fallon McBride's story in the previous day's *Clatsop County Examiner* about the four dead teenagers. Breakfast and news chat were an early Friday morning ritual for Joshua Latham and seventy-year-old Stan, a ritual Joshua was glad he'd initiated. His fiancée, Paige, didn't complain about the Male Bonding Breakfasts at Stan's either, claiming that having Joshua out of the house gave her an extra hour alone to lie in bed and be ugly and stinky before he came back to pick her up for work.

Today the men were having scrambled eggs and whole wheat toast with strawberry jam that Stan had made himself, an accomplishment, Joshua suspected, because Stan's hands were shaking pretty badly these days. "Your sister needs this case like she needs herpes," Stan said. "How's her shoulder treating her?"

"She doesn't complain about it, but I know it still hurts sometimes. Like when it rains."

"Which means she's in pain from November until March. Goddamn. Must have been awful for her, going back to that same place where she got shot to investigate the deaths of those four kids. What do you suppose possessed 'em?"

Joshua shook his head. Since leaving the seminary and becoming a social worker, Joshua had seen depressed kids by the truckload. Abused or neglected at home, ignored or bullied at school, the kids often ended up at Friends of Families, seeking asylum. They were considered "at risk" by their teachers, burdensome by their parents, losers by their peers. 3F House, as everyone had come to call it, serviced teens from Oregon's north-coast communities and was a place they could hang out for an hour or two, talk out problems with a counselor, maybe play a game of chess to help escape the negative self-talk that plagued the kids during most of their waking hours. Yet, as miserable as many of them were, they were hanging in there, finding something in the challenging world around them to cling to.

"Maybe they thought that life gets to be too much sometimes."

Stan rose to get more coffee and Joshua thought of Lily Howard, who never missed a counseling session at 3F House. Lily had endured more agony than those twice her age. When she was fifteen, the modest frame house she had lived in with her mother caught fire. Lily survived the blaze by climbing out her bedroom window. Her mother, overcome by smoke and disoriented, struggled to find an exit. From the flat roof of the garage Lily screamed, urging her mother to follow the sound of her voice. For brief minutes, her mother screamed back then Lily heard the worst sound of all—silence. When firefighters pulled the body from the wreckage, they saw Mrs. Howard's blackened handprints marking a desperate path along a corridor wall, moving in the wrong direction. Two years later, Lily still had nightmares, still awoke to the smell of smoke, heard the crackle-snap of flames. Entries on her blog were dark, disturbing, and fraught with verbal flagellation—an errant lit cigarette from Lily's pack of Virginia Slims Superslims had caused the fire that had killed her mother. For Lily, life really was too much.

Stan returned with the coffeepot and poured. "A shame to give up, especially at that age. How did those kids know something better wasn't around the next corner?"

Joshua shrugged, guessing that the next corner was simply too far away. There were days when he wondered if anyone was completely happy anymore. Then he would cross the threshold to the log cabin next door, throw his arms around Paige and realize that at least he could count himself among the lucky.

"Like that bunch in Washington," Stan continued, putting jam on another piece of toast. "Remember those five people, did that flying Wallenda routine off the side of the cliff? 'Suppose you read they didn't even know each other. Met on the Internet, decided to buy the farm together. 'Collective illness,' I think one of the papers said. I guess misery really does love company."

That was the profound nugget Fallon McBride had used to begin this morning's article. The reporter had written, too, about a phenomenon known as the "Werther effect," so named after the publication of Goethe's *The Sorrows of Young Werther* in 1774, in which many young men emulated the title character's suicide, prompting a ban of the book in several countries. Collective illness indeed. And highly contagious.

McBride had painted a grisly mental picture for *Examiner* readers—the teens had "gone out in style," dressed to impress. If they were unable to make a mark in their young lives, they had certainly made one in death. Celebrity status. Except these celebrities, at press time, were still nameless.

"Teenagers crave attention," came the quote Fallon gleaned from a noteworthy area psychiatrist, who expressed profound shock and sadness when he heard the news. "Adolescent commiseration is a common trait," Dr. Samuel J. Risk explained, "a teenager's way of discovering where he belongs. But when commiseration is centered on mutual despair and hopelessness, the repercussions can be tragic."

Joshua was reaching for the milk pitcher when he glanced over at the small television set on Stan's counter. His friend, Risk, was being interviewed on "Daybreak Portland." He asked Stan to turn up the volume.

Risk's dark beard and thick black hair were impeccably groomed. He wore a crisp blue shirt with a white collar, but Joshua knew that Risk was equally comfortable in jeans and a T-shirt and that he wasn't above hoisting a few beers and cooking up a batch of chili for Super Bowl parties. "All teenagers seek a mirror for their experiences," Risk was saying. "When that mirror reflects others who also feel isolated and disillusioned, they may decide that death is the only solution. And in a group, dying becomes less frightening. Sometimes a public display, like the one in Cypress Village, is an effort to give death a sense of meaning and purpose."

When questioned by the interviewer about the recent group suicide that had occurred in Washington state and the belief that the deaths were the result of an Internet pact, Risk went on to add that he had grave questions about the press even alerting the public to such a disturbing occurrence.

"The doc makes good sense," Stan told Joshua. "Shouldn't print this kind of stuff in the papers. Just gives people ideas."

The interview concluded with Risk listing the warning signs of someone in danger of committing suicide, among them a recent upswing in mood after a period of depression, giving away possessions, withdrawal, lack of self-care. Parents were urged to keep the lines of communication open at home and to insist on medical help for any child thought to be suffering from symptoms of depression. The program's host added that anyone having information about the identity of any missing area teenagers was asked to call local police.

Joshua glanced at his watch, polished off the rest of his toast and gulped coffee. "Time for me to get a move on. Need anything from town today, Stan?"

"Can't think of anything, 'cept maybe a busty blonde housekeeper."

Last week Stan's request had been for a nicely stacked redhead who could bake a decent pie. Joshua laughed. "I'll see what I can do."

Forty minutes later, Joshua was encamped in his office. Friends of Families was located in a turn-of-the-century house on one of the least gentrified streets in Cypress Village. Inside, the characteristic Victorian trimmings remained—high baseboards, ornate staircase, wide-planked floors. The home's original living and dining room were designated quiet areas, where the kids could get homework done, play a board game, read in peace. The third floor, a twenty-by-twenty-foot space with a sloped ceiling, was reserved for group meetings, in-the-round discussions that were scheduled every Monday and Wednesday at seven o'clock.

Joshua enjoyed being in his office first thing in the morning. He had the room at the front of the house, its bay window affording him a nice view of the treetops. The house was quiet then; the other counselors didn't report for duty until two, giving him a blessed few hours to sort through mail, respond to e-mail and return phone calls. His rear end had barely warmed the chair when his phone rang.

The caller identified himself as Ken Ishiguro, a visiting lecturer in Japanese studies at Willamette University in Salem. He had heard about the work Joshua did with area teenagers and wondered if he could help his nephew.

"He's very depressed," Ishiguro said. "And after reading about those young people and how they died ..."

Joshua should have mentally prepared for this. Fallon's article would have every parent pressing the panic button, concerned that their teenager's moodiness might be something more serious. Well, better that than not to care at all. Joshua had certainly seen his share of that sort of parent. But Ishiguro had said nephew, not son.

"Excuse me, Mr. Ishiguro," Joshua said, jotting the name down, not trusting his memory, "but you said your nephew is depressed? Usually, clients are referred to me by their teachers or family doctors ..."

"Yoshi doesn't go to school. He's seventeen. And he won't see a doctor. Only you. I showed him an article about you from the newspaper."

Yoshi refused to see a doctor? Therein could be the root of the problem. Depressed or not, Yoshi was running the show. "And Yoshi's parents? Do they think their son's depressed?"

"Yes, yes, they know of Yoshi's problem. That's why he's staying with me in America. They can't handle him. He's bringing much embarrassment to his family."

"Yoshi's parents live ..."

"In Japan. Hirakata. A small town between Osaka and Kyoto. But Yoshi loves America and everything about it. When I moved here in August, I agreed to bring my sister's son with me, thinking the change would do him good."

"But there's been no improvement."

Joshua heard only a sigh from the other end of the phone. "Perhaps," Ishiguro said eventually, "you should see for yourself."

Joshua ran an index finger down his day planner, looking for an opening. He might be able to set something up later in the day, once the rest of the staff arrived. Then Yoshi could see how the centre was being run, maybe meet some of the other kids as well as have enough time for Joshua to assess the young man's needs. "Could you have your nephew here at 4:30 today?"

"No, no. It's impossible."

Joshua was flipping the page in his Day Timer now, scanning for spaces between his colorful chicken-scratched entries. "I'm afraid the next available time won't be until next Wednesday. Same time. 4:30."

"No, that won't work. Yoshi is hikkii."

"Excuse me?"

"He doesn't leave his room. He hasn't almost since the day he arrived here. And not for the last year in Japan. My nephew is *hikikomori*. You will have to come to him."

"I'm sorry, Mr.—" he glanced at his paper "—Ishiguro. But perhaps you're familiar with the expression 'I don't make house calls.' Friends of Families and its counselors work strictly from our location here on Sutter Lane. Perhaps you could check our website, read our mission statement—"

"I already know everything I need to know," Ishiguro said abruptly. "You will change your mind."

Joshua heard the resounding click in his ear. He hung up as well. Hikikomori? Was that the term the man had used? And what did it mean? Joshua wrote the word on a scrap of paper, guessing at the spelling.

The uncle had said Yoshi hadn't left his room. Not the apartment, his *room*. How could that be? The boy had to eat, use a washroom. And what about his friends?

Intrigued, puzzled, and just a little pissed at having had someone hang up on him, Joshua booted up his computer then typed in the word "hikikomori." Within minutes he found himself immersed in a culture he knew nothing about, held rapt by the reasons why over a million Japanese youth were taking to their rooms and refusing to come out. "Japan's Lost Generation," one article called the hikikomori youth, and Joshua was nearly finished reading it when he heard the downstairs door open, then shut. Only 8:45. One of the other counselors? Faye always announced her arrival with a cheery hello-it's-me up the stairs, and Robb's trademark greeting was "Hey ho, let's go." Hearing neither and feeling a niggle of concern, Joshua swiveled in his chair. "Hello?"

He heard soft footfall on the stairs, someone treading cautiously, unsure. Then a slightly built Asian man appeared in the doorway to his office and introduced himself. Joshua rose and shook the hand of Ken Ishiguro.

CHAPTER 5

It was a characterless, ground floor apartment in a drab, low-rise building, but Ken Ishiguro hadn't been looking for charm when he rented the place in August. He told Joshua his priorities were a reasonable price tag and privacy in a location far enough away from his teaching colleagues at Willamette and anyone else who might be tempted to drop by for a visit. Unit 104 adhered to the standard apartment blueprint—L-shaped living-dining area, a galley kitchen, two bedrooms and a bathroom down a dark hall. No surprises here, Joshua thought at first, but he was wrong. Entering the second bedroom was like being struck in the face with a shovel.

He was at once gripped by the pervasive stench of body odor. Then his eyes adjusted to the dim light and beheld the curious surroundings. The walls were painted flat black, a backdrop for the collection of posters that lined the room. The place was a shrine to James Dean. There were several posters of the actor, one in partial profile with Dean clutching the V-neck of a torn sweater, another of him playing chess, yet another of him sprawled across a leather chair.

Comic books towered in corners; they were stacked on the bedside table; they fanned across the single bed. A power bar held plugs for a microwave, toaster, mini-fridge. Techno-gadgetry occupied another area—a plasma TV, a cell phone, a Sony PlayStation. A computer sat on a desk in the corner, its screen saver a Japanese cartoon character karate-chopping his way from left to right. The land of the rising gizmo.

It was ten p.m. Most people Joshua knew would be winding down for the evening, exhausted after rigorous days at school or work. At ten o'clock, some hikikomori were just waking up.

Joshua asked himself how he had allowed himself to be talked into this. He was the charity's director. He oversaw the work of the other counselors, got constant updates on the teens in their care, but he rarely took on a kid's case himself. And he had never visited one of the youth at home. He repeated as much to Ishiguro, protesting that his nephew's illness might be beyond his scope of expertise and that perhaps the boy needed a psychiatrist. He had been reaching for his Rolodex to give Ishiguro the number of a therapist when the diminutive man held up his hand. "No. It must be you. Yoshi will only see you."

Within Joshua was a can't-say-no gene. Since childhood, he'd been a champion of the underdog, defending classmates from playground bullies, choosing the weakest athletes first to be on his gym squad. At age eleven, he'd lassoed his parents and twin sister Carolyn into organizing a blanket drive for Portland's homeless, and he cajoled hotels and discount stores into providing bottles of shampoo and bars of soap for people living on the streets. The Lathams "Takin' It To The Streets" project had been featured in the *Oregonian.* For Joshua, turning his back on someone in need had never been an option. Now here he was.

He thought briefly of Paige, propped up in bed reading a book, wearing something silky. She had shot him a wistful smile as he left. He could probably be having great sex now instead of staring at the walls of a James Dean funhouse.

A gaunt youth wearing an oversized Polo hoodie and jeans peered from behind a folding screen.

"This is my nephew, Yoshitomo Tagawa," Ken Ishiguro said. While Joshua reached out for a jive handshake, the finger-curl clutch, Ken was already excusing himself. "I'll leave you two to get to know each other." Then the door shut.

Joshua's hand was still extended but Yoshi hadn't shaken it. The boy had disappeared back behind the screen. Joshua cast another glance around the room, noticed for the first time that the window was covered with a dark blanket. "I like what you've done to the place."

The young man said, "I called Martha Stewart, but she was booked solid." His voice was flat, expressionless.

Joshua smiled at nobody. "The good ones always are. Mind if I pull up some carpet?"

"Whatever."

Joshua dropped from where he stood, settling cross-legged onto a comic-book-free zone in the middle of a small rug. He sensed the young man was now seated as well.

"My name's Joshua. Big James Dean fan, huh?"

From the other side of the screen, silence.

"It'd be easier to talk if you came out from behind there."

But Yoshi didn't emerge. So Joshua recited what he knew about James Dean, his love for fast cars, his interest in photography, his relationship with Liz Sheridan, the actress who played Jerry Seinfeld's mother on television. "Three films in just over a year. Two Oscar nominations."

There was no way of knowing whether Yoshi was impressed with Joshua's knowledge of his idol. Joshua searched his memory. "*Giant. East of Eden* ..."

"*Rebel Without a Cause*," Yoshi added, his voice expressionless. "Seen it fifteen times."

"Imagine what he could have accomplished if he'd lived."

"'If he can live on after he's dead, then maybe he was a great man,'" Yoshi told him. "Dean said that. Dying turns a lot of people into legends."

Joshua noted how fluently Yoshi spoke English. All Japanese began to learn the language in the seventh grade, but Joshua expected to encounter a stumble, a misused word, an incorrect verb tense. Was it the boy's admiration for America that made him want to speak its language so expertly? His worship of James Dean? Perhaps chat rooms, e-mail and television were Yoshi's teachers.

"I'd settle for being less legendary, but alive," Joshua said.

"'There is no way to be truly great in this world. We are all impaled on the crook of conditioning.' Dean said that too," Yoshi told him in his flat voice. "He rocks big time."

Joshua tried to steer the conversation away from Dean but Yoshi refused to be engaged. It was James Dean or no one. More minutes ticked by. From behind the screen, a banana peel was lobbed in the direction of the wastepaper basket but it missed its target, landing on a comic book.

After a long awkward silence Joshua said, "What has your uncle told you about this visit, Yoshi?"

"Not much."

"You know I'm a social worker ..."

Nothing.

"And that I've been asked to help you. Get you to work through some of your problems."

"Who says I have problems?"

"Yoshi, you can't live like this, in here, forever."

"Why not?"

"It has its limitations."

"Advantages too."

"Enlighten me."

Joshua wished he could see Yoshi's face. Was he rolling his eyes, humoring his uncle by allowing this greenhorn Westerner into the sanctum? Was there a grimace, a pinched frown to indicate he couldn't wait for this to be over? Yoshi's voice was giving nothing away. It was a one-note drone—no inflection, no commas, no periods. There were a lot of words, but nothing Joshua hadn't already learned from the boy's uncle. He wondered how talkative Yoshi would be without the screen separating them.

After another long pause, Yoshi said, "There's no pressure here. I don't have to be a part of any rat race. No one tells me how hard I have to study or how difficult it will be for me to get a good job if I don't get into a good university. Here, I have the things I need."

"Because your uncle gives them to you."

"It was our agreement. He gives me food and shelter, and I agree to let a counselor come and talk to me. I'm supposed to offer you coffee, too."

Joshua saw a jar of Maxwell House instant and knew the caffeine would keep him up all night, but he somehow doubted he'd be getting much sleep anyway. "Sure. Coffee sounds good."

"Everything you need is behind you."

Joshua rose, opened the small fridge and poured part of a bottle of water into a mug. "Are you having some?"

"No."

Joshua put the mug in the microwave. While he waited for the water to boil, he puzzled over the laissez-faire approach Ishiguro, indeed Yoshi's entire family was taking to his illness. This wasn't some silly phase. Yoshi was sick. He needed help, but instead his family had been enabling his condition, giving him exactly what he required to remain a recluse. Joshua wondered what he would do if he had a son like Yoshi. Remove the bedroom door, unplug the computer, the TV, the PlayStation, and march him kicking and screaming back into the real world. Tough love. But Yoshi was Japanese, and Joshua sensed his withdrawal hinged on far more than merely pressure to compete in school. He needed to know what triggered Yoshi's retreat in the first place. It was one of the reasons that drew him to this apartment after adamantly expressing his refusal to Ishiguro. Yoshi was a challenge, his illness one that Joshua hadn't seen before. The more the boy's uncle talked, the more fascinated Joshua had become.

He found milk in the fridge and a bowl of sugar on a shelf and stirred both into the mug. When he settled once more a little closer to the screen he heard Yoshi's monotone voice again. "So what do you think? Am I crazy? My parents think so. They're afraid I'm *mukatsuku.*"

"Sorry? Mukatsuku?"

"Dissatisfied. Angry. Some hikkii feel like that. Much has been made of the phenomenon in the press. There have been reports of Japanese teenagers hijacking buses, being violent toward their parents, assaulting elderly strangers on the streets. They say that when some hikkii have no outlet for their anger, they *kireru.*" For

Joshua's benefit he added, "They snap. That's what my parents were afraid of. I think they're relieved I'm in America."

"They were afraid of you?"

"Many Japanese parents today are afraid."

"Coming here. Your choice?"

"I thought it would be different here, away from my parents. I think America is cool. But in case you haven't noticed, Oregon is a pretty Caucasian state. I don't exactly fit in."

"Plenty of Caucasian kids feel that way too, Yoshi. And to answer your question, no, I don't think you're crazy. But, like all of us, you need a little support to get you over the rough patches." Joshua paused, hoping that his directionless smile was penetrating the screen that separated them. "Plus I suspect you haven't had many people to talk to."

"I have friends," Yoshi said defensively, the first hint of any emotion. "I chat with them all the time." A finger emerged from behind the folding screen and pointed to the computer.

"Virtual friends aren't quite the same thing. You're a young guy. Watching movies, playing video games and chatting online are fine to a point, but what about dating? Don't you sometimes think about taking a girl out, holding hands, all that good stuff?"

"I can get sex anytime I want. I don't need to leave the room for that. See that pile?" Yoshi gestured toward a short stack of comic books beside his computer. "*Seijin manga*. Some very good porn comics in there. Plenty of hot girls online too. Who needs dating? I don't need to spend money on a girl, listen to her talk all night about how she's going to find a rich man to marry. My way is better. Uncomplicated. The virtual world isn't wrong, it's just different."

"Maybe so. But I'm here to show you that the real world doesn't have to be so bad either, and my goal is to ease you back into it. I suspect that's what you really want, too."

"Maybe. Someday. But not now. I'm not ready."

"Yoshi, this is going to sound harsh, but right now, I'm not sure you know what's best for you. The next meeting we have will be face to face, because the minute I leave this room, I'm telling your uncle to get rid of this screen."

"Bastard."

"Not the first time I've been called that." Joshua drained his coffee, rose and said, "That'll do for our first session. Except for one more thing. When I leave, I'm taking one of your gadgets with me."

"Bullshit you are. You can't just come in here and take my stuff—"

"Correction. Your uncle's stuff. Now make a choice, or I'll choose for you."

In the silence that followed, Joshua imagined Yoshi scanning the room, his gaze traveling from his PlayStation to his computer to his television. Eventually Yoshi said, "The toaster."

Joshua rose and unplugged the appliance. "Good choice," he said. "But think carefully. Next time, I'm taking two things away."

"Yes, you are a bastard, all right," Yoshi replied, but there was no malice in his voice.

"Everybody's good at something. And Yoshi? When I take this toaster, you won't go all kireru, will you?"

He heard Yoshi sigh, then the soulless voice returned. "In order to kireru, you need to feel emotion. Me? I'm already dead inside."

CHAPTER 6

busridersforum.com
November 27, 2009 01:03
Join Date: August 15, 2009
Location: Oregon
Posts: 18
Jim Stark
Suicidal Tendencies
Still here. Too bad. SkiBum and the rest had what it took to get the job done, and with style. Asphyxia doesn't damage the body, so I know they died a beautiful death. I am jealous, but I'll be riding soon.

November 27, 2009 01:17
Join Date: Sept.20, 2009
Location: Oregon
Posts: 31
Nightshade
Suicidal Tendencies
Good to have you back, Jim. I'll be on the next bus. Wanna ride with me?

To all my friends here, thanks for caring. I want you to know that I'm a good student, I love my family, and I love my best friend. I have tried to be kind to everyone. I hope people will remember me as a good person. Be at peace. I am.

November 27, 2009 01:26
Bella Donna (moderator)
Suicidal Tendencies
Real nice to have you back, Jim. But everyone here knows you're all talk. You haven't got the guts to catch the next ride. Well, am I right? Man or mouse, Jim?

November 27, 2009 01:34
Suicidal Tendencies
Bella Donna (moderator)
Warning! That last Bella Donna post wasn't me! We have a troll on the forum so be warned, everyone. Goading isn't allowed. I've removed the offensive post, but probably not in time for some of you. Jim Stark, we're your friends here. Don't listen to sadistic trolls who come here to hurt us.

November 27, 2009 01:56
Join Date: May 23, 2009
Location: Oregon
Posts: 46
C3PO
Suicidal Tendencies
Jim Stark, it doesn't take courage to die. It takes courage to live, but if you're fresh out of courage, then dying's definitely the way to go. I'll be boarding with Nightshade—maybe we'll see you, maybe not.

In any case, wish us well.

The Suicidal Tendencies thread was hopping tonight. Nightshade was upset about the mini-flame war ignited by the false Bella Donna. She stepped in to pacify. *Hey, chill everybody. We're all we've got. Come on, big hugssss.*

The Monitor rolled his eyes.

The last posting of the night came from Killcrazy in Belgium, wanting to know about the person posing as the site moderator, Bella Donna. "Who was that asshole?"

The asshole, you miserable fuck, is me.

The Monitor shut off his computer, knowing the real site moderator could never unmask him because he had set up an untraceable account using a stolen credit card. He had hundreds of free e-mail accounts so his private messages also disappeared into a cyber-void. He paid cash for a new laptop every few weeks, checked into low-rent motels and sent messages or visited Internet cafes in seedy areas, their proprietors not caring whether their patrons were accessing kiddie porn or urging pathetic fools to kill themselves. He changed on-screen identities often; the masquerade was half the fun. With a few keystrokes and a wicked imagination, he could be anybody.

The identity he most preferred was that of a monitor, in suicide parlance, a person who is appointed by a group who has entered a death pact. Traditionally, the monitor's role was to ensure that everyone's demise would be smooth and painless, often with the monitor being the last to go. In this case, the title wasn't quite accurate for two reasons—one being that the Monitor had no desire to kill himself, and the other being that he had no intention of ensuring anyone's death be painless.

The group at the Aerie had been disappointing in that regard. It had taken them over an hour to drain the bottle of scotch, mere minutes to die. One by one they had simply slumped over in the car. *Pfffffft*. It might have been a poetic ending but it was hardly a dramatic one.

Next time would be different.

Next time would be epic.

CHAPTER 7

THE CLATSOP COUNTY EXAMINER

Saturday, November 28, 2009

Do You Know This Girl?

Local police are seeking the public's help in identifying a young woman whose body was found in Cypress Village early on November 26.

The deceased, a white female, was wearing a size 14 mauve floor-length gown with an empire waist and matching shoes, size 9. Height is 5′4″ and weight is 160 lbs; hair is mid-length, medium brown. Age is estimated to be 14-17. She has a moon-shaped scar on the inside of her right knee and a recent flare-up of rosacea. Her given name may be Brenda.

Also listed as deceased are Heather Conklin, 17, of Boise, Idaho; Tim Schultz, 15, of Eureka, Ca., and Kevin Randolph, 18 , of Marblehead, Mass.

Anyone with information is asked to call the Cypress Village Police Dept. The investigation is being handled under the direction of Sergeant Carolyn Latham. Pictures of the clothing worn by the missing girl can be viewed on the Cypress Village Police website.

Two days after Fallon McBride's second article appeared in the *Examiner*, the phone in Carolyn's office rang twice. The first call was from Gregg. Her ex wondered how she was doing and whether she needed anything. He'd read about the four dead teenagers in the paper and that the police were still seeking the identity of the remaining victim. He hoped she wasn't pushing herself. Gregg had been calling her more often lately, usually on Fridays, but this was only Monday, and here he was again, with one additional twist to the usual formula—he wanted to buy her lunch. What was going on with him anyway? She agreed to meet him for a mid-afternoon coffee then cursed herself for caving in. Even now, her ex-husband was still getting his way.

The second caller's voice was high and squeaked like a rusty door hinge. "Sergeant Latham? This is about the girl in the paper. The one whose name is Brenda. I might know her."

Carolyn's hand flew across her desk. She clicked on a pen and said, "Yes?"

The caller was from Lincoln City, two hours down the coast highway. The boy's name was Matt Lawlor, and he was obviously making the call from his cell phone at school. Carolyn could hear lockers banging and the general murmur of crowd noise.

"Could I meet you someplace? I can't talk here. We're not supposed to use cell phones between classes. I've got a double lunch."

"Name the place. If I leave now, I can meet you at eleven."

Lincoln City was ranked as one of the top twenty-five retirement communities in America, with its tax-free shopping, huge outlet mall and seven miles of sandy beach. It was a great place for watching spectacular sunsets and turbulent winter storms. Winds blew most of the time. Carolyn had always loved the power of the wind, loved being buffeted around and messed up by it, and loved seeing whitecaps churn up on the ocean. Regrettably, this wasn't a day for a walk along the shore. Driving down the highway, Carolyn checked her voice mail every fifteen minutes. No other calls had come in about the mystery girl, only Lawlor's.

The coffee shop was right on Route 101, and Carolyn entered, looking for a six-foot-something blond wearing black jeans and a red T-shirt. She spotted him in a dark corner, hunched over a magazine and getting stern looks from one of the servers behind the counter. “Matt?”

The boy looked up.

“I’m Sergeant Latham,” she said quietly. “What’ll ya have?”

“Same as you’re having,” he shrugged, looking nervous.

Carolyn ordered two tall decafs, returned to the table and said, “Can’t have you getting back to class late. Maybe you should just start talking.”

He was a sophomore. Carolyn wrote down the name of his high school, double-checked the spelling of his surname. She sized him up as being one of the popular kids—good-looking, neatly dressed yet trendy. His growth spurt hadn’t quite reached his voice, a flaw that some adolescent bully might have picked on if the kid wasn’t so tall and well muscled.

Brenda, the girl he thought might be missing, was in his home room. She lived across the street from him, and he’d known her since kindergarten.

“Tell me about her,” Carolyn urged. “Everything you can remember.”

“Physical stuff? She’s got brown hair. ‘Blah brown,’ she always said. Kind of naturally wavy. It would always go fuzzy in the damp weather. She was kind of big—not exactly fat—just … shapeless. And not very pretty.” He looked down, ashamed to be admitting it. “But she could be really funny. She always had good jokes.”

“Did others think she was funny?”

“Sometimes. But behind her back lots of them laughed at her.”

“Why was that?”

Hesitation now. Carolyn sensed this boy had a huge weight to remove from his shoulders and that it had been sitting there for some time. Judging from the furrowed brow on what should have been a smooth young forehead, Matt Lawlor was reliving some kind of pain. Was it Brenda’s? And was Matt talking about the same girl Carolyn had found dead at the Aerie?

“She tried too hard. You know, to get people to like her. Because of that, they didn’t. People were pretty mean to her.” His face flushed red. He pressed the coffee mug to his lips and stared at a smudge on the table.

"Guys? Girls? How were they mean?"

"Guys, mostly," he replied, focusing once again on Carolyn, his gaze flitting everywhere on her face. "Specifically, the basketball team. But everybody knew."

"Knew what, Matt?"

"That Brenda was a head ski."

Carolyn was too long out of school. The jargon had changed and working with juveniles wasn't her forte, but the phrase Matt had just uttered drew a shiver. She nudged her coffee to one side, already sensing that another sip would burn like battery acid in her stomach.

"A head ski," she repeated.

The boy's face flushed deeper. "Yeah, like she'd perform oral sex on somebody to get a date."

"And you said everybody knew this?"

He took another long drink then said, "Stuff like that doesn't stay quiet long."

"Okay, Matt. You've lived across the street from Brenda all your life. Did she ever confide in you? Were the sex acts against her will?"

"How many guys would you blow if they didn't give you another look? Uh, sorry. But you know what I mean. She never felt she had a choice. She said if she didn't do it, they would spread lots of rumors that she'd done worse. And she only confided in me once. That's what she told me."

"When was this?"

"About a week ago. Said as long as she stayed in that school, she'd always be a head ski. She could never work her way up to being a little woman."

"You've lost me."

"It's what they all aspire to. The little woman is a girl who has a steady boyfriend and she has sex with him. The little women look down on the head skis."

Little woman. Charming. She had no clue what young girls had to put up with, what hideous rites of passage they had to endure to feel a part of something, to be accepted.

"You're pretty tall, Matt. Play any basketball?"

"I'm on the team, yeah."

"You and Brenda. Tell me about it."

"I never made her do anything! I was never with her like that!"

"Okay, Matt, I had to ask."

"She offered," he blurted out. "She offered but I turned her down. She said it would be different with me. Because we'd known each other so long. She said I was always nice to her. But I never did anything about stopping the others. And I laughed when they laughed. So that makes me the worst kind of prick, doesn't it?"

Carolyn couldn't answer him. She didn't know. "When did Brenda make this ... overture?"

"Last week. When we had that talk. Monday, I think it was."

"All right, Matt. Now here's the question I should have asked first. You saw the article in the *Examiner*. What makes you think your neighbor Brenda is the same girl as the one we're describing?"

"The scar. That half moon scar on the inside of her knee? I was with Brenda when she got it. We were young. She fell off her bike. Landed on a piece of twisted metal. And she hasn't been in class since Tuesday."

"Her last name, your Brenda?"

"Koch. Some of the guys used to call her Susie Kochsucker."

Nice. "Did she know?"

"Sure she did."

Susie Cox. Brenda Koch had booked her final hair appointment online using a G-rated version of her hated nickname. *Oh, you poor kid. You poor, miserable, lonesome kid.*

Carolyn had always wanted children, but Gregg had fluffed her off, Gregg who would soon have two of his own. Carolyn dreamed of attending school plays, baking birthday cakes, lining her kids up for pictures with Santa, cheering them on in sports or music or whatever they chose to pursue, teaching them how to drive, buying them clothes for the prom. Was she hopelessly naïve? Was every environment today a battlefield, with only the prettiest, the tallest, the loudest, the meanest surviving? How could she have protected someone like Brenda?

Brenda Koch was in the morgue, stiff and still and cold. Carolyn felt a rush of anger at what had befallen the yet unclaimed child. She longed to wrap her arms around that big-but-not-exactly-fat body to bring some warmth back into it, to somehow send a message that someone did indeed care, if too late.

"And Brenda's parents—have they knocked on your door, asked whether you've seen their daughter? They must realize that she's missing."

"Brenda's only got a mom, and it wouldn't surprise me if she didn't."

"How can that be?"

"Brenda could do pretty much what she wanted. Her mom didn't care. She cleans rooms at one of the motels, tends bar a couple of nights a week. She's pissed up most of the time. No one on the street has anything to do with her. Brenda once told me she could probably take a shuttle to the moon and her mom wouldn't even know she was out of the house."

Matt glanced at his watch then he shot Carolyn a guilty look. "I gotta go or I'll be late."

"You don't by any chance have a picture of Brenda? Yearbook photo, anything like that?"

Matt shook his head. "Brenda didn't like having her picture taken. She always made sure she was sick when it came time for school photos."

"Then just give me the address of the Koch place."

He gave it to her, along with directions on how to find it. "It's her, isn't it. Brenda. She's dead." His voice broke a little but the boy quickly recovered. A full-blown attack of conscience would strike soon.

"I can't say anything definite at this point. Someone will have to identify her. But Matt? If the girl we found is your neighbor, Brenda, then maybe your talking to me, your reporting her as missing … maybe that'll somehow make up for those times when you didn't do the right thing."

It wasn't much to offer the boy, but it was all Carolyn had.

CHAPTER 8

CAROLYN CONTINUED SOUTH ON 101, past the Tanger Outlet Center and into the Nelscott District where Brenda Koch and her mother lived in a yellow frame house. There was a silver Ford Escort in the driveway, with perforated rust patches around the wheel well and tail lights. To add a cheery touch to the sad exterior of the place, someone had stuck faded silk geraniums inside a plastic decapitated swan.

Mrs. Koch greeted her at the door wearing a bathrobe and a constipated grimace. "If you're sellin', I'm not buyin.'"

Carolyn produced her ID. "Cypress Village police, ma'am. You're Mrs. Koch? Brenda's mother?"

The grimace deepened, and a trio of vertical grooves formed between the woman's eyebrows. "I'm Irene Koch. What's this about?"

"Mrs. Koch, I wonder if I might come in. I need to ask you some questions about your daughter."

The door opened wider, and Carolyn abandoned the headless swan to enter the Koch living room. She sat on a lumpy moss green sofa, trying to ignore the pile of tabloid magazines on the coffee table with headlines that screamed about this week's anorexic starlets.

The Koch woman was growing out a spiral perm. Her hair was still damp from the shower, and the lavender soap she'd washed with barely covered the smell of stale booze that seeped through her pores. She perched on the edge of a leatherette recliner, chipped toenail polish peeking from beneath the hem of her robe. "Has Brenda skipped school again? I've already talked to her about—"

"No," Carolyn cut in, "but has that happened often, Brenda cutting classes?"

"Had some trouble for a while. Just didn't want to go to school. She mentioned something once about some teasin' and carryin' on, but I told her to toughen up. Kids'll do that, I told her, and if she let it bother her, they'd just keep it up. Cigarette?"

Carolyn shook her head. Irene Koch reached for a pack of Merit lights. "Mind if I do?"

"Actually, I'm allergic," Carolyn lied.

Koch's hand retreated into the pocket of her robe.

"Mrs. Koch, when was the last time you saw your daughter?"

"Last Wednesday," she offered casually. "At breakfast. I remember because she woke me up, and I was none too pleased. I worked late the night before. Anyway, she dragged me into the kitchen, and what do you think was there? She had a stack of pancakes on my plate, a glass of orange juice, some strawberries—the works. Even nuked the syrup in the micro."

And instead of going to school, she got on a bus for Cypress Village, had her hair done, drank herself numb then killed herself. But first she had to torture her mother, leave her with a lovely memory to cling to so that Irene Koch would finally feel something more than indifference toward her daughter.

"You didn't wonder where she'd been for almost a week?"

The woman swept her hand as if shooing a fly. "Brenda can take care of herself. Can't keep tabs on these teenagers all the time. They need their freedom. It's how they learn to get along in the world. I was on my own at sixteen. Seems my daughter's inherited my independent streak. Besides, Brenda often took little … vacations, she called them. Went different places to think."

About being a head ski, Carolyn thought bitterly. And how it was that countless blow jobs later, she still didn't have anyone to care about her.

"Didn't the school call, wonder why Brenda hadn't been in class?"

"Someone left a message here yesterday, asked if she was sick. I didn't get around to calling them back yet."

"Mrs. Koch, does your daughter own a purple dress? You know, a fancy one? Full length?"

"Good Lord, no. What would she need it for? Besides, we couldn't afford anything like that. I work two jobs to keep this place going. What's with all these questions about my daughter? She's either done something wrong or she hasn't."

"I'm here because we found a girl in Cypress Village, and we think her name is Brenda. But she was wearing a formal purple gown, and you say your daughter didn't own one. Did Brenda have a part-time job, earn herself some spending money?"

"Woulda been nice, but no. Too busy studying, she always said, but I know she spent more time on that damned computer in her room than hitting the books. And I've got the report cards to prove it."

An evening gown was a cumbersome thing to steal. Where had Brenda found the money for it? Surely the boys' basketball team wasn't a paying clientele. Carolyn wondered if Brenda, callused over by the shabby treatment and abuses of the past year, had taken her skills to the street.

"Mrs. Koch, do you keep any cash around the house? Emergency money, that kind of thing?"

"Sure, I bring my tip money home, but I'd never tell Brenda where I hide it."

"Perhaps if you could check ..."

The woman was already out of the chair and headed for the kitchen. Carolyn saw her drag a chair across the linoleum and step onto it, reaching deep into a cupboard over the refrigerator.

"That little bitch! She cleaned me out!" She jumped from the chair and reentered the living room, brandishing a copy of an old Pillsbury cookbook. She riffled the pages. "I had almost four hundred bucks in here!"

Enough to buy a dress, some shoes, pay the salon and perhaps treat her new friends to a pizza before dying.

"Please sit down, Mrs. Koch. There's a picture I'd like you to look at."

It was an awful photograph. Death by asphyxiation due to carbon monoxide poisoning renders the flesh cherry pink. As much as Irene

Koch would never win any supermom awards, she didn't deserve to see her daughter this way.

"It's her," she said. "It's Brenda. Now you tell me what happened."

Carolyn told her as much as they knew, that four teenagers had somehow become acquainted on the Net and formed a suicide pact, carrying out their plan last Wednesday evening. Their deaths would have been quick, if that was any consolation, due to their ingestion of enough barbiturates and booze before lighting the barbecue inside the car. Carolyn didn't speak of her conversation with Matt Lawlor, nor did she mention the school bullies who had tormented Brenda for a solid year.

After a time, Irene Koch nodded. "That daughter of mine always was a deep one." Then she added, "Well, her father can pay for the funeral, and that's for sure."

"I'm very sorry, Mrs. Koch."

The woman said nothing, just reached for her cigarettes, shook one from the pack and lit it.

"One more thing, Mrs. Koch. I'd like to take Brenda's computer with me. There might be some information on it that would be helpful to the police."

Brenda's mother inhaled a lung full of nicotine, looked hard at Carolyn and said, "Get the fucking thing outta here."

CHAPTER 9

BRENDA KOCH PURCHASED HER MAUVE satin gown from the sale rack at a bridal shop in Lincoln City. The saleswoman didn't have the heart to tell her the color did nothing to flatter her skin tone, and she had tried to steer Brenda toward a dress with sleeves as well, but the girl's mind was made up. She wanted the mauve dress.

By the time Carolyn returned to the village, it was already dark. Ziggy was eager to get at the Koch girl's computer and see what the teenager had been up to online in the weeks before she died, but Carolyn told him to go home. "Time enough tomorrow, Zig. It's acceptable to be conscientious *and* have a life."

Not that Carolyn knew much about having a life. She had called Gregg on her cell, canceling their coffee date. Gregg was eager to reschedule, just to touch base, he'd said. The only thing Carolyn wanted to touch base with right now was her mattress.

Entering the empty condo left her awash with desolation. What had she been expecting—the pat-pat-pat of little bunny slippers across the floor, chubby arms that smelled of talcum powder wrapped around her neck, some house-husband greeting her with a kiss and a freshly baked carrot cake? A knot of sorrow lodged in her throat and stuck fast. She tried to swallow it. She blinked hard, determined there would be no more tears, not for her failed marriage, not for her broken, scarred body, and not for all the things that might have been. That should have been. That she felt she deserved. If tears fell, they would be for Brenda Koch, that insignificant other who was passed around, passed over and left no choice but to die in the company of strangers.

She had gone into Brenda's bedroom to remove the girl's computer. It was a genderless room, unadorned walls painted a dismal gray, unlined curtains so faded their floral pattern was barely discernible. Left on her own, Carolyn searched through Brenda's closet, the teen's meager, drab wardrobe further testimony to the notion that pretty clothes would be a waste on an ugly girl. A dresser drawer revealed a collection of old-lady underwear—nylon briefs in various versions of white, two brassieres yellowed with age. Other than a tiny pot of raspberry-flavored lip balm, Carolyn found no cosmetics in the room. A clock radio rested on the bedside table, but there was no sound system, no telephone, no poster of a favorite rock star. The room could have belonged to somebody's grandmother.

Thinking about the Koch girl made Carolyn forget her fatigue. Moments later she went back to her Explorer to get Brenda's computer. It was a prehistoric IBM clone, the tower's heft causing Carolyn's shoulder to burn as she lifted it onto her dining-room table. No computer genius, it took Carolyn nearly an hour to plug in all the wires and make sure she had things hooked up properly. The machine took forever to boot up, the "please wait ..." directive forcing Carolyn to do exactly that. At least the old dinosaur had manners. Just as the array of icons appeared on the screen she heard a knock at her front door.

Ziggy peered past Carolyn and saw the computer. "I knew you'd start without me, C.L.," he said. "Is that any way to treat a geek?" He grinned and pushed past her into the dining room. "Hope you've made coffee."

"It's decaf," Carolyn answered.

"Then put a shot of something in it while I try to figure out what Brenda Koch has been up to."

On her way into the kitchen, Carolyn spied her bedroom door wide open, her stuffed teddy bear tucked neatly under the covers. Quickly she closed the door, felt herself go warm and hoped Ziggy hadn't caught a glimpse of her faithful bedmate. Hardly fitting for a patrol sergeant's résumé. Additional qualifications: sleeps with Pookie Bear and night light.

The night light kept the shadows away. Now that she lived alone, Carolyn didn't like awakening in a pitch dark room, and besides, dark bedrooms signified groping, fondling, and sweaty, whispery sex, and she hadn't been getting any of that lately.

"Baileys or Grand Marnier in your coffee?" she called from the kitchen.

"Yes."

Carolyn splashed both liqueurs into a pair of heavy ironstone mugs and returned to the dining room. Ziggy had found time to shower and Carolyn caught traces of sandalwood soap as she pulled her chair alongside his. He had rolled his sleeves up, revealing dark hair on his arms that Carolyn hadn't taken notice of before. His brow furrowed in concentration as he stared at the screen.

"I'll be damned," he said.

"What?"

"Seems our girl—Brenda, is it?—didn't much care who saw her personal mail. She didn't bother to erase any of her messages. Lucky for us."

"Probably figured her mother wouldn't even be interested enough to read it."

"Sounds like you had quite a day in Lincoln City. Mother was a real piece of work, I take it."

"That's an understatement. I'll fill you in on her later. Right now, what does Brenda's computer tell us?"

"For one thing, she's not inundated with a ton of e-mail. At least not compared to the amount my daughter gets."

Ziggy's only child, a delightful 15-year-old named Amanda, was in his words, a "girly girl." Though both studious and athletic, Amanda was also into clothes, hairstyles, make-up and talking on the phone with her friends. After nine o'clock, when homework was done and no more phone calls were allowed, the e-mail flew in.

"And most of the messages that the Koch girl received were signed with pseudonyms. Look." Ziggy pointed to the screen. "Killcrazy. Monitor. C3PO. Nightshade. Not school acquaintances, but online friends."

"Here's a first and last name though, Zig. Jim Stark. I'll check with Brenda's principal tomorrow, see if there's a Jim Stark enrolled at the high school."

He nodded. "Time to see what websites this girl was accessing."

Ziggy dragged the mouse up to "View" then scrolled down to "History" and clicked on "three weeks ago." Only one website appeared, a pro-choice site for suicide. "Christ on a pogo stick. This is why parents need to be computer literate. Welcome to the world where almost anything can happen with very few consequences."

Before their eyes was a compendium of suicide methods, from A to Z, and from the supposedly painless to the completely insane. The site contained a complete reference of lethal drug dosages and advised what drugs to ingest to avoid upchucking and choking on one's own vomit. In case someone didn't know, suicide by self-immolation was ranked as an excruciatingly painful way to die. Deliberately crashing a vehicle into an abutment or wall also earned a thumbs-down, since the participant could survive the accident and be handicapped for life. Instructions were provided on how to administer a fatal cut, though this method came with a warning—death could be slow. And there was always a chance of being rescued, adding up to a real waste of effort.

A smorgasbord of self-destruction. Carolyn quelled a shiver. "Do you always check on Amanda, see where she's cruising on the Net?"

"Constantly. We keep our computer in the kitchen, and our family's got one e-mail address. When Amanda gets mail, we all get mail."

"She doesn't grouse about the lack of privacy?"

"She tried it once, but she knows the territory that comes with being a cop's kid. Besides, she's crazy about me."

Carolyn knew that was true. Ziggy was a great dad. He glowed every time his daughter brought home her report card, scored a basket, helped out around the house. He didn't even mind so much when she nicknamed him Ziggy Pop, after the punk rocker Iggy Pop, though Ziggy told her that unlike the musician, he drew the line at smearing peanut butter all over himself, and he wasn't about to cut himself with broken bottles, either. Amanda thought her father was pretty cool for a cop, and Ziggy counted himself lucky. Amanda was the daughter most people wished they had.

Ziggy took a long drink. "Just what I need. More hair on my chest."

"Too strong?"

"Are you kidding?"

Both read through a mile-long list of terms of use, limitation of liability paragraphs, and disclaimers. The moderators and administrators of the site warned that they were not trained to be medical-health practitioners, nor did the site pretend to be a substitute for legitimate therapy or counseling. Users of the site and its links could not hold the contributors. to the site liable for any decision made or outcome of such. Carolyn's eyes were grainy from the fine print.

"Sewn up nice and tight, isn't it?" Ziggy said. "In short, if you die, it ain't our problem, hoss. Anyway, let's see what interesting links this site takes us to. Maybe we'll find out where Brenda met some of her online friends."

Links connected users to several online counselors. There were chat rooms and forums as well, and Ziggy played around with those, jumping back to the original site when he didn't find what he wanted. No Geezer. No Jim Stark.

Carolyn topped up their coffee, cut a bagel in half that was supposed to be the next morning's breakfast and shared it with Ziggy. "I don't get it," she said, looking over his shoulder. She pointed to a link. "What's that?"

"Cute. Very cute. 'Catching the bus' is a euphemism for committing suicide. Let's see what we find."

Busriders.com was a forum, or message board where a user could post thoughts or opinions, provided one followed the rules. No hateful or obscene messages. No posting of chain mail, spam or other such cyber junk. No off-topic messages. Users were cautioned to not divulge personal information and not to commit privacy violations by asking for another's address or phone number.

Respect the opinion of others. In short, if someone wanted to die, step aside and let 'em.

"Okay, C.L, put on your eyeshade. We're going to lurk in here for awhile."

"Lurk?"

He shook his head in dismay. "You still communicate with a quill pen and papyrus?"

She gave him a shove. "Sorry, Zig, but while you were busy boning up on who-gives-a-damn compu-jargon, I guess I was out in the real world."

"Point made." He smiled. "We're going to read the posts, get a feel for the culture of the web board, see who's who. But I won't register. May not even need to."

Ziggy entered the forum and scanned the discussion threads. Desperate—RU? Own worst enemy. No Peace. Demons in my Head. Ziggy clicked in, scanned, clicked out. He and Carolyn read a debate between two posters on whether the human brain still registered thought and pain once a head had been severed from the body, one of the participants arguing that he'd read about a ten-minute window, whereby a guillotine victim actually realized what had happened. Conclusion—chopping one's head off wasn't the best way to go. "Too fucking bizarre," Ziggy said and exited the thread. After clicking on another topic, Suicidal Tendencies, he said, "Bingo. Meet Brenda's cyber friends."

The online nicknames appeared—Monitor, Jim Stark, Nightshade, Geezer, Killcrazy. An Internet suicide club. The only place where Brenda Koch could find people to listen to her was in cyberspace. On busriders.com, a message board populated by depressives, Brenda had found the support she needed. *You want to kill yourself? Well, so do I. Let's get together.*

Ziggy and Carolyn stared at the screen for the better part of an hour, alternating between the forum posts and Brenda's private messages in her e-mail. Monitor, whoever she really was, emerged as a grandmotherly type who had somehow taken the others under her wing. She was the voice of understanding, of compassion, of reason. She made no judgments. She knew grief, illness, loneliness and also knew full well about the overwhelming desire to be done with it all. She posted on the web board often and PM'd Brenda every two or three days. Carolyn wondered whether Tim Schultz, Kyle Randolph or Heather Conklin had private messages from the Monitor on their computers.

The site moderator, Bella Donna, was a strict taskmaster. Jollyfolk, the term she gave to those who tried to dissuade participants from expressing sad thoughts, were ceremoniously banned from the site. A troll, masquerading under several pseudonyms including the moderator's, was openly derisive about any stalwart who had chosen to tough out a misery-laden life. Had the troll sent private messages to the others? Phone calls to Boise, Marblehead and Eureka would answer that.

"I think we're onto something here, Zig."

Ziggy nodded then yawned widely and looked at his watch, an Omega that his wife Ilona had splurged on the Christmas before. "Too bad it's so damn late. Not much more we can do tonight," he said, rising and taking both coffee mugs to the kitchen sink. He rinsed them out then put them in the dishwasher. When he returned to the dining room, he shut down the computer and began repacking it. "I'll take this with me, hook it up at the station tomorrow. Now get some sleep. I mean it."

Wanting a thing didn't make it happen. Long after Ziggy's RAV4 pulled out of the visitor's space in front of her unit, Carolyn tossed in bed. Pookie Bear was little comfort. When slivers of daylight filtered through her blinds, Carolyn was still haunted by the final message Brenda had left for her cyber friends and the nickname the unloved, unmissed girl had chosen for her cyber-identity—SkiBum.

CHAPTER 10

"MOST MEN FALL ASLEEP AFTER sex, but you want to watch a movie?"

Joshua knew Paige had a point, but since returning home from another meeting with Yoshi, he was wired. It was a little after midnight, and his bedroom frolic with Paige had done little to relax him.

Paige reached for her pajama top. Joshua reached for the remote.

"What are we watching?" she asked, stifling a yawn.

"*Rebel Without a Cause.*" Joshua popped the DVD into the machine. "Haven't seen it in ages. Guess how many times Yoshi's watched it?"

"Yoshi's got nothing else to do. We've both got work in the morning."

"I'll keep the volume low. And the answer's fifteen. He's seen it fifteen times."

"Joshua, you've seen this kid twice and he's already gotten under your skin. What gives?"

It was true. Joshua had never met anyone like Yoshi. "I can't explain it. Yoshi's given me no reason to like him, but I do. Other than comics and James Dean, he's got no interest in anything. I bought him a book on Dean, gave it to him tonight. Worth the twenty bucks just to see a brief flicker of excitement in his eyes."

"And get you on his good side, I assume."

"Let's hope so. This is a smart kid, Paige. His uncle told me he was at the top of his class back home."

"If he's so smart, why's he living like a hermit?"

"At some point, for some reason I've yet to find out about, the bottom fell out of Yoshi's world. Ishiguro told me Yoshi became moody, distracted, insolent toward his mother. One day, he caught a cold and stayed home from school. He never went back."

"Wait a minute. His parents couldn't make him?"

"Yoshi locked himself in his room. Threatened to set the house on fire if his mother interfered."

"She didn't call the police?"

"People in Japan think having a hikikomori kid is a family problem. Calling the police alerts the neighbors and brings shame upon the family. Most parents choose to suffer in silence and hope their child will pass through the phase over time. One family had their son lock himself in their kitchen. Their solution? Build a new kitchen. Another family was banned from their own house and had to live in their car."

Paige shook her head in disbelief. "So it's agoraphobia times ten?"

"Not really. An agoraphobic will gladly see friends in his own home. A hikikomori doesn't want to see anyone, anywhere."

"Where's Yoshi's father in all this?"

"He works in Tokyo. Keeps a small apartment there and takes the train home every other weekend."

"Leaving his wife to manage the problem of Yoshi on her own."

"It's complicated, Paige. Moving the family to Tokyo would be too expensive. And traditional Japanese are reluctant to ask for outside help, especially not with family problems. Even when elderly men are mugged on the street—it's called *oyaji-gari*—they keep their mouths shut about the violence. Having to admit that a couple of punks roughed them up for a few thousand yen would be a huge blow to their pride."

"How long are you going to counsel Yoshi at his uncle's place?"

Joshua knew what Paige was thinking. She hated being alone at night. Paige spooked at shadows and jumped at sudden noises. Hushed, quiet nights were worse.

"A few more sessions, tops. Then it's out into the cruel world for Yoshi."

He felt her burrow closer.

"Just keep the night of December fourteenth free. Uncle Spence is coming over, remember?"

Paige worshipped her uncle. During her estrangement from her parents, he had been the voice of reason. Millicent and Jerome Greene had been utopian wackadoos, more concerned with the faithful flock that assembled for their prayer meetings than being parents to Paige. After their fatal car accident, Spence stepped up to the plate as Paige's surrogate father and Paige adopted his surname, Rowan. For the first time, Paige felt the warmth of real affection and delighted in hearing her uncle call her "Angel Heart." Now Spence lived in a nursing home in Portland, a right-hemisphere stroke making it impossible for him to live on his own. But Paige and her uncle clung to the tradition of decorating the Christmas tree together on the fourteenth, the anniversary of Spence's wife's death. Sprucing up the cabin for the holidays was their way of paying tribute to her.

"I'll be here, don't you worry."

"Good. Now watch your movie."

Paige rolled away from him and curled up on her side. Joshua slipped a hand under the blanket and let it rest on the soft curve of Paige's hip. He thought back to their earlier lovemaking and how connected they were, how connected they always were. It made him wonder how someone like Yoshi could choose isolation, a life with little human contact.

He heard Paige sigh, felt the gentle rise and fall of her body. On the screen the opening credits rolled, with James Dean's name appearing at the top of the list, in the role of troubled teen Jim Stark.

CHAPTER 11

On Tuesday morning, Carolyn consumed an extra large coffee and a raspberry bear claw at her desk. Some breakfast of champions. She was so tired even her eyelashes hurt. Her sciatic nerve wasn't up for another drive to Lincoln City, so she sent one of her officers to interview Brenda Koch's teachers, catch some gossip from the basketball team, and find out anything about the girl's last days.

Ziggy hadn't yet arrived with the Koch girl's computer. Carolyn wondered how he had explained working so late last night to Ilona. She wondered why it mattered. Ilona had come from a family of cops so if anyone knew the ramifications of marrying a police officer, it was Ziggy's wife. Knowing Ilona, she had probably fixed Ziggy a cup of tea when he got home, maybe massaged his aching shoulders and hands, which were just starting to display knobby, arthritic knuckles.

Checking her watch and still seeing no sign of Zig, Carolyn placed a call to the officer in Marblehead who'd called to report Kevin Randolph as missing. Ted Tarrant sounded young. His voice was deep and friendly, even as he spoke about a nasty storm that was currently battering the Massachusetts coast.

"The Randolphs look like they've been in a war zone," he told Carolyn. "No way did they see their son as suicidal."

They admitted that a few months ago, Kevin had seemed withdrawn. He'd stopped playing tennis, wasn't interested in hanging out with his friends. Then they claimed he suddenly pulled himself out of his funk and was looking forward to the family's ski holiday in February. But Carolyn realized that Kevin hadn't turned a corner at all; he had simply made peace with his decision to die.

"I tell you," Tarrant said, "I hope I don't have to deliver too many messages like that in my career. Losing a kid, especially that way, has got to be the worst."

Or not having a kid at all, Carolyn thought bitterly. Another thought followed. *Oh, get over yourself.*

"First time for you? Delivering bad news?"

"Guess I must sound pretty green. Been on the force six months."

If she were in Massachusetts instead of across the country, Carolyn would probably have given Tarrant a reassuring clap on the back, tell him he did just fine, made sure he got out with other officers at the end of his shift for a drink. She found herself wondering what he looked like. She imagined him as sandy-haired, with a wind-burned complexion and incredibly white teeth.

"Well, I hope you're sitting down because I've got more bad news for you." Then Carolyn filled him in on what had turned up on Brenda Koch's computer.

"Shit," Tarrant said. "A suicide pact? Made on the Net?"

"It explains how four kids from different states found each other. Kevin wound up here because he didn't want to die alone."

Tarrant swore again. "Well, as awful as it is, there's no crime in starting up a website like that. Talking about suicide isn't illegal. We can't go shutting down every site that crosses the line of decency."

Carolyn wished they could. The world could be a dark place, dark and ugly, the virtual world, the same. The shadowy realms didn't need any more monsters crouching in the corners, especially the kind that lurked on the Net, waiting to prey upon the impressionable young, or to add further inspiration to the minds of the already depraved. If Gregg could read her thoughts now, he would likely tell her to stop being so fucking naïve.

"It's not going to be easy to prove a direct causal link between busriders.com and what happened here," Carolyn said.

"Besides, even if we were successful in getting the site shut down, it would just pop up somewhere else."

"Officer Tarrant—"

"Ted, please."

"Ted, what if I were to tell you there could be something more going on here than just cyber suicide?" She explained the flattened patch of grass near the spot where the teens had parked, the champagne cork, and the notion that someone could have watched the four die. "I can't prove it. Not yet. But if someone gave those kids a push toward their final act or outlined a plan in their private messages, we've got complicity in suicide. Being present at the scene would make that person a principal in a homicide."

"Wasn't there some guy in your state, a few years back, who tried to coordinate a Valentine's Day suicide pact on the Net?"

"Yes. He was charged with solicitation to commit murder and conspiracy to commit manslaughter. Was trying to get the participants to record the act on webcams. Probably a good idea if you get the Randolph boy's computer and see what you find."

"I'll get it if I have to steal it."

The two exchanged e-mail addresses and fax numbers. Carolyn spent the next two hours on the phone with police in Eureka and Boise, having similar conversations with contacts there. She then spoke to Lieutenant Perri Carver in Washington.

Carver's voice carried a soothing tropical lilt. "How can we help you?"

"Check the area near where your victims took their leap. Scout for any lookout points, any place where someone might have settled in to watch them die. And watch for any signs of ... celebration. Like a liquor bottle. Anything."

"Those five jumped in August," Carver said. "Even if there was something there then, that's not saying it's there now."

Carolyn knew it was a long shot but she had to try.

By the time she hung up, Ziggy had arrived and was at his desk keying in furiously. "Trying to see if I can decipher any of the pseudonyms on Brenda Koch's computer. Maybe somewhere along the way, someone got careless and leaked some personal information. We can only hope."

Carolyn stood over his shoulder and caught another whiff of sandalwood. She stared at the screen, but Ziggy was scrolling through messages too fast, making her nauseous. She averted her eyes and looked instead at the framed photographs on Ziggy's desk—one of Ilona on horseback, another of his daughter Amanda crossing the finish line at a track meet. Carolyn glanced over at her own desk. Not a photograph in sight.

When her phone rang again, she barely heard it. Ziggy said, "Aren't you going to get that?"

Carolyn went into her office and picked up the receiver.

Crap.

As always, her ex wouldn't take no for an answer. Time to have that coffee they'd missed out on.

This was turning into a shitty day all around.

"Be careful out there," Ziggy called to her. He was no fan of Gregg Holt.

"Don't worry," Carolyn told him as she headed for the door, "I'm wearing my Kevlar undies."

Gregg had suggested meeting at The Rocks, an upscale restaurant with floor-to-ceiling windows and an expansive view of the Pacific. Carolyn countered with her own choice, Marley's, a small beanery near the station where most of the cops hung out.

On the way there, Carolyn wondered why Gregg was so insistent on meeting. They had ironed out the financial details of their divorce months ago. Already she felt her stomach tighten, her fault for having consented to meet him in the first place. Why had she? Curiosity, she supposed, and she wanted to kick herself.

What Marley's lacked in décor it more than made up for in great food. Cholesterol seekers could indulge in rib-sticking options, but Marley's also had lighter fare and a tapas menu. Carolyn walked past a row of chrome and vinyl bar stools to a booth at the far end of the restaurant. She whisked a few crumbs from the tabletop, grabbed a laminated menu that was wedged behind the sugar dispenser and sat down. Through the slats in wooden blinds, she could see Gregg's Escalade squeezing into an angled parking spot. Minutes later, her ex emerged from the vehicle, a cell phone attached to his ear. When he entered the restaurant and spotted her, he gave a broad smile, snapped the phone shut and sidled into his side of the booth.

"You're looking well, Carolyn," he said, shrugging out of a topcoat. "Have you ordered?"

"Just got here. Thought this was just going to be coffee."

Gregg smiled then took a cursory look around the place, wrinkling his nose at the exposed brick walls and the array of fake greenery. "I've never been here before. Food good?"

"Burgers are legendary. Club sandwich is a mile high."

When the waitress appeared, Gregg ordered a julienne salad and mineral water. "Shall we make it two?"

Carolyn shook her head. "Burger please," she told the waitress as her stomach rumbled. "And a Diet Coke."

"Gravy on the fries?"

"Why not? I'm feeling reckless."

Several minutes of awkward conversation passed along the what's-new-with-you vein. Then Gregg asked her about the four who died on Signal Hill.

"That's the last thing I want to talk about. Next?"

"Had to have been rough on you, finding them up there."

"That's not what I call changing the subject."

After a brief attempt at looking contrite, Gregg tried again to coax her into discussing the investigation. Why was Gregg so titillated by the teens' suicide? Granted, it was big news in Cypress Village, but Carolyn vividly remembered how the teens had looked in the rental car and she didn't want that image flashing through her mind while she was eating her lunch. Another knot formed in her stomach.

"Gregg, you never took an interest in my work while we were married. What's up?"

"Maybe I should have, Carolyn. Taken more of an interest."

"Bit late now, don't you think?"

Gregg huffed.

The food arrived and Carolyn smothered her burger with mustard and ketchup. She dug in while Gregg complained about

Nadia's weight gain, little Gillian's toys scattered everywhere and his beachfront condo covered in drool.

Finally, when she was unable to tune him out any longer, she said, "Gregg, what gives? All you've done is complain about your new life. Do I have to remind you that you chose that life?"

"Carolyn, I just want us to be friends."

"Friends? You've got to be kidding."

"There's no reason for bad blood, is there?"

"Let me see. You had an affair. Got Nadia pregnant. Walked out on me. Now there's another child on the way, and here I sit, the one you always told to wait, saying there would be plenty of time for kids later. No, there's no reason for bad blood."

"Sounds like you've waited a long time to get that out."

"I guess I have. And I'm sure you'll understand why I don't want to dance at your wedding."

"That's just it. I'm not so sure I want a wedding."

Carolyn gulped Coke. Gulped again. "That has nothing to do with me."

Gregg looked crushed. Defeated. He shoved his plate away, the salad barely touched. "I'm not happy with the way things have turned out, Carolyn. This isn't the life I wanted."

Carolyn wanted to hit him. Slap him. Pummel some sense into him. Instead she fished around in her oversized handbag until her hand closed around her wallet. She slammed twenty dollars onto the table, muttered something about accepting responsibility and stormed out before she could say what she'd really been thinking since learning of Nadia's first pregnancy, that her ex had an ego the size of Mount Hood, and if he wasn't happy, it served him right.

Back at her office, she closed her door and let loose a litany of swear words, a few of the old standards and some new hyphenated ones as well. Once she had finished cussing out her ex-husband, she directed a vivid string of adjectives at Sam Burke, the cook at Marley's. His burger lodged in Carolyn's stomach like a sack of ball bearings, the acid bubbling up and down her esophagus for the remainder of the afternoon.

At home, she busied herself to distraction. She paid bills, got caught up on her laundry, scrubbed the grout on her shower tiles. Eventually she climbed between fresh sheets with Pookie Bear and turned on the television.

This isn't the life I wanted. Well, welcome to the club, Gregg.

Carolyn's life wouldn't have won any prizes either and if someone asked her right now if she was happy, she knew what she would tell them. But things would get better. She knew that as much as she knew anything. The improvement would begin the minutes she found the bastard who had watched Brenda Koch die.

CHAPTER 12

A PLATTER OF CANNOLIS SAT ON the counter in the Friends of Families kitchen, courtesy of Rose Pezeshki who worked part-time for Joshua. Auntie Rose, as everyone called her, helped with fund-raising and light housekeeping. She loved being around the teens, despite Joshua's occasional reminders that she wasn't a counselor, and she was always showing up at 3F House with food. She made a mean Linzer torte, and her English trifle and Pavlova weren't shabby either. Calories across countries, Rose would say. She tore through the place with dervish-like energy, to the point where the youngest counselor, Robb Northrup, once asked, "Hey, Auntie Rose, what are you running from?"

That line hadn't earned him a smile and Joshua knew why. Rose had plenty to run from. Rose knew about pain, knew it when she'd cut her daughter down from the basement rafter, tasted it when she tried frantically to breathe life into cold dead lips. More heartache came when her priest refused to bury her only natural child on consecrated ground. Rose's suffering continued when her husband left her the day after the funeral, leaving her a one-line message on the back of the phone bill. *No reason to stay now.*

Joshua thought Rose's tragedies explained her devotion to Lily Howard, who was now the same age as Rose's daughter had been when she'd found her. "I'm scared for that girl," Rose had told him once. "She reminds me so much of my Lori." Rose had a huge, loving heart, and she needed to feel needed. She was the doting den mother, the mortar that held the place together.

Counselor Wes Bertram hovered over the plate of pastries, sporting an icing sugar moustache. He seemed to be debating having a second one then patted his expanding waistline, turned his back on the calories and headed upstairs. The two hundred pounds he used to carry as solid muscle on his six-foot-something frame had long since softened into a doughy paunch.

Bertram, or Big Bert to the kids, was leading the evening's discussion. The topic—Broken Dreams—was close to Wes's heart. Bertram had big dreams once and so did the man who'd come to scout him for pro ball. Now, at forty-four and hobbled with a bum patella, Wes was no longer certain he had much of the dreamer left in him. His youngest child, who had just turned five, was undergoing a rigorous course of chemotherapy to shrink the neuroblastoma that was pressing on her spinal cord.

Within the walls of 3F House there was a lot of baggage.

Joshua made himself a cup of coffee and sat at the kitchen table. He was reminded of his last visit with Yoshi, the room lit only by the glow from the computer screen. As promised, he'd removed the kettle and microwave from the room and returned them to Ishiguro's kitchen. For a brief moment, Joshua saw a glint of anger flash in the boy's eyes, but it disappeared with his next blink. Yoshi, it seemed, preferred his computer and PlayStation to food. His supply of saltines, peanut butter and junk food would soon run out, then what? Yoshi would have to leave his room, wouldn't he?

Joshua managed to get Yoshi to open up a little about life in Japan. He had attended a prep school, more accurately known as a cram school, between his regular classes. Japan was undergoing a long overdue educational reform, Yoshi explained, but it was too little too late. Though there was a slight shift to higher-level thinking and individuality, the old ways still permeated the fiber of Japanese society. Generations who'd been raised on rote learning and deference to authority didn't change their stripes overnight. Non-conformity was a huge no-no, but Yoshi had no desire to become a grey-suited corporate warrior like his father.

There was fierce competition for the prestigious schools, and this competition led to bullying. Or dropping out. Or worse.

"You mean suicide?" Joshua asked.

"Sure," came the monotonous reply, not delivered from behind the shoji screen this time, but over a copy of one of Yoshi's *manga*.

Joshua picked up a sampling of the boy's comic books and leafed through them in the semi-darkness. Plenty of depictions of oral sex and intercourse acrobatics filled the pages. Even the more innocuous issues, clearly targeting readers far younger than Yoshi, were highly sexualized. Primary school children gaped lasciviously at their teacher's breasts, their fantasies about seeing them naked outlined in overhead bubble clouds. Yoshi glanced over, waiting for a reaction. Joshua didn't give him one.

Manga and technology were rooting Yoshi into a ten-by-ten black box. He lived in a false society of his own making where he wasn't held up to scrutiny, where he wasn't accountable. Joshua wondered what Yoshi would do when he was relieved of his techno stuff. Would he be forced back into the real world? Or would he stare ahead into nothingness, a formless blob waiting to disintegrate.

Ishiguro and Yoshi's parents were carrying on with their lives, saving face while Yoshi was swept into a very small, very plugged-in corner.

Come out, don't come out. It makes no difference.

Except to Joshua.

The big issue, the one that kept Joshua awake nights, was *could he help this kid*?

He needed another meeting with Ken Ishiguro, but Yoshi's elusive uncle always seemed to be too busy. He would check his calendar, he said, and get back to Joshua next week.

Joshua's preoccupation with Yoshi was interrupted by the sound of raised voices coming from the next room. He went to the doorway.

Auntie Rose, staring wide-eyed at her cell phone, was ashen. Chad Malvern, still wearing his private-school blazer and gray flannels, was asking Rose if she was all right.

"Look at you, pretending like you fucking care."

The remark came from Gavin Polley, a streetwise kid with an array of piercings and tattoos that set him apart from most of the adolescents in Cypress Village. He was scarily intelligent but had a penchant for self-harm, his body a road map of lacerations and scabs. His kid sister had chosen a more perilous method to cope with the Polleys' contentious divorce, by dying a year ago from a drug overdose. Polley was slowly rallying from his grief and had made a few friends at 3F House, Chad Malvern not among them.

"Something wrong, Gav?" Malvern said.

"You're wrong, rich boy. All wrong."

Joshua stepped into the room. "What's going on here?"

Malvern sat down, looking small and weak, eyes glassy. "I just asked Auntie Rose if she was okay. She got another one of those crank calls. Then Gavin went ballistic."

Polley's face was purple. "Such bullshit. Can't anybody see it? He's got you all fooled!"

The others were rooted in place—Auntie Rose, Lily Howard, a few other teens who'd come to study. Wes Bertram came down the stairs.

"Fucking reptile!" Polley pointed at Malvern. "Him with his 'yes ma'am, no ma'am.' Why don't you tell them what you're really up to in your spare time, Malvern? You low-life piece of dogshit."

Bertram stepped toward Chad Malvern who looked ready to upchuck his dinner. "Come on, Chad. What say we take a walk?"

Joshua led Polley upstairs to his office where he continued his accusations against Malvern. He called him a manipulator, a snake charmer, a fraud. "He's trouble, Mr. L. The worst."

Beyond the cryptic references, Polley would say little. Regardless of how he felt about Malvern, Polley wouldn't rat him out. Some adolescent laws were sacred.

CHAPTER 13

busridersforum.com
Dec. 1, 2009 23:04
Join Date: April 9, 2009
Location: Belgium
Posts: 74
Killcrazy
Suicidal Tendencies
I'm ready to die, but I don't want to see it coming. I've always been accused of being irresponsible, and now I don't even want to accept responsibility for my own death. Ironic, right? Almost got enough money to hire someone to kill me. When it happens, I won't know how, I won't know where. My family will mourn, but at least they won't hate me. They'll hate the bastard who killed me. Plus they'll still be able to collect a death benefit. Everybody wins.
So I won't say goodbye, just "see you on the other side."

Pilgrim responded with another farewell. *Wish me smooth sailing too. I am done.*

Jim Stark's message was: *Too bored to live, too lazy to die. How's everybody else?*

Time for the Monitor to stir the pot. As Mr. Bator, he keyed in: *Better than you, Jim, you miserable, good for nothing f**k. Enough whining already. Buy a gun and do us all a favor. Or ride with everybody else.*

Geezer's reply came minutes later, telling everybody to ignore the troll. He'd been flat on his back all day, the painkillers just starting to take effect, but there weren't enough of them. He was ready to share the ride. C3PO was coming aboard as well. Love to everyone.

Jim Stark responded, *Now's as good a time as any.*

The Monitor keyed in his own grandmotherly reply: *I hate to think of anyone suffering needlessly. We treat our sick animals better. The next rainbow you see? That will be me, sending you my warmest wishes from Eden. Bless you all.*

Then he shut off the computer and laughed. Yes, bless you all. Everyone knew that within Eden lurked a serpent.

Next he used a disposable cell phone to send private messages to Geezer, Jim Stark, Blackjack, Pilgrim, C3PO and little Nightshade, who had already said her goodbyes. Painless deliverance, he promised. Until we are together.

How they disgusted him.

Whiners. Nothing more than a bunch of pathetic, snivelling, snotty-nosed whiners. They had no clue about suffering. Wouldn't know a real problem if one came along and bit off chunks of their collective asses. They mewled, blubbered, pleaded to die. And they would get their wish. A service easily and freely provided. The painless part—now that was a bit trickier. After all, there were no guarantees, were there? Things always went wrong, didn't work out exactly as planned. That's what kept things interesting, those little glitches that were beyond human control.

Human control. The Monitor smiled, paid for his coffee and left the Net café.

CHAPTER 14

THERE WAS NOT, NOR HAD there ever been, a Jim, James or Jaime Stark registered at the high school Brenda Koch had attended. Nor did Stark attend school with any of the other victims of the tragedy that had taken place at the Aerie. Carolyn wasn't surprised. In fact, she wanted to kick herself for not realizing that Jim Stark was another pseudonym, like Susie Cox. And Jill Munroe.

Late the night before, in the midst of a fitful sleep, Carolyn rolled over, nearly squashing the stuffing out of Pookie Bear. Then she sat up with a start. Jill Monroe. The name had bothered her the second her hairdresser uttered it. The jumble of thoughts that had left Carolyn restless eventually meshed together into a cohesive memory. She should have put it together sooner.

A swimsuit poster. A diamond-bright smile. A feathered hairdo that Carolyn had begged her mom to let her have, even though she was only five years old. Her wish at that age had been simple—when she grew up, she wanted to be just like Farrah Fawcett. The character the movie star had played for only one season on the television series "Charlie's Angels" was named Jill Munroe. The athletic angel. Heather Conklin, the Boise victim who'd adopted the alias, had been a dancer.

The officer Carolyn had sent to Lincoln City had returned with grim news about Brenda Koch. Yes, the flag was flying at half mast and someone had placed a bouquet of flowers in front of her locker, but most of the people, staff and students alike, reported not knowing Brenda very well. She didn't seem to mix well with others, one of the teachers said. Had Brenda ever seemed depressed? Been referred to a counselor?

Embarrassed looks. Shrugged shoulders.

Damn them anyway, Carolyn thought.

Ziggy appeared in the doorway to Carolyn's office and leaned against the jamb. "Close up shop, C.L." He and Ilona were going to their daughter's Christmas concert. Ziggy threatened to humiliate Amanda in front of her friends by taking their camcorder.

He looked every inch the doting parent, with new cords, a denim shirt and his hair gelled into a spiky buzz cut. Very cool.

"Enjoy the show, Zig," Carolyn told him, thinking again how lucky Amanda was and how she wished Brenda Koch could have known such a father.

"What's on for you tonight?"

"You mean after I elbow my way through the crowd of men trying to beat down my door? Not much."

"Ah, the single life. Must be tough to narrow it down to just one."

"Yeah, it's hell."

At home, Carolyn made a spinach salad, poured pinot blanc and heated some leftover lasagna. Then she called the only man in her life, her brother.

Paige answered instead. Joshua was in Portland attending a lecture given by Samuel J. Risk. The psychiatrist had volunteered for several tours of duty with Doctors of Mercy and was giving a talk about his experiences. Joshua had met Risk when he was a struggling seminarian and had consulted Risk when he became unsure of his priestly calling. He continued to use the humanitarian as a sounding board, often over a pitcher of beer after racquetball.

"Dastardly behaviour," Carolyn said, "deserting you on a night when there should be romance in the air. Is that any way for an engaged guy to behave?"

"Joshua's been counseling some kid who won't come out of his room, so I haven't seen much of him lately. You want to come out for coffee?"

Carolyn thought about it then said, "Thanks, but I think I'll just turn in. Long day today, and tomorrow doesn't look much better."

"Those four kids—Carolyn, it must have been awful. I haven't quite known what to say to you about it—"

"If only someone had gotten to them sooner, right? Don't we all wish."

"And on Signal Hill—"

"Yeah, that didn't help."

After hanging up, Carolyn went to her bedroom and fished a pair of striped pajamas from a dresser drawer. She hung them on the hook inside her bathroom and started running water in the tub. Following her divorce she'd switched from wearing silk nightshirts to cotton or flannel pajamas. They didn't ride up and leave her bare-assed in the middle of the night, and besides, she looked cute as hell in pajamas. She switched back to drinking white wine as well, sneering at her ex's notion that true wine aficionados only drank the robust reds.

She secured her hair into a messy topknot and settled into the tub, the smell of bergamot wafting up from the water. She took a lingering look at her body. She had always been a devoted fan of her breasts, the two kids, as she called them. They would never cause men to salivate when she entered the room, but they would never have an issue with gravity, either. Her stomach was taut, her waist narrow, her legs slender but muscled. She ignored the puckered scar on her shoulder and hoped her next bedmate would too. Maybe once the investigation was over she would devote more time to stepping up her love life, which was now humming along at zero.

After a good long soak, she gave her apple-scented soap the whirlwind tour then got out of the tub and dried off. She threw on a terry bathrobe, slipped on a pair of socks then padded over to her dining-room table and booted up her computer. A pop-up ad appeared—meet sexy singles online. Find a friend, a soul mate, a life mate. Oh sure.

She read some Hollywood gossip, which reminded her of the stack of tabloids on Irene Koch's coffee table.

Susie Cox. The other online aliases rushed back at her—Nightshade, Geezer, C3PO—the false names making it easier, safer for the users to communicate their darkest, most horrible secrets.

Jill Munroe.

Jim Stark.

On a hunch, Carolyn typed Stark's name and ran a search. Seconds later, she was greeted by a long list of Jim Starks, among them a realtor in Lansing, a hardware store owner in Pensacola, a poet in the Netherlands. But the Jim Stark she sought didn't exist. At least, not in real life. She suspected the Jim Stark who participated in busriders.com was a fictional icon, one who blazed across a movie screen then too quickly disappeared. And James Dean had played the troubled Stark in *Rebel Without a Cause*.

CHAPTER 15

THE DINER HADN'T SEEN A customer in thirty years. Most of the small-paned windows that faced the road had been shattered by pellets, thanks to joy-riding yahoos out for a night of target practice. Stenciled lettering above pale window frames advertising fries, soft drinks and burgers had faded from black to barely gray. Inside, layers of chalky dust settled everywhere like thick foam. Tiny anonymous things skittered and chittered and clicked in the corners. During daylight hours, the sagging structure and peeling roof appeared pathetic and somber. At nightfall, the place hunkered against the deep purple sky like a crippled beast, silent, foreboding, waiting. It was perfect.

The driver parked the BMW behind the building, and the group entered the diner through a side door that had been wedged ajar with a brick. The eldest male, who'd brought a flashlight, went in first.

Hello, Geezer.

The others followed: another male, then three women. The second man seized the flashlight and trained the beam along the L-shaped counter. "She said it would be behind here," came his hoarse whisper. "Let's hope our Monitor is true to her word."

Geezer and the women shuffled into the center of the room; the other male, clearly accustomed to being in charge, went behind the counter then ducked out of sight.

"I've got a question." A woman's voice. Drunk. Or high. Maybe both.

C3PO. I'd know you anywhere.

"Why are we whispering?" she giggled. "There's no one within miles of this dump."

"Yeah, no one," said another of the women, the youngest. "Creepy, isn't it?"

"It's what we asked for," Geezer said. "No frills."

"That's right," said the one behind the counter, standing upright again. "Don't think of it as creepy, Nightshade. Think of it as rustic."

"Where's the Monitor?" Nightshade asked. "She said she would meet us here. And so did Jim Stark."

"What are you worried about? The rest of us are here. Not getting cold feet again, are you?"

"No," she shook her head, adamant. "I've taken care of business. E-mailed my folks, sister and best friend. I used a time delay. But it doesn't seem right to catch the bus without Jim. Maybe we should wait."

Geezer looked at his watch. "It's time," he said. "We agreed. Jim Stark will have to catch the next one."

"Then if all systems are a go, let's belly up to the bar." The younger man produced a partial sleeve of plastic glasses and a screw-top wine bottle with its label washed off. The bottle was full of clear liquid. There was a note, too.

Everything is arranged, my dears. I won't be riding with you this time ... unforeseen circumstances ... but I've looked after you. Be at peace,

The Monitor.

He read it aloud. Then with his sleeve, the man wiped an area of the countertop clean.

Nightshade let a small sob escape. "No Monitor either? I think we should wait. At least until Jim shows up."

Geezer shook his head. "I've waited long enough."

C3PO said, "Me too. Make mine a double. I'll have Jim's share. And drink a toast to The Monitor, wherever she is."

"Allow me the honor," said the man behind the counter, who began pouring equal amounts into five glasses.

"Doesn't anyone want to say something first?" Nightshade asked. "You know, like a poem or a prayer or something?"

"Sure, I'll say something." The man made a dramatic flourish of recapping the bottle. "Life's a bitch and then you die."

Geezer shot him a look. "No need to be insensitive. How about you, Nightshade? Anything you want to say?"

The young girl thought for a moment then shrugged. "I guess not. Except—it was nice knowing you all. Thanks for being my friends. Thanks for understanding. I'm glad I'm not going through this alone. You make it less scary."

"Can we just get on with it?" This from the oldest female who'd yet to speak.

Other than Nightshade, not a particularly sentimental group.

"It won't hurt?" Nightshade again. "She promised us it wouldn't hurt."

The man behind the bar reached across and patted her hand. "Something to put us to sleep. Then something else to stop the heart. Just like with animals being euthanized. Quick and painless, okay? Sorry if I was an ass before. Been driving all night. I'm just tired."

"We're *all* tired," said the older woman. She raised her glass and drank. Then the rest drank, their facial expressions contorting, a reaction to the bitterness of the liquid.

They sat beside each other on the filthy floor, backs against the wall of broken windows. Nightshade rested her head on Geezer's shoulder. They waited. They were very quiet.

Occasionally, a car passed by on the road, headlights briefly putting the diner on shabby display. An owl hooted in the distance. The night creatures continued to scuttle across the linoleum. Nightshade drew her feet close to her body, hugged her knees. The younger man, who had driven them all to the spot in his car, checked his watch.

"What was that?" C3PO whispered, glanced toward the pass-through behind the counter. "I thought I heard something back in the kitchen."

"Shhh," said Geezer. "Try to relax."

"That's just it. I can't. I feel so ... jumpy. Maybe we should turn off the flashlight."

"No," Nightshade said suddenly. "I mean, can we please leave the light on?"

Geezer nodded. He draped an arm protectively around the young girl's shoulder. "Relax, everybody," he said again. "Deep breaths."

They were quiet again, listening to the sounds of each other's breathing, lungs filling and emptying. C3PO lay down in a fetal curl on the tiles, pulling her oversized hoodie snugly around her. She closed her eyes. Moments later she rolled over to face the opposite wall. The older woman flexed her jaw, dropped her head forward and massaged her neck, a puzzled frown settling on her face. Nightshade began to whimper.

Geezer cleared his throat. Swatted at something with too many legs as it hurried across his ankle. Swiped out again as the creepy crawly scuttled toward Nightshade.

After a time, the young man checked his watch again. "Fifteen minutes," he whispered. "Something's wrong. I'm not even tired."

"I'm wide awake too," the woman complained. "And I did what I was told. My stomach was empty when I came here. But so far, I've only got a stiff neck and a sore face."

"My neck hurts too," Nightshade cried. "Really bad."

Minutes later, Geezer's arms and legs went into spasm. His howls of agony filled the diner, the jarring noise triggering violent convulsions in the others. Nightshade screamed. Her back arched convexly, her head and heels still on the floor. No one was in a position to offer assistance, each of them helpless as the poison consumed them, sending their bodies into repeated and worsening spasms. In unison they became contorted, jerking puppets on a grimy and insect-infested stage. They screamed, howled, begged.

"Christ Almighty, make it stop!"

"Somebody help us!"

"Hurts … oh God, it hurts!"

High-pitched shrieks.

Gutteral moans.

Agony-filled entreaties to Savior or Satan.

"No more! Please!"

"Let it be over! Let us die!"

Nightshade had no words, only more screams, all her muscles constricting at once.

In the midst of the horrific scene, the door leading to the kitchen swung open and the gloved figure entered the room carrying a stainless steel bowl and spoon in one hand, a flute of champagne in the other. Plastic bags covered a pair of black shoes. "Good evening, my dears."

"Who—who are you?" The eldest woman forced the words out through clenched teeth, her jaw rigid.

"Why, I'm your Monitor, dear."

"B—but you can't be! You're—"

"Taller than you expected? Yes, a lot of people have said that. And younger, too."

"You said there wouldn't be pain!"

"Look at us!"

"What's gone wrong?"

"Actually," the Monitor said, resting an elbow casually on the countertop, "nothing's gone wrong. This is exactly how I envisioned your deliverance."

Geezer cried out again, back arching almost continuously now. "Can't breathe." There was a gasp then another convulsion.

"You promised us!" hissed the younger man.

"We trusted you," moaned C3PO. "This isn't fair!"

"Oh my dears, life isn't fair. You already know that. You've been whining about that for months now. You've all had it so tough, haven't you? Your boring jobs, your impossible parents, your little aches and pains. Doesn't it all seem so trivial now, now that you truly know what pain is?"

"What did you give us?" the man huffed, his words barely audible above the screams of the others.

"*Strychnos nux vomica*. Strychnine. One hundred and fifty milligrams each. Absolutely fatal. No turning back now. Tastes like the devil, too, at least that's what I've been told. I mixed it with a little maple syrup. I hope you appreciate that."

He broke composure to flash them a warm, Monitor smile.

"Death from either asphyxia or sheer exhaustion. The body, you see, isn't meant to continually jackknife like that. The slightest stimulus, from bright light—" the Monitor paused and directed the flashlight at the group. The one calling herself C3PO emitted a tortured hellish groan. "—to loud noise, can aggravate your symptoms." With that the Monitor pounded the stainless bowl with the spoon.

In a macabre synchronicity of motion, they convulsed, yowled, gasped and one by one, they breathed their last. Nightshade, the youngest and the strongest, lasted nearly an hour, proving to the Monitor a quote attributed to Anne Sexton. The poet, before her eventual success with suicide, said, "The body is a damn hard thing to kill."

CHAPTER 16

Carolyn and Ziggy were working late, a half-eaten, meat-lovers pizza shoved to one side of Carolyn's desk. Ziggy's wife was out with her reading group, and his daughter was working on a major assignment for her Spanish class, so he had no reason to rush home. Carolyn didn't need to rush home either.

Earlier, she and Zig had met Heather Conklin's parents. The couple had driven from Boise to collect their daughter's ashes. They also insisted on seeing the place where Heather had died. Ziggy drove them to the Aerie, answered as many of their questions as he could with as much sensitivity and compassion as he could muster without breaking down himself. There wasn't a course or seminar that could adequately prepare him for speaking to two people who'd just had their hearts ripped out. He told the Conklins what he knew, that a boy from Massachusetts named Kevin Randolph had rented a car and driven the teens to this spot. It had all been planned weeks in advance, the details finalized on the Internet. The dress Heather had been found in was one she'd worn to a dance recital the previous year. Her princess dress, Mrs. Conklin said. That was what Heather used to call it.

Neither parent had noticed any sign of depression. Their daughter worked hard at school, was dedicated to the ballet. They never pressured her, never drove her to perfection. There was no stage-mothering. Heather was thin but there was no evidence of an eating disorder. Her appetite was as hearty as any growing teenager's. She dated occasionally. A nice boy named Paul came by the house some Saturday nights, chatted politely with the Conklins before taking Heather out to a movie or for a bite to eat. It all seemed too good to be true, Mr. Conklin said, in case Ziggy was skeptical, but that's how it was. Ziggy nodded, understanding. He told the couple he had a daughter who sounded a lot like Heather. As soon as he said it, he told Carolyn he wanted to tear out his tonsils. His daughter was still alive.

The Internet was the devil, Mrs. Conklin said, and she and her husband were slated to appear on a Boise cable show the following week to discuss its evil lures. Ziggy understood that, too. He patted the hood of the Conklins' car as they drove away, Heather's princess dress hanging from a hook in the back seat. The urn containing her ashes rested up front between them.

Carolyn felt for those parents, and she felt for Ziggy, too, just as she had for Ted Tarrant in Massachusetts, who'd had to face the Randolphs with news of their son's death. The experience with the Conklins seemed to imbue Ziggy with a new resolve. Despite the fatigue tugging at the corners of his eyes, he was lurking in busridersforum.com, checking out the Suicidal Tendencies thread to see what had been posted there. There was only one message, from a new poster, someone calling himself LethalDose. *Hope to see you all soon.*

Ziggy reached for a bottle of spring water and guzzled. "Pizza was salty. What do you think of the name Fading Away?"

"I much prefer Takacs. More continental. More swarthy."

"Very funny. I mean for my online nick. I can't very well type 'hi, I'm the police.'"

"You're right. And Fading Away resonates better than I'm-going-to-slit-my-throat-any-second."

"Now we just need to come up with a legitimate reason why Fading Away wants to kill herself."

"Fading Away will be female?"

"Let's make her as vulnerable as possible. And she'll be pseudononymous, too. I'm going to use a chain of re-mailers. They'll wipe out our electronic ID info and we'll be reallocated to an anonymous ID. Basically, we're creating a complicated trail so that what we post on the message board can't be easily traced back here. Sure as hell that's what our Net-ghost is doing."

"Great. So what you're telling me is—"

"Before we throw Fading Away to her cyber-wolf, you have to realize that Internet crimes are mega-tough sons of bitches to crack. We may never catch this bastard."

"You're just trying to cheer me up."

"Wish I could. As clever as I think I'm being here, and believe me, I'm still a Net neophyte, our cyber-freak is probably light-years ahead. The software I'm using is fine for a start, but it and my limited expertise will only take us so far. This little online stunt could be as useful as a fedora to a headless man."

Carolyn squeezed the bridge of her nose. She was getting a headache, which she would take over one of her sciatica attacks any day. Still, she wished Ziggy had something more positive to say. They were only nine days into their investigation and the prognosis had already dipped from bleak to grim.

Ziggy drained what was left of his bottled water, eyed the pizza then stood and put the box out of harm's way on top of Carolyn's filing cabinet near the door to her office. "Plus," he said when he returned to the swivel chair beside hers, "he could turn out to be a fourteen-year-old geek who gets his jollies from manipulating others. Stalkers live for one thing—to disrupt their target's routines, their everyday lives. Fucking almighty power trip, see?"

"Let me hazard a guess at this creep's profile. Intelligent, like you said. Highly computer literate. But lonely. Isolated."

"Because?"

"Because he hasn't got the courage for any face-to-face contact. It's easier, more comfortable for him to remain—what was your word?—pseudononymous. But I disagree with you about the fourteen-year-old geek part. Remember how we got onto this hideous hell-train in the first place. We think our freak may have watched those people die. Does that sound like something a young teenager would do?"

"Look, don't get me wrong, C.L. I've met a lot of Amanda's friends at the sports games, the school concerts. Guys and girls.

Studied them like any overprotective father. Most of 'em are great. Raised right, the whole bit. But a few I've come across—well, let's just say I wouldn't mind seeing them move to another planet. And it only takes one maladjusted kid to cause a whole mother-frickin' shitload of trouble."

"Okay, I'll keep an open mind."

Carolyn appreciated Ziggy's point. Notorious serial killer Edmund Kemper was fifteen when he shot his grandparents. The two youths who had lured two-year-old James Bulger from a shopping mall in Liverpool were ten. They had committed repeated attacks on their helpless victim because, in the words of one of the boys, "he just kept getting up." Carolyn also remembered reading about a fourteen-year-old who'd bludgeoned his much younger neighbor with a baseball bat then hid her body under his waterbed. Yes, the unthinkable could happen, but up until now the image Carolyn had of the person who'd crouched at the top of the Signal Hill wasn't of a teenager. She had envisioned a cunning, ruthless puppeteer, one who relished taking people at their most vulnerable, their most miserable; once ensnared, it was a simple matter to douse them with gasoline and toss them a match. Could such manipulation have been committed by a youth? She didn't want to believe it, but she thought again about poor James Bulger, lured so tragically to a terrible death and knew it was possible.

"How about an illness?" Ziggy said.

No, thanks, already got one, Carolyn wanted to say. "You mean for Fading Away, of course."

He nodded. "She'll need a reason to die. Something that will make the virtual bus-riding community sympathetic."

It was a no-brainer. "Sciatica," Carolyn announced simply.

Ziggy arched a brow in her direction.

"You know the old saying—'write what you know.' The posts will sound authentic and convincing because I'll be writing them." Though Carolyn hadn't experienced a full-blown episode in a while, there were times when white-hot pain radiated from her buttocks down to her legs, forcing her to her medicine cabinet for anti-inflammatories. Once, a particularly grueling attack had been aggravated by a sneeze. The pain had lasted a week and she eventually succumbed to medicated oblivion, popping pain-killers like peanuts. During more benign bouts of her condition, Carolyn considered herself lucky to escape with only an aching hip. An old lady hip, Gregg used to call it.

"Sciatica it is," Ziggy said.

"And Fading Away will be in her mid-thirties. She'll live in the Pacific Northwest, be divorced with no kids. Again, why make something up when the truth works just as well?"

"You're right. We'll be less likely to get tripped up and caught in a lie. You'll be okay with this?"

"Absolutely," Carolyn answered, her voice sounding surer than she felt. What was she worried about? She would choose what to reveal, what to keep hidden. It wouldn't be a problem. "Fading Away will have some of my stats, but she'll be pushed to the point of desperation. She'll be alone, lonely, unable to work at the job she loves because of her illness. How's that sound?"

"Sounds like you can start drafting up your first post to the group." Ziggy nudged a pad of paper toward her. "I'm going to try some of my online wizardry to see if I can locate our forum moderator, Bella Donna."

"Good luck with that. Bella Donna could be living in a cave in Afghanistan for all we know."

"Possible, but somehow I don't think so. Quite a few of the bus riders are posting from Oregon or our neighboring states. Plus we've had a group suicide right here in our back yard. I think Bella Donna is local. And sure, she's denying that she posted that message to Jim Stark a while back encouraging him to finish the deed. It's easy to blame hate mail on a troll. But there's still a fifty-fifty chance that Bella Donna did write that stuff, in which case she's not just pro-choice, she's pro-suicide."

"Ziggy, if she's the one tipping the web board participants over the brink and we find that she actually watched those kids suffocate themselves, then we may have a psychopath on our hands, one who could be in danger of escalating. But if all she did was watch, we've got nothing. Discussing suicide isn't against the law."

"Yeah, but what if we can prove that Bella Donna not only watched those kids die but also supplied them with the charcoal? Or outlined the plan for them to follow? Then we've got her on solicitation to commit murder."

"Correction. *Someone* will have her on solicitation to commit murder. She may not be in our jurisdiction."

"Now who's trying to cheer who up?"

Ziggy stood up and left her office to park himself at his own desk to try and root out the ISP for busriders.com. Carolyn could hear keystrokes clacking furiously, interrupted by intervals of swearing. Occasionally she looked up from her own writing to see the sergeant rake a hand through his short hair. His sleeves were rolled up, his necktie loosened. His face was etched into an angry grimace so it wasn't difficult to conclude that the elusive Bella Donna was still at large. Carolyn shared Ziggy's frustration. As far as computers went, Ziggy was their expert, but even he admitted his skills were woefully inadequate. Cypress Village police didn't have the money or the resources to continually update programs or send officers for training. With every day that passed, their knowledge became obsolete as technology advanced with lightning speed. If Bella Donna, or someone else, was truly a conspirator to murder, Carolyn might have no choice but to involve the FBI. She hoped it wouldn't come to that.

She checked over her written draft to busriders.com, made a few improvements, walked around her desk and took the sheet over to Ziggy. "Check this out. See if it sounds cyber-like. I'll make coffee."

She returned minutes later with two steaming mugs. "I put in a couple of those Irish coffee-flavored creamers that you like."

Ziggy took the mug. "Always knew you cared, C.L."

Carolyn felt her face warm. She said quickly, "What do you think?"

"Of the coffee? Great." He looked up and smiled then returned his attention to the sheet of paper. "Let's give it one more look."

Carolyn leaned over her partner's shoulder and reread the page.

`busridersforum.com`

December 3, 2009 22:00
Join Date: December 3, 2009
Location: Pacific Northwest
Posts: 1
Fading Away
Suicidal Tendencies
Can anyone help? I've been lurking on this web board for a while, getting to know some of you, wondering who I can trust. I just need to know someone understands. On a desperation scale out of 10, I'm sitting at 12. Can't work at a job. Am in agony all the time.

I have sciatica, and if you don't know what that is, try to imagine pain so bad that you pray someone will sever your body at the waist just so you can get some sleep. Imagine there's no comfortable position to sit in. Imagine someone sticking knives in you all the time. That's what it's like for me.

Doctors have tried everything, but some cures are worse than the disease. My father had sciatica too, and he eventually lost control of his bladder. Do I have that to look forward to? I've been reading Geezer's posts—you sound a lot like me, Geezer. I'm alone, too, and wanting it all just to end. I'm so tired of hurting, so tired of everything.

"That true?" Ziggy asked. "About your dad?"

Carolyn lowered her head.

"Sorry. None of my business." He cleared his throat. "I think Fading Away's post works. Kind of numb, reaching out, but fed up, too. And you don't reveal too much too soon. That's good. Let your story evolve as you gain more comfort with the group, but for our purposes, we'll still have to move along more quickly than we normally would if we intend to draw out Bella Donna or any of the others." He drank coffee and Carolyn watched his Adam's apple bob as he swallowed. His fingers were curled around the heavy mug, his gold filigreed wedding band glinting off his ring finger.

Carolyn stood up, removed her hand from the back of Ziggy's chair. "I'll type it and send it then?"

"Let's do it from this computer. You'll have to register to post on the board and check the option that says you want to receive mail. We'll set up an e-mail account, too. And C.L? Any communication you have with the group, will you run it by me?"

"Zig, you know that's not practical. If people are online in the middle of the night, and Fading Away is supposed to be suicidal, she'll be awake, ready to respond with her own message. But if I'm in doubt, I'll err on the side of caution and wait." Then she rolled her eyes. "Cyber gurus, you're all alike."

Ziggy spent a few minutes registering Fading Away on busridersforum.com then he typed in Carolyn's first posting. Fading Away was now part of the suicide message board. With any luck, she would be accepted by the group and her infiltration of the forum would lead to the unmasking of the bastard who'd originated the site. If Bella Donna or anyone else had watched the four teenagers die on Signal Hill, then Carolyn had to stop the sicko. But if there was more than watching going on here, Carolyn hoped that whoever might be responsible for urging the foursome to end their lives wasn't on any kind of accelerated schedule. It would take time for Carolyn to be convincing; it would take time to draw out a circle of a trustworthy few. Carolyn prayed she had the luxury of time.

Ziggy was about to log off the computer and shut it down when his phone rang. "Hey, Mandy," he said when he heard his daughter's voice. "What? Take it easy. I can't understand you."

Carolyn could hear Amanda crying through the receiver.

"Is it your mother?" Zig was frantic. "What's wrong? ... Are you sick? Amanda, calm down ... I'm coming right home."

He slammed the phone down and hurried to a metal coat rack where his windbreaker hung.

Carolyn rushed over to him. “Zig, what it it? Is Amanda okay? Is it Ilona?”

“I don’t know,” he answered, his face a mask of confusion and panic. “She was hysterical. I couldn’t get anything out of her.” He wrestled with his jacket then bolted for the door.

“Call me if there’s anything I can do!” Carolyn hollered after him.

But he was already gone.

CHAPTER 17

IT WAS A HIDEOUS TABLEAU, the bodies frozen in grotesque, contorted postures, rigor having set in immediately, for some in mid-convulsion. Their eyes bulged. Their faces were suffused with blood. Their lips were drawn back, each of the five displaying a toothy, maniacal rictus. The diner that had once been the best place to get a burger was now a chamber of horrors.

Sergeant Zygmunt Takacs, his face chalky, drew near the body of the youngest victim, a whippet-thin girl with a tangle of auburn curls. He got down on one knee and made the sign of the cross. "Jesus, Mary and Joseph," he whispered. "Melly, what have you done?"

"Zig?" Carolyn stepped closer and gently put her hand on his shoulder.

"Melissa Waller," he said, his voice hoarse. "She's Amanda's best friend. Came camping with us last summer. Greatest kid. Always at the house. Just like having another daughter." He closed his eyes, spread his hand over his face. "Son of a bitch."

"Why don't you slip outside for a while, get some air."

He waved off the offer, cleared his throat and stood. "Let's get the job done."

Unlike those who had died at the Aerie, the five at the diner had brought ID with them to their final resting place. The oldest male was Bill Armstrong, 64, from British Columbia. The other man's wallet was located in the glove compartment of the BMW parked outside. Neal Bloome had made the trip from Reno, choosing to die out of state and away from his wife and three sons. Their photos were clipped to the sun visor of his car. Dozens of business cards for Bloome and Ross, Attorneys at Law, were contained in a small silver case in the console between the front seats, along with a Coldplay CD and a partially consumed roll of Lifesavers.

Lying beside Melissa Waller was a mid-twenties blonde, her stringy hair all but obscuring her face. She was clad in an ankle-length paisley dress, dark leotard and lace-up boots. A navy crocheted shawl lay nearby which Carolyn assumed belonged to her as well. Once the initial photographs of the victims were taken, Carolyn gingerly swept the strands of hair away from the woman's face and gasped.

"My God. This is Shana Pascal."

Ziggy leaned in. "From the Cat?"

Carolyn nodded.

The Cheshire Cat, a trendy café in the village, boasted the best fair-trade coffee and homemade pastries along the Oregon seaside. Carolyn was a regular customer, and Shana served her almost every morning. Carolyn thought the young woman seemed pleasant enough but during their few chats, she sensed Shana was lonely, adrift, as if still searching for a place to belong.

She hadn't found it.

The ME surveyed the scene before him. Thomas Trahern was a fit man in his early sixties. He sported an admirable head of gray hair and a matching walrus mustache which he stroked as he said, "Never seen anything like this in my career, but if this isn't strychnine poisoning, I'll turn in my bone saw. Poor bastards. Got to be the worst way to go."

Ziggy looked ready to break. He pursed his lips, blinked hard and backed away toward the counter.

"He knows the young girl," Carolyn explained to Trahern. "And I've met this one." She nodded at Shana.

"Damn. Sometimes I forget what a small town this is. Are they all local?"

Carolyn shook her head. "Just the two. Then we've got Reno, Vancouver," she pointed to Neal then Bill, "and this woman's from Orem, Utah."

Trahern bent toward the eldest female, a plain-looking woman wearing a baggy sweatshirt and track pants. June Kinzel, according to the ID in her purse, was forty-seven, single and an elementary schoolteacher. A pocket-size calendar showed dates set aside for staff meetings, parent interviews, a class trip. Also in her purse was a worn leather-bound copy of *Pearl of Great Price*, one of the four sacred texts of the Mormon faith. "Do me a favor," Trahern said. "Lift up her sweatshirt."

With a gloved hand, Carolyn raised the pale pink fabric. Beneath the sweatshirt, the woman wore a one-piece white cotton vestment that Carolyn recognized as a temple garment, its neckline resting just below the collarbone. Mormons who had been formally endowed in the faith wore the garment to remind them of their promise to live a righteous life. It was meant to be a spiritual shield and protection, and some Latter-Day Saints believe it also protected the wearer from physical harm.

Not this time, Carolyn thought.

"Just as I suspected," Trahern said, looking at the drawstring pants loosely tied and slung below the woman's rounded belly.

June Kinzel was pregnant.

"About four months along, I'd say," Trahern offered. "Just starting to become difficult to conceal her condition from her friends, family, and co-workers. If the baggy sweatshirt didn't fool me, chances are it didn't fool too many others either."

"Wonder what her Mormon friends thought about it," Carolyn muttered, although that thought wasn't foremost in her mind. She mourned for the child, imprisoned in a womb full of poison. She wondered if it had suffered, hoping that a merciful God would have ended its struggle quickly.

"Strychnine." Trahern shook his head. "Out of all the pharmaceuticals they could have ingested, why pick the substance that would cause the most agony?"

"Maybe they didn't choose," Carolyn said quietly. "I suspect someone chose for them. These people may have been conned into thinking they would have a peaceful death."

"Well, it was anything but." Trahern enlightened Carolyn on what the five had experienced in the time leading up to their demise, choosing his words carefully. He was describing the tortures of the damned.

"The baby too?"

Trahern sighed. "Let's not even think about it."

"Hey, C.L.," Ziggy called to Carolyn from the lunch counter, his voice shaky. "Check this out."

Carolyn cast her gaze to where Ziggy pointed. The counter, like the rest of the diner, was thick with dust. Except for two places. There was a clean rectangle, about a foot square, at the end of the bar near the diner's side door. Almost directly opposite the spot where the five had died was an irregularly shaped circle on the countertop that was also dust-free.

"What do you make of this?" Ziggy asked. "Is this where they drank the stuff?"

Carolyn examined the countertop and thought before forming her response. Her mind traced the imagined movements of the five, from the time they entered the diner until they lay together to die. She tried not to dwell on what each was thinking, especially the pregnant woman and fifteen-year-old Melissa Waller. "My guess is they gathered at that end, where the area is wiped clean. Bloome's black sweater has a lot of dust on the right sleeve. This smaller smudge here," she said, "is something else. My instinct says an elbow."

Carolyn turned to face the dead, her elbow hovering above the smudged area. She affected a casual stance, ankles crossed. "Bastard stood right here," she said. "Stood here, leaned against the counter and watched them die." She refrained from elaborating upon the details Trahern had quietly shared with her, how the victims had endured excruciating pain, likely howling in agony as they were gripped by seizure after seizure. Too awful to imagine, much worse to know that Amanda's best friend had met her end that way. She could spare her partner and friend that.

"There are other possibilities for the smudge, C.L. We can't be sure."

"No? Look."

Patrol Officer Ken Howe, armed with a forensic kit, was carefully following a path through the grimy floor toward the diner's kitchen, spreading black powder everywhere. "Someone came from back here," he said. "Didn't have the decency to leave us one tread mark from his shoes. Looks like the bastard wore bags over 'em. But here's something interesting."

Ziggy and Carolyn moved in single file to where the investigator stood. On the dusty floor, someone had traced a picture, or rather, a symbol.

"Son of a bitch," Ziggy muttered. He stooped for a closer look.

Clearly etched on the dirty tiles were two thick parallel lines, several inches apart, joined by shorter perpendiculars, one of the short lines jagged and broken.

Carolyn crouched. "What are they? Train tracks?"

"Or bars on a jail cell," Ziggy offered.

Howe snapped pictures. "Reminds me of a cold-air return. You know, those grates in floors ..."

Ziggy tilted his head. "What's it supposed to mean?"

Carolyn put a hand on Ziggy's shoulder to steady herself then rose. "I think that's what we're supposed to figure out. Time to do some research into gang graffiti, symbolic language, hieroglyphics. Whoever put this here is sending us a message."

"Son of a bitch," Ziggy said again. "Melissa ..." His face grew pale.

Carolyn patted him firmly on the back. "I know, Zig. It doesn't get any worse."

"Could one of them have done it?" He gestured toward the bodies, averting his gaze from his daughter's friend.

"It's possible," Carolyn said. "But here's a thought. If they drank poison, where's the bottle?"

It was true. The shelves behind the bar were devoid of glassware. There were no bottles, glasses or jars anywhere. A sixth person had been at the diner. And he had taken the container with him.

When Carolyn told Ziggy this he said, "But why? These people decided to kill themselves. They made ... arrangements. So someone comes along and watches. What's the reason for taking the container away? Unless he actually supplied them with the stuff. Then it's murder. Why point a finger at himself?"

"Don't you see? That's the *fun* part. He wants us to know he's been here. Just like he did on Signal Hill when he left that champagne cork beneath the tree. That was no accident. See, it wouldn't do for just the victims to grab all the headlines without our mastermind getting so much as an honorable mention. He's clever, and he thinks it's time we knew it."

The three stared at the symbol as if time would reveal its meaning. As soon as Howe had finished getting his photographs, Carolyn walked a wide circle around the strange drawing. It was no use. The lines were still just lines.

She joined Ziggy who had returned to where the five lay. He was staring at Melissa Waller who lay rigid beside her adult companions.

"That could have been Amanda," he whispered.

"No, Zig," Carolyn put her arms around him, tried to make her touch warm, comforting, strong. Somehow to her it felt like something else. "Amanda's got you and Ilona," she said quickly. "She's always known that. She'd never have a reason—"

"Melly had good parents too, C.L. And a little sister she adored. Oh, God."

Carolyn felt Ziggy's weight sag in her arms.

He broke from her grasp. "I've got to tell them."

"No way. I'll do it myself just as soon as—"

"No. It's gotta be me. I'll go over there now."

"You should be with Amanda. She needs you."

"She'll have me soon enough."

"Zig—" Carolyn hesitated, the question needing to be asked, but she hated having to ask it "—do you think Amanda might have known something about ... what Melissa had planned?"

"We'll know tomorrow when I bring her to you for questioning."

Carolyn nodded, understanding.

"Way I see it," he said, "I've got a couple more shitty hours left to be a cop, then I can go home and be a father. Let's hope I don't screw up either job."

Five more dead. No, six. Carolyn thought once more of the baby, June Kinzel's four-month-old. Womb to tomb. Did the baby suffer? *Let's not even think about that.* ME Trahern had looked away.

Carolyn pushed the horrific images from her mind and tried to suppress a fresh set of shivers that traveled the length of her body. She still had work to do. Terrible work.

By the time she reached Signal Hill it was 4:00 a.m. She parked and took several moments to breathe deeply. She forced herself to remove her stare from the hulking dark silhouette of the Aerie.

Local youths had already made a pilgrimage to the scene, placing flowers and candles at the entrance to the driveway where the four teenagers had died. Some had written poems, made cards. Someone had left an old tennis racket.

Carolyn directed her gaze toward the spot where she suspected the audience of one had planted himself. He would have waited among the pines, watched the Neon drive up the hill. He would have been there from the beginning. He would have given himself time to spare. Did he use the time to consume a full bottle of champagne? Carolyn didn't think so. He wouldn't have run the risk of getting caught for drunk driving. He would have passed the time creatively. Because he was a creative bastard.

She zipped up her weatherproof jacket, grabbed a flashlight and a disposable camera from the glove box and stepped from the car. Among the trees, the ground was sodden and her socks and shoes quickly became soaked. More chills. She crouched low, searching the area where she believed the monster had hunkered down, waiting for the show to begin. She circled each pine and spread branches apart, training the flashlight's beam along tree trunks.

Pine needles scraped across her cheeks, caught in her hair, poked at her eyes. She kept on. It was here somewhere. She knew it.

Her senses were on high alert. She listened for an occasional car passing along the road below, an owl hooting, perhaps a mouse skittering among the underbrush. On Signal Hill, it was crypt quiet. She trod carefully though she knew she was alone, took shallow half-breaths and continued her sweep of the trees. It wouldn't be far away. He would want it to be found.

She returned to the spot where she had noticed the flattened patch of grass and sat on the wet earth. She was numb with cold, exhausted to her marrow, but it didn't matter. She wouldn't be sleeping much, not at all if she didn't find what she'd come for. Again, she shone the beam against the base of the trees that surrounded her but saw nothing.

Carolyn faced her vehicle, about sixty feet away. *You sat like this*, she thought, *sheltered by these low branches. They wouldn't have been looking for you. They only came to die.* But perhaps he'd begun his evening further back among the trees, stepping closer to the driveway only when the Neon appeared. That was it. He was a master gamesman, after all. No point in making it too easy.

She stood up again, futilely wiped at the seat of her pants and moved farther away from the gravel drive in a straight line from where she'd been sitting, flashlight moving in a slow, low arc. She searched the area for over an hour, circling back, retracing steps, each tree and patch of ground looking the same as another.

Perhaps she had been wrong. Maybe one of the victims had drawn the symbol in the dust, not a sixth person after all.

Carolyn pushed branches aside and returned to her car. Her hand was on the door when she looked up at the Aerie. The wood and stone retreat beckoned to her from its perch at the top of the hill, and she found herself moving toward the house. Gooseflesh crawled across her skin. Hair rose on her arms. *He's in jail*, she told herself. *You're safe here.*

Mission-style lanterns flanked the front door and gleamed brightly. If her mysterious sixth person had been on this porch, he had left no clue. No symbol. Carolyn circled the perimeter of the large house, forcing herself to cast aside her fear as she approached the side entrance.

You're fine, she thought. *Find the damned symbol. Then you can go home.*

Another thirty minutes yielded nothing. Perhaps she would try again in the daylight. Bring another officer with a fresh set of eyes.

When she returned to the Explorer she realized what she had overlooked.

CHAPTER 18

THE TAKACS FAMILY HAD SPENT a rough night.

"Amanda's on the edge of her last nerve," Ziggy said after he closed the door to Carolyn's office.

Ziggy's daughter sat just outside the door drinking tea from a Styrofoam cup. She slumped in a formed plastic chair, her body seeming to cave in on itself. Her usually neat hair was hastily drawn back and held with a clamp, several disobedient strands hanging in her face. She looked small, dumbstruck and fragile.

"Looks like her dad is, too," Carolyn said, trying not to stare at the dark circles under his eyes. "Did any of you get any sleep?"

"Not a hell of a lot," he admitted. "Mandy cried all night. Threw up once too. Eventually we all got out of bed and sat on the couch in the family room. Didn't say much, just kind of held hands and stared at some old movie on the television. Had to put a blanket around her to stop her from shaking."

"Poor thing," Carolyn said, gazing out at her through the half glass in the door. Others were trying to go about their business, not quite knowing what to say to Sergeant Takacs's daughter, whom they adored. "Did she tell you anything, anything at all?"

"I didn't ask. I didn't want to make her tell the story twice. When she did talk, it was just to tell us what a good friend Melly was, how much she'll miss her. C.L., if there was any way I could have spared my daughter this—well, I'd march headlong into hell if I thought it would help."

"I know you would, Zig. Tell you what. You bring Amanda in here. The sooner she tells us what she knows, the sooner she can get home, get some rest."

Ziggy nodded and opened the door. "Come on in, Mandy."

Amanda Takacs entered, her pale complexion mottled, her lips red and swollen. She braved a trembling smile for Carolyn who wanted to wrap her in a hug. Bad idea all around, she knew. Amanda was struggling to keep fresh tears from erupting. Instead, Carolyn directed her to a chair and offered the girl more tea, which she refused.

"It's just like I told you, Amanda," Ziggy said. "Sergeant Latham's got some questions for you. Tell her everything you know. Everything. I'll be at my desk if you need me, okay?"

"I'm fine, Dad."

"'Course you are." He kissed the top of his daughter's head, gave her shoulder a strong squeeze then left, pulling the door closed behind him.

Carolyn pulled her chair from behind her desk and positioned it close to Amanda's. "Amanda, I can't tell you I know how you feel because I don't. But what I'm sure of is that you have two parents who are crazy about you, and they'll get you through this. I wish I could promise that you'll feel better next week, or next month, but I can't do that either. I don't know how long it'll take before this stops hurting."

Thoughts strobed through Carolyn's mind. Gregg packing his bags. His lover pregnant. Then Carolyn getting shot, once in the shoulder, once in the back, and just for a moment, not giving a good goddamn whether she came out of it or not.

Older wounds. Her mother, running off to trip the light fantastic with her dance instructor, months before her parents' silver anniversary. Her father suffering a fatal heart attack a year later. Maybe some hurts were always with you.

"Melly was my best friend," Amanda said. "At school they called us the M&Ms. You know, Melly and Mandy."

"From what your dad told me, Melissa was a special girl."

"She was. She was smart and good at sports, and she was always ready to have a laugh. She was just the neatest person to be around."

Carolyn allowed Amanda to reminisce about her friend. Melissa Waller had been popular, not in a swing-your-pompoms way, but more like the kind of girl others could count on. She was easy to talk to. Guys were interested, but Melissa was choosy. She could have gone on dates both nights of every weekend, but she didn't accept many offers. Often she preferred sleeping over at Amanda's, watching scary DVDs, eating nachos and flat-ironing her friend's hair. Both Carolyn and Amanda smiled when Amanda told of how she and her friend had shoved inflated balloons inside their pajama tops and performed a riotous version of "Nine to Five" for Ziggy and Ilona. Ziggy had captured the entire duet on his camcorder.

More stories emerged as well. Of long bicycle rides in summer, trying out for sports teams, planting trees for their church's youth group project. With the telling, Amanda's face softened and her voice lost its tremor. Perhaps healing occurred more quickly in the young, Carolyn mused, wishing for Amanda's sake that it was true.

"Amanda, here's the hard question. Did Melissa ever talk about wanting to kill herself?"

The girl shook her head vigorously. "She was happy. Always happy."

"And yet ..."

The silence hung in the air. Carolyn looked up. Ziggy cast occasional glances into the office, ever the concerned parent, wondering how his little girl was making out.

"Melissa was your best friend," Carolyn said, her voice urging, coaxing. "She would have told you things, things she wouldn't have shared with anyone else. Was everything all right at home?"

"It was great. Melissa loved her parents. And her sister. Everything was cool. I think she—she may have got caught up in something ..."

Carolyn waited.

Amanda swiped at a tear. Eventually she said, "The people she met on the Net. They were ..."

"Depressed," Carolyn offered. "Suicidal?"

A nod. Head hung low.

"What happened to Melissa—" Carolyn continued "—came as a surprise to you?"

"Yes." Hesitation, then, "No. I mean—"

Carolyn waited. The truth, or the part that Amanda knew of it bubbled close to the surface. She glanced around nervously at her father. Carolyn followed her gaze. Ziggy was furiously hammering keystrokes, staring at his monitor. Had there been a response to Fading Away?

Amanda fiddled with her ring, a small peridot birthstone she wore on her pinkie. She cleared her throat, asked politely for another cup of tea. Carolyn stayed put. "Sure, Amanda. In a minute. But something's on your mind. Talk to me."

"He'll kill me," Amanda said, looking again at her father.

"Who, him?" Carolyn raised her chin in Ziggy's direction. "He hasn't got a killing gene in him."

"Do we have to tell him?"

"Yes. Whatever it is, your parents will be made aware. But you've been through a lot. And you'll have tough days ahead. Your mom and dad love you and will support you through this. Somehow I don't think they'll banish you to an icehouse in Antarctica."

It was as if all the air had gone out of the girl's lungs. She looked about to burst into tears and must have sensed it because the words tumbled out at once. "It was a joke. We didn't mean anything. We were babysitting Melly's sister. Nothing was on TV."

"So you logged onto the Net ..."

"We'd heard about a message board, and we were curious. We read the posts then decided to post a message of our own."

"Both of you?"

Amanda nodded, still not meeting Carolyn's eyes. "You know, some kids steal. Tease other people. Melly and me, we never did. We've never even tried smoking. But this—this is the worst thing we've ever done."

Tears flowed but Amanda withheld the sobs. She had to get this over with. Carolyn reached over, pressed a tissue into the girl's hand and held it there a good long moment. Then she gave the hand a reassuring squeeze. *Okay, continue now. Out with it.*

"In September we registered as Nightshade," Amanda said, wiping her eyes. "Clicked onto a thread with the title 'Suicidal Tendencies' and posted some dumb message about being depressed.

It was just to see what would happen. Who would respond. What they would say. We wondered if we could fool anyone."

"Wait a minute." Carolyn searched her memory, separating Nightshade from Killcrazy, Geezer and the others. "Amanda, I've checked out that message board. Nightshade wrote that her parents were divorced, that the blended families were getting together for the holidays and she didn't think she could stand it."

Amanda's rejoinder was simple. "We made that up."

Like an assignment for an English composition class. Create a story. Hook your reader. Suspend disbelief.

"A few times during the next week or so, we'd post again, read the replies, but I got tired of it. Told Melly it was lame. I stopped being Nightshade but I guess Melissa didn't."

Carolyn tried to recall the number of posts Nightshade had made to the site. She would have to check, but she thought the number was high. Melissa wasn't going to give up her online community just because her friend wasn't joining in. For some reason, Melissa needed support, and she had clicked with a group of depressives. Perhaps, like any adolescent, she just wanted to be listened to. She had sought validation and she got it.

You want to die? We understand. We're here to help.

"After you stopped, did Melissa keep talking about the message board, what messages she was sending and getting back?"

"She tried a few times—you know, like 'Geezer sounded really depressed today. I hope he's gonna be okay.' After a while, I just wasn't interested. It was like Melly paid more attention to her cyber friends than the rest of us. Almost as if she was addicted."

Not almost. Melissa Waller *was* addicted, drawn into a downward spiraling group who sucked her in with them. Did she interpret Amanda's lack of interest as a snub? Despite statements to the contrary, Melissa couldn't have been as happy as Ziggy's daughter claimed.

"I should have kept listening," Amanda said, her voice drained of inflection. "I should have been a better friend."

"Don't do that to yourself, Amanda. We can't control what others think and do. Melissa had choices—"

"But what if she didn't think she did?"

Carolyn paused, confounded. Everyone had choices. Melissa could have stopped posting on the web board. She could have gone to a movie last night, not climbed into Bloome's BMW with people she'd never met before. Even at the diner, she could have run, could have spilled the poison down the sink. No one held a gun to her head. At least, not in the true sense of the word.

"Amanda, your father told me Melissa sent you an e-mail last night. Mind telling me what it said?"

"I printed a copy."

The girl reached inside the front pouch of her hooded sweatshirt and with a trembling hand, presented Carolyn with her friend's final message.

Carolyn unfolded the sheet and read.

Hey, Mandy,

By the time you read this, I'll be gone. Please don't be sad. You know I hate it when anyone's sad. I'm catching the bus with my friends, and they'll take care of me. We're going to that spooky old diner out on Miller's Road. I made a promise, and you know I always keep my word. There are, and have been, things I couldn't share with you. I hope you'll understand. You are, and always will be my very, very best friend, and I'll love you forever.

Hugsssss,

Melly.

A promise is a promise. Had Melissa Waller played a dangerous game, pretending to be suicidal, telling the forum group that she intended catching the bus? Too much stalling, any reneging on the deal and she would have been ostracized, branded as a fraud, a cheat, a liar. *Nightshade? Catching the bus? Lol.* Melissa had backed herself into a dark, cobwebby corner, yet Carolyn thought there were still many times she could have backed out. Had she disappeared from the message board, perhaps the group may have believed she had actually killed herself. How would they have known any different?

Melissa went ahead and kept her promise, got in the car anyway. It was then that an idea dawned.

There are, and have been, things I couldn't share with you.

"What do you think Melissa meant by this?" She underscored the line with an index finger.

"I don't know. We told each other everything."

Almost everything, Carolyn thought. But some things were too difficult to speak of. *You are, and always will be my very, very best friend, and I'll love you forever.* Sometimes the fear of rejection overruled honesty. "Amanda, is there anything else you want to tell me, anything else I should know about Melissa?"

She shook her head. "I really don't understand why I'm talking to you. Melly ... killed herself. What does that have to do with the police?"

"All suicides have to be investigated. Death under suspicious circumstances, until we can rule everything else out."

Amanda seemed satisfied with that explanation. She stood up, but as she put her hand on the knob she turned back to Carolyn and said, "Melly's death. Was it peaceful, do you think? When you saw her, was she—"

"Very peaceful," Carolyn said quickly.

Amanda seemed satisfied with that as well. Some lies were definitely worth telling.

CHAPTER 19

JOSHUA FINALLY MANAGED TO PIN Ken Ishiguro down for a meeting. The man had been disgruntled and impatient on the telephone earlier in the week, but Joshua refused to be dismissed or relegated to some vague date in the future. Ken quickly apologized and followed up with an invitation to dinner, which earned Joshua a scathing look from Paige. When Joshua entered Ishiguro's kitchen on Friday night, Ken was chopping daikon with a lethal-looking cleaver. Other vegetables, in bite-sized pieces, were set on the counter in individual bowls. Water for rice boiled in a large pot on the stove. A small dining table was nicely set for two—wine and water goblets, an orangey-red tablecloth, metal chopsticks laid across square black plates. Ishiguro clearly liked to entertain and Joshua thought that having Yoshi living with him must be cramping his bachelor style.

"Like to cook, Ken?"

"A hobby of mine. In Japan I was always having parties or going to parties. I enjoyed an active social life." He looked down the hall toward Yoshi's room. No light seeped from beneath the space under the door. Still asleep. "Not like now. I have a lot of friends at the university, but I can hardly invite them here." As an afterthought he added, "I miss it. The cooking. Setting a nice table. Decent conversation. Laughter."

Joshua nodded. With Yoshi, there wasn't much to laugh about.

Over a delicious seafood stir-fry, the two men discussed the changes taking place in Japan, a culture where change was feared. Ishiguro spoke of the current employment slump. "Some are calling it a Super Ice Age. Even if young men want jobs, they have a difficult time finding them. Firms are cutting back, not hiring. This is an easier solution than to fire a corporate man who has provided many years of loyal service. With the economic downturn has come a new mindset. Being unemployed no longer carries the stigma it once did, and many young men, rather than pursuing full-time work are turning their backs on responsibility and becoming freeters."

When Ishiguro eyed Joshua's puzzled expression, he explained, "They take part-time jobs or casual work while they try to figure out what to do with their lives."

"And their parents can afford to support them indefinitely?"

"That's right. They choose recreation over work, pleasure over pain. For many, even romantic relationships represent too much work. They prefer to visit prostitutes or have online encounters. There are no complications. It's hard to argue. Hikikomori like Yoshi have given up. They are spoiled, used to getting what they want and getting it quickly."

"The repercussions must be huge."

Ishiguro nodded. "In Japan we have a demographic time bomb. Our birth rate is declining. People are living longer. If the hikikomori problem is not addressed, over a million potentially productive workers will be removed from what is already a dwindling pool."

"And when their parents aren't able to care for them anymore, they'll be a burden on your welfare system, am I right?"

"Yes. And our elderly will have no one to care for them. I believe the expression is 'we're screwed.'"

"Let's hope not. Meanwhile, I'll try to do whatever I can to get Yoshi to realize his own potential. I suppose a Freudian would ask about his relationship with his mother."

Ishiguro smiled, offered more wine, but Joshua politely shook his head. "Yoshi loves his mother," the man said. "And she dotes on him. Because of their closeness, Yoshi may be feeling tremendous pressure to please her. With Yoshi being the only son, multiply that pressure by one hundred."

"And Yoshi's father, is he very demanding?" Joshua wished he could have a face-to-face meeting with Yoshi's parents. Getting information about Yoshi's home life second-hand wasn't his preference, but somehow he doubted Mr. or Mrs. Tagawa would be more forthcoming with insight into their son.

"No more than any other man who wants to be proud of his son. But the shame Yoshi has caused my brother-in-law ... it has become easier for him to remain in the city instead of coming home on weekends. Yoshi has nearly destroyed his parents' marriage, his father's health. Since Yoshi went hikkii, my brother-in-law has developed ulcers. He has lost much weight, become an old man. My sister says it is like being married to a stranger."

"It must have been tough for you to watch the family suffer because of Yoshi."

Ishiguro nodded. "She is my only sister. We are very close."

"What about Yoshi's friendships? School?"

"Yoshi did well in school. He had bonded well with his *kumi* ... this is a group formed in kindergarten. They stay together until graduation. They eat lunch together, play and study together. Yoshi once came home crying because he'd witnessed a case of *nakama hazure*—one of the students had been cut off from the group because he had gained weight. Yoshi feared the group would someday shun him too. He was devastated by the bullying that the other boy endured."

"But Yoshi was never victimized?"

"If he was, he never spoke about it."

"Mr. Ishiguro—"

"Ken."

"Ken, I'm trying to understand the root of Yoshi's illness. What might have precipitated his withdrawal. I can appreciate his problem might not be attributable to only one source, but so far what I'm hearing is that Yoshi comes from a traditional Japanese home—a distant father and an overprotective mother, both of whom wish to see their son be successful. No disrespect intended. But is there something else? Something I'm missing?"

Ishiguro set down his chopsticks and steepled his fingers in front of his face. There was an interminable pause. Joshua could hear Yoshi stirring in the room at the end of the hall, wheeling his desk chair across the parquet floor. Down in the apartment's outdoor lot, a car horn beeped. Joshua picked absent-mindedly at a snagged fingernail and wondered whether he should repeat his question, when at last Ken Ishiguro lowered his hands from his face.

"What is it the French say? *Cherchez la femme.*"

Yoshi was sitting on his bed eating dry Cornflakes from the box when Joshua entered his room. The overhead light was on. To Joshua's relief, the folding screen hadn't returned, not that there would have been space for it. The room qualified as a state of emergency. Comic books were strewn everywhere. Sheets and blankets were pulled from the bed and clothing littered the floor.

Yoshi was propped in a corner, surrounded by debris from a diet of soda crackers, potato chips and root beer. For the first time he faced the center of the room instead of his computer in the corner and Joshua was able to get a good look at the boy. Yoshi was tall and reedy, his slender body swallowed up by enormous pants and an oversized T-shirt. Even his socks were big slouchy things that wrinkled around his ankles. Scattered acne scars marked his cheeks. His eyes were red, as though he'd been crying. This time, when Joshua extended his hand, Yoshi shook it.

"Nice to finally meet you," Joshua said, his foot crunching down on a chocolate bar wrapper. "There's got to be a basketball team somewhere just waiting for you to show up."

Yoshi didn't respond.

"Everything okay?"

"Why shouldn't it be?" the boy said, too quickly.

Joshua glanced around. "Things seem to have ... gone a little downhill in here."

"Didn't know you were coming tonight."

"Fair enough. Want some help straightening up?"

Yoshi shook his head. "I'll get around to it."

Joshua cut a path across the floor and sat on the chair in front of Yoshi's computer. Beside the monitor was one of the boy's *seijin manga*. Clearly, Yoshi was a breast man. This comic book though, appeared brand new. The pages weren't dog-eared or tattered, and there were no fingerprint smudges on the cover. A gift from Yoshi's uncle? More likely the boy had ordered it online.

There were logistical questions about the hikikomori life that Joshua needed to have answered. Following his customary opening chatter about nothing in particular, Joshua came out with, "I've gotta ask. What about the bathroom? When do you go?"

Yoshi used the washroom at night when his uncle was asleep, took showers then too, although Joshua noticed he hadn't had one lately. Yoshi's parents sent him a generous monthly stipend, so much for food, so much for incidentals. Like pornographic comics and video games. He admitted to occasionally raiding his uncle's refrigerator but never to ripping off Ishiguro's money. "He keeps his wallet under his pillow," Yoshi said.

And Yoshi didn't need Ishiguro's money anyway. He never went anywhere. No movies, no restaurants, no dates. Though Joshua could see a closet crowded with clothes and dresser drawers crammed so full they wouldn't shut, these things still couldn't account for the ridiculous amount of cash the Tagawas sent their son. What could Yoshi possibly spend it on?

Puzzling to Joshua as well was why Yoshi, who never ventured outdoors, owned an olive drab water-resistant jacket and a pair of hiking boots.

Eventually Joshua broached the subject that he hoped wouldn't turn Yoshi's face back toward the wall. "Ever e-mail anyone back home? Friends from school? Girlfriend maybe?"

Yoshi shook his head, chomped more cereal. "My Japanese friends are lame. And I don't have a girlfriend ..."

"Anymore, you mean."

"That's right. I don't have a girlfriend anymore. We're over. Way over." Yoshi's speech carried with it the same emotionless monotone as always. He may as well have been reporting that the fish weren't biting or that Swiss cheese was full of holes. But this time, the voice held a persistent quiver.

"I remember how rough that was," Joshua said. "My first break-up. I was dumped for another guy. Same with you?"

Again the boy shook his head. "Not exactly ..."

Joshua waited, his mind scrolling through the possibilities.

At length Yoshi said, "It was a Prada bag."

"Come again?"

"Aoki wanted a Prada handbag. I couldn't buy it for her—my mother would have roasted my balls for dinner. So Aoki told me she knew how she could get one."

Yoshi waited for Joshua to fill in the blanks but his face must have registered his confusion. The boy, exasperated, heaved a sigh. "Let me tell you how it is. In Japan, young women don't want to live like their mothers, cooking, cleaning, running a house on their own. They want independence, freedom to travel. They want to shop all the time. If they're not lucky enough to marry rich, they don't want to marry at all. So they live at home, take part-time jobs and go on *arranged dates*. This puts money in their pockets for designer clothes and a couple of trips to Hawaii every year."

"Arranged dates," Joshua repeated. "Sounds like a polite way of saying prostitution."

Yoshi smirked.

Joshua paused to let the idea sink in that an overpriced handbag that would be out of style in a year could be worth more to a girl than sustaining a friendship with someone who cared for her. "Was it serious, your relationship?"

Yoshi shrugged. "She was just a girl."

Joshua suspected she meant much more to Yoshi. Yoshi was the sensitive boy who had cried, fearing the constant threat of being shunned by his kumi. Underneath the bravado and wooden affect, Yoshi had a tender heart and it had been crushed. Aoki's desertion may have been the nightmare that hurled Yoshi into his hikikomori existence.

"It would be a huge deal to me, if a girl treated me like that," Joshua said and meant it. "I'd be feeling pretty lost. Desperate, even."

Yoshi's reaction was like a cobra strike. "I'd never kill myself over some stupid girl."

"Ever thought about it, though? Harming yourself? Plenty of teenagers toy with the idea at some time or other."

Yoshi flinched then his eyes welled up. He blinked rapidly then lowered his gaze. "Suicide's no big deal. Nothing in Japanese laws or religion tells us it is wrong. You know, in Tokyo they've installed mirrors on some subway walls? It's supposed to discourage people from jumping in front of the trains. And if someone dies on the tracks, the government charges the surviving family members for the delay in rail service. What bullshit. If people want to jump, let them jump. What's everybody so scared of? One minute you're breathing, the next minute you're not."

The electronic generation. Every manner of violence and death could be played out on a screen. With the touch of a reset button, the characters pop instantly back to life, ready for another battle, another opportunity to be crushed, beheaded, blown to bits. Joshua knew this distorted understanding of death was compounded by the advances of medicine and increased life expectancy. How many young people had even experienced the death of a loved one? Held the hand of an ailing relative, kept a bedside vigil at a hospital?

"Death is the end of the line, Yoshi," Joshua said. "There are no second chances."

Yoshi crunched another handful of cereal, put the box on the floor with the rest of the garbage, and mustered a look of bored resignation. He followed this with another shrug then said, "Easy come, easy go."

Once Joshua had gone, Yoshi checked his e-mail. His mother had sent her weekly message, saying she missed him. She hoped he was fine and making many friends in America. His father, as usual, was working hard, but had come home for a visit last Sunday. She had cooked him a nice meal. Yoshi responded with his usual: I'm fine. I miss you as well. Say hello to father.

He opened a private message from Killcrazy who was looking for Nightshade, wondering why she hadn't answered his e-mail. Had she CTB? Yoshi shuddered and tried to swallow but his mouth was dry. He typed back, *Beats me.*

His last message came from Geezer. He shivered then realized some sadistic bastard was playing a joke. It had to be a poser. Geezer couldn't be sending the message. This was probably someone wanting to sell him porn or Viagra. Last week's spam had been rife with offers of hot girls from the Ukraine. Curious, Yoshi opened the message and craned his neck toward the four words that appeared across his screen.

Semper respice post te.

He recognized the language as Latin and scribbled the message on a scrap of paper. With a few keystrokes, he accessed a Latin-English dictionary and carefully typed the sentence into the space provided, double checking his spelling.

When the translation came into view, Yoshi blinked hard, blinked again, and heard a small "no" erupt from somewhere within. Cold rippled along his spine, spread across his shoulders like icy fingers. He backspaced, deleting the Latin. He'd made a mistake. He would try again. He one-finger typed the words once more but the same message appeared.

Always look behind you.

CHAPTER 20

Carolyn sent Ziggy home with Amanda shortly after the girl had left her office. "Stay there," she told him. "Amanda needs you, and there are enough of us here to hold things together."

That wasn't exactly true. One of the officers was vacationing in the Costa Rican rainforest, and another was home with the flu. Two more were investigating a smash-and-grab at a convenience store near the elementary school. That left the nasty work of notifying police in Utah, British Columbia and Nevada to Carolyn and another harried officer, their work made even nastier by a phone call from Fallon McBride, who wanted the story on the diner suicides for the evening *Examiner*. Ziggy, still reeling from his daughter's involvement as Nightshade, hustled Amanda out the door, muttering that her Internet privileges would be reinstated when she got married.

Though Carolyn was tempted to call Ziggy several times during the afternoon she refrained. She forced herself to wait until well after she'd eaten dinner before punching in his home number. "Listen," she said when he picked up, "I didn't want to talk about this while you were in this morning. Saw no sense in having Amanda hanging around longer than she needed to, especially with McBride's nose twitching, but I may have stumbled onto something. You're not the only one who was up all night."

"I thought you looked like hell, but I was too polite to say so."

"Lucky for you I'm not the sensitive type. After I left the diner, I went back to Signal Hill."

"The Aerie? What f—? Oh, I'm not going to like this, am I."

"Those six lines, Zig. The ones we found in the dust. I found the same symbol—"

"Where? We didn't see anything that night."

"That's because we didn't know what to look for. Took me a while, and I've got the scrapes to prove it, but I found it. When I didn't see anything on the property I paid a visit to the impound lot. It's there, Zig. On the rented Neon. Scratched into the paint. On the roof of the car."

"Lord love a fucking duck." He paused then added, "Still, one of the riders could have done it, C.L. You know, before getting into the car. Maybe these people that entered into the pact all agreed that they'd use the same symbol."

"For what purpose? You think people who really want to die have the wherewithal to get artsy, not to mention climbing on top of that car? I'm telling you, someone else was on the Hill with those kids that night."

"Son of a fucking bitch."

"I've been on the computer since I got home last night trying to find out what those lines could mean. Tell you this much. They're not railroad tracks. Or any of the other things we guessed."

"What then?"

"Zig, I think it's a ladder. With the top rung broken."

"A ladder? Is that supposed to mean something?"

"Ask any religious group. Virtually all of them have adopted the ladder as a symbol. The Hindus have something called—wait a sec …"

Carolyn cradled the receiver between her ear and shoulder, shuffled papers.

"…the ladder of the Brahmins. It stands for the seven worlds of the Indian universe. Followers of Kabbalah know about the Ladder to the En Sof. Don't even get me started on the Rosicrucians, the Alchemists and the Theosophists."

Ziggy sighed. "You've left out the Christians."

"No, you just didn't give me a chance to turn the page. We usually show the ladder with a sponge affixed to a reed. Symbol of the crucifixion. While we're at it, you may as well throw the Freemasons into the mix, too. They use the Jacob's ladder as a symbol to show progress from earth to heaven."

"You really didn't sleep much, did you."

"Been on the phone with Washington State, too. Asked them to give the North Cascades National Park another look."

"You're thinking there's another ladder symbol near where those people jumped?"

"A hunch."

"Which, if found to be true, means we've got a real psycho on our hands—"

"Who's organized, mobile and loves running the show."

"But what's the guy's motive? Power? Is he some nerd who can't get people to listen to him in real life, so he manipulates the bejeezus out of them on the Net? Or is he just another impotent freak who can't get it up."

Carolyn smiled. It was a running gag between them. Every time they busted someone and tried to guess what led the person to commit a crime, Ziggy cited erectile dysfunction as the cause. Or inadequate dietary fiber. People got ugly when they're bunged up, went the theory.

"My instinct is telling me there's more to it this time, Zig. Like punishment. Maybe that broken rung is meant to show that the victims, in thinking about ending their lives, have lost their footing ..."

"And as a result, won't gain entry into heaven."

"So he's judge, jury, and executioner."

"Jesus on a trapeze."

Carolyn listened to dead air for a long moment then she told Ziggy to get some rest and look after his daughter. When she hung up and logged onto her computer, she found three replies to Fading Away's post. One was from Bella Donna. It said simply: Glad you found us, but sorry you needed to. The other, from Killcrazy, was even simpler. Geezer caught the bus. Jim Stark was more gracious. Welcome to the club, he posted.

Geezer. Carolyn assumed that to be Bill Armstrong, the man from Vancouver. Divorced, she'd learned, and suffering from acute fibromyalgia. In her communications with the Canadian city's police, she discovered that Bill had grabbed a flight to Portland early on Thursday morning. Armstrong's ex-wife, whom they described as a broomstick rider, received a greeting card via snail mail on Friday at her office. On the front was a picture of a kangaroo and the bright red caption: Just hopping with excitement ... Inside, Armstrong had written a brief note. *Hi honey, I hope you're well. Now I am, too.* Lenore Armstrong hadn't understood the point of the card, not until a police officer appeared at her office door just as she and a few co-workers were debating which pub they'd descend upon to jump-start the weekend.

Carolyn kicked off her shoes and took a few minutes to type Fading Away's next message on the Suicidal Tendencies thread. She and Ziggy had agreed on what should be written, so Carolyn spoke of her chronic sciatic pain, of being held captive and tortured by her own body. Just before she hit SEND, she added: I wish I could have caught the bus with Geezer. We're so much alike.

Carolyn was running water for her bath when the phone rang. It was Paige. She had read the paper and was stunned. Fallon's article, "Suicide Spree Grips Village," wasn't subtle. Subtlety wasn't one of Fallon's attributes, so Carolyn wasn't surprised that the newswoman didn't hold firm to her earlier vow to keep news about the suicides low-key. If a spree didn't grip the village before, it sure as hell would now.

"Come to The Rocks with Joshua and me on Sunday night," Paige said. "Take your mind off all this horror for a while."

"Paige, you're sweet, but I know you and Josh have spent precious few moments together lately. A third wheel at a romantic restaurant isn't something you two need."

"Don't be so hasty. I'll have Joshua to myself all day tomorrow. By seven o'clock on Sunday night, I'll be sick of him. Now come on. None of us have ever been to The Rocks. It'll be fun."

Carolyn considered the idea. She hadn't been anywhere decent in ages. Going for drinks after work at Marley's didn't count, and that strange lunch she'd had with Gregg counted for even less.

"The Rocks, huh?" she said, already feeling her dark mood shift. "I'd better get busy and shave my legs and everything."

"Just the legs will do," Paige answered. "You don't need to shave your everything."

Wishing Paige goodnight, Carolyn hung up and eased into the bath. A good meal, and good company. She needed both. If anyone could lift her spirits it was Joshua and Paige. She began to look forward to the evening.

The Rocks was built to capitalize on the scenery. The restaurant cantilevered over the Pacific, and three walls of windows afforded diners spectacular views of frothy waves crashing against the floodlit boulders below. The interior was sleek and modern, everything in muted pearl-gray tones, making the place at dusk appear to float on the horizon. Carolyn wasn't a fan of minimalism. To her, the restaurant seemed stark and unfinished, and though she'd chosen her best black crepe skirt and a jade silk blouse, she felt at odds with her surroundings. Perhaps it was more than the skimpy décor making her uneasy. The Rocks was where Gregg liked to dine, and he'd been enjoying a meal with his lover at the restaurant the night Carolyn was shot. Luckily Gregg wasn't around to witness Carolyn on a date with her twin brother and his fiancée.

Joshua and Paige looked sweet together, all smiles and hand-holding. They ordered wine and Carolyn asked, "Josh, what's this I hear about you visiting some reclusive teenager?"

Joshua tried to explain hikikomori to Carolyn while Paige picked at a breadstick, clearly disinterested in the subject of Yoshitomo Tagawa. When he was finished, Paige said, "Those house calls are ending soon, and Joshua will be keeping regular hours again."

He nodded. "Yoshi's been a challenge."

"That boy's got to come out of the apartment sometime, doesn't he?" Carolyn said. "Sounds like the sooner the better."

Paige shot her a grateful look.

When their meals came, the conversation shifted to Dr. Samuel J. Risk and his humanitarian work.

Carolyn read an article about Risk in the previous day's *Oregonian*. Risk had gone to Africa in October of 2003. Exactly two years later, he was in a tented camp in Muzaffarabad, ministering to victims of the earthquake that had struck India and Pakistan. One thousand homeless. It was Risk's seventh mission.

Paige had read the article too. "But Risk is a shrink. What could he do for those poor people?"

"He helped establish a rehab program for the victims of trauma. Basically, he would just walk around between the tents," Joshua said, "introduce himself, explain why he was there. Sometimes people would just start unburdening themselves. Risk spoke about one woman who could hear her daughter crying out from under the rubble for three days. When the daughter was finally found, it was too late. And the mother can't stop hearing the cries."

Carolyn said, "When I hear stories like that, it makes me realize I have nothing to complain about."

She thought about Nightshade, Geezer, Brenda Koch and the others. Everyone's definition of hell was different. "Sounds like the presentation made quite an impression on you, Josh."

Joshua nodded. "Brought you an audio copy of the lecture." He removed the disc from his inside jacket pocket and slid it across the table. "Actually, I wouldn't mind signing up for a stint with DOM sometime."

"DOM?" Paige said.

"Doctors of Mercy."

"But you're not a doctor."

"The organization needs social workers."

Paige turned to Carolyn. "And I thought I didn't see much of him this week." To Joshua she said, "What does that involve?"

"Getting all my vaccinations updated, for starters. A debriefing in Europe, then placement in the field."

"You've already checked into it?"

"Just did a little reading. No big deal."

Frown lines creased her brow. "Where would they send you?"

"They place their volunteers where they're needed. No one gets a choice."

"Someplace dry, I hope. I'm sick of all this rain."

"Um, Paige, you wouldn't be allowed to go. There are no facilities for couples."

"But I could stay nearby, visit?"

Joshua shook his head. "It doesn't work that way, I'm afraid."

"I see," she said, her tone clipped.

Carolyn interjected, sensing this was going from bad to abysmal. "How long would you be gone, Josh?"

"We don't even know if they'd accept my application. I mean, I speak French and Spanish, so that's an asset. I'm in reasonably good shape, I've got experience dealing with young people, but not a lot with adults. It could go either way. But I'm still just in the thinking stages with this. No need to pack my suitcase yet."

"How long, Joshua?" she repeated.

"I'd be interviewed by a Human Resources Officer at their west coast office. They'd do a background check, and if I'm accepted, I'd enter a pool of volunteers. Placement could occur anywhere from two weeks to six months following that."

"Would you answer the damn question?" Paige said. "How long?"

"Could be six months."

Paige's face glowed red. Quietly, she folded her napkin and laid it on the table, rose and left the restaurant.

The argument continued during the short ride home. It had begun to rain and the wipers slapped against the windshield. The pavement was gloss black, oily and slick.

"Nice move, Joshua. Waiting until you had your sister present before letting me in on your little fantasy."

"It's not a little fantasy," he countered, "and that's not what I was doing. I kept trying to emphasize that it was just something I'm thinking about. You're the one who jumped the gun and assumed it was a *fait accompli*."

"Given that you've done all kinds of research into it, what do you think I'd assume?"

"Paige, I know it's a lot to take in, but just give it some thought. I think it's something I could be good at."

"Aren't you forgetting something? You already have a job, one you're good at. One that takes up more than enough time. What will happen to 3F House if you go gallivanting off to some remote corner of the globe?"

"I'd hire a temporary director until I got back. The others can manage just fine. They know what they're doing."

"All right then. Think about this. We've been together less than a year. You were considering the priesthood once. You gave it up, left the seminary. Why?"

They'd covered this ground more than once. His goal was to work with youth, but with so many scandals rocking the Church, people pegged him for a pedophile and steered their children clear when they saw him coming. That cut him deeply. He envisioned a life ahead with more pain than pleasure, his future in the hands of bishops who would control where he lived and with whom, his social life populated with men, men and more men. In the end, he knew he couldn't bow to an idol of celibacy. St. Catherine of Siena's words resounded clearly in his mind. "If you are what you should be, you will set the world on fire." More soul-searching and countless sessions with Samuel Risk led Joshua to the decision that he could light more fires from outside the church than from within.

"You know the answer to that, Paige. I decided I like women. A lot. I wanted a life filled with affection, with kids. That's why I think I should do this now. Before we start a family. If I didn't think our relationship was strong, I wouldn't even consider going. But listening to how Risk's experiences changed him, well—"

"Funny," Paige huffed. "You're looking to change and here I sit, liking you just fine the way you are."

Joshua was about to say more when he was distracted by movement beyond his side window. A lanky figure in an olive-green swamp coat and dark baseball cap emerged from a convenience store and was running down the street, head lowered, shouldering into the wind. Joshua did a double take, glancing left as the man hurried down the sidewalk. He heard Paige's stern tone cautioning him to keep his eyes on the road. He did as he was told. Joshua had seen enough to know that the figure racing through the darkness, a plastic bag clutched under his arm, was Yoshi.

CHAPTER 21

THE TENSION WAS STILL PALPABLE in the cabin for the remainder of the night, but by morning, it was tinged not with anger but with profound sadness. Paige returned from walking Parker, their chocolate lab, and upon seeing Joshua, muttered a grouchy good morning as she entered the screened-in porch at the back of the house. "I thought you'd have left for work by now," she said, wiping the dog's paws on an old towel she kept in a basket beside the door.

Joshua glanced at his watch then rose. "Guess I should be going," he said, "but I was waiting for my goodbye kiss."

He'd been stalling, not wanting to leave for work with things so rotten between them. He had tried to explain his feelings again after they'd settled into bed last night, but Paige didn't want any part of it. She was as tired of hearing about Dr. Samuel J. Risk as she was of hearing about Yoshi. "Something's missing, Joshua," she said, the fight gone from her voice. "For you to even consider leaving for a period of at least six months means something's wrong here. With us. Or maybe just with me. Maybe I'm not giving you what you need."

He tried to protest, to declare she was everything he wanted. More. But this other need of his was separate from them. He had a chance to make a real difference. To do some good.

"You're not a seminarian anymore, Joshua. And you're not a missionary. You made your choice. I thought you were happy about it."

She rolled away from him. The discussion, such as it was, was over. Even when he spooned in behind her and wrapped the quilt around them, he felt her body stiffen. She didn't grasp his arm the way she usually did, and pull him closer. Instead she raised her arms over her face and clung to her pillow. They had lain awake for some time, not speaking, not moving. Joshua wasn't sure how much sleep either of them had gotten, but this morning, even an icy shower with needlepoint jets drilling his skin didn't remove the feeling he'd had every ounce of his energy sucked out of him. Two cups of strong coffee didn't shake the feeling, either.

Paige stepped over and gave him a perfunctory peck on the cheek. "You have a good day."

The permafrost layer she'd surrounded herself with didn't fool him. She was hurting badly and he'd caused it, the last thing he wanted. What could he do? Pretend he'd never mentioned Doctors of Mercy? Tell her right now he wouldn't think any more about going, that he wouldn't leave her, not for a second?

Eventually he said, "Are we all right?"

She turned from him, sat on the couch and patted the cushion beside her. Parker jumped up and sprawled across her lap. "A supportive, dutiful partner would probably say something like 'go, with my blessing. Do what you have to do. I'm proud of you.'" She wouldn't look at him, Instead she petted her dog, focusing on the lab's shiny coat.

The words he expected followed.

"Joshua, I wish I could be that person. But I'm not. Not now. I'm sorry. The timing feels wrong."

He nodded, his heart sinking. Welcome to the impasse, he told himself. The land of wait and see.

Paige had survived a relationship with a domineering partner who'd tried to reshape her into his version of the ideal woman. She'd dyed her hair flaming red, bought a closet full of slut clothes and transformed herself into what she thought he'd wanted, but she still wasn't good enough. In the end, she fled and had spent considerable time and energy regaining her self-esteem and discovering who she really was. Now that she had found someone she could truly be herself with, she was receiving the same message from Joshua, that she wasn't worth sticking around for. Paige was right. In terms of their relationship, the timing was wrong. In fact, it was lousy. But he couldn't ignore the magnetic pull of his can't-say-no side.

"I love you, Paige," he said but she still didn't look up.

Joshua left for work. He played the radio loud in his Jeep and tapped the steering wheel to the beat of some generic hip-hop song. He would throw himself into work, attack the teetering files on his desk, make calls, have a staff meeting late in the day, and pay one important visit to Ken Ishiguro's apartment. Maybe if he and Paige stayed busy for a day or two, they wouldn't feel so wounded. Then they'd be able to talk again, find some middle ground. But where would that be? The more he thought about it, the more he wanted to volunteer. Paige didn't want him to. There was no middle. None that he could see.

When he arrived at 3F House, Joshua was surprised to see Robb Northrup's red Focus parked at the curb. Robb wasn't due at work for hours, and he usually spent Monday mornings doing the books for his father's funeral parlor.

Joshua entered and saw a disheveled Robb leaning over the banister at the top of the stairs. "Talk to you a sec, Josh?"

"Sure. Okay if I grab a coffee?"

Minutes later, he ascended the stairs, mug in hand, and found Northrup seated in his office keying in something on his laptop. When Joshua entered, Robb quickly slapped the laptop shut.

Robb swiveled his chair around and said, "I need to leave 3F House."

Joshua nearly spilled his coffee. "Goes without saying, I didn't see this coming."

"If you want, I'll give you time to find another counselor, but I'd really like to go sooner rather than later."

"Sounds kind of urgent. Anything I can help with?"

Joshua had noticed changes in Robb over the past few months. The counselor was easily distracted, impatient, apathetic. Joshua had confronted him about it, gotten nowhere.

"I need a break, that's all."

He looked at the man's heavy-lidded eyes, ringed with gray circles. "Robb, anyone can see you haven't been sleeping. Is it your father? Is he pressuring you again?"

The Northrup family owned the funeral parlor in the village, and it was a business Robb's father wanted his son to continue. Hadn't the business provided a nice life for the family? Didn't the Northrups have the respect of the community? Robb was tired of the lectures, tired of reciting his list of "yeah buts" to deaf ears.

"Got nothing to do with the old man. It's this job. I talk and I listen, but nothing seems to do any good. Tell you the truth, I'm fed up to here with these kids. So, see, Josh, I'm not what you'd call counselor material."

Joshua sensed there was more to the story. "When I hired you two years ago, you were one of the most compassionate people I'd ever met. You couldn't wait for those kids to come through the door so you could work with them. What's changed?"

"Me. I've changed." Northrup's voice had a curious edge.

"No chance this'll turn around? Maybe just some time off ..."

"No," Robb insisted. "I've got to get away."

Joshua nodded. "Any plans?"

He shrugged. "Maybe travel. See a bit of the world."

"You'll be missed."

Awkwardly, Robb leaned forward and extended his hand. "Thanks."

The counselor's shirt sleeves were rolled up twice, exposing a small tattoo above his left wrist that to Joshua resembled a spinal column with testicles. He knew Robb had another tattoo on the back of his neck—a winged hourglass that also symbolized the brevity of life, a *memento mori*. Robb had that tattoo inked when he was a teenager and claimed it was the stupidest thing he'd ever done. He told Joshua it was the reason he wore his hair long.

"See you've treated yourself to a new tattoo."

Robb glanced at his artwork. "It's an *aya*. An Adinkra design. Meant to symbolize the fern. Because ferns are hardy, whoever wears the symbol can supposedly stand up to adversity."

Joshua wondered what kind of adversity Robb Northrup was faced with. Behind Robb's tale of job burnout, Joshua felt there was much more behind the counselor's decision to leave, and quickly. Was he in some kind of trouble?

Joshua shut the door to his office, logged onto the Net and keyed in "Adinkra symbols." He found beautiful designs—variations on squares, circles and hearts. Many of the symbols were symmetrical, reminding Joshua of kaleidoscopic patterns. Among these, he located the *aya* and clicked on it. Robb had been right, that it did indeed represent the fern. The symbol was often worn by African kings to show fearlessness and to indicate they had outlasted much difficulty. One of the most widely understood meanings of the symbol, and one which Robb failed to mention, was that it stood for defiance. It meant: *I am not afraid of you.*

CHAPTER 22

Joshua arrived at Ken Ishiguro's apartment at eight o'clock. The professor wasn't home. He had told Joshua that he had a faculty reception to attend but that Yoshi was aware of Joshua's wish to stop by. Ishiguro instructed the building superintendent to let Joshua into the apartment.

Joshua suspected that Ishiguro had made up the story about the reception, that in reality he preferred not to be around once he learned what Joshua had in mind for Yoshi. The man had agreed that sterner measures needed to be taken with his nephew. He was outraged to learn that Yoshi had been spotted outside the apartment and felt that these past months, he'd been played for a fool. Still, that didn't mean he wanted to be under the same roof as his moody nephew if the fur started flying. That privilege belonged to Joshua.

Yoshi was in his room, his gaze magnetized to his Play Station, his neck craned toward the action on the screen. He wore enormous black painter-style pants and a white Gucci T-shirt. His feet were bare. A laundry basket full of neatly folded clothes lay atop the bed, reminding Joshua of the next law he would hand down to Yoshi's uncle—stop doing the kid's laundry. There would be no more shopping for Yoshi's food either, and no leaving bags of groceries outside the bedroom door. It was time for Ishiguro to reclaim his apartment and his life. The days of Yoshi's bedroom door being used as a barricade to the outside world were over.

Joshua's hand closed around the screwdriver in his jacket pocket. "Yoshi?"

The boy grunted, eyes still staring straight ahead, fingers working at warp speed.

"Yoshi, it's customary to stop what you're doing when a guest arrives."

Still no eye contact. On the screen a body keeled over. "It's not our regular night. Why are you here?"

"We need to talk."

"Correction. You need to talk. I need to kill another terrorist."

Joshua bit his lip and gave himself time to rein in his temper. It had been a long day, what with Paige freezing him out and Robb Northrup wanting to leave 3F House. The last thing Joshua needed was this surly kid working him like a joystick. He glanced around the room, his eyes drawn to Yoshi's closet and the olive drab jacket wedged between several pairs of jeans. On a hook inside the door was a dark baseball cap and, as Joshua suspected when he reached for it, it was still damp. Likewise a pair of Air Jordans with caked mud and grass between the treads.

The route from the apartment building to the convenience store where Joshua had spotted Yoshi was scant blocks along a major street with sidewalks along both sides of the route. So where had Yoshi picked up the grass and mud? What had this kid been up to?

Yoshi continued with his game, his back to Joshua.

I'm good at games too, Joshua thought.

He kept silent. Right or wrong, it was time to take charge. Joshua began removing items from Yoshi's mini-fridge. He carried armloads of soda, juice and milk down the hall and transferred them to Ishiguro's fridge. Crackers, peanut butter, jam, and potato chips went into the kitchen cupboards. Joshua unplugged the refrigerator and removed the thermostat. He returned the small appliances Yoshi had been hoarding to a cleared space on the kitchen counter. If Yoshi was aware of what was taking place behind his back, he didn't let on.

Next, Joshua used the screwdriver to remove the chain lock from Yoshi's bedroom door. At the sound of metal hitting metal, he thought he saw the boy flinch. Finally, Joshua took the jacket, the damp sneakers and baseball cap from Yoshi's closet and laid them on the bedroom floor, dead center. Then he strode over to where the boy sat, still trying to save a Las Vegas bank from a terrorist attack and yanked the plug on the computer.

"What the fuck! I was massacring the bastards. Did you *kireru*?"

"No, Yoshi, I didn't snap. Want to go for a walk?"

"You really are crazy. Too much pressure at work or something. Take a vacation." The boy rose and moved around his desk to the power bar and its tangle of wires. Joshua stood on the cord.

"I asked you a question," Joshua said. "Do you want to go for a walk? You've been cooped up here long enough."

Yoshi sat back down and rolled his eyes. "Do I have to explain hikikomori to you again? Didn't you get it the first time?"

"Oh, I got it, but there's hikkii and then there's hikkii, am I right?"

The boy frowned, brows knit into a sharp V. Then he tapped his temple with an index finger. "Too much rain, Joshua. Your brain has gone soggy."

"You're right. We have had a lot of rain. Turn around." Joshua pointed to the wet clothes on the floor.

At first Yoshi could only stare blankly at Joshua. Joshua leaned against the wall, crossed his arms over his chest and nodded again at the pile. Yoshi turned.

"You're not going to try and tell me the tenant upstairs has a leaky toilet, are you?"

Yoshi remained mute.

"You went out last night," Joshua stated. "And that's not the first time. I gave your description to the owner of that all-night convenience store on the corner. He's seen you in there at least twice a week, usually around three or four in the morning, when I'm sure your uncle is sound asleep."

The boy's Adam's apple bobbled with his audible swallow. His earlier cockiness was gone, and his gaze flickered about the room with the panic of a trapped animal.

After a time Yoshi admitted leaving the apartment building on several occasions. Mini-excursions of necessity, he said. Sometimes at four in the morning, a guy just has to go on a potato-chip run. Other hikikomori did the same, under cover of darkness.

"Stands to reason, Yoshi, if you could leave the apartment, you can also leave this room. So let me tell you how it's gonna be going forward. You want something to eat, you go down the hall and fix it. You do your own laundry. Your uncle already has a full-time job. He doesn't need another one looking after you. Nothing's wrong with your legs, your arms or your brain. I suggest you start using all three."

Pretty damn radical, Joshua thought, given that he had only met Yoshi two weeks ago. But after seeing the boy outside last night, he had begun to suspect that Yoshi was playing the hikikomori card to suit his own purposes. It was time to determine the true extent of Yoshi's illness.

"Plus, there's a discussion group on Wednesday night at 3F House. I'll pick you up at 6:30. Your uncle can drive you home."

Joshua expected anger. He was certain Yoshi would deliver some sarcastic barb about Western tough love bullshit. He expected too, that Yoshi would shut down temporarily, refuse to speak altogether or at least direct hate stares at him. Instead, his lip quivered. His eyes welled up. Eventually he managed to stammer, "No. It's t-too s-soon. I'm n-not ready."

"You can't be alone anymore, Yoshi," Joshua told him, his tone gentler. "You're drying up inside. You need real friends, real experiences."

"I'll have those someday," he mumbled.

"Why would you even want to wait? Yoshi, the time is now. You said you wanted to change, to get better."

"I do." He cast his gaze at his laundry basket and fixated on a pair of faded denims on the top of the heap. "But other things are more important now."

"Such as?"

"Keeping safe. I'm safe in here."

"Safe? From what?"

The boy wouldn't answer.

"Yoshi, what's with the mud and grass on your shoes?"

Yoshi merely shrugged. "Must have stepped in something."

"When you went out last night, did something happen?"

"No," he replied after a long pause. "Nothing happened last night."

"And nothing will happen on Wednesday night, either. You'll be all right at 3F House. There's a great bunch of people over there. You'll like them."

"You don't understand."

"Help me then. Help me understand." Joshua motioned for Yoshi to sit down while he returned the damp clothes to the closet.

"It's different now."

"How different? What's changed?"

But Yoshi wouldn't say. He remained focused on his freshly washed jeans.

"You know, Yoshi, sometimes 'safe' isn't all it's cracked up to be. I don't mean people should run around being reckless with no regard for their personal safety, but when you run scared all the time, you don't grow. In order for change and growth to happen, you have to step out of your comfort zone, take a chance now and then. And I'll be right beside you."

"The whole time?"

Joshua nodded.

Yoshi asked about the kids who dropped in at 3F House. What were they like? What were their hobbies? Did any of them like computers? How well would he fit in, being Japanese?

Joshua thought of Gavin Polley with his silver studded lip, uppercrust Chad Malvern with his prep school manners, and Lily Howard with her dark moods. Yoshi would fit in as well as anybody. "You'll be just fine. Be nice to have people to talk to, won't it?" He glanced over at the black computer screen. "Real people, that is."

Grudgingly, Yoshi agreed. "Maybe you could bring them all here instead?"

At that, Joshua smiled. "'Fraid not."

The boy blinked then focused on Joshua. "I have a bad feeling."

"About?"

Yoshi shrugged again. "Just do."

"Yoshi, I understand. This is a big step. Unfamiliar. It's okay to feel nervous. But you said you wanted my help. Here it is. Take it."

"I don't want to do this."

"Hate to play the bastard here, but you haven't got much choice. If you don't agree to come, I pack up your computer, put it in my Jeep and you won't even have a virtual friend to call your own. So come on, Yoshi. You know what James Dean said?"

The boy raised an eyebrow.

"'Live as if you'll die today.' Well, that's how you should be living. This is your chance to emulate your idol. Don't blow it."

"What if I do die today?"

Joshua gave Yoshi an appraising look. "You seem healthy enough to me. But a half life is no life. At least try to take this step, Yoshi."

After a long pause, Yoshi said, "You're sure you'll be right there?"

Once more, Joshua gave Yoshi the reassurance he seemed to so desperately need. Then he asked, "Have you eaten tonight?"

"No."

He accompanied the boy to the kitchen where he watched Yoshi make a peanut butter and banana sandwich. He coaxed him into eating it at the kitchen table then made him remain there a little longer to drink a glass of milk. Back in Yoshi's bedroom, Joshua plugged in the computer and he passed his most pleasant hour of the day receiving expert instructions in the art of terrorist annihilation. At ten p.m. when he rose to leave, Yoshi asked him if he could stay.

"Just a little longer," he said. "Uncle Ken should be home soon."

So Joshua stayed, thinking Paige couldn't get any angrier with him. Twenty minutes later, he heard Ishiguro's key in the lock. After bidding Yoshi good night and reminding Ken about Wednesday's meeting, Joshua headed across the parking lot to his car.

He drove with the radio off, wanting to keep distractions to a minimum. Suddenly there seemed to be a lot to sort through, not the least of which was the question, "Would the real Yoshitomo Tagawa please stand up?"

Yoshi had always been satisfied with online companions, with virtual sex, with games and comics. And he craved his privacy. Relationships were too complicated, not worth the trouble. Yet when Joshua had tried to leave, Yoshi begged him to stay. He was visibly relieved when his uncle returned home.

On previous visits, Yoshi had been a reluctant talker, but a courteous one. Tonight, he was different. He'd been belligerent, angry. Joshua knew that anger was a perfect defense mechanism for someone who was hurting. Or afraid. And there were definitely moments tonight when Joshua sensed that Yoshi was indeed afraid. Had Yoshi been pissed that his uncle had gone out for the evening and left him alone? Was that why he was so intensely mesmerized by his computer game, because he desperately needed the distraction, to lose himself so he wouldn't think of what was really disturbing him?

I'm safe here.

From what?

Though he concentrated on the road, Joshua continued to see the fear in Yoshi's eyes, particularly when the boy noticed that the chain lock was missing from his bedroom door. As if he was terrified of what might come in.

Joshua shook off the notion. He was reading too much into this. Still he couldn't help wondering where Yoshi had gone on his other night runs. Just to the convenience store, or further afield? The image of the mud-and-grass-caked sneakers flashed through his mind.

Tonight, Joshua had seen too many changes in the boy, each metamorphosis coming within minutes of the previous. Yoshi the Indifferent. Yoshi the Nasty. Yoshi the Weak. Yoshi the Child.

There was another possibility, one that could also account for Yoshi's abrupt changes in temperament, and one Joshua hadn't wanted to consider. It could all be an act.

CHAPTER 23

Carolyn lived for her job. Despite her love affair with police work, she knew there were still times when it was a bastard of a profession. On a daily basis, she fought for respect from her colleagues, some believing she'd been promoted simply because she'd gone and got herself shot. She and Ziggy supervised fourteen patrol officers, but her Rambette image was never far away, the hated nickname earned when she ignored a suspect's demand for a soda from the vending machine. The arrogant bastard had turned his wife's face into mashed eggplant, and Carolyn was on the verge of getting him to admit it when he suddenly broke out in a sweat and began to shake. Though the hypoglycemic episode was quickly remedied with a glass of orange juice, the suspect threatened to sue until it was discovered that he wasn't wearing his Medic Alert bracelet and had skipped breakfast. In anticipation of being brought in by police, he'd concocted his own medical emergency. But Carolyn became known as a hard-ass and the Rambette name was born.

Most days, she pushed reams of paper. She gritted her teeth when guilty sons of bitches went free because of some legal loophole. She tried her damnedest to help people manage their lives only to have them show up in handcuffs the very next week. Thanks for listening. Time well spent.

To add to her list of professional gripes—too many funerals. Within the space of ten days, Carolyn would attend three—Shana Pascal's, Melissa Waller's, and Brenda Koch's. Though Carolyn had never met Brenda, she felt a connection to the girl. Of course, Carolyn would be keeping a careful eye on the mourners, wondering whether one of them was weeping phony tears, secretly reveling in the devastation wrought by the deaths of so many people.

It was beyond optimistic to expect the person they sought to appear at one of the victim's graves, hanging back from the others who grieved, averting his eyes from the police. The one who'd toasted the deaths at the Aerie and who'd shuffled his bag-covered boots through diner dust had already seen what he wanted. The process of dying was the kick, the high, the ultimate. Watching the bereaved toss clods of dirt on shiny coffins would be, Carolyn imagined, anticlimactic.

When Ziggy arrived at work and poked his head through her office doorway, Carolyn asked, "How's Amanda doing?" A natural question, but she still felt like a horse's ass for asking it. How did she think she was doing? Her best friend had just killed herself, for God's sake.

If Ziggy thought she was an idiot, he was too polite to say. "Well, she's not comatose," he told her, "but she's the next thing to it. Hopefully, once the funeral is over with, she'll start to rally. It's tough. On all of us."

"I can imagine," Carolyn said, noting the purplish circles under Ziggy's eyes. "Will a strong cup of coffee help?"

"No, but I'll have one anyway."

While Carolyn poured from a Proctor Silex, she thought of Melissa Waller, the girl Amanda Takacs had professed was always happy. Carolyn knew the very real statistic on teen suicide and how a large number of those who'd succeeded in the act had been struggling with issues of their sexual identity. She'd gone back to the busriders message board and reread all of Nightshade's posts, zeroing in on the girl's sad words—*if anyone knew who I really am,* what *I really am, it would kill them*. Nothing could stop Ziggy or Amanda from reading Nightshade's messages as well, but Carolyn hoped they wouldn't. Melissa intended to take her secret to the grave, and perhaps that was where it belonged. Carolyn couldn't begin to predict what effect the truth would have on Amanda.

Ziggy sat down and said, "Just in case you thought I was loafing around at home yesterday, I've got a scoop for you. Guess who I found?"

Carolyn turned, handed him a man-sized mug and slid her chair around in front of her desk. "Jimmy Hoffa?"

"Close. Bella Donna. Pays to stay up to date with the latest software. Also helps to have a hacker in my back pocket."

Over the last five years there had been several arrests up and down the Oregon coast dealing with computer fraud. Police had exposed dozens of phishing and pharming schemes. By forging e-mails or planting malicious programs into a consumer's computer, a fraudster could expose the user's personal ID. Law enforcement had also uncovered several phony appeals for funds to be sent to homeless and displaced victims of 2005's Hurricane Katrina. The tsunami in Thailand the previous year had produced hundreds of scams, among them offers to locate a missing loved one for a fee. Ziggy's contact was likely one of those he'd busted. Hopefully, whoever it was now stood on the good side of the law.

"Bella Donna is a neighbor of ours. Actually lives just up the highway in Astoria. And I'm meeting with him later today."

"Wait a minute. Bella Donna is a him?"

Ziggy nodded. "It's done all the time. He's a poser. In chat rooms, on message boards and forums, the guys masquerade as girls, the old farts pretend they're young, the poor claim they're rich. In psychiatric circles, it's known as the Mardi Gras Phenomenon. Put on a mask and speak without consequence. At least half of the people who post are spouting complete bullshit. In other words, nobody is who they say they are. Bella Donna's real name is Brady Field, and he's a cardiologist, originally from Atlanta."

"Cardiologist?" Carolyn was stunned. Of all the images she had formed of Bella Donna, a successful doctor wasn't among them. Weren't doctors in the business of saving lives? "He'd be making a decent buck," she said. "And I should think he'd have plenty to keep his brain occupied. So why in God's name would the good doctor create a suicide website?"

"What I got from him on the phone is that eleven years ago, he was a miserable son of a bitch. His only child died shortly after birth, causing his marriage to hit the shitter. Field entered into a doomed love affair with a medical student and so began the descent into the mother of all depressions. He started busriders.com, aware that those who talk in public or to friends and family about suicide run the very real risk of getting locked in the cuckoo hatch. The forum was designed to be a place where folks with suicidal feelings could discuss their innermost thoughts, fears, and frustrations without threat of repercussion. His claim is that the site doesn't in any way encourage suicide, but it doesn't condemn it either."

"Terrific. So Field thinks he's doing these wretches a favor by giving them a place to congregate and talk about killing themselves."

"Something like that. Unfettered communication can be pretty liberating. Especially if in your everyday life, you're strung tight as a banjo. Field says he saw the forum as a worthwhile effort, a place where people could be understood rather than be judged. He was quite surprised to learn there was such an overwhelming need for the site. No way did he anticipate it becoming such a fly trap for the suicidal."

"You must have wanted to jump through the phone and rip off his eyebrows with your bare hands."

"I was thinking about parts further south, but yeah, it was tough to listen to."

"Well, eleven years have gone by, and Brady Field's message board is still with us. Is that supposed to convince us that the site serves a valid purpose, that writing about suicidal feelings is somehow therapeutic?"

"No. Field takes credit for turning his own life around. He got a divorce, moved across the country and bought a cat. He's happy, bless his little black heart."

"Sniff out anything wrong about him?"

"Too early to tell. We talked for ten minutes, max. But I want to look the bastard in the eye. If he's been aiding and abetting those web board participants to kill themselves, I'll make sure he serves the full sentence."

"Uh, all due respect, Zig, I think you have a problem."

"What's that?"

"You're a little too close to this thing. You spent all yesterday at Amanda's side because her best friend killed herself. You said yourself that Melissa Waller was like your own daughter. Now you've found the guy who created the forum that Melissa and Amanda posted on. I wouldn't blame you for wanting to drag Field behind your car on a gravel road, but we need information from him. We won't get anywhere if you piss him off."

"I'll be a lamb," he said through a tightened jaw. "Really."

Carolyn shook her head. "I'll go to Astoria, Zig."

Ziggy looked wounded. "He's expecting me, C.L."

They seesawed awhile, until it was decided that they would both pay a not-so-social call on Dr. Brady Field.

When noon came, Carolyn ate a wilted salad at her desk. By one o'clock, she and Ziggy were buckled into a Crown Vic and heading north on US 101. Ziggy had the radio playing during the forty-minute drive, his excitement at having located Bella Donna overshadowed by his cell phone call to his daughter, who was still in her pajamas and hadn't yet eaten anything. He muttered a soft "love you, little girl" to Amanda then lapsed into a thoughtful silence.

They passed Seaside, stirring up Carolyn's memories of the Prom, a two-mile paved walkway that had been built in the '20s. She and Gregg had sat on one of the many benches lining the path, their gaze drawn to the magnificent homes on one side and the dunes on the other. Some heated necking had taken place on those dunes.

When the car circled onto the roundabout and exited onto Marina Drive, more memories surfaced, this time of fourth-grade trip to the Maritime Museum, Joshua deciding then and there he would be a sailor when he grew up. A year later, after a tour of the Firefighters Museum, he had changed his mind. His entering the seminary after high school was a career choice Carolyn hadn't seen coming. When he left the seminary and pursued a degree in social work, Carolyn thought he'd finally found his niche, but with his recent interest in Doctors of Mercy, it seemed her twin still wasn't sure what he wanted. She hoped he would figure it out soon.

Ziggy shut the radio off and asked Carolyn to consult his scrawled directions. Minutes later they located the home of Dr. Brady Field. The house was a contemporary sandstone structure perched at the top of a winding road. The landscaping was lush, the shrubbery neatly clipped but not, Carolyn noted, pruned into the ridiculous unnatural humps, blocks and balls so often seen. A small sign advertising the doctor's security system poked out from among the branches of a carpet juniper. A black Audi A8 sat in the double driveway.

"What do you think, Zig, close to a million?"

"In and about. Nice view of the Columbia. Big lot. Our doctor friend is doing okay."

"Can't wait to see the inside. Let's go."

Dr. Brady Field greeted them at the front door wearing tan chinos, a denim shirt and Topsiders. He looked to be in his mid-forties, his hair just beginning to be salted with gray. He was tall and solidly built with a large meaty hand that dwarfed Carolyn's when he extended it. Catching his surprised look at seeing not one but two officers, Carolyn introduced herself and explained that she thought it best to accompany Sergeant Takacs, given his close involvement with one of the diner's casualties.

She and Ziggy were ushered into a spacious foyer with an open staircase that seemed to float from the middle of the hallway to the next level. The doctor was a fan of white—the walls, the banister, the bleached maple floors. At the far end of the hall was a large living room with a sharply sloped ceiling and a two-storey brick fireplace. They sat on a pair of matching white loveseats, separated by a Plexiglas cocktail table loaded with thick art books. Carolyn wondered if Field had cracked the spine on any of them.

He offered them fruit juice, herbal tea, wine if it wasn't against the rules. They refused, but the doctor helped himself to a glass of shiraz that he had decanted on a nearby glass-and-chrome serving trolley. Carolyn thought of the Dom Perignon cork she'd discovered on Signal Hill and decided that if the cardiologist were to drink champagne, he would certainly be able to afford the best.

A Himalayan cat sauntered haughtily into the room, its blonde-white fur and pale gray ruff a perfect complement to the décor. It wound around Field's ankles then jumped onto his lap and settled in, directing a look of scorn at Ziggy. "Neither of you are allergic, I hope?" Field asked.

"No," said Carolyn.

"Love cats," said Ziggy, who didn't.

"Dr. Field," Carolyn began, "Sergeant Takacs has filled me in on the telephone conversation you had with him yesterday." She summarized the highlights, stating when the doctor had created the pro-choice suicide forum and his reasons for doing so. The doctor stroked the cat's fur, sipped wine and nodded as Carolyn recited the details. "Doctor, you make it quite clear on the site that your forum is not a place for people to come and save others or to talk them out of ending their lives."

"Doing that would be a violation of the purpose of the forum," Field explained. "One of our basic principles is that of free choice. None of us can presume to know what's best for someone else. Are you aware of how many newsgroups exist on the topic of suicide?"

Both Carolyn and Ziggy shook their heads.

"At last count, somewhere around thirty thousand worldwide. Yet we like to think we're one of the few who can welcome anyone to our forum in a non-judgmental and caring environment."

"So no one is allowed to post a comment advising a depressed participant to seek psychiatric help?"

"Interventionists and trolls would be banned from the site by the site administrator or one of the moderators. Philosophically, most of us feel ambivalent toward mental health practitioners. P-docs vary widely in their abilities to effectively treat their patients, and since they're bound by the laws of their particular jurisdiction, they don't always act in the best interest of their patients. Often they function more as agents of social control."

Ziggy cleared his throat and Carolyn shot him a quick look. So much for doctors supporting each other.

"Along those same lines," Field continued, "we clearly state in our disclaimer that we don't pretend to be a substitute for the knowledge held by P-docs."

Ziggy cut in. "You mentioned a site administrator. Would that be you?"

Field sipped wine and nodded. "I control all facets of web board operation."

"As a cardiologist, I would have figured you'd have a pretty packed schedule."

"Which is why I have a team of moderators who also monitor the site. They're able to ban users, delete topics, edit posts. For instance, if someone posts offensive material, tries to invade someone's privacy or engages in any kind of bashing, that would be removed. If profane language is used, a moderator replaces the swear word with a couple of stars."

"They wouldn't be able to catch everything right away though, would they?"

"True. Some things do get by them, but they can't control that. There's a disclaimer stating we can't be held responsible for what may appear in the forum. The moderators do the best they can to remove objectionable material as soon as they see it."

We can't be held responsible. Carolyn wondered if the elegant doctor's skin was sprayed with a non-stick coating.

"But you don't consider trading tips on the best rooftop to jump from to be objectionable?"

Field didn't blink. "I do not."

"Would goading someone to commit suicide be considered objectionable?" she asked.

"Yes, of course," he answered in a rush. "And without doubt, there are some vicious sites out there, but mine isn't one of them. I specifically state in the Terms of Use that any messages advocating suicide, murder-suicide, or offers to kill a suicidal person are forbidden. I'm aware you're here because you are investigating the deaths of those five people at that diner. I can only conclude that they somehow met on our forum, but I can assure you that my moderators reported no suicide pact messages posted on our site."

"No. Your participants are smarter than that. All of those arrangements—where to die, how to die—are planned in Private Message."

Field sipped wine, unruffled. "I can't control that. If there's some supposed suicide epidemic going on, it has nothing to do with me."

The Himalayan reacted to the change in its owner's tone. It stood, arched its back and looked Field square in the eye. Apparently satisfied that no harm was coming to its chief meal ticket, the cat curled up in the opposite direction and within moments was asleep again.

"Doctor Field," Carolyn said, "I'm sure you created your forum with the best intentions. But what we're dealing with here is not just a random group of people who didn't want to die alone. We now know that a group in Washington State plus four adolescents from across the country have accessed your message board. And we also suspect that when it came time for them to die, they had some help."

That was mostly true. Carolyn couldn't be sure about the jumpers in North Cascades National Park. If someone had watched, he had done so from a distance. Police, at Carolyn's request, had revisited the area but hadn't yet found evidence of complicity. Nothing to link those deaths to the atrocities that occurred in Cypress Village.

"But that's murder," Brady Field said, his voice as calm as if he was commenting on his wine's bouquet.

"Promoting a suicide, and reckless endangerment," Ziggy said. "Both felonies. Melissa Waller, the young girl who died at the diner, was my daughter's best friend. You might know her as Nightshade. And when Melissa stayed with us for a week this summer, I didn't see any sign of a girl who would willfully ingest strychnine. But young and impressionable kids like Melissa can get sucked into a situation beyond their control."

Field winced. He glanced over at the bottle of shiraz on the trolley but remained seated, likely out of respect for his cat. "The thought that someone could be using my message board to dupe people into killing themselves—"

"That someone is looking at serious jail time," Ziggy said, leaning forward. "And I'll make damn sure it happens. Ten years is a good chunk out of a cardiologist's life, isn't it?"

The man's face went as white as his walls. "You don't mean I'm a suspect?"

Ziggy smiled. "You're what we would call a 'person of interest.' It would be helpful if you would cooperate, give us a list of your moderators, your forum participants along with their online nicknames ..."

"I can't do that."

"We'll be serving your Internet Service Provider with a subpoena."

Brady Field pursed his lips, an unbecoming expression. Carolyn thought he now resembled his cat.

"It's awful," the doctor said, "about those people. All of them. But if someone hung himself, would the victim's family rush to sue the manufacturer of the rope? Neither I, nor busriders.com is responsible for those deaths. You're going to ask me to shut down the site, aren't you? It cuts to the very core of the First Amendment. It—"

"Easy, Doctor Field," Carolyn said, noting that at no time did the doctor asked to be addressed as Brady. "We're not going to ask you to shut it down. At least, not yet."

"That surprises me."

Carolyn let his statement hang in the air. Field wasn't stupid. He would make the connection soon enough.

"Besides," Ziggy muttered, "you'd just start it up again under a new name."

For the briefest moment, Carolyn was certain she noticed the corner of Field's mouth twitch. An almost smile.

Ziggy rose and so did Carolyn. The cat opened one eye then jumped from Field's lap and like a thing possessed, suddenly darted up the open staircase in pursuit of invisible prey. As the doctor accompanied them to the door, Ziggy repeated his pronouncement about the subpoena.

"We all do what we have to do," was the doctor's smug reply. The color had returned to his face. At the door it was as if someone had slid a pulpit in front of him. Field spoke again in defense of free speech and the valuable service his website provided. He professed himself a proponent of Oregon's physician-assisted euthanasia law. Carolyn absorbed it all. The doctor's opinions and his zeal to deliver his rapid-fire thoughts though they hadn't asked, was indeed making him a 'person of interest.'

In the car once more, Carolyn said, "Zig, in your gut, do you think it's him?"

With barely a pause came the answer. "I didn't see anything today to tell me it isn't."

Carolyn nodded.

"Tell you something else," he said. "I'm glad I run every morning. I'm glad I'm not overweight. I'm glad heart attacks don't run in my family because C.L., no way would I ever let a cold bastard like that cut me open."

CHAPTER 24

On the ride home Carolyn felt sick inside, wanting more than anything to have Brady Field shut down busriders.com. She knew too, that Fading Away had the potential to lure in the killer, be it Field or someone else. But how long would that take? And how many others might die in the meantime?

In the e-posted responses to Fading Away, Carolyn had been relieved to find no mention of another group eager to catch the bus. Perhaps even the suicidal reached a plateau every so often and needed a break from the all-encompassing task of planning their deaths.

Ziggy was more talkative, pulling Carolyn from her own dark thoughts into his. "I just don't get it, C.L.," he said. "You think you know your own daughter and then something like this happens. We thought we raised Amanda right, you know? Ilona stayed at home to be a full-time mom. We always ate supper together as a family. We took Amanda to church. Put her in activities. Cheered her on at every damn thing she ever tried. Then she gets on the Net with a friend and pretends she wants to kill herself? What the hell is that about?"

"Think back to your high school days, Zig," Carolyn said. "You probably did some dumb things, too. Got drunk. Maybe took a turn behind the wheel of someone's car when you didn't have your license. Mooned some old lady. Why did any of us do those things? Attention. Recognition. Acceptance."

"I thought Amanda had all that."

"Sure she did. From you and Ilona. But when kids grow up, gain a little independence, they want those things from other people. They're after a tougher audience, one who doesn't love them unconditionally. Earning acceptance from an outside group represents a challenge, see?"

Ziggy's fingers curled tightly around the wheel. "But why this group? Why busriders.com?"

Counseling was Joshua's domain. Was there anything Carolyn could say to console her friend? She searched her mind frantically for the right words, each phrase sounding trite, overdone, banal. Eventually she settled on, "They were different, Zig. There were people of all ages in the group. It was an adventure, a kick to see what she could get away with, see who she could fool, and all done from a distance. What Amanda thought was a safe distance."

"Yeah, and we know how that turned out."

Carolyn nodded sadly, thinking about Melissa Waller, lassoed into something that got too big, too powerful for her to escape. "But Amanda didn't stick with it. She bailed out of being Nightshade early in the game. There's got to be some comfort in that."

"Some," he said grudgingly. "Make no mistake, C.L. I love Mandy more than oxygen, but right now, I'm as pissed at her as I ever wanna get. I'll support her through this awful thing, I'll sit up with her for months if I have to, get her professional help, whatever she needs. But a part of me wants to shake her, ask her what the hell she was thinking."

"It's okay, Zig." Carolyn reached across the console, gave his forearm what she hoped was a reassuring squeeze. She saw his fingers loosen from the steering wheel then he patted her hand with his left one in a good-buddy gesture. Carolyn wanted to say she would be there for him, if he felt like talking, anytime, but she pursed her lips tightly instead, thinking he must already realize as much. She resisted the urge to lace her fingers through his, turning abruptly away to stare out the window as a light rain spackled her view of the ocean. The rest of the ride back to Cypress Village passed in silence.

By quitting time, the rain was pelting a fierce tattoo on Carolyn's office window. She decided to wait out the weather and clean up her desk—avoidance tactics, she knew. Going home to an empty house was a dismal prospect. Maybe in half an hour the storm would let up, and she wouldn't have to race to her car with a newspaper over her head. Her umbrella, as usual, was in the wrong place, this time tucked snugly in the back of her Explorer along with her jacket. Ziggy had already gone home, muttering a hurried "see ya, C.L.," as he turned up his collar.

Carolyn didn't envy the evening Ziggy had ahead of him. The Takacs family would likely spend more catatonic hours in front of the television. She could imagine Ziggy and Ilona whispering, tiptoeing, muffling all the usual household noises, careful not to further upset their already fragile daughter. And Ziggy would be guarding his own emotions too, holding in check his anger at Amanda's days or weeks of foolishness, her cyber thrill ride that had gone horribly sour. Where was Ilona in all of this? Ziggy had mentioned little about his wife, what she was feeling, how she was handling it. Was she somehow blaming Ziggy? Was he blaming her?

Carolyn spun out of her chair and went to the window. She was thinking far too much about Ziggy and his family, investing too heavily in problems that weren't hers. Why was that? Not enough to do? Hardly.

Far from letting up, the rain was getting worse, streaming in opaque sheets against the pane. On the inky pavement below, blurred yellow headlights cut through the darkness then disappeared. She should have just gone home, fixed herself a mile-high ham sandwich, poured a glass of something then climbed into a tub full of bubbles. She had a scented candle on her bathroom counter, one Paige had given her. Mandarin pineapple. What was she saving it for? Later she'd light the thing, grab one of the dozen books she'd been meaning to read and get involved in some poor fictional character's misery. It wasn't much of a plan, but it beat the hell out of not having one at all.

She would give the rain fifteen minutes to behave itself then she would head home. While waiting, Carolyn typed busridersforum.com on her keyboard. There were several responses to Fading Away, mostly sympathetic. Killcrazy from Belgium urged her to find a better doctor, someone who had more current knowledge about effective pain management. The Monitor called her 'dear' a lot and sounded much like a doting grandmother who wanted everything to be right with the world but was at a loss about how to make that happen. "I just want your pain to end, Fading Away," she'd written. "However that's meant to be."

A new poster who called himself Shooter was a real prince. *If it's all as bad as you say, why are you still around?*

Carolyn formed her own brief reply.

busridersforum.com
December 8, 2009 23:00
Join Date: Dec. 3, 2009
Location: Pacific Northwest
Posts: 2
Fading Away
Suicidal Tendencies
Thanks, everyone. Read your posts. No energy today to say much or do much. Feel everything is weighing too heavily. So lonely, in such pain, and I'm just …

Fading Away

P.S. Shooter, I hope you find a friend who treats you better than you treated me.

There was another quick reply from the lovable Shooter. *Who needs friends?*

Very nice. Carolyn checked her watch. She'd given the storm an extra five minutes to no avail. Rain hit the window like machine-gun fire. Rivulets flowed down the street, and passing cars sent up huge fans of water as they sped through puddles, everyone eager to be home.

She was reaching for her windbreaker when the phone rang. It was Lieutenant Perri Carver. Washington State.

"Storming where you are?" she asked. "Weather's kicked up here big time. Coast Guard can't keep up with the calls." Carver's voice was hoarse and phlegmy.

"Sounds like the weather isn't agreeing with you either."

There was a loud sneeze at the other end, then, "Can't seem to shake this damn bug. Anyway, got something you might be interested in."

Carver told her about a trail, one used by more experienced hikers in North Cascades National Park. It led to a high ledge and a scenic lookout. Anyone standing on the bluff would have been able to see the quintet of jumpers clearly from across a rocky chasm.

"He left something, didn't he," Carolyn said.

"Guy fancies himself an artist. Painted something on a rock near where he could have sat. We wouldn't have thought much of it if you hadn't twigged us. It was the last place we were looking, and we were just about to pack the whole business in and have a good laugh at you people south of us for spawning some bizarre theory."

"What did you find?" Too much chit-chat, Carolyn thought, edgy. Get to the bloody point.

"The date. August 25th. The day the jumpers died. And a time. 2:00 p.m."

"Any chance one of the jumpers painted it there, you know, before hiking the other trail?"

"Anything's possible, but in this case, I doubt it. Like I said, the trail is challenging. One of the casualties was HIV positive. Advanced. He was lucky to hike to his own death. There was a teenage girl, a middle-aged woman, neither particularly fit physical specimens. Nor were the other two. So hiking two trails? Not in a day. Could have gone to the lookout days before, of course."

Yes, Carolyn thought, but that's not how it happened. The person who masterminded the group suicide in the park sat and watched. And recorded the exact time of the jump. It had been agreed upon. All for one and one for all. Musketeers with a death wish.

"Below the date," Carver continued, "he painted the letters R.I.P. And there's something else, too."

The gravelly voice at the other end paused.

"A symbol," Carolyn stated simply.

"That's right. And I'm sending it to you as we speak. Looks like—"

Carver sneezed again. Blew loudly into a tissue.

"Save your voice," Carolyn told her. "Let me guess. It looks like a ladder. With a broken rung."

CHAPTER 25

JUST WHEN SHE THOUGHT SHE'D seen the sickest of the sick. Carolyn recalled the coldness of the bastard who'd shot her last year, the one who still gave her nightmares. Now she was faced with chasing down another monster, one who had an ice cube for a heart and who delighted in seducing the vulnerable on the Net and watching them die. No, watching them *suffer* and die. He was stepping up the thrill, making the suicide experience more tangible, more close up. The disturbing thought, one that plagued Carolyn as she headed for home, was: How would he top the strychnine? Death didn't get any uglier. Would he have to become a hands-on killer, feel his victims' blood ooze between his fingers as he thrust a knife into their flesh? Or would he remain content with manipulating them from a distance, perhaps watching as they pulled a trigger, sent an explosion of brain matter across a pristine white wall.

As her condo came into view, Carolyn realized she didn't want to go home. Not yet. Not alone. She checked her mirror then quickly pulled into a driveway, backed out and turned the Explorer toward town. There would be people at Marley's. She could sit at the bar, have a decent meal and eavesdrop. Marley's would have more distraction potential than her television or a stack of books. She couldn't concentrate anyway.

The restaurant's parking lot was nearly full. Carolyn eased the Explorer into a narrow space between two SUVs then jumped puddles toward the green awning that jutted from Marley's entrance. By the time she reached it, her feet were soaked, her puddle-jumping skills not what they used to be, and when she checked her appearance in the entryway mirror, she saw a drowned muskrat staring back at her.

Quickly she grabbed a comb from her purse, smoothed stray tendrils into her ponytail then made her way to a vacant stool at the counter. She shrugged out of her jacket, waved away the menu, and ordered a roast beef sandwich with a half-pint of Guinness, reasoning that the iron from the beer might pump some energy through her veins. She felt sapped dry.

It was a bad night for people-watching. Carolyn was surrounded by such achingly normal folks that she wondered if any of them would stir if she stripped naked and danced a jig on the bar. When they were younger, she and Joshua used to size up strangers, give them fictional names and biographies. But now she couldn't spot an aging chanteuse or an international spy among the lot. Perhaps the fault was Carolyn's. Maybe she had simply lost her imagination.

A new waitress was working the bar, her eyes ringed with gloppy coats of mascara. Aspiring poet, Carolyn decided. Ms. Limpid Pools.

She wondered if their cyber killer could sit in a crowd like this, chowing down on the evening's fish and chip special, perhaps tapping a fellow diner on the shoulder, asking to borrow the ketchup. Carolyn suspected he would consider himself too superior to bend an elbow with the people at Marley's.

The raccoon-eyed barmaid was discussing the Signal Hill suicides with a gloomy drunk two stools over. It was only natural, she explained, that the four teenagers would choose Cypress Village as their place to die. The cypress tree, after all, was a symbol of death, of despair, of mourning. Oh brother, Carolyn thought, wondering whether she could cancel her order and go home.

By the time she saw him ambling toward her, it was too late. Ms. Limpid Pools picked that precise moment to set Carolyn's sandwich in front of her. "Hi, Gregg," she said when her ex approached. To her dismay, he perched on the stool next to hers, setting a pint of pale ale on the bar. She wondered when the red wine connoisseur had switched camps.

"Just getting home from work?" he asked.

"Yeah. You?"

He nodded.

She looked over her shoulder. "Where's the family?"

"Home. Thought I'd drop in here for a bite to eat."

"I thought The Rocks was more to your taste. Suddenly you're a Marley's convert?"

"Guess I just felt like something different."

She handed him a menu and he ordered a steak sandwich, no onions.

"How's the shoulder?"

"Healing nicely."

"And the sciatica?"

"Only hurts when I'm awake."

He laughed. She drank.

When their meals came Gregg proclaimed the steak sandwich surprisingly tasty, as though he'd expected Marley's to specialize in cremated boot leather. Then he asked her about Christmas. "All set for the festive season?"

"The wreath's on the door," she answered, deciding at once that tomorrow, for sure, she would buy a tree, invite Joshua and Paige over to help her decorate it.

"If you've got no plans, you could come to our place for dinner."

What the hell? Gregg didn't appear drunk, but the draft beer must have destroyed part of his brain. It was the only explanation Carolyn had for why Gregg would be inviting her to spend Christmas with his pregnant girlfriend and their year-old child. "Um, no," she said when she could find her tongue. "I don't think that would be a good idea. In fact, I might be going away for the holidays."

She hadn't thought about it, but suddenly, a Christmas vacation seemed like a good idea. She could head up to Alberta, ski the south face at Lake Louise. She had some unused days left.

It was a door she shouldn't have opened. Between bites, Gregg began to wax nostalgic about the ski holidays they used to take. They'd gone to Telluride, Deer Valley, Snowmass. They'd had midnight soaks in the hot tub with drifts of snow surrounding them, the evergreens twinkling with Christmas lights. His and hers massages. An invigorating guided snowshoe trek through the Colorado backwoods, and hot apple cider around a campfire. He nudged Carolyn's memory about her one and only black diamond run, skiing down a slope aptly named Hanging Valley Wall, her knowing with absolute certainty that she would crash into a tree before ever reaching the lodge. She'd made it, though, safe but exhausted, with Gregg cheering her on. Thankfully, he didn't need to remind her that, back in their slopeside condo that night, the sex had been mind-blowing.

Gregg ordered another beer and Carolyn switched to coffee. "Does Nadia ski?"

Gregg shook his head. "Not much of an athlete, I'm afraid. Can't swim to save herself, either."

"Oh. That's too bad." Carolyn knew that Gregg would live in the water if he could. He swam, snorkeled, scuba dived, and dreamed of someday owning a sailboat. "But I'm sure you've got other things in common. And you have a daughter. Any pictures?"

"Just this small one." From his wallet, Gregg produced a stamp-sized photo of Gillian, a round-cheeked cherub with wisps of blonde hair framing her pink face.

Carolyn studied the picture, at the little girl's wide blue eyes, her smiling bow lips. "She's got your mouth."

"You think?"

"She's very cute."

And you're very lucky, she thought. I hope you realize it.

Gregg grabbed for the check when it came. He asked about her condo, how things were working out there. Did she have enough space? Were the neighbors good? Did she feel safe?

"It's great," she told him. "There's plenty of room. And I'm thinking of getting a dog."

"You'd be a great doggie mom."

He swiveled on the stool and signaled for the check. "Rain seems to have let up. Let me walk you to your car."

Carolyn felt his hand on her back as he ushered her through the exit. He was just being gallant. A polite gesture, she told herself.

"I love the smell after a good rain," he said, inhaling deeply. "Everything washed clean."

"Smells like worms to me."

Gregg laughed then said, "I don't want to alarm you, but—"

"What? What's wrong?"

"I know I'm surprised—"

"What is it?"

"It almost seems like we're getting along."

Carolyn laughed with him. "No, that can't be. You must be mistaken."

When they neared her vehicle Carolyn fished her keyless remote from her pocket. The lights flashed and she heard the click.

She wasn't sure whether she paused too long or whether Gregg was merely standing too close, but suddenly his hands grasped her shoulders and his mouth was on hers. He was tender, familiar, and she found herself responding, lips parting as his arms came around her. Gregg had always been good at this, the prequel to lovemaking. As rotten as she might feel, as tired as she could get, she could always lose herself in his kiss, in his embrace that was both comforting and arousing. Was there ever a time when she didn't want him? No, and that was the problem. She heard a moan and realized it was coming from her.

"No," she said, breaking the kiss, wedging the heels of her hands between them. "Tell me that didn't happen."

"It did, Carolyn." He leaned in close again.

"A mistake." She shoved away from him. "The beer—"

"You had half a pint. You're not drunk."

"Then I'm crazy. I've hated you for months. Maybe I'm tired of hating you. It takes too much energy. But this—" She felt sick. "Never again."

"Carolyn, this thing with Nadia. It's all wrong. I'm not in love with her. I was a jerk, I know. I rushed into it. Because of the baby. But it's wrong. I can't do it anymore."

The ground pitched under her. "I don't want to hear it. I can't hear it. Go home. Work it out. Leave me alone."

She fumbled for her car door, wrenched away from him as he reached for her again.

"Carolyn, wait. Don't leave it like this. We have to talk."

Somehow she managed to climb into the vehicle, lock the automatic doors and ram the key in the ignition. She made the trip home going ten miles under the speed limit, not out of caution for the slippery pavement but to compensate for her real desire to put her foot to the mat and keep on driving. Once inside she peeled off her clothes and took a shower instead of a bath. What was wrong with her anyway? She'd been obsessing over Ziggy. Had she really wanted to take his hand when they'd driven back from Brady Field's? Then there was Ted Tarrant's voice, a faceless rookie who lived across the country and was probably ten years her junior. Now Gregg. Pathetic. She scrubbed vigorously at her skin, raked fingernails through her scalp as she shampooed, would have slapped herself if she thought it would help.

In plaid pajamas, she padded to the kitchen, poured a glass of chardonnay and returned to the bathroom for her scented candle. Tomorrow she would get a Christmas tree, decorate the damn thing herself. And she'd check the classifieds. There had to be a puppy somewhere that needed a good home.

The smell of mandarin pineapple wafted toward her nostrils, and her breathing returned to normal. Carolyn scanned the TV listings, eyed the pile of books, read the cover blurbs of the first four on the stack. Then she went to her computer and booted it up. The Suicidal Tendencies thread was unusually inactive now. Perhaps the lovable Shooter had gone to bed. Carolyn scrolled through other threads to see whether the regular posters had gone elsewhere. Then she checked her e-mail. Three messages. Ted Tarrant had sent a video clip. Crazy cat stunts. Very cute. She didn't respond. She opened a message from Perri Carver in Washington State. She was still trying to locate witnesses who may have seen a lone hiker in the state park the day the five jumped, but so far, she was coming up dry. What she did learn was that the symbol found on the rock at the lookout in North Cascades National Park had been painted with Martha Stewart's Picket Fence, available in thirty-six stores throughout the state. A popular color, according to a staffer at Carver's local hardware store. Very crisp and cool.

Just like the interior of Brady Field's house.

Carolyn drank wine and opened her last e-mail.

My dear Fading Away,

I've been so worried about you. You sounded so despondent in your post earlier. Wondering how you're feeling and if there's any way I can help. Just ask,

The Monitor.

What good could the Monitor do? She didn't have much time left, her earlier postings revealed. She was an old lady with terminal cancer.

Or so she claimed. Carolyn thought of what Ziggy had said about posers—in cyber communication, everyone pretends to be somebody else. Had the Monitor offered assistance to the others? Lured the victims to their deaths with her good Samaritan routine?

At once, Carolyn realized, Who could be less threatening than a sick old lady?

CHAPTER 26

JOSHUA ENGAGED THE CHILD-PROOF SAFETY locks in his Jeep, a precaution in case Yoshi decided to bolt from the vehicle at a stoplight and make a desperate dash back to his uncle's apartment. It had taken Joshua twenty minutes to convince Yoshi to slip on his jacket and get into the passenger seat.

"You'll stay with me?" he asked.

Joshua assured him he would. Again.

"And the others, they're okay?"

"Nice group of people. And you'll like Wes. He's leading tonight's discussion."

"I'll be safe?"

"Absolutely. Yoshi, what are you so afraid of?"

"Nothing." During the short ride from Ishiguro's place to 3F House, Yoshi listened to music on his iPod and kept his hands occupied with a bag of corn chips. His dark eyes peered from beneath the brim of a baseball cap and darted everywhere as if expecting some childhood nightmare creature to spring from behind a tree and ambush the car. Re-enter Yoshi the Child. Joshua wondered which of the teen's many faces would be revealed once he entered 3F House and met the others. Would he become sullen and testy like the other night? Or would he withdraw and say nothing, only making eye contact with the hardwood floors.

Earlier in the day, Joshua had met with his friend Samuel Risk at a Stumptown Coffee Roasters in Portland. Joshua had banking business in the city, and Risk was between sessions. Over mugs of Trapper Creek decaf Joshua gave Risk a summary of Yoshi's background, his fascination with computer games, porn, and James

Dean, as well as his painful break-up with his girlfriend, Aoki; Joshua was also worried about how he had handled things with the boy last night.

"You're doing the right thing, Joshua," Risk told him, to his relief. "That boy's got to get out in the world, painful as it might be in the beginning."

"I feel like a heartless shit, pushing him into this. What if he isn't ready?"

"But without a nudge from you, his social skills will be reduced to the equivalent of a gnat's."

"I just don't want to make a mistake with him. He's so fragile."

Risk pointed an admonishing finger. "You're being too hard on yourself. You know the cure rate's only about thirty percent for a hikikomori kid. If Yoshi doesn't pull out of it, you can't blame yourself."

Joshua knew he would anyway, but aloud he told Risk he was right. Then he broached the subject of his interest in Doctors of Mercy and his desire to spend time in the field.

"What does your fiancée think about that?"

"Plainly put, Paige thinks I'm a flake."

"Ouch. That must have hurt. But do you suppose she has a point? You've got a good thing going with her, Joshua. Hate to see you screw it up."

"Me too."

"Humanitarian work's not for everybody. You wade through a heap of misery to get to that glimmer of hope. I get a clearer picture of you sitting in an easy chair—cardigan, newspaper, couple of kids running in and out of the room."

"I think about that, too. Except the cardigan part."

The two made small talk for a few more minutes then set a tentative date for a racquetball game.

"Last time you cleaned my clock," Risk said. "Any chance you'll go easier on me next time?"

"None," Joshua replied with a smile.

Then Risk glanced at his watch and reached for the check. "Time for me to make a move."

"Next one's on me," Joshua told him.

"Good," Risk said, grabbing his jacket from the back of the chair. "We'll have dinner. Somewhere expensive."

"Don't push it."

They agreed to meet for breakfast soon.

When the Jeep pulled up along the curb in front of 3F House, Yoshi waited until Joshua had killed the engine and had stepped out and around to his side of the vehicle before getting out. Warily, the boy scanned the length of the street then looked behind him. Joshua planted a firm arm around Yoshi's shoulder and led him up the front walk. Inside, Auntie Rose, her right hand wrapped in gauze, was serving muffins to Chad Malvern who was hunched over a pile of books on the dining-room table. Rose, along with the rest of the staff, had been coached about Yoshi, his hikikomori, his relationship with his parents and uncle, his heartbreak at losing Aoki. They were informed that getting the boy out of the apartment was a huge deal and that Yoshi would be nervous. Even petrified. Joshua told Rose not to overdo it.

She rushed over with muffins and tried to make eye contact by peering under the brim of his cap. "You must be Yoshi. So nice to have you here."

A corner of Yoshi's mouth struggled to turn upward, the feeble attempt at a smile so fleeting most would miss it. He declined the muffin with a trembling raised hand.

"I'll wrap one up for you to take home," Rose said, and catching Joshua's eye, retreated to the kitchen.

Joshua ushered Yoshi over to where Chad Malvern sat, still in his school uniform and trying hard not to stare at the new kid. Joshua introduced the two, and Yoshi nodded shyly. Malvern sprouted a wide grin and stood to shake hands. After a hesitant moment, Yoshi shook.

"Big essay due next week," Malvern said. "Poor planning on the teacher's part, I'd say. She'll spend her Christmas break marking. I'm going scuba-diving in the Caribbean. You dive?"

Yoshi mumbled a quiet "no."

"Coming up for discussion, Chad?" Joshua asked.

"No, Mr. Latham." Chad was the only 3F kid who called Joshua by his surname, despite Joshua's insistence that the formality wasn't necessary. "Polley's up there."

"There's room for you, too, you know."

"I think I'll just stay here, get my work done. Yoshi can hang here if he wants."

Yoshi took another step closer to Joshua.

"Think I'll introduce Yoshi to the others," Joshua said. "But maybe you two can talk later."

"I'll be here until about ten, sir," Chad answered with another disarming smile. "That's when my dad's picking me up."

Malvern's dad, a globe-trotting software company CEO, usually gave his son cab fare to get to and from 3F House which freed up his time to scout around for a younger, prettier wife than the one he'd just divorced. Chad's father put on a good fatherly show during school breaks, whisking Chad off for wilderness treks, ski excursions, white water rafting. The day-to-day parenting, not nearly as much fun, was what nannies were paid for. Joshua had clapped eyes on Keith Malvern only twice, but it was clear where Chad got his smooth ways. Chad was a little too yes-sir-no-sir for Joshua's liking, with a fawning politeness he thought might be masking a go-fuck-yourself-sir attitude. Teachers at the private school Chad attended thought 3F House could help Chad develop a more consistent work ethic and help him better relate to people his own age. The debonair Chad had been suspended twice for cyber bullying. One more strike and Chad would have had to slum it in the public school system.

Upstairs, Joshua introduced Yoshi to the group and told them Yoshi was from Japan.

Gavin Polley spoke first. "Hey, I heard that they have these cool karaoke bars where they let you smash plates to let off steam. You ever been to one?"

Yoshi's gaze darted from Gavin's sleeve of tattoos to the four corners of the room.

Prodding information from Yoshi was like trying to push a snowbound car out of a ditch. Rock the vehicle, spin the tires, and with momentum, traction and luck, the car would eventually lurch forward. Yoshi lurched too, struggling with the attention thrust on him. He executed a halting, noun-verb two-step as questions about geishas, Japanese schools, and the cost of a steak dinner were hurled at him. Wes Bertram motioned Yoshi to a chair and said, "Easy, guys. Yoshi's just come in the door. Save the inquisition for our next meeting."

Joshua slipped out of the room. By the time he got downstairs, Ken Ishiguro had already left a message with Auntie Rose. He wouldn't be able to pick Yoshi up. Would Joshua mind driving him home?

"Dammit," he said to Rose. "Did he give a reason?"

"He just said something had come up. But I could hear the something giggling in the background."

Great. More indifference. Just what Yoshi needed. Ken Ishiguro was going to get laid tonight and Yoshi would be pawned off on Joshua. Was there any hope in hell of this kid getting better? Joshua swore again.

"Poor kid." Rose struggled to wrap two muffins in tin foil favoring her left hand.

Joshua took over. "What happened to you?"

"Burned myself on the stove. You know me. Always rushing." With her good hand she gestured at the muffins. "These aren't a cure, but maybe they'll show that boy that somebody cares. He's such a nervous kid. It's bad enough his parents are too embarrassed to help him, now he's got an uncle who doesn't give a shit either. Excuse my French."

Joshua finished wrapping the muffins and returned the rest to the fridge. "Hope you had a doctor look at that hand."

"Don't worry about me." Then she lowered her voice. "What kind of girl would leave a boy like that? He seems so sweet. Not like—"

Their conversation was cut short by a hollow thud coming from the other side of the front door. Chad Malvern looked up from his stack of books. Rose eyed Joshua curiously then moved toward the noise. When she opened the door she gasped.

Lying on the stoop was a dead raccoon.

Joshua hurried over. "What the hell? How'd that get here?" He stepped over it and ran down the sidewalk toward the street, glancing in both directions. Seeing no one, he returned inside.

The color had drained from Rose's face.

"I'll get that thing out of here," Joshua said. "Someone's idea of a joke, I guess."

"What's going on?" Chad Malvern asked, rising from his spot at the dining-room table.

"Nothing, Chad," Joshua said quickly. "Stay put and get your work done. Your father will be here soon."

By the time Joshua disposed of the animal and came back inside, the discussion upstairs was over, and Chad had cornered Yoshi into a one-sided conversation. Rose was putting on her coat, her complexion still ashen.

"Time for us all to call it a night," Joshua said. "Don't let that prank shake you up, Rose. Come on. I'll walk you to your car."

She nodded. When Rose was safely behind the wheel, car doors locked, Joshua went back inside and turned to Yoshi. "Seems your uncle is delayed, so I'm taking you home."

Whatever relative ease Yoshi had experienced while inside 3F House disintegrated when he stepped outside. Once again, he pulled his baseball cap down and Joshua saw him scan the street, his cyes widening as a black Hummer with tinted windows pulled up to the curb. "That's Chad's father," Joshua told him just as Chad entered through the front door and hurried by them. The elder Malvern enjoyed living large and driving large, the behemoth Hummer screaming for attention in a village of eco-friendly hybrids.

In the Jeep, Joshua said, "Well, what did you think of the gang?"

Yoshi locked his door then belted in. "They're okay. Polley's cool."

"What about him?" Joshua jutted his chin in the direction of Malvern's Hummer as it turned a corner up ahead.

"Him not so much." Despite Joshua's urging, Yoshi didn't elaborate.

Joshua was still pissed at Ishiguro. "You can be really proud of yourself," he told Yoshi, compensating for his uncle's detachment.

"That was a big step tonight. It took guts, and the others seemed to like you, too."

Yoshi nodded politely but seemed more intent on surveying the street, gazing fixedly at a lone man who strolled along the sidewalk with a pair of Westies. Moments later, his attention turned to his passenger mirror. Reflexively, Joshua checked his rearview mirror as well. "Only two cars on the road and that obnoxious bastard's riding my ass."

When Yoshi twisted to look over his shoulder, the car tailing theirs flashed its headlights. *Wink, wink.*

"What the hell does he want? We're in a residential area. He can't pass, and I can't go any faster."

At the next intersection the car took a right. "Big deal," Joshua said. "All that just so he could turn?"

Yoshi sat wordlessly in his seat. In his clenched fists, Auntie Rose's muffins were massacred, with crumbs and bits of blueberry shooting through the crumpled foil.

"Hey, Yoshi, ease up. What's wrong? Was it that car? Guy was just being a jackass."

"Yeah. A jackass."

"You've had a big night. You're bound to be a little edgy."

"Yeah," came the one-note drone again. "Don't tell that nice lady what I did to her muffins."

"Your secret's safe with me. Anything you want to talk about?"

"No," Yoshi said, his voice dropping to a whisper. "Nothing."

CHAPTER 27

YOSHI BOILED WATER, MADE TEA but his shaking persisted. A hot shower offered relief as long as he stood under the warm pulsing jets, but as soon as he toweled off and put on pajamas he was trembling again. He felt chilled, as if someone had plunged him into an icy lake and held him there. The apartment thermostat registered 72 degrees. He cranked it up to 75.

He had invited Joshua to stay with him until his uncle got home, but he refused. No telling when Ken would return, Joshua told him. Maybe they could order a pizza, destroy a few more on-screen terrorists? Joshua shook his head. He hadn't seen Paige all day. He wished Yoshi a good night, congratulated him again on his first foray into society, and left.

Now Yoshi was alone.

He could never leave the apartment again. Not for *manga*, not for food, and not to meet with those kids. They had talked about dreams. Goals. What they wanted to accomplish within the next five years. Lily, with her pretty heart-shaped face, wanted to become an actress. Gavin, the cool one, wanted to go to an art college, become the next Andy Warhol. When the question had been put to Yoshi, he'd balked, tried to shrug it off, but Bertram, the washed-up footballer, said "no passes." Eventually, feeling the weight of everyone's stare, Yoshi mumbled that when he got better, if he got better, he'd like to go to Cholame, California.

"What's there?" Polley had asked. "I've never heard of it."

It was the place where James Dean had crashed his Porsche Spyder on September 30, 1955. An ardent Japanese fan, Ohnishi, had erected a chrome cenotaph there in 1981.

Yoshi would never get to Cholame. He would never go anywhere. His home was inside this apartment, in this room with its black walls, its heaps of comic books, its gadgetry. It had been enough once. It would be enough again.

He should never have left it, not tonight. He cursed Joshua for leading him to think that there were better things waiting beyond the walls of his room, cursed himself for starting to believe it might be true. He knew now that the only thing waiting for him outside was danger.

His real goal, the one he couldn't tell the group about, was simple—he wanted to stay alive.

That car. That fucking car. It had winked at him. He was sure of it. And when he turned, the driver had raised something toward the rearview mirror. For a brief moment, Yoshi caught a glimpse of the object in the shadows. A champagne glass. No. His imagination, it had to be. He was sleep-deprived. Tense. Plagued by night screams and gut-squeezing guilt. There had been no glass. Couldn't have been.

Yet even before he opened his e-mail, he knew.

Hello Yoshi, or should I say Jim? So very nice to see you again and so sorry you missed your bus. But you were treated to a fine danse macabre, *no? Come to the dance, my young friend.* Quod fuimus, estis; quod sumus, vos eritis. *Until we meet,*

The Monitor.

Yoshi trembled. He wasn't anonymous anymore. The bastard saw. The bastard knew.

He didn't make it to the bathroom. Supper came up as he sat at the computer, his stomach wrenched with spasm after spasm. Afterward, he cleaned up as best as he could and hurried through the small apartment, closing blinds and checking locks before collapsing tearfully on his bed, his back pressed firmly to the wall.

He had gone out after midnight once since *that* night. No one had followed him. He was sure of it. He had been careful. He looked over his shoulder constantly, alert for suspicious movements, a slowing car, a solitary stranger following too closely. *Semper respice post te.* The chilling e-mail message had shaken him at the time, which was what it was meant to do. But he thought it was only spam, sent by someone posing as Geezer, a troll who lurked on the message board. A sadist. A sick fuck. Probably sent the same message to some of the other riders too. Yoshi remembered wanting to kick himself for his paranoia. He was anonymous, wasn't he? The ISP would have had no reason to divulge his true identity. And even though he'd been spotted, even though those cold eyes had stared right at him, well, that didn't matter, did it? A person needed a name to go with the face.

Yet somehow he had been found. He had looked behind him and the headlights had *winked*. It wasn't a coincidence, nor was it the action of some road-rage bully, as Joshua had thought. Yoshi now had every reason to be paranoid, to be deathly afraid. That first warning had come not from some hacker sadist, but from the Monitor.

When his stomach finally settled, Yoshi Googled *danse macabre* and read about early frescoes and paintings that depicted all levels of society, from the highest emperor to the lowliest peasant, being led into Hell by skeletons and decaying corpses. Death—the great equalizer. He learned of the legend of the three men who meet their three dead ancestors along a road. In the ancestors' warning, translated from the Latin: *You are, what we were; you'll be, what we are.*

Yoshi had intended to catch the bus that night with the others. His uncle had been in his room, grading essays with '80s music blaring through a headset clapped to his ears. He wouldn't notice that Yoshi was gone, wouldn't go into his room to check on him. He never did.

Midnight. That was the agreed upon time. Yoshi assured the other riders he would meet them at the diner. There were few cars on the road but Yoshi had underestimated the time he would need to pedal his uncle's 10-speed from the apartment to the firetrap that had once been a restaurant. He was out of shape, puffing breathlessly after the first four miles. He had fallen once, too, unable to see a pothole in the dark. By 11:45, he knew he was still too far away to make it, but he kept pedaling. Perhaps they would wait. Perhaps they had been held up, too.

He heard the screams from the road.

Yoshi flung the bicycle to where it caught against the thick spines of a neglected gorse hedge and raced toward the decrepit building. He had only been at the window for seconds, horror-filled seconds, but it was long enough. Geezer, the oldest, was already dead, but the others were in the throes of some throat-gripping agony. They spasmed, they convulsed, they jackknifed, they shrieked. And Nightshade—oh, Nightshade. Her ear-splitting cries were still in his head.

Across the room, enveloped in shadow, a figure leaned against the counter, observing. *Rejoicing*. Yoshi could just make out the glass of champagne in the watcher's hands and was certain he could hear a quiet chuckle being carried on the night wind.

For a split second, he sensed that their eyes met. Cold eyes? He'd only thought that they were cold. He couldn't really see them, or much of the face. By then he was running, staying low as he tore across the scrubby land, the screams of the others following him, begging someone, anyone, for swift death.

Yoshi pedaled furiously for only a half-mile in the opposite direction from which he'd come, realizing the watcher might drive by, looking for him. He found a dense copse of maples and jumped from the bike. He hoisted the top tube onto his shoulder and ran for the trees, heart hammering as he neared his only shelter from predatory eyes that would scour the roadside in search of a lone cyclist.

He stayed in the woods for most of the night, crouched behind a fat tree trunk, becoming a watcher himself as cars rolled sporadically by: a dark Mercedes, two vans, a couple of hatchbacks, one red, one white. A scooter. An Audi or Saab, he couldn't tell which, then a silver SUV. He tried to keep track, ready to note if any vehicle passed along the road more than once. He didn't think so but he couldn't be sure. He was lying on wet ground, the cold worming its way through him, chilling him to the core. And there was a block of time when his attention had been removed from the road. He had turned away to vomit. Even that had come up cold.

He had left them there. His friends. Geezer. Pilgrim. C3PO. Blackjack. And Nightshade, who still screamed, even now.

What could he have done? He had no information for the police. He hadn't seen the Monitor clearly. It had been dark. He'd been gripped by the horrific spectacle of the others' deaths. He'd run like hell.

Yoshi had seen plenty of cop shows. The police couldn't protect him. They might even have used him as bait to catch a killer.

Then he heard sirens. By the time Yoshi decided it was safe enough to leave the woods, the diner was a crime scene. He pedaled past, didn't stare at the ambulances, didn't stare at the police vehicles, nor at the media already setting up camp. He gave the scene a cursory glance, as any curious onlooker would then continued on, head low. A respectful posture for the dead.

By the time Yoshi returned to the apartment, it was early morning. His legs burned, his throat was raw, and his lower back felt as if a fist had pummeled it. He pushed his pain aside and waited another forty-five minutes, this time hunched behind the concrete half-wall of the apartment parking lot, until he saw his uncle drive away in his Toyota hatch.

Inside the apartment, he guzzled water, for no other reason than to give him something to throw up. He spent the day e-mailing Killcrazy, Bad Attitude and nearly a dozen other bus riders, telling them that Jim Stark was alive and well but would no longer be posting on the Suicidal Tendencies thread. He warned them about posers on the web board, those who only pretended to be kind, who pretended to want to help. He blocked all messages from the group, its administrator and the Monitor. He removed the site from his "favorites" list and deleted all his visits to busriders.com from his computer's history. *Sayonara*, Jim Stark.

Coupled with his fear was a deep emptiness, one that settled and grew in the pit of his stomach. He felt cloaked in a thick, black shroud. Losing Aoki had been the worst, he thought, until now. To save himself, he had just cut himself off from all his friends, and he wouldn't be meeting his new ones again, either. Gavin Polley. Lily. Big Bert, the football guy, who was okay. 3F House was a cool place, but he couldn't go there. He would have to find other friends. There were countless message boards, chat rooms. He would begin again.

Joshua would be disappointed. His uncle would be pissed. Maybe they would try to force him from the apartment, grab him under the arms and drag him into Joshua's Jeep.

He couldn't explain why that wouldn't be possible. If the watcher had managed to get a good look at him, the fact that Yoshi was Asian wouldn't have escaped those eyes. How many Japanese teenagers were there in a place as small as Cypress Village? Yoshi guessed there weren't many. If any. To expose himself to his enemy would mean his death. And he wouldn't see it coming.

The Monitor could be anybody.

Yoshi would not leave the apartment. And no one could make him. In the kitchen he opened drawers, searching until he found one of his uncle's knives. He removed it from its slot and took it to his room.

CHAPTER 28

THE FIVE WHO HAD JUMPED to their deaths in Washington State had been in the ground for just over three months. Heather Conklin's ashes were in a decorative urn at her parents' house in Boise; the two boys who had died with her had been buried quickly and quietly. Brenda Koch was given a no-frills funeral, her casket looking not much better than a project constructed by first-year woodworking students. The mourners, as Carolyn had suspected, were few. But earlier, it seemed as if the entire population of Cypress Village had gathered for the funeral of Melissa Waller, cramming into the church and listening dumbstruck as Amanda Takacs delivered a simple but touching eulogy for her best friend.

At her desk, Carolyn ate a bland chicken sandwich, washed it down with a bottle of cranberry juice then surrendered to her craving for a Mars bar. She accessed busriders.com, typed in another desperate message as Fading Away and read the posts already entered. Killcrazy, the poster from Belgium, was still around, not sounding any happier, but not saying he wanted to end it all either. A new poster, one who called himself Strait Razr, had a message for everyone on the thread: stop whining and just f***ing do it. Clearly Bella Donna and the other moderators weren't online to delete the post.

Carolyn thought about Dr. Brady Field and wondered why, if he had turned his life around, he would still commandeer a web board for the suicidal. Was he truly an altruistic soul who wanted to reach out to those who were suffering? When Carolyn and Ziggy had visited him, she'd seen nothing in the cardiologist's manner to indicate a generous spirit, or even a particularly compassionate one.

Though Field had expressed shock when he learned that the deaths on Signal Hill and at the diner might be linked to his site, he'd exhibited more concern that freedom of speech be protected than a killer caught. And Carolyn detected a pervasive air of 'nobody tells me what to do.' But would the well-heeled doctor have revelled in telling others what to do? Would he have delighted in the knowledge that the desolate, the downtrodden, the hopeless, would die if he wished it so? And had he driven to Washington State two months ago?

Carolyn sought out the darkest corner of her imagination and pictured the scene at the diner as ME Trahern had described it, bodies jolting as if struck by forked lightning, the protracted agony of ceaseless spasms. She conjured an image of Field in the diner, leaning casually against the dusty lunch counter, perhaps drinking champagne as if he'd snagged Standing Room Only space at a local dinner theater. The picture was clear. She could easily envision Field in the role.

Envisioning didn't make it so. Carolyn thought once more of the so-called suicides. Jumpers in Washington—watcher on mountain across a chasm. Signal Hill—watcher in nearby bushes. The diner—watcher scant feet away. *Close, closer, I'm right on fucking top of you.* Maybe she'd been coming at this all wrong, wondering what would come next. Assuming she didn't catch the bastard. Perhaps she needed to work backwards. Again she heard Perri Carver's gravelly voice telling her about the symbol on the rock in North Cascades National Park. And the date. August 25th. R.I.P.

Arrogant. The perpetrator had hiked to a rocky lookout, by Carver's account, a challenge in itself. He had sat, an audience of one, and watched as his protégés plummeted to their awful deaths. He may have looked down at their crumpled bodies, distorted limbs splayed on jagged rocks, and lifted a glass in a self-congratulatory toast. Arrogant, too, because he had thought to bring paint to that hellish place to leave a lasting and mocking tribute to the five. He was certain they would jump, and certain of the time they would do it. The confidence of a first-timer? Suddenly, Carolyn didn't think so.

She rummaged through the stack of files on her desk and located the information she and Ziggy had gathered on Brady Field. Before his move to Oregon, Field had been a southerner. Atlanta. With a marriage that had bit the dust. And an affair with a med student. Between the ex-wife and the spurned lover, Carolyn reasoned that at least one of the women would have a story to tell. But first she needed to contact police in Atlanta, find out whether there had been any mass suicides during the mid-to-late '90s when Field had been practicing in the city. Failing that, she would ask about any suicides that struck a wrong note and might have given rise to the suspicion of murder. She would ask whether the police had any dealings with Field, whether the good cardiologist had ever been arrested. She made a note as well to try and locate any of the nursing staff who would have worked with Field. No one could expose a doctor with a God complex better than a nurse.

Carolyn's computer pipped. She had mail. She clicked on her envelope icon and read.

Dear Fading Away,

I haven't heard from you and I'm so worried. I hope you're not in any pain, though we're all suffering, aren't we? If you're still with us, remember my offer—anything you need, I'm here, though not for much longer.

The Monitor

Great. A persistent depressive. Just what Carolyn needed. Still, it was important to continue the charade. She positioned her fingers over the keys and began.

To my friend, The Monitor,

I haven't written because my agony is so horrendous, I can barely sit in the chair to type this e-mail. My legs feel like they've been stabbed with hot knives, the pain so bad sometimes I think I could go blind. Painkillers put me in a different kind of hell, a fog-filled stupor replete with garbled sentences, a staggering gait and huge black holes in my memory. I wonder what I've said, who I've hurt, what dangers I may have inflicted while strung out. I'm seeing a pain specialist next week—another one. Meanwhile I cling to filaments of hope, feeling deep down that I should just give up. I've never been a quitter, and it's hard to admit that I may have reached the end, but really, how much more can anyone expect of me? I've tried so hard, but no one should be forced to live like this. I can't take much more.

Fading Away ...

Carolyn was dismayed at how easily the words flew across the page, how with a few simple keystrokes and a tap of the SEND button, complete lies could be manufactured. No accusing face to stare back at her, no narrowed gaze, no third degree. Her story would not be questioned. In truth, she never felt better. She hadn't had as much as a dull backache in days.

How many lies had Brady Field told? He had posed as Bella Donna, a female. He may even have been one of the message board's trolls, urging its participants to get on with the business of suicide. Perhaps his ex-wife, his former lover, or a member of the nursing staff at Northside Hospital would expose more lies. As Carolyn looked for the number for Atlanta PD, her computer pipped again.

Dear Fading Away,

I can help you. Won't you let me, while I still can?

The Monitor

Too damn persistent now. What kind of help was the Monitor offering?

Only one way to find out. Fingers poised over the keyboard, Carolyn typed.

Yes, Monitor. I'd like your help. I am ready.

CHAPTER 29

"What has that no good hound gotten himself into?"

Rebecca Holland, the former Mrs. Brady Field, didn't believe in mincing words, and for that, Carolyn could have teleported herself through the phone and kissed her.

The cardiologist's ex-wife was a renowned event planner in the Atlanta area with a coffee-table book and a series of videos to her credit. Charity galas and celebrity weddings had put Holland's name in *People* magazine, in which she'd been quoted as saying her life was sublimely full, too full for romance, too full for marriage. The article had been written in her pre-Field days. At some point the doctor and his charms had altered her position on matrimony.

"We're just trying to clear him as a suspect," Carolyn said, using the stock line that really meant *we're going to nail his sorry ass.*

"Suspect?" came the throaty drawl. "Let me tell you right now, whatever you suspect him of? He did it."

"Would it be an understatement to say that you and Dr. Field didn't part on friendly terms?"

Raucous laughter erupted from the other end of the phone. "Brady's lucky to have left Georgia with his testicles intact. My family is a little old-fashioned, Sergeant. We don't take philandering lightly."

Holland had checked out Carolyn thoroughly before consenting to the phone interview. Once the woman had determined Carolyn to be who she said she was, there was no holding her back. According to his ex, Brady Field's eyes had begun to rove on their honeymoon. The sultry women on the isle of Capri were the antithesis to Holland, with her pale skin and white-blonde hair. For years she ignored the warning signs of infidelity, preferring instead to square her shoulders and ride out what she termed a marriage's growing pains. It was the pitying, embarrassed glances of others that finally gave credence to her suspicions—Brady Field was a stalker, a hunter. He reveled in the seduction, the dance, the chase. Capture? That was nice too, but fleeting and meaningless without the ability to control the captive.

From her conversation with Field's ex-wife, Carolyn could readily discern that Holland was not the type to be reined in. She had been a financially independent, successful entrepreneur before meeting Field—that had been part of her allure—and she wouldn't cave easily to being told what to do by the supercilious doctor. A young and malleable medical student who worshipped every shit he took would be more to Field's liking. Enter Stacey Haas and the disintegration of the Field-Holland union.

"When your marriage ended, was Dr. Field despondent? Did he ever try to woo you back?"

"Sure he did," Holland said, sarcasm oozing from each syllable. "For three whole days. But that's only because he's a sore loser and the divorce was my idea. Despondent? Brady? Don't make me laugh."

Something was amiss here. In Ziggy's first conversation with the doctor, Brady Field claimed he had created busriders.com because he'd been suicidal. He needed a forum to vent his feelings without fear of repercussion and wanted to give others the opportunity to do the same.

"You're an extremely busy woman, Ms. Holland. Is it possible that, as your marriage was —?"

"Imploding?"

"—ending, you could have missed some indication that your husband was severely depressed? Even suicidal, let's say?"

"Now I think we're talking about two completely different men, Sergeant. The Brady Field I lived with for three years would be far too conceited to kill himself. He wouldn't deprive the world of his presence. You've heard the expression 'the world is your oyster?' Well, Brady believed that wholeheartedly. Nobody else's oyster, just his."

Carolyn paused, trying to process what was being said with what Field himself had explained. That the man was a whopping narcissist had been obvious after spending only minutes in his white-on-white trophy house, but the possibility that he'd lied to Ziggy about his suicidal feelings hadn't occurred to Carolyn. It should have. He'd lied on the Net, leading visitors to the web board to believe that Bella Donna was female. But perhaps the bitter, scorned Rebecca Holland wasn't the most reliable source of information.

"Would it surprise you, Ms. Holland, to know that your ex-husband started up an Internet web board where suicidal people could post messages?" Carolyn explained the philosophy of busriders.com and the types of posts found there, as well as Field's alter ego as Bella Donna.

Carolyn heard an audible intake of breath then a long silence. Eventually Holland said, "First things first, what a horrible thing to come up with. Leave it to Brady to tap into others' misery and take advantage of it. I wonder if anything is sacred anymore. Am I surprised that Brady would concoct such a site? Understand this, Sergeant. There's only one thing Brady relishes as much as being the center of attention. Can you guess what that might be?"

Money came to mind. But Carolyn didn't have time for guessing games. New posters were accessing Field's forum every day. How long before another group would decide to catch the bus? And how long before Field or someone else would offer to put together a plan to hasten their demise? He had to be stopped.

"I could save on this long-distance bill if you'd just tell me."

"Control, Sergeant. Brady thrives on it. If, as his on-screen persona, Brady becomes privy to dark secrets and can fictionalize some of his own to gain sympathy, can you imagine the thrill he would feel? The rush he would get from knowing he'd fooled not only one but possibly hundreds of people? Ooh-wee. Right up his alley."

Yes, Carolyn thought, just as it would be up Field's alley to drink a toast while watching others twitch in their final agony.

"And if I know Brady, he wouldn't be content with only one web persona. If he's admitted to being Bella Donna, my guess is he's also masquerading as someone else. You know, all the better to fool you with, my dear."

Carolyn was on side with Rebecca Holland on this too. Brady Field was indeed a conquistador, one who was on a never-ending search for something new, something bigger, something better. She was reminded of a song she heard occasionally on an oldies station. *Those kicks just keep gettin' harder to find.*

Strait Razr. Encouraging everyone to stop whining and just do it. Brady Field?

Carolyn wondered exactly how many disguises were in Dr. Brady Field's closet.

CHAPTER 30

Carolyn wasn't surprised to learn that Dr. Brady Field hadn't been too popular with the nursing staff at Northside Hospital in Atlanta. It had taken some deft slicing through red tape and an "I'll have to check with my supervisor" before she was able to finally connect with someone who would agree to speak with her about the cardiologist. She spent interminable minutes on HOLD listening to appalling pan flute versions of pop tunes before surgical nurse Gemma Dobbs came on the line to echo the sentiments of Field's ex-wife. Brady Field was a staunch member of his own fan club. According to Dobbs, the doctor's feet were in no danger of ever being callused or blistered—he was too busy walking on clouds. Even early in his career he was condescending to the nurses. Impatient. Dismissive. If he hadn't been such a brilliant and skilled surgeon, he would have been intolerable. Then of course, there was his affair with the medical student. The going-away party for Field had been small and had ended early in the evening.

Stacey Haas, Field's lovestruck protégé, had not attended. Months into her affair with Field, the twenty-seven-year-old had come to her senses. Her Svengali had become an omnipresent shadow, his looming presence bearing down with each breath she took. "He wanted to know my every thought," Haas lamented to Carolyn on the phone. "I felt like a lab rat, with Brady watching me eat, exercise, study. Some nights I'd wake up to find him staring at me, just hovering over my pillow. It was creepy."

Some time later, her period was late. Field, who had made a habit of going into her purse, counted the days since the circled date in her calendar and calmly explained he would arrange for an abortion. "No discussion, no asking me how I felt. I still get chills when I think about it." The pregnancy scare turned out to be a false alarm, Haas's menstrual cycle thrown out of whack by stress.

Then came the job opportunity at Legacy Good Samaritan. Field would have taken the position if it was offered to him. He hadn't asked Haas what she thought about that either. "He assumed I would pack up everything and join him. Instead, I wrote him a curt goodbye note and changed the locks on my apartment. I never heard from him again."

"Sounds like you dodged quite a bullet there," Carolyn told her. She had been prepared to dislike Haas, to cast her as the temptress who had lured Field from his marriage. She remembered keenly the blamefest she'd engaged in after Gregg had left her, directing accusations at her errant husband, his younger lover, and herself, a dizzying Bermuda triangle of finger pointing. But Haas was a victim, too, and Carolyn was sympathetic.

"Bullet?" Haas said. "More like a cannonball. Not a day passes when I don't regret meeting him. And believe it or not, I've been to lunch with his ex. Rebecca Holland is a remarkable woman."

"And the two of you engaged in some Field-bashing, I'm sure."

"Yes, there was some of that," Haas admitted. "I'm just relieved to know she doesn't blame me for the failure of their marriage. When I think of how dumb—"

"Go easy on yourself," Carolyn told her. "If Rebecca Holland doesn't blame you, then you shouldn't blame yourself."

"No one likes to feel like a fool, Sergeant."

"I hear you there."

"There was something else," Haas said, her voice low. "Once, in the OR, Brady was finishing a complicated surgery on a four-year-old girl. We waited for him to restart the child's heart, but instead he said, "Imagine how those parents will feel if I have to tell them their only child died on this table. We could have a miracle here, or hell on earth. I'm taking bets. What'll it be? Who's for a miracle?' Sergeant, I wanted to grab that tiny heart and restart it myself. We all stood by helpless, watching, and he loved it."

Haas scoffed at the idea that Brady Field had ever entertained thoughts of suicide. She claimed no knowledge of busriders.com though she recalled that Field spent an inordinate amount of time on the Internet, often late into the night. "I thought he might be accessing porn sites, and I'm being facetious here, but I was grateful that whatever he was into meant he was leaving me alone."

Carolyn gave Haas her work number and office e-mail then ended the conversation. Her throat was dry and her neck ached. She stood, did a few brisk laps around her desk, finished off with some shoulder shrugs and a bottle of sparkling water.

At noon, Ziggy called from Portland to report that the staff at Legacy Good Samaritan Hospital spoke well of Field and considered themselves lucky to have him. The hospital was named one of the top one hundred in the U.S. for cardiovascular care and had been so honored three times in six years. The facility was the only hospital in Portland to receive the recognition in 2006 and was setting benchmark levels of performance in a range of cardiovascular services. Field probably enjoyed a share of the credit for this praise as well. "I still wouldn't let him cut me open, C.L. I don't care how good he is."

"No one blowing a whistle on the guy?"

"According to one intern there—name's Lyndon Kerr—Field is a frickin' genius. Claims he's chosen cardiology as his specialty because of Field."

Carolyn rolled her eyes. Not what she wanted to hear. "Come on, Zig. There must be something."

"I managed to corral one nurse," Ziggy mumbled, his mouth full of what Carolyn guessed was some kind of sandwich. "She gave me a watered-down version of what you've already heard."

"How do you mean, watered-down?"

"Field's still on staff, so a nurse speaking ill of a doctor is akin to career suicide. I had to assure her of my complete discretion. She ushered me into a visitors' lounge and told me she secretly nicknamed the doctor Jack Frost. Said that in the operating room, Field is an iceman. Rarely breaks a sweat, even during grueling procedures that go on for hours. Oh sure, he slips the Zen-like music into the CD player, gets everybody to relax, but this nurse says the atmosphere is just plain creepy. Says it's almost like watching a robot at work."

"Any inappropriate behavior toward the nurses? Flirting? Off-color remarks?"

"Nothing. It's like nobody's in the room with him. There's a huge wall between him and them, and she claims that's how Field likes it."

"No blight on his professional record? No slip-ups? No operating while intoxicated?"

"As a surgeon, he's flawless. It's as a human being that Field falls short."

"So what we've got here is a damn good doctor who nobody likes."

She heard Ziggy swallow. "Peanut butter or roast beef?"

"Smoked turkey," he replied. "You think I'm so predictable."

"No, I've always thought of you as a culinary pioneer."

"Besides, the hospital cafeteria was out of roast beef. Listen, C.L., Brady Field might be a hateful son of a bitch, but he is in the life-saving business, and by all accounts, he goes to the wall for his patients. Given that, what would be his motive for killing Melly Waller and the others?"

"Maybe he sees them as unworthy."

"He didn't even know Mel—them."

"But he thinks he does. Get into his head for a moment, Zig. Sure, the doctor pulls out all the stops for his patients. He is a brilliant man. No argument there. But his patients are fighting to stay alive. What about the ones who could care less? The suicidal crowd on the web board? Screw 'em. In fact, why not help them out? If they hold the value of life so cheaply, then better to get 'em off the planet. Field giveth, Field taketh away."

There was only one problem. During the years that Brady Field worked at Northside, there had been no reported incidents of mass suicides in Atlanta. In the state of Georgia, suicide claims the lives of about nine hundred people per year, the suicide rate highest among seniors. The preferred method for self-termination was firearms; jumping to one's death barely represented a hairline sliver on the pie chart. In Georgia, the suicide rate had declined since 1980. The state was one of the few that had a comprehensive report on suicide and after studying the statistics and speaking to the Director of the Division of Public Health, Carolyn could find no parallel between any suicides that had occurred during Field's tenure in the south and the mass hysteria that had recently gripped the Pacific Northwest.

Perhaps Carolyn was wrong. Perhaps the Washington jumpers were Field's first victims after all. Or perhaps Field wasn't the guy.

Carolyn listened to the cautionary cop's voice in her head telling her to keep the net wide, her mind open. Focusing and fixating on Field could be a dangerous tunnel to crawl into, especially if, while she was chasing down more clues to link Field to the crimes, another killer, the real one, struck again.

But she wasn't ready to absolve the doctor. Not yet. Too many things about him stunk.

At once, another thought intruded, competing for attention. Where had Ziggy been calling from?

Legacy Good Samaritan.

I can help you. Won't you let me, while I still can?

Carolyn had received e-mail from a Samaritan of her own, an e-mail she'd dismissed because she had more important things to do. She remembered Strait Razr, the obnoxious correspondent who urged everyone to stop whining and just do it. Would a group of depressed individuals fall victim to such a blatant dare? It was possible, but more probable, Carolyn thought, that they would be gently cajoled, coaxed, and comforted by the promise of a quick, painless release, one offered by a kindly, compassionate soul. A Samaritan. The Monitor.

Brady Field? Ex-wife Rebecca Holland had suggested that if the doctor had passed himself off as Bella Donna, he could easily be two or three other posers as well. It was time to locate Shana Pascal's next of kin. Hopefully the dead girl's computer and cell phone were still in her apartment, ready and waiting for Carolyn to check for e-mail and text messages from a sinner disguised as a saint.

If not Field, then who?

CHAPTER 31

LOOSE ENDS. THEY REPRESENTED AN intolerable sloppiness. Poor planning. Lack of foresight. For nine days now, the Monitor had been agonizing over what to do with the very loose end that called himself Jim Stark.

Stark had not kept his date with the group, a horrendous breach of ... contract, in some respects. The others had been true to their word, arriving at the diner precisely at midnight, the late hour making it easier for Nightshade to sneak out of her parents' house and into Jackpot's waiting car. If anyone were to have reneged on the agreement, the Monitor would have bet on Nightshade. Poor little gay *caballera*. How she had screamed. Worth the price of admission.

Jim Stark, on the other hand, was an enigma, emotionally in the dregs but too benumbed to take action. A solo act—which the Monitor guessed involved solo sex as well—Stark had insisted on finding his own transportation to the diner. It was a plan the Monitor tried to discourage, but Stark had been adamant. Such obstinacy had served only to make Stark late for the rendezvous, placing him, not inside the diner where he should have been, but at the window, watching, listening. And now he knew.

The Monitor had only caught a glimpse of Stark but it was enough. The boy's Asian eyes widened as he viewed the spectacle for those frozen few seconds before he fled. Now Stark had once again cut himself off from everyone, no longer posting on the forum.

He had retreated to his hikikomori world of beeping gadgets, black-out curtains and James Dean reruns. The Monitor didn't know exactly how much Stark had seen, whether it had been too dark to make out the champagne glass, the facial features in the shadows.

There had been nothing in the papers, no lurid headline about a teenager witnessing the grisly sight at the diner and offering a description to a sketch artist. Or were such things already happening behind the scenes without the knowledge of the press?

The Monitor didn't think so. Stark had buried himself deeply. He would be frightened. And he trusted no one. Almost no one.

Action had to be taken, and quickly. Even with Stark locked in his room, the risk of discovery was too great. The boy had to be lured from his safe haven, and The Monitor knew exactly how to do it.

CHAPTER 32

Carolyn spent Saturday afternoon decorating her first Christmas tree alone. It was a four-foot balsam that had probably been cut down in July. The needles would be all over her rug within a week, but impracticality be damned, she just couldn't abandon the poor thing. It had been propped against a cold chain-link fence and was in drastic need of water and affection. When she and Gregg divorced, she had retained custody of the holiday decorations and colored lights, so she festooned the tree with as much regalia as the spindly branches could withstand then poured herself a glass of wine, her first toast to the season.

Her thoughts for much of the day revolved around the dead and their families who had little choice but to soldier on after the mass suicides. What would Christmas be like for Melissa Waller's parents and her kid sister? Would Lenore Armstrong, Geezer's ex-wife, be praying things could have been different somehow? Would she be wishing away all the petty arguments that, over the years, could erode a marriage? Was Brenda Koch's mother silently grieving the loss of her daughter, or had she already donated the girl's clothes to charity and rented out her bedroom?

Carolyn knew that she needed to pull away from the victims, that obsessing over them was casting a suffocating blanket of gloom over her. Focusing on the killer, which occupied the largest part of her thoughts resulted in a slowly simmering anger that grew and fermented and exploded into a rage more powerful than anything she'd ever felt. *Mad or sad, Carolyn. Pick one.*

She walked with her wine glass to the dining-room table where the case files were stacked in three neat piles on either side of her computer. North Cascades National Park. The Aerie. The Diner. Absent-mindedly she opened the first file on the top of the diner pile. Neil Bloome. The lawyer from Reno. Online nick = Jackpot. Carolyn read through the inventory found in Bloome's car, picturing clearly in her mind his family photo, his breath mints, his CD collection. Something scraped at the surface of her memory. Shana Pascal—C3PO. As it turned out, Shana didn't own a computer, so she had to have accessed the message board from a cyber café.

Immediately Carolyn went to the Aerie pile and pulled the folder belonging to Kevin Randolph, the well-heeled kid from Marblehead who'd died with the others in the rented car. She pulled Heather Conklin's file as well, the budding ballerina from Idaho, and scanned the information found there. What Carolyn had missed before suddenly leapt from the pages. Quickly, she shuffled more folders until she located the one with the posts from busriders.com, beginning in late August, the day the five in Washington jumped to their deaths. She riffled through pages until she found the post she sought. In November Geezer had written: *So PM me, if like me, you're ready to go*. Police in British Columbia had checked Bill Armstrong's computer, searched through his private messages but found no instructions from anyone telling him to go to the diner, to get in Neil Bloome's car. Deleted? Sure. But deleted messages were still retrievable and as yet police hadn't uncovered anything in the deceased's private mail.

Except a phone number. Neil Bloome had surrendered his phone number. To the Monitor.

Carolyn did a cross-check. The number Bloome listed in his private message to the Monitor didn't match his home phone number.

A cell phone. Of course. But there hadn't been a phone found in Bloome's car, nor in his jacket pocket. Kevin Randolph and Heather Conklin didn't have cells with them, either. A teenager without a cell phone? Every adolescent on the planet subscribed to the wireless religion, cell phones clapped to their ears like an extra appendage. So where were the phones?

Dumped. Because the killer told them to. The victims had received their instructions—where to go, what to bring, whom to meet—via a text message on their cell phones. Which they likely smashed into pieces and flung into a trash can once the plan was in motion. Carolyn paged through all the files. Not a cell phone anywhere. The Monitor, whoever he or she was, had thought of everything. On the computer, the persona was a caring, grandmotherly figure who wanted to help, one who loathed suffering. On the cell phone was evidence of a darker, more evil conspiracy. And that evidence was now likely shattered and strewn among discarded coffee cups, empty cigarette packages and moldering scraps of food in garbage cans across several states.

Carolyn grabbed for her Rolodex, a duplicate of the one she had on her office desk and punched in the number for Ted Tarrant in Marblehead. He was off for the day, but Carolyn left a message for him to return her call. She did the same with Lieutenant Perri Carver in Washington State, and again with her contact in Boise, hoping that at least one of the Monitor's victims had conjured the strength for a brief act of defiance and not destroyed his cell phone.

She booted up her computer. It was already the twelfth of December, and with Christmas looming, Carolyn was certain some of the more despondent members of busriders.com would be making their misery known.

There were postings galore.

Killcrazy from Belgium wrote:

Hi, all. Don't know about you, but I miss Jim Stark. Nice that he at least told us he wouldn't be posting anymore, but it's always hard to lose a friend. Can't help wondering what happened and why he's not here. Does anyone know if Jim caught the bus?

Strait Razr responded with his usual snide manner. Or hers. *You've heard of the expression "shit or get off the pot?" Maybe Jim finally shit. Good for him. Me, I keep searching for that perfect, painless method. Doing my research but nothing yet. I'll let you know.*

Brady Field, logging on as the moderator Bella Donna, offered his words of wisdom.

We all hope for the best for Jim Stark, wherever he is. A reminder to Strait Razr—if and when the time comes, remember we do not discuss methods on this board. To do so will get you permanently banned. Big brother is always watching.

It wasn't long before the posting Carolyn had been waiting for appeared. The Monitor made her grandmotherly presence felt ten minutes later.

I worry about Jim too, as do the rest of you. He's been so down for so long I feel he won't be with us for too many more days. I can only hope that when his final deliverance comes, he will go peacefully to the next world. Jim, if you're lurking out there, know that you are cared for and we want to help.

I'll just bet you want to help, Monitor, Carolyn thought. I think you've been plenty helpful already.

Reading the posts gave her a chill, so Carolyn drank the rest of her wine in a single gulp then went to boil the kettle for tea. She wondered what Brady Field was trying to prove. Big Brother is always watching? Did that mean that Bella Donna was going to more closely moderate the message board? Or was it a warning to posters that the police were online?

Outside, dusk had begun to settle, the sky fading from pale blue to gray. A stiff wind blew. Carolyn plugged in the lights on her Christmas tree and used a remote control to light her gas fireplace. When she heard the kettle's whistle, she went into the kitchen and made what her mother would call "a proper pot of tea," using loose Irish Breakfast tea leaves and a sterling-silver strainer. She found one of her mother's favorite cups and saucers in an upper cabinet and wished she'd bought a cookie at the bakery earlier. Sometimes, the ceremony of making tea served to calm her down and slow her racing mind, but tonight, it was having the opposite effect. She swallowed the scalding tea almost as quickly as she'd consumed her wine, but the hot beverage did little to quell the gooseflesh that rose on her arms.

Cold fear.

She needed Ziggy. She needed to tell him what she was thinking and together they needed to plan her next post as Fading Away. He would call her a mad fool, of course, except Ziggy would be more colorful in his description.

All due respect, C.L., this time you're a fucking lunatic.

To catch the Monitor she might indeed need to be a fucking lunatic. As long as she didn't wind up being a fucking dead lunatic.

CHAPTER 33

Joshua made another stab at restoring domestic harmony by making brunch reservations at the Redwood Inn. He and Paige had settled on a truce of sorts and agreed to revisit the discussion about his humanitarian yearnings at a later date. Joshua was hoping that a three-month moratorium on the subject would suffice. Paige insisted on six months. Six months it was.

After nine o'clock Mass on Sunday, Joshua intended to stop for a bouquet of flowers for Paige, another smoothing-over effort, this one interrupted by the twitter of his cell phone. Ken Ishiguro sounded like a man half crazed. Could Joshua come? It was urgent. Yoshi had really done it this time. And Ishiguro was afraid, both for Yoshi and himself. Then he hung up.

Joshua tried Ishiguro's number, but Yoshi's uncle wasn't picking up. Afraid? What had Yoshi done?

For a brief moment he was tempted to ignore the call. Both Ishiguro and Yoshi were masters of manipulation, and Joshua was growing weary of having his chain yanked, yet in the end, he steered his jeep in the direction of Ken Ishiguro's apartment. He heard Paige's voice in his mind telling him he was over-investing in Yoshi, falling prey to both the boy's hikikomori machinations and his own fight-for-the-underdog complex. He heard the voices of countless lecturers as well, warning him about crossing the line with a client. The choir in his head was right. Joshua knew that he had to stop, that these home visits were inappropriate and that he'd strayed perilously far from a prudent counselor's role. Yet the voice he obeyed was the one that rang out not in wisdom but in desperation. Yoshi could be in danger.

Joshua had been so busy congratulating himself on Yoshi's emergence from his cocoon on Wednesday night that he'd been repressing the nagging thoughts that occasionally flickered to his forebrain.

I'd never kill myself over some stupid girl.

Joshua couldn't help wondering if the statement was a case of Yoshi protesting too much. Did Ishiguro fear the same? If what Joshua suspected were true, Aoki had been important to Yoshi, so important that her severing their relationship had sent him racing for the shelter of a micro-universe, one in which he felt safe and in control. *Easy come, easy go,* Yoshi had said once and Joshua had pounced on it. Yes, Yoshi had toyed with the idea of killing himself, had even posted messages about suicide on a popular message board. All talk and bluster, he admitted to Joshua. He didn't have a plan. Planning involved energy and ambition. Yoshi had neither.

Did Joshua believe that? Or had Yoshi's suicidal feelings returned? As Joshua approached Ishiguro's door, he saw a young blonde emerge, wearing the guilty look of someone who'd just been caught with her panties around her ankles. When she realized Joshua was about to visit the apartment she'd just left, she cast her glance toward the patterned carpet and quickened her step to the elevator.

Ken Ishiguro, clad in a robe, offered no greeting, merely stepped to one side to allow Joshua entry. His thin lips sliced a straight line across his face. Stern eyebrows tented over bloodshot eyes.

"What's going on here?" Joshua said. "And who was that?"

"I would have introduced you," Ishiguro replied, closing the door, "but my manners are less than satisfactory when I have only had two hours' sleep."

For a brief moment Joshua thought the man was referring to an exhausting night of lovemaking then reasoned that wouldn't account for Ishiguro's ugly mood, nor would it explain the urgency of the phone call.

Joshua cleared his throat. "Where's Yoshi? Is he all right?"

Ishiguro grunted. "In his room. Probably sound asleep. Hikkii bastard."

Strong words for the normally reserved professor, Joshua thought. "Wait a minute. Yoshi's sleeping? I'm obviously missing something here," he said, barely controlling his anger. "You called me on a Sunday morning. Made it sound like Yoshi had set the place on fire."

Ishiguro retreated to a corduroy sofa and tried to smooth his disheveled hair. Joshua sat in an armchair and leaned forward.

"You have no idea what it is like to live with a boy like that," Ishiguro said, jutting his chin in the direction of Yoshi's bedroom door. "He nearly drove his parents mad, and now I may be going the same way."

Only four nights ago, Yoshi had been at 3F House, blending in, making new friends. He had seemed fine. A little nervous, but fine. What had gone wrong?

"Tell me what happened."

"The other evening I suggested a walk, just as you advised. A short trip, just down the front sidewalk and back, to get Yoshi accustomed to being away from the building. He told me to go to hell. I did all the things you said, Joshua. I praised him, told him he had made such progress by going out with you, meeting new people, moving freely around the apartment."

"All that sounds good, Ken."

"Yes? So that is why he waved a knife at me. He told me if I ever tried to make him leave the apartment again, he would cut out my eyes."

"Yoshi's got a knife?"

"My filleting knife. He took it from the kitchen."

Joshua remembered the night Yoshi's uncle had cooked for him, how he'd expertly de-boned a salmon for their stir-fry in a matter of seconds.

"He keeps it under his pillow," Ishiguro added. "And he says he'll use it on you too."

Ishiguro paused to allow that thought to sink in, then he rose and paced the length of the living room, again raking hooked fingers through his unruly hair. "My brother-in-law, Yoshi's father, pays the rent on my apartment. It was an ... incentive for me to bring

Yoshi to the States. But no amount of money is worth this. Yoshi exists simply to punish me now, for trying to help him get well, and especially for introducing him to you."

"Punish you? What has he done?"

Ishiguro's face flushed. Eventually he stopped pacing and sat once more. "Twice this week," he began, "I have tried to entertain a female companion, but Yoshi has made it impossible. At two this morning, he woke us by singing in the shower. At four, he burnt toast and set off the smoke alarm. An hour later we heard his headboard thumping against the bedroom wall. He has also purchased a new lock for his door. The only way I know he is even in his room is because I hear him. I haven't seen Yoshi since Wednesday night."

Joshua stood quickly. "I need to talk to him."

"It will not do you any good. He will not open the door."

"Then I'll talk to him through it until he opens up. I've got to make sure he's all right. And somehow we've got to get that knife out of there." Joshua had heard of websites started by sadistic youth, urging their online friends to webcam their suicides so others could view the act. He wondered what Yoshi had gotten himself into. And what had caused such a cataclysmic backslide. He hurried down the corridor toward Yoshi's bedroom, his uncle following closely.

Joshua called Yoshi's name between rapid-fire hammer strikes on the door. His knuckles reddened. Ached. Yoshi didn't respond.

Ishiguro raised his fist to the door and pounded. "Yoshitomo! Goddamn it!"

"Easy, Ken."

"No! I will not take it easy!" Ishiguro turned from the door to face Joshua, his complexion crimson. He took staccato breaths. "I have had enough. Yoshi is not our problem anymore, Joshua. I will call my sister to send a plane ticket. Yoshi must go back to Japan. Before I kill him myself."

CHAPTER 34

JOSHUA PLEADED WITH KEN ISHIGURO. He needed more time. In the States, Yoshi had a better chance of getting well. In Japan, with parents who would rather sweep their son and the shame that came with his illness out of sight, Yoshi would be doomed. For some hikikomori, their condition degenerated to the point where even television, computer games, virtual friends and comic-book fantasies represented too much effort. Those souls were lost, trapped in a cyclic existence of eating and sleeping, functioning more like a family pet than a human being.

"Give up, Joshua," Ishiguro said. "What is Yoshi to you anyway?"

"He's a boy who needs help."

"Many other teenagers also need your help. You would be better off devoting your time and energy to them."

"This is a setback, Ken. It happens. No different than an alcoholic taking a drink. It's not a complete failure. Yoshi *was* making progress."

Wishful thinking, Joshua speculated. In a few short weeks Yoshi had been persuaded to emerge from behind a screen, surrender his creature comforts, abandon the security of his room and venture to 3F House. It had been too much too soon, and now the boy was doubling back, rebuilding the barricades, keeping himself safe.

"He is locked in his room with a knife. That sounds like more than a setback to me. How can I close my eyes at night? Can you promise he won't attack me in my bed?" Ishiguro waved off the futility of his question. "Of course you can't."

"More time, Ken," Joshua repeated.

Challenge junkie. Paige had accused Joshua of being exactly that a few nights ago. Whether it was working with Yoshi, volunteering with a charitable organization or even moving in with Paige, who'd been working on her own relationship issues, Joshua thrived on leaping over hurdles, just as he'd done for his high school track team. Nothing pumped adrenaline through his body like overcoming an obstacle. Carolyn, his twin, possessed the same gene. When Paige had made the observation it had stung, but now Joshua thought she might be right.

Without waiting for an answer from Ishiguro, Joshua turned and continued down the hall. He stood outside Yoshi's room and tentatively jiggled the door knob, but he already knew the door would be locked.

"Yoshi?" he called.

"Go fuck yourself," came the voice from the other side.

"Anatomically impossible," Joshua said. Hearing no response, he added, "Bit of a step back, Yoshi, that's all. You'll be fine. We'll take things slower."

"There is no 'we.' Go away."

"Can't do that."

Excruciating moments ticked by. Joshua, his ear to the door, could hear Yoshi tapping away at his keyboard. Computer game? E-mail?

"Yoshi, how 'bout a game of 'let's make a deal'?"

"I have everything I need. You have nothing to bargain with."

"You're wrong there, my friend. The deal is, you unlock the door. You surrender the knife. We'll talk."

He listened to Yoshi's flat laughter. "You're fucked in the head. Go home."

"Not gonna happen, Yoshi. See, you didn't let me finish. You unlock the door, you surrender the knife, and I won't call the police."

The keyboard clacking stopped.

"That's right," Joshua continued. "The police. The moment you threatened your uncle with the knife everything changed. You're now considered dangerous both to yourself and your uncle. Perhaps your uncle didn't want to lose face by calling the cops, but that sort of thing doesn't bother me. Once they get here, they'll have this door down in seconds, you'll be cuffed and taken to a luxury suite with a metal mirror and a concrete mattress. No comic books, no computer, no television." He folded his arms across his chest. "I believe you were saying I had nothing to bargain with?"

"You can't do that," Yoshi replied, the sardonic edge gone from his voice.

"Sure I can. You're not going to hold your uncle, this apartment, or me under siege. This standoff can end two ways—you do as I say and we talk this out, or you end up in jail. Up to you, but you haven't got much time to make your decision. I've got reservations for brunch."

After another long pause, Yoshi said, "I think you're bluffing."

"Think what you like." Joshua retreated down the hall, his footsteps echoing on the parquet floor. He reached Ishiguro's living room before he heard the chain slide across. The bedroom door opened.

"Wait."

Joshua stopped and looked at Ishiguro, sitting on the sofa, absently thumbing through a magazine. "What am I waiting for?" he called over his shoulder.

"We can ... talk. For a minute."

Joshua directed a stare at Ishiguro's cordless phone and the man nodded. He took the phone and moved toward Yoshi, who was standing in the bedroom doorway in sweats and bare feet. "Root yourself to the spot and point to where the knife is."

Yoshi pointed. "Pillow."

The next minutes were spent with Joshua quietly telling Ishiguro to get dressed, take all sharp knives down to his car and lock them in the trunk, along with razor blades and anything else that could possibly be used as a weapon. There was no way to absolutely murder-proof the place, but at least Ishiguro might have been able to catch a few hours' sleep without worrying whether he would be stabbed in his bed.

Yoshi had turned off his computer. Whatever he'd been up to in the moments before the door opened remained a secret. Joshua sat on the bed. "I seem to remember you telling me to fuck off," he said.

The boy rolled his eyes. "You pissed me off big time. I'm not ready to go out. I have to stay here."

"This room is so important that you'd harm your uncle or me to stay in it?"

"I do what I have to do. I'm not going outside."

"The kids at 3F House really liked you. And so did Big Bert."

"They like me so much, they can come here."

"How do you think your uncle feels?"

The boy shrugged. "We don't talk about feelings."

"Well, I suspect he feels betrayed. He's brought you here to help you, and you tell him you'll cut his eyes out. He shares his apartment with you, and you lock yourself in your room and take all the good stuff with you. He brings a girlfriend home, and you sabotage his date."

At this Yoshi smiled.

"Not funny," Joshua said. "Not one bit. You care so little for your uncle? Well, he's had it with you. He's about to ship you back to Japan."

The boy's eyes went glassy. "I won't go. Not now."

"*You* can't. *You* won't. Yoshi, you don't call all the shots. Life doesn't work like that. Your uncle is fed up with being manipulated, and so am I."

They danced around another half hour of conversation, with Yoshi insisting that he could not go outside, that it wasn't safe. Returning to Japan was not an option.

Joshua broached the subject of suicide again, reminding Yoshi of what he'd said about Aoki being "just a girl," not worth killing himself over. "I sensed you might be protesting a little too much," Joshua said. "And I've been worrying about you. You haven't seen or heard from Aoki in months. And you're a long way from home."

Yoshi waved off the concern. "I already told you. I have everything I need. No reason for me to slice open a vein."

Joshua noticed that at the mention of Aoki's name, the boy's eyes sparked to life. He tried to get Yoshi to open up more about his ex-girlfriend, hoping Yoshi might begin to heal instead of drawing inside himself.

Yoshi went mute.

"Okay," Joshua said after listening to endless minutes of dead air. "You don't want to talk. Fine. No point in me hanging around."

Another shrug.

At the end of the visit, Joshua was no closer to discovering what had brought about the boy's setback. He checked his watch and realized he had just enough time to swing back to the cabin, pick up Paige and make their brunch date for noon. He was cutting it close, a fact that Paige would surely notice.

His energy as a challenge junkie was waning. For a brief moment he wondered whether Yoshi should return to Japan. Perhaps his parents would swallow their pride and get their son to a psychiatrist who specialized in hikikomori. From what Joshua had read, there weren't many of those, and the few who existed weren't experiencing much success.

It was still early in the game, Joshua told himself. He could do so much more if given the chance. He couldn't admit defeat, not this soon.

If he let a kid like Yoshi cut him off at the knees, what good would he be to Doctors of Mercy? To be sure, Yoshi was a tough case. But he was only one kid, and he was here in the U.S, with a host of resources available to him. If Joshua couldn't help him, how could he think he'd be of use to thousands in a third world country with little or no support?

He needed to get his chops back, catch a second wind, regain some confidence. A few quiet nights of professional reading might afford him a chance to regroup and give him a fresh start with Yoshi. He would phone Risk, get some reassurance from his friend. Once he reenergized, Joshua could attack the challenge of Yoshi with renewed vigor. He could be more objective. Not take everything Yoshi said and did so personally. Shake off the obsession. He could do it. He knew he could.

CHAPTER 35

On Monday, Joshua left 3F House at exactly five o'clock. Paige's early morning reminder of her uncle Spence's visit still resounded in his head. Wes Bertram jokingly accused Joshua of being whipped, a macho expression he loathed, yet somehow, it stuck with him and it stung. He did seem to be doing a lot of bowing and scraping lately, striving for a toehold on his relationship with Paige while muddling through at 3F House.

When Robb Northrup showed up for his shift, he wanted to know whether Yoshi would be at the Monday night discussion.

"Not unless James Dean himself rises from the grave and personally drives Yoshi here in his Porsche," Joshua said. "Don't hold your breath waiting for him."

He puzzled over Robb's curiosity about a boy he'd never met then resolved to put Yoshi and 3F House out of his mind. This night with Uncle Spence was important to Paige, and Joshua was determined to put on a festive face.

By the time Paige returned to the cabin with her uncle, Joshua had secured the Fraser fir in its stand, and he'd strung six sets of lights around the tree. Mulled cider simmered on the stove; a pan of seafood lasagna from a gourmet shop in the village bubbled in the oven.

Spencer Rowan looked frailer than when Joshua had visited him a month earlier. He wondered if Paige's uncle had experienced another ischemic attack, knowing that mini-strokes often plagued those who'd already been victims of a more serious episode. Death by degrees. The man's mouth was turned down at one corner and appeared frozen; he shuffled into the living room as if unsure of the solid floor beneath him. But he managed a reasonably solid handshake and protested vigorously when Paige began to help him remove his jacket.

"Go in the kitchen and stir something," he told her. "I want to grill your husband about the eligible women he knows. I need a date for New Year's Eve ."

Paige laughed, kissed her uncle on the cheek and said, "Okay, you miserable old coot."

Spence's eyes twinkled.

Joshua motioned toward the easy chair by the fireplace and insisted Spence take it. He pulled up an ottoman and sat down. Parker, sensing an animal lover, ambled over for a head scratch then curled up on the rug.

As soon as Paige was beyond earshot, Joshua whispered, "How are you feeling these days, Spence?"

"Can't complain, for an old fart. Have to get up in the middle of the night for a pee, but so does everybody else I know."

He doesn't want us to worry, Joshua thought immediately. Sitting close to him, Joshua noticed more changes. A slightly droopy left eye. Sallow skin. The distinctive ketone smell of his breath, an odor he remembered as his grandmother lay dying.

"Listen, Josh," Spence said, his voice tremulous, "Paige told me about this volunteer thing you're thinking about."

Ah. So here we go. Josh patted the man's hand. "We agreed to call a halt to discussing it for a while."

Spence nodded. "She'd kill me if she knew I was talking to you about it. But that really shook her up."

"I know. And I think it's great that you feel so protective toward Paige."

"She's like my daughter," he said, his breath labored.

"Don't get yourself worked up over this, Spence. We're fine. Really."

"You're a good man, Joshua. But your best quality is also your biggest flaw. You have kind of a—now, don't take this the wrong way—Samaritan complex. Someone needs a hand, you're there.

Trouble is, the human race is supposed to work as a team. You think it's all up to you."

"That's not quite true. I—"

"But it's not quite false, either. Spread yourself too thin, you're good for shit." A deep lung wheeze. "So what I'm saying is, don't neglect the people right under your nose."

Joshua shot Spence a worried smile. "Who's the social worker here?"

Spence grinned out of one side of his mouth. "Bet you're sorry the stroke didn't affect my speech."

When neighbor Stan Gardner appeared, the four gathered around the table and feasted. Paige had cut her uncle's lasagna into bite-size pieces. During the meal, Joshua caught Stan sneaking sidelong looks at his friend of forty years, trying not to appear shocked at the changes he was seeing. Stan and Spence reminisced a little, Spence choking up when he spotted the Christmas tree in the dining-room alcove, standing in the very spot where he and his wife, Gayle, had erected their one and only tree, just months before she died. They drank a toast to Gayle and talk turned to current events.

"Read about that awful business in Japan?" he asked.

Spence said, "At the base of Mount Fuji, yes." A cough. "What the hell gets into people?"

Joshua had read the article the men were speaking about in the *Oregonian*. Three cousins had tried to set themselves on fire in Aokigahara, a densely wooded area at the foot of Japan's most famous mountain. It made Joshua think once more of Yoshi, on how he'd closed himself off again, and to what dark place the boy's inner thoughts might have travelled.

Stan filled Paige in. "You know that forest in the article was listed in a suicide guidebook as being one of the most perfect places to die? In one year alone, police picked up seventy-four bodies among the trees. In another forest nearby, police put up a sign about how precious life is, hoping it would act as a deterrent. Cops routinely go on corpse runs, sweeping through the woods to scout for cadavers."

Paige swallowed. Reached for the wine bottle. "Didn't anyone try to pull the book from the shelves?"

"Police demanded that sales be restricted to those over eighteen," Stan said. "Still, you can't hold a book responsible for the strange things going on in that country. In the 1930s, some 19-year-old jumped into a 1000-foot volcanic crater on Oshima. Guess what happened in the months after that?"

"Bunch more people did the same thing," Spence offered.

"Three hundred more, to be exact. Then there was that weird case in the '70s when that writer committed *seppuku* in front of his university students. He was supposedly protesting the Westernization of Japan."

"Seppuku?" Paige asked.

"Ritual decapitation and disembowelment. We peasants call it *hara-kiri*. Literal translation is 'stomach cutting. The ceremony involves—"

"Maybe we should change the subject," Joshua cut in. "Not exactly cheery holiday talk."

"You're right," Stan said, "though you've got to admit, it's interesting that a culture can be so fascinated with suicide that it creates a vocabulary around it. Suicide of an entire family, suicide of the elderly, suicide between lovers—each has its own word. There's even a word for suicide to relieve guilt, but don't ask me what it is."

Paige stood and started clearing plates. "I can't help but think we've got the same kind of phenomenon going on here. Some kind of contagion. Those people in the diner, the kids on Signal Hill, that group in Washington … it's awful. Sick."

"Joshua's right," Stan said. "Let's change the subject." He raised his glass. "Here's to our good health. And to life."

They all toasted. The ghoulish talk was further diverted by the appearance of an apple crumble Paige had picked up from the bakery and reheated. Again, Spence's dessert was cut into manageable chunks and liberally covered with ice cream which melted into vanilla soup before he was able to finish it all. Everyone waited. Joshua was pleased to note that there was nothing wrong with the man's appetite.

After the meal, they trimmed the tree, though several times Spence had to sit down and rest. Then they piled into Joshua's Jeep for the return trip to the nursing home in Portland. Paige had wanted her uncle to stay over. "Are you kidding?" he said. "Whole slew of widows will miss me if I don't get back tonight."

They drove slowly along the main street of town, and Spence reminisced about Cypress Village before the artsies and outdoorsies had discovered it. "Bunch of motels, a grocery store and a gas station. Looks a lot better now. Hey, what's going on over there? Is that a dope deal?"

Paige heaved an exasperated sigh from the back seat and gave her uncle's shoulder a playful shove. "Oh, Uncle Spence. Every time you see more than two teenagers together, you think it's a dope deal."

Joshua glanced through the passenger window. Six teens—four boys and two girls—were gathered on the sidewalk in front of Beale's bookstore. The group looked like they'd come from shooting a Gap ad, all clones of each other in polo shirts, V-neck sweaters and khakis. Joshua recognized preppy Chad Malvern in the center of them. Seeing Chad mixing it up with people his own age came as a relief.

By the time they reached Portland, Spencer Rowan was snoring heavily in the passenger seat. One of the nursing home staff came to the Jeep with a wheelchair and helped Spence in it. "Limousine service tonight," the lanky staffer told Spence. "I wouldn't do this for just anybody, but it looks like you've had a full day."

Paige kissed her uncle on the top of the head. "'Night, my old coot."

Still groggy, Spence reached up and smoothed a hand across her cheek. "'Night, Paige." Then, "I love you."

"Love you too."

Joshua saw her eyes well up as Spence was wheeled into the building.

"I really do love him," she said.

"He's quite a guy."

"He looks so small, so helpless."

Joshua put his arm around her, led her to the Jeep. "His color's just off a bit today. Tomorrow will be better."

They arrived back at the cabin at midnight. Their phone rang at ten minutes past. Spencer Rowan hadn't even made it to the elevator before succumbing to a massive heart attack. He died sitting in the wheelchair.

CHAPTER 36

The Monitor assembled everything he needed into a neatly organized kit. Contained in a leather duffel bag were several pairs of gloves, a brand new plastic sheet, a tensor bandage, and a chloroform bellows. The bellows was a decidedly low-tech device, a double-ballooned instrument with a red rubber tube and a nose cone mask, available on the Net through any number of medical supply companies. Though primitive in design, it would be an efficient vehicle for transferring chloroform into a pair of waiting lungs.

He was delighted with his choice of drug. Chloroform had an interesting history. Prior to its discovery, the surgical theater was comparable to a torture chamber. A doctor's approach to dealing with patient pain ran the gamut from hypnosis to a single shot of alcohol to opium, all administered *post*-op. Other surgeons felt the key to caring for their patients' well-being was to operate with speed, leading many to time how quickly they could perform various procedures. If speed wasn't the answer, then applying snow and ice couldn't hurt. He had even read a report of one doctor who had fitted his patient with a helmet then used a wooden mallet to render him unconscious. The hat and hammer method. Very scientific. No small wonder that early operating rooms were located in remote areas of hospitals, often in lofty towers, where the patients' screams couldn't be heard by those awaiting similar fates.

Then came chloroform.

Chloroform had once been the preferred anesthetic administered during childbirth; carefully measured doses allowed the patient to remain conscious but in no pain. Even Queen Victoria lauded the drug's capabilities and requested it when giving birth to Prince Leopold. The Catholic Church was rumored to have condemned it, however, proclaiming the pain of childbirth to be God's will. Luckily, Queen Victoria was an Anglican.

Chloroform was popular on crime shows. He'd even found a website devoted to showing freeze frames in which victims, usually female, were incapacitated by the dreaded soaked handkerchief over the face. Users could scroll down to see shots of Pamela Anderson or Lindsay Wagner wide-eyed and helpless seconds before the drug rendered them unconscious, their struggles, gurgles and heaving cleavage duly commented upon.

In real life, chloroform had much more to offer than what the small screen presented. Invariably upon regaining consciousness, the victim vomited, often profusely, the vomitus sometimes bloody. He supposed that didn't make for good television viewing. There might be salivation, stupor, a feeling of pressure inside the person's head. If the dose was low.

High doses were lethal. Eventually, the drug was abandoned in hospital surgeries in favor of ether. Chloroform was considered too risky, too toxic, and it was often blamed for causing fatal cardiac arrhythmias. Sudden sniffer's death.

He loved that phrase.

He also loved that chloroform served as an immediate and efficient antidote to strychnine poisoning. He wondered if anyone else would appreciate the irony.

The drug was also used in the production of Teflon, which he found amusing. Very little stuck to Teflon. The added bonus? Chloroform eliminated rapidly from the body. It was forty times sweeter than sugar. Sweet indeed. He couldn't have chosen better.

The Monitor was pleased with the location in which the next scenario would be played. The building was nearly invisible in the shadows of a mind-your-own-business neighborhood, hidden from passersby on the street. He gained entry using bolt cutters on the combination lock and made note of the equipment stored there. He was delighted when he spotted the sturdy beams that criss-crossed the ceiling.

The place was small, with no windows. There were no barking dogs in the vicinity, no insomniacs watching late-night TV who might have inadvertently looked out from a bedroom window and spotted a person stealing into a back yard. Perfect.

It was nearly 2:00 a.m., the time for young lovers to be reunited. The Monitor stepped from his vehicle and crept stealthily between the houses. When he reached his destination, he saw that the combination lock hadn't been replaced. He went inside, flattened himself against the wall behind the door and waited. Soon, the Japanese beetle would enter the web.

CHAPTER 37

For the first time in almost two years, Yoshi felt alive. He was taking control. A man of action. He pedaled through the dark village streets and breathed deeply, filling his lungs with fresh air. He caught himself humming.

This must be what happiness feels like.

Happiness tinged with dread. Behind darkened windows, all was quiet. Even the night creatures—crickets, owls, bats—were silent. Still, Yoshi was wary, the occasional passing car giving his heart an adrenalin shot. None of the vehicles slowed. None flashed their lights.

He remembered the car that had followed Joshua's Jeep the night he had gone to 3F House. *Wink. Wink.* He didn't know how, but that Monitor bastard had found him. He had only been out of the apartment one other time since he'd witnessed the horror at the diner. Three nights later, he foolishly summoned his courage and ventured the short distance to the convenience store for a new supply of snacks and Red Bull. Joshua had spotted him that night. Perhaps the Monitor had spotted him, too.

None of that mattered now. Soon he would be completely rid of the psycho Monitor and busriders.com. He would stop hearing the screams. Stop seeing the watcher in the shadows. He hoped.

The only deviation from their plan was the note he'd left for Joshua. He genuinely regretted having to say goodbye to him; regretted too, having been such a shit. Joshua was a decent man, and he cared about people. They hadn't known each other long, but Yoshi felt that, given more time, they might have become friends.

Her first e-mail had left him skeptical.

I miss you so much.

He typed back: Rich boyfriend dump you?

Then so many messages, rapid-fire.

No, Yoshi, I was wrong.

You were my first love. I'm so sorry for everything. Let me make it up to you.

You can't, he replied.

I have thought of harming myself.

You were always such a drama queen, he keyed in and waited.

With you, I can be strong. Without you, I am dead.

What does that have to do with me?

For seconds, it had felt good, dishing it out. Then it felt awful, horrible. His fingers poised to send an apology when another e-mail appeared.

I've been lurking on busriders.com. You may know me as Lotus. I know you're Jim Stark. I knew it immediately. Then: *I sense danger. Something's not right.*

Yoshi remembered Lotus. She had posted only once, sharing her misery. The Monitor had responded. *Help is closer than you think.*

No! Yoshi keyed frantically. Do not accept help from the Monitor. You are right. There is danger.

I would feel safe with you.

For a brief moment, he allowed his heart to sing. Then, still cautious, still smarting from cruel words and crueler rejection, he sent another e-mail.

If you love me, prove it.

How?

Be with me. Here.

It is difficult.

Life is difficult, he responded. If you don't come, your words mean nothing.

After an agonizing wait, her message appeared. *Yes, Yoshi. I will come.*

He was blocks from his destination. Their meeting place. His pulse quickened when he spotted a car, a dark Volvo station wagon, parked at the curb near the intersection. He could make out the shadowy contour of a man behind the wheel. Had he been followed?

He felt dampness between his legs. Perspiration, he hoped. Yes. A few trickles of sweat. Nothing more.

He swung wide of the car, the visor from his ball cap shielding his face, and kept pedaling, half expecting to hear the click of a door opening. He heard only the whir of the bicycle's tires.

She had texted him earlier from the airport. *My plane has just landed. I'm on my way.*

Not much farther. In his pocket, his phone vibrated. Another text.

I'm waiting. ♥ you.

He pedaled faster. One more block. Half a block.

Soon. Very soon.

When he reached the house, he resisted the impulse to fling the bicycle onto the lawn and race into the back yard, arms open wide. Everything had to go according to plan. He could not attract attention. Carefully, he dismounted and walked the bike along the narrow sidewalk between the houses. The rear yard was a wall of solid black. It was tomb quiet.

It was an odd meeting place, but the only one he knew. He could have taken a taxi to the airport and met her plane but this was the final test—she had to come to him, make the effort. She owed him that.

Yoshi approached the door of the shed and depressed the thumb latch. He was enveloped by more darkness and the faint odor of something sweet. Perfume?

"Aoki?" he called softly. "Are you here? Aoki?"

CHAPTER 38

Spencer Rowan was buried on a cold, rainy Thursday.

Black clothes. Black cars. Black umbrellas.

After the funeral, Carolyn joined Joshua and Paige at the cabin and offered to cook them a decent meal. She and Joshua were raiding the refrigerator and cupboards when Paige entered the kitchen, clad in frayed jeans and one of Joshua's shirts, sleeves rolled up to the elbow and Parker clinging to her hip. The dog keenly sensed her grief and was shadowing her everywhere.

No one was thinking much about food, but Carolyn went through the motions anyway. She minced garlic, removed the zest from a lemon, and chopped parsley. Angel hair pasta boiled on a back burner.

Joshua uncorked a chilled bottle of Pinot Grigio.

"I wish he would have stayed with us on Monday night," Paige said, taking the glass Joshua was offering her. She swiped a fresh tear, cleared her throat. "If he had to die, why couldn't it have been here, in this cabin with me holding his hand? The thought of him sitting in that awful wheelchair—"

Joshua draped an arm around her shoulders, gently stroked her back. "I know, hon. But maybe he knew what was coming. Maybe he wanted to spare you."

Carolyn nodded. "You were lucky to have Spence in your life, Paige. I know he was like a father to you."

Paige swiped a fresh tear. "He was the best."

Joshua wondered how different the past two years might have been for Yoshi if he'd had a father like Spence, someone who was at home more often and would have raised his son to express his feelings, to cope with setbacks and disappointments and heartache. Joshua hadn't thought about Yoshi in days, and now he felt guilty. Since learning of Spence's death late Monday night, Joshua had barely left Paige's side, making only two brief appearances at 3F House to open his mail and touch base with his staff.

I'm safe here.

Joshua had been so certain Yoshi had been turning a corner in his illness, then suddenly for no reason that he could fathom, the boy retreated once more into hikikomori hell, this time feeling he needed a knife to protect himself. From what? Joshua needed to call him. Perhaps tomorrow, if Paige was feeling a little better, he could steal away for an hour and meet with Yoshi. The boy would surely need some comfort and hopefully, during the conversation, Joshua could discover what lay at the root of Yoshi's meltdown. If Yoshi even knew himself.

Paige refused a second glass of wine and, pleading exhaustion, went to bed, taking Parker with her. Joshua and Carolyn cleared the kitchen table, loaded the dishwasher then moved into the living room with the wine bottle.

"Appreciate you coming to Spence's funeral," Joshua said, topping up his sister's wineglass when they settled on the sofa. "I'm sure you're swamped with looking into those deaths at the diner. And the Aerie."

Carolyn waved off the thanks. "All I've done lately is go to funerals. Such is the extent of my social life." Then she caught herself. "Sorry, Josh. I didn't mean to sound casual or uncaring. I'm just tired."

"Any progress on the investigation?"

"Maybe if there was progress, I wouldn't be so exhausted. This wine will probably go straight to my head. You know something else? I don't care." Carolyn took a long sip, then another. "I love Italians. I love their grapes."

"Enjoy," Joshua said. "You can crash in the guest room tonight."

"Might just do that," she sighed. "Josh? Ever think some problems are beyond your capabilities, that try as you might, you just won't be able to solve them?"

He thought of Robb Northrup, burned out and desperate for a fresh start. He thought, too, of Yoshi and Paige, both suffering. Was he doing any of them any good? Was he a good friend, a good counselor? Would he be a good husband? "I have my moments," he answered. "I think everybody does."

"I hope my promotion to patrol sergeant wasn't a mistake. I hope my entering law enforcement wasn't a mistake."

"You're a great cop, Carl," he said, using the nickname he used to tease her with when he claimed to wish for a twin brother.

She hazarded a slight smile. "Don't mind me. I'm just in a funk."

"Funerals and Christmas. Bad combination. You'll bounce back. And you'll get to the bottom of why all those people died here, too."

"It's bigger than you think, Josh. And it's evil."

He caught his sister's faraway look, a haunted stare into nowhere that chilled him. He'd seen her troubled before, and not so long ago, remembering her agony after the shooting, that pain worsened by another fresh wound, Gregg's announcement that he was leaving her. Now, as if she hadn't gone through enough, Carolyn was left to determine why nine people had killed themselves in her jurisdictional back yard. Yes, it was evil.

"I'm right here waiting to listen," he said gently. "And you know I can keep a secret. It's that ex-seminarian thing."

Carolyn shook her head and slouched into the cushions. "Can't say much. Besides, if I start talking about the job, I'll never get to sleep. Think another glass of wine will hurt?"

Joshua refilled both their glasses. Carolyn abruptly changed the subject. "How's your techno-geek, the kid who doesn't leave his room?"

"Thought I'd made some progress with him, but I was just kidding myself. Yet idiot that I am, I like him."

"You're not an idiot, you're just a softie. So he really never comes out?"

"Rarely, and then only after midnight when most people are in bed. His waking hours consist of staring at his computer screen, his comic books or his James Dean posters."

"James Dean?"

"Idolizes him. Apparently he's huge in Japan. Yoshi's seen *Rebel Without a Cause* at least fifteen times. Maybe he identifies with the Jim Stark character, I don't know—"

"Who?" Carolyn shot upright.

"What'd I say?"

"You said Jim Stark." She was on her feet. "Joshua, I've got to talk to this kid."

"Carl, it's not that easy. He's been going through some stuff and—"

"I don't give a damn what he's going through! I need Jim Stark."

Joshua stood up. "What's going on?"

Carolyn was already at the door, grabbing her coat from the hall tree. "Take me to him, Joshua. Now."

CHAPTER 39

Ken Ishiguro abandoned his phone manners. He had been on his way out the door when Joshua called from his mobile in the Jeep to say he was on his way to see Yoshi and was bringing a friend.

"I take it we're not welcome guests," Carolyn said. "I could hear the guy griping from here."

"Understatement. He had a hot date."

"Doesn't bother me a whit if I've delayed some horny guy's orgasm for an hour."

"Are you going to tell me what's going on? Why the urgency to meet Yoshi, and what is this business about Jim Stark?"

Once more Carolyn dismissed his questions. "I need time to think," she told him. "Can you turn off the radio?"

He could feel his sister's edge-of-seat tension, saw through his peripheral vision her steepled fingertips tapping together in triple time. He realized her stress was contagious when he caught himself squeezing the steering wheel in a death-grip. He was speeding too, and Carolyn, the cautious driver, didn't notice. Joshua exhaled slowly, loosened his hold on the wheel and eased up on the gas pedal. They passed the main few blocks of the village in silence. Potted evergreens festooned with red bows and twinkling lights heralded a merriment Joshua didn't feel.

By the time they made the turn into Ishiguro's apartment complex, he thought his sister would spontaneously combust. "Relax, Carl, we're here."

He pulled into the last vacant visitor's spot and glanced across the lot toward Yoshi's bedroom window. It was dark. Still asleep?

It was 10:30. By now Yoshi was usually awake and elbow-deep in *manga*.

Ishiguro's face matched his mood. Prominent fissures marked his forehead. Frown commas framed his mouth. "I have a late date," he snipped when he opened the door to Joshua. "I am entitled to some kind of life, you know."

Joshua quickly introduced Carolyn, said she just had a few questions for Yoshi and assured Ken they wouldn't be long.

Ishiguro looked at his watch then pointed his chin down the hall in the direction of Yoshi's room. Joshua put a finger to his lips, a signal for Carolyn to remain quiet. When he knocked on Yoshi's door, there was no answer.

"Yoshi? Wake up. I need to talk to you."

Still nothing. Carolyn looked at him, her expression full of questions.

"Yoshi, I know it's not our regular night, but this is important."

Ishiguro tapped an impatient foot on the parquet.

Joshua knocked again. "Yoshi?"

"Is he even in there?" Carolyn whispered. She jiggled the knob but the door was locked.

In four determined strides Ishiguro was at the door and pounding it furiously. "Yoshitomo! Enough of this. Open the door immediately!"

Joshua pressed his ear to the door but heard no movement. The small hairs on the back of his neck rose. A potato-chip run? No. Too early for that. Yoshi always made his pilgrimages to the convenience store after midnight.

I'd never kill myself over a stupid girl.

"Yoshi!"

Carolyn gripped his shoulder. "We'll go around to his window, Josh. Come on."

They shoved past Ishiguro and raced out of the apartment and around the building to Yoshi's window. Some tenant, perhaps Yoshi himself, had used the area as a personal refuse dump. The ground was littered with pizza boxes, candy bar wrappers, Styrofoam take-out containers. The acrid stench of dog pee wafted up from the garbage.

Joshua kicked aside crushed pop cans. Hands cupped at his temples, he peered inside but saw nothing except a veil of black. Frantic, he nudged the window upward with the heels of his hands and crawled over the sill into the room, Carolyn following.

He felt his way across the room, sliding his feet along the floor, calling Yoshi's name as he went. When he reached the far wall, he felt for the light switch and clicked it on.

The room was neat. Comic books were stacked in symmetrical piles, the bed was made, the laundry was put away, the empty basket sitting in a corner near the closet door.

The closet. Joshua edged toward it. What did he expect to find on the other side of the bifold doors—Yoshi hanging from a necktie?

He didn't know what to expect.

Slowly he slid the doors apart.

The olive drab swamp coat was gone. So was Yoshi.

"Joshua?"

He turned to where Carolyn stood, in front of Yoshi's computer. She handed him a white envelope with his name printed in green ink on the front.

Ishiguro called from the other side of the door. Carolyn crossed the room and let him in. The man scanned the room as if expecting Yoshi to materialize from somewhere under the bed.

"When did you last see your nephew, Mr. Ishiguro?" Carolyn asked.

The man cast his glance to the ceiling, his head shifting almost imperceptibly from side to side as he traced back. "Monday," he said at last, meeting Carolyn's gaze. "Yes, Monday. But I didn't see him. I only heard him."

"Heard him? How do you mean?"

"Music. He was playing music. And singing. I never heard him sing before."

"What time was that, Ken?" Joshua asked. "Do you remember?"

Again the skyward glance. "I had just finished dinner. About seven thirty."

"And you haven't heard anything since? You didn't think to check, see if he was alright?"

Carolyn gently tapped Joshua's arm. "Mr. Ishiguro, you had no reason to suspect Yoshi wasn't in his room?"

"Why are you so worried?" the man said. "He's probably just gone out for more comic books. You saw him once, Joshua. You know he sneaks out. And you wonder why I didn't check up on him? This is the same boy who had a knife under his pillow. I was afraid. What was to say he didn't go out and buy another knife? You have no idea what my life has been like these few months." His eyes shifted from Carolyn to Joshua. "Neither of you."

Long moments ticked away. Joshua held out the single sheet of paper contained in the envelope Yoshi had left for him. He said, "I don't think Yoshi's gone out for comic books this time."

Carolyn and Ishiguro stepped closer, until they were on either side of his shoulder, and read.

Joshua,

Thank you for trying to help me. I think I was a challenge for you, right? Please tell my uncle not to worry. Perhaps he will send the same message to my parents. I am, at last, truly happy and have known all along that there could be only one thing to free me from the hell that has been my life these past two years. My savior has come and I am going home.

Yoshi.

CHAPTER 40

"It's unthinkable. He lives under the same roof as his nephew and doesn't know Yoshi hasn't been around since Monday? It's not like Ishiguro lives in a mansion."

Carolyn felt heat rise to her face. She didn't pretend to understand hikikomori, Yoshi's angst, or his uncle's frustration with it. She only knew that having Yoshi disappear right out from under his uncle's nose went way beyond weird. She wanted to give Ishiguro's rounded shoulders a violent shake.

They were in Joshua's Jeep again, heading back to the cabin, both hoping that Paige was sleeping through their foray into the night. If she awoke to an empty house, she would be upset, though Joshua had left a note saying he'd be back soon and that Stan was a phone call away.

"I know how it must seem," Joshua said, "but we aren't even sure that Yoshi slipped out on Monday night. The letter has no date on it. Yoshi could have left the apartment five minutes before we got there."

"But Joshua, in your good heart of hearts, what do you really believe?"

He sighed. "That he left on Monday night. And that note's been sitting there for four days."

"What do you make of that note? Why after two miserable years, is Yoshi suddenly happy? Can hikikomori sufferers turn on a dime like that?"

"I don't know. That's the damnable part of all of this. As far as Yoshi's disorder goes, I'm still learning. I've been groping my way along ever since I met him."

"Don't beat yourself up. You haven't known him that long. But did you ever get the impression Yoshi might be suicidal, that perhaps he consented to come to the States for one reason only—?"

"To die?"

"So his parents wouldn't be disgraced. When bad news crosses oceans, it gets diluted. He might have thought it would be easier on them if they heard the news via a long- distance phone call rather than have to discover their son's body by breaking down his bedroom door. Sorry, my tact seems to have retired for the evening. You're worried about him, aren't you."

Joshua nodded. "I knew Yoshi was depressed, and that he's a complex kid with a complicated illness. He spoke pretty casually about death, you know, 'easy come, easy go,' I think he said once. Don't forget, he comes from a culture where death is preferable to dishonor. Still, when I asked Yoshi if he'd ever thought about killing himself, he was adamant that he wasn't considering anything of the kind."

"Just telling you what you wanted to hear, you think?"

"I don't know. Could he have been playing me, saying anything to get me off his back? Sure, it's possible. Though I hate like hell to admit it. Still, I never imagined he'd take off and—" Joshua slammed the steering wheel with his hand. "You're not thinking Yoshi's a part of what's been going on ... those other deaths?"

"Steady," Carolyn said gently. "Keep your eye on the road. Gravel shoulder here. And I haven't said anything of the kind."

"I didn't say you'd said it, I said you'd been thinking it. Is that why you flinched at the mention of Jim Stark? What does a movie character have to do with those people dying?"

The Jeep hit the gravel shoulder and skidded several times before regaining traction on the pavement.

"You're jumping to crazy conclusions, Josh, and we're going to get into an accident if you don't smarten up. Now let me ask you something. During those times you spoke with Yoshi, did he ever mention having a savior, someone who was looking out for him? Some kind of good Samaritan? Or maybe someone called the Monitor?"

Joshua considered the question for long moments, his lips pinched tightly together. "Monitor? No. He never told me about anyone like that. Yoshi had virtual friends, people he'd met on the Net, but I never knew anything about them. The savior he wrote about in that letter is a mystery."

"Maybe Yoshi's computer will reveal more."

"Carl, you don't think Yoshi's just run away, do you? There's more going on here. That's why you asked for the computer."

"I don't know yet, Josh. Let's hope it's something as simple as Yoshi needing some space. And go easy on yourself about not bonding with him. Yoshi wrote that letter to you after knowing you for a few weeks. He didn't leave any such message for his uncle."

Joshua didn't seem to take comfort in that. Still frowning, he scanned the side of the road as if expecting Yoshi to emerge from the darkness to flag down the car. Carolyn remained mute as the Jeep hugged the centre line.

"Josh, what's your honest impression of the uncle? Does he care for Yoshi?"

"In his way. Ken brought Yoshi here, after all. Awfully good of him. Although ..."

"Although?"

"Last time I talked to him, Ken let it slip that the Tagawas were not only giving Yoshi a generous living allowance, they were also paying Ken's rent."

"Huh. Easy for Ishiguro to be magnanimous when it doesn't cost him anything. When you talked to Yoshi's uncle, did he ever do or say anything that was ... what am I trying to say? Off-putting?"

Joshua bit his lower lip, furrowed his brow in concentration. If he noticed that Carolyn hadn't answered his question about Jim Stark, he wasn't saying. "Off-putting? Everything about Ken can be off-putting if you don't know how to take him. I won't deny that he irks me and that it's easy for me in a private moment to slip into blaming both Ken and the Tagawas for enabling Yoshi's condition, but honestly, as far as caregivers go, I have to tell you, Ken's not the worst I've seen. Not by a long shot."

"You wouldn't call him ... manipulative? Cold?"

"Ken is reserved, yes. Manipulative—yeah, there could be some of that, too. But if anyone was pulling strings in that apartment, it was Yoshi. You didn't care much for Ken, did you?"

"He didn't appear too worried about Yoshi being gone. I sensed he was more concerned that his nephew had taken his bicycle."

"Ken said he was going out to look for Yoshi. As soon as we left."

"I was more under the impression he was going to make up for lost time and hightail it to his date's apartment."

Joshua nodded again, as if he knew it too. "So what do we do?"

"*We* don't do anything. You get us back to the cabin, and you'll take care of Paige. I'll pick up my car and drive around awhile, see if I spot Yoshi at any of the usual hangouts."

"What does he look like?"

Joshua gave her a description.

"I'll get the patrol officers to keep their eyes peeled. Then I'll boot up Yoshi's computer, see if I can find out who his savior is and why a kid who hardly ever goes outside is suddenly missing for four days. At least Ishiguro didn't balk when I asked him for the computer. Almost as if he was trying to remove every trace of his nephew."

"Carl, you don't think Ishiguro is somehow involved in Yoshi's disappearance?"

"For all we know, the kid could just be on a walkabout. Might be somewhere right now peeing himself, knowing he's got you worked up about that note. As maddening as that would be, that's the best case scenario. Teenagers do some crazy things to get themselves noticed. On the other hand, while I don't want to worry you, what I saw in that apartment put the small hairs on my neck on high alert."

"That being?"

"Ishiguro's words, actions—and non-actions—indicated to me that he's relieved his nephew is gone. 'Yoshi is a challenge. You don't know what it's been like ...' For a grown man, Ishiguro spouted plenty of me-me-me. With Yoshi out of his life, things get better for him. The question is, how far would he go to improve his own situation?"

She saw Joshua grimace, as if he'd swallowed a tablespoon of vinegar. Maybe what she said wasn't palatable, but as time and her investigation wore on, Carolyn found herself sadly lacking the requisite social graces. She had good reason to believe that Jim Stark was Yoshi and that she'd been a step closer to uncovering more about busriders.com and its participants. Yoshi could have answered some questions. She could have sweated him awhile. Perhaps the kid wasn't the harmless young recluse that Joshua believed him to be. Whether cunning or shy, Yoshi was now in the wind and the Monitor's identity was still a mystery. So was his next move. Adding to Carolyn's growing list of things that were pissing her off was that the offshore ISP that guarded Brady Field's client list was ignoring the subpoena she had requested.

Joshua asked her once more about Jim Stark and where she'd heard the name before. "Just something I've been working on," she replied, and Joshua didn't press for more.

Overhead, clouds stacked upon more clouds scudded in from the shore. It wouldn't be long before the sky opened up, making it difficult to spot Yoshi. Or his savior.

"That doesn't look good," Joshua said, glancing up just as the first drops hit the windshield.

"No," Carolyn agreed, "it doesn't look good at all."

CHAPTER 41

JOSHUA REMEMBERED YOSHI QUOTING JAMES Dean. *Dying turns a lot of people into legends.* Was that Yoshi's intention, to go out with a bang like his idol?

Long after Carolyn had left to search for the boy, Joshua paced in front of the fireplace and wrestled with the whys and wherefores of Yoshi's disappearance. Had Yoshi merely escaped what he perceived to be pressure by running away? It didn't fit. Yoshi had been determined to remain in the safe zone of his room, so determined he had threatened his uncle with a knife when Ishiguro had suggested a short walk.

Besides, where would he go? Yoshi's previous nocturnal escapades had been brief, and had taken place in familiar territory. That Joshua knew of. He remembered once more the mud on the soles of Yoshi's shoes and knew there was more to the boy's excursions in the dark than he had admitted to. Was his fervent bid for safety just an act? A way of manipulating Joshua and Ishiguro into minding their own business?

Perhaps Yoshi wasn't running from something at all, but rather *to* something. His savior. What did he mean, writing that in his note, and why had Carolyn mentioned someone called the Monitor?

His sister had posed her questions about Yoshi carefully, using her official, gentle cop voice, not wanting to upset him. Much too late for that. A hikikomori kid, one who was frightened and adamant about protecting his safety, was missing. Day four.

Yoshi hadn't been abducted. That much was certain. With Ishiguro's help, Joshua and Carolyn now knew that some things were missing from Yoshi's room—a backpack, a pair of jeans, a black

Giants cap with orange lettering, an iPod and the James Dean book Joshua had bought him. His money was gone, his passport as well. Ishiguro pointed to the drawer where Yoshi kept the allowance his mother sent every month. The boy could be walking around with four hundred dollars, give or take. Not the actions of a suicidal kid. Unless, like the others who had formed a death pact on the Net, Yoshi needed traveling money to get to an agreed-upon destination.

Yoshi, dammit, where are you?

Joshua glanced at the clock on the mantel. Midnight. He stopped pacing and placed a call to Ishiguro to ask whether Yoshi had returned. Ishiguro wasn't answering. Out looking for his nephew, Joshua hoped, or on a date, as Carolyn had suspected. Minutes ticked by, with Joshua tempted more than once to start up the Jeep and cruise the streets for some sign of the olive-green swamp coat. He could call the cab companies, find out if a boy matching Yoshi's description had requested a taxi; check the late-night coffee shops, go to the convenience store where Yoshi had bought his *manga* and ask the owner if he'd spotted him. Then he realized that Carolyn was likely doing exactly that. One cop in the family was enough.

Joshua tiptoed into the bedroom where Paige was still sleeping soundly. He undressed and slipped beneath the blankets, careful not to disturb her. The next few days would be rough. Paige would need him, and he would give her one hundred percent of his attention.

Beside him, Paige stirred then opened her eyes. "I called out to you before," she said, her voice small, quivery. "I guess you couldn't hear me."

He rolled over and wrapped his arms around her, stroked her hair. "I'm here now."

"I miss him already, Joshua. I miss hearing him call me 'Angel Heart.'"

"I know."

"Now I'm really an orphan."

When she began to cry, Joshua felt as he had the day he'd fallen in love with Paige, knowing that she was a woman he would protect with his life. While he realized he couldn't prevent her from going through the inevitable pain of losing her beloved uncle, he didn't intend to leave her stranded while he obsessed about a boy he'd only known for a few weeks. It was up to the police and Ishiguro to find Yoshi. For the first time, Joshua was beginning to feel his head was screwing itself on straight and that he didn't have to be the patron saint of lost souls and hopeless cases. His place was here.

"You're not alone, Paige," he whispered as her sobs abated. "You've got me."

CHAPTER 42

THE MONITOR WAS PATIENT. HE scanned several area newspapers for recent developments in Cypress Village. He found instead the usual tree-hugging protesters competing for space with a new or possibly resurrected crop of anti-euthanasia activists. The latter appeared every few months or so in the editorials to dispute the state's physician-assisted suicide law. The current protest revolved around a doctor from Clackamas county who was routinely prescribing lethal doses of Nembutal to his elderly patients rather than trying to treat their depression. The law had been designed to cover those with incurable diseases, those of sound mind who had been pronounced by at least two doctors as having less than six months to live. The Clackamas medico, who had clearly fudged the legal line, was being sued by the survivors of one Mabel Sloane. "My mother wasn't just some old lady," son Walter was quoted as saying, "she was *my* old lady."

A person couldn't be too careful.

The police would make no connection between The Monitor's earlier work and his most recent. The chloroform bellows was now deposited in the bottom of a Dumpster behind a Taco Bell in Eugene; the rest of the detritus of Monday night's affair had been pitched down an incinerator chute in a friend's Salem apartment building.

The boy had brought few possessions—his wallet, a book about his idol, James Dean, an extra pair of jeans and some underwear, a small silver friendship ring. Jim Stark must have purchased the ring online. Or perhaps he'd even had it in Japan, saving up for just the right time to give it to his precious Aoki, a right time that never materialized.

Jim Stark. Yoshitomo Tagawa. Anyone who participated in an ALT forum could be traced with a little cyber ingenuity. The Monitor had posed as a Samaritan, a mewling do-gooder in whom the others quickly confided. He could claim to be Lotus, even though he had no clue who Lotus was. He could also easily masquerade as a besotted teenaged girl.

I have missed you so much. We are meant to be together. I can't wait 2CU. Our love is forever,

Aoki.

At first, Stark was doubtful. Aoki had hurt him. Could he just forget about that? He wouldn't be burned again.

More love mail, more cyber kisses, and Stark began to weaken, swallowing the bait like Kobe beef. He didn't blink at the new e-mail address because he wanted so badly to believe. Almost.

Stark needed proof. She claimed to love him. But how much?

Simple answer. She would have to leave her family, leave her home, come to America. Anything to be with Yoshi, her first and only love.

Aoki? Can it be? After all this time? If this is true, my life can begin again.

The Monitor imagined the trembling keystrokes as arrangements were made. The meeting place. The time.

The Monitor had felt giddy thinking of the arranged rendezvous. It was as though he actually was a smitten schoolgirl, flush with the prospect of reuniting with an old love. He curbed his delight, focused on the painstaking details of the task ahead of him.

Lovely.

This time, the Monitor left no symbol. No *requiescat in pace.* No broken ladder drawn in the dust of some spilled fertilizer. He'd worn a rain-resistant suit. Gloves. A rubber bathing cap over his hair. He had spread a painter's plastic drop sheet over the floor before he'd walked on it, rolled it up when he left. The only fresh footprints came from a pair of size nine Nikes. He recalled how they'd pinched his feet when he slipped them on, how his feet canted unnaturally to the inside as he'd walked toward the place where the stepstool and ladder were stored.

He took care to tie the sleeves of the jacket the way a left-handed person would, having watched Yoshi emerge from 3F House carrying a Zip-Loc bag in his left hand. The Monitor had made sure by posting a question on the forum: did more left- or right-handed people have suicidal feelings? Yoshi had volunteered the information eagerly.

The Monitor had used the tensor bandage to bind Yoshi's arms to his sides. It wouldn't do to have him rouse from his chloroformed stupor and untie the knot around his neck. Instead, trussed like a mummy, when Yoshi regained consciousness, he struggled, kicked, but succeeded only in tightening the noose. It had been a prolonged death, but it was neat.

The Monitor returned his attention to the newspapers, reading for pleasure now. He chuckled at the comics, did the crossword puzzle and skimmed the entertainment pages to see what was playing at local theatres. He hadn't caught a movie in a while. He decided on dinner out instead. He thought about a few possibilities in Portland then changed his mind, instead making reservations at The Rocks for eight o'clock. He always enjoyed the food there, the ambience even more so, especially now, knowing the restaurant was within sniffing distance of the scene of the crime.

CHAPTER 43

THE MORNING AFTER LEARNING OF Yoshi's disappearance, Joshua called Ken Ishiguro from work. No, Yoshi hadn't turned up at the apartment, nor had he telephoned or e-mailed. Ken had already informed the Tagawa family in Hirakata about Yoshi's vanishing act and assured them that the American police were doing everything possible to locate their son. Joshua listened for a frantic tone in Ishiguro's voice, some sense of worry or anxiety, but all he was able to pick up was the man's eagerness to beat the morning traffic into Salem.

Joshua left two messages with Carolyn, but by noon he still hadn't heard back. He checked in with Paige often, too, rushing home with a sandwich from Marley's when he learned she hadn't eaten. He was just returning to 3F House at one thirty when he spotted a shaggy-haired stranger standing in the shrubbery in front of the house and peering through the window.

"Excuse me?" Joshua called from the curb. "Help you with something?"

From time to time, backpacking drifters making their way from Seattle to San Francisco showed up at the house looking for a meal, a bathroom, or a place to crash. Joshua would routinely explain that his charity served thirteen- to eighteen-year-olds and that there were neither meals nor boarding facilities provided. Then he would hand them the address of the nearest shelter and firmly but kindly send them on their way.

This one had no backpack. The man turned toward Joshua's voice but made no move to step away from the window.

Joshua drew nearer and guessed the stranger was in his late twenties. He reminded Joshua of a praying mantis—small head, gangly limbs, and bulging eyes that darted everywhere with the frenzied paranoia of a speed freak.

"Rose around?"

"Rose?"

"Pezeshki. Know where she is?"

"Afraid I don't," Joshua replied. "She's not inside and she's not in the bushes. Mind stepping out of there?"

The man took two long strides out of the shrub border and onto the porch, his lanky frame now fully visible. He wore dirty denims, sneakers, and a fatigue jacket, the collar turned up to partially hide the raging case of cystic acne that covered his neck and jawline. Long fingers tapped a frantic beat on his outer thigh.

"Know when she'll get here?"

"I'm sorry. I didn't catch your name?"

"Never threw it. About Rose?"

Joshua set his jaw, wondering how ugly this was going to get. During the seven years that he'd been running 3F House, he had only called the police once, when one of the kids, high on PCP, cornered Faye in her office and threatened her with a pair of scissors. This guy looked on the edge of losing it too. Joshua was about to say that he couldn't divulge information to strangers about his volunteers or employees when he heard a car door slam behind him.

"Kyle!"

"Speak of the devil," the man said when Rose Pezeshki emerged from her hatchback.

Tension sparked in the air between the two. "Joshua, this is Kyle," she said. Rose trained a steely gaze at the man. "My stepson."

Joshua's arm budged automatically but quickly returned to his side when Kyle didn't reach for a handshake. Instead Joshua nodded and for that received an indifferent glance before Kyle focused on Rose once more.

"Could use a little help," he said.

"I gave you money last week," Rose said, her tone clipped.

"Doesn't go as far as it used to." He made an effort to flash an engaging smile, made less so by the appearance of yellowed teeth.

"Kyle—"

Joshua touched Rose's arm, careful to avoid the gauze on her right hand. "I'll just be inside. Let you two sort this out."

He moved quickly and unlocked the front door, hovering in the hallway in case the scene on the porch grew worse. Joshua had never known Rose to be without a smile but the pinched frown she directed at her stepson spoke volumes about their relationship. Even from where Joshua stood, midway down the corridor, he could hear their voices.

"You're not taking my car, either. Last time you brought it back with an empty tank and hundreds of miles on it. Lord knows where you went, but it couldn't have been to a job interview, like you said. No more lies, Kyle. And I won't let you hurt me, either."

"Don't be such an old lady. At least spot me a few bucks."

"No. You want money, go ask your father, wherever he is."

"Dad's a little short this week."

"And I'm a little short every week. What I gave you last Monday was enough to get you on a bus out of here. Why are you still around?"

Kyle's laughter wormed its way through the door. "My travel plans have been postponed."

"Sorry to hear that. Goodbye, Kyle."

The front door opened.

"You still blame me, you stupid bitch?" Kyle shouted to Rose's retreating back. "I didn't make Lori put that rope around her neck!"

Then Rose was inside, her face crimson with anger. For a moment, she leaned against the door and stared at Joshua, chest heaving with short gasps of breath then she dissolved into tears. He stepped forward, wrapped his arms around her and let her sob.

"That's the way, Rose. Let it out. You'll feel better."

It was minutes before she calmed down enough for Joshua to guide her to a sofa in the living room, slip her topcoat from her shoulders and sit beside her, ready to listen.

"How much could you hear?" she asked.

"Enough to know that Kyle doesn't sound like a very considerate stepson."

Rose found a trace of humor in the remark and let out a small laugh. "Joshua Latham, ever the diplomat. I try to see the goodness in people, Joshua, but it's hard sometimes. And Kyle keeps his goodness well hidden."

"Tried to shake you down for money. That much anyone could pick up."

"And it's not the first time. When I gave him fifty dollars last week, I really thought he would go away," she sniffed. "Shows what I know."

"Does he live around here?"

Rose shrugged. "I think he has friends up and down the coast that let him sleep on a couch or in a garage. When they get sick of him, he finds different friends."

"No job?"

"Nothing steady."

They were tiptoeing across an icy surface, testing for cracks. Joshua knew there was more to Kyle's story than Rose was telling, his drug abuse, for one. He wondered how savvy Rose was to her stepson's physical symptoms, but it was clear to Joshua why Kyle needed money.

The room was silent for long minutes. Rose kneaded the top of her left hand with her thumb until a red patch appeared. Indian sunburn, he and Carolyn used to say when they were kids.

Rose wasn't getting to her feet. She was summoning her courage, Joshua realized, so he gave a gentle nudge. "Rose? About what Kyle said ... your daughter's death. Something about blaming him."

She hung her head and let out a sigh then laced her fingers together, hands quiet now. "I do blame him. For Lori's death. I blame myself, too. And her father. We should all share the burden."

"That's the horrible thing about suicide. Aside from losing your loved one so tragically, you're left with so many questions, wondering what you could have done differently—"

"It's all that and more, Joshua. You see, I suspected Kyle ... and Lori—well, that something was going on. Something horrible. I couldn't get Lori to open up about anything, and when I told my husband what I suspected, he refused to believe it. He said hateful things to me. Kyle was his precious son, after all. According to him, I was jealous of their relationship, and I'd never really accepted Kyle. Two nights after we argued, Lori was dead."

"And your husband left."

"Yes. He and Kyle packed their things into our van and left the day after Lori's funeral. I had no idea. But I wasn't sorry."

"What you suspect Kyle of ... you have proof?"

Rose shook her head. "Intuition. Strong intuition. I'd walk in on things, things that made my skin crawl. Kyle was always finding some excuse to barge into Lori's bedroom. I scolded him about it, said that teenage girls had a right to expect some privacy."

"How did he react?"

"The same way he always did when I took issue with something he did. He'd tell me to stop being an old lady. I'd come into the house and find him standing too close to Lori, or chasing her around the house and trapping her up against a wall, his arms boxing her in. And I'd see their faces—Kyle would be laughing. Lori looked scared to death. Joshua, if I could turn back the clock ... it should have been me and Lori in that van, with our bags packed, running away from those two. Now, having Kyle showing up is like reliving every shameful moment I've tried to forget."

Joshua assured Rose that Kyle would not be allowed anywhere near 3F House and he'd inform the other counselors as well. He added that if he continued to harass Rose for money, she should consider getting a restraining order.

"Do you think your stepson would ever try to hurt you?"

"He already has." She held up her bandaged right hand.

"Kyle did that?"

"I didn't burn myself on the stove like I told you. Kyle scalded me. With the tea kettle. So I gave him money. And my car keys. What else could I do?"

"But you stood up to him out there just now—"

"Which I couldn't have done unless I knew you were close by. We'll see how brave I am once it gets dark and I'm alone. If Kyle comes to my apartment looking for money and I don't give him any—" She resumed kneading her good hand. "Sometimes I think my stepson is capable of anything."

Especially during the tweaking stage of methamphetamine abuse. A user, running on days without sleep, could become violent with little or no provocation. Joshua didn't want Rose to become a victim of her son's aggression. She had been victim enough already.

"How old is Kyle?"

"Twenty-six."

"Really? He looks older."

"He hasn't chosen an easy path for himself."

"Rose, you realize—"

"That he's got a drug problem? Yes. He's been in rehab once already. Did a lot of good, didn't it?"

"Maybe you've seen the last of him, at least for a while."

"Hah. I thought I'd seen the last of his father the day he left, too, and yet there have been times when I swear I've spotted him around town. Always with his head down, hurrying away." She shook her head. "Stress. It does funny things to the imagination."

"Not possible that your ex actually is in town, maybe keeping tabs on Kyle?"

"I hope not. Believe me, my ex-husband isn't someone I want within a hundred miles of me. He hasn't been right since I told him what I suspected about Kyle and Lori."

"Not right?"

"In the head."

That was all Rose would say. Joshua thought of the dead raccoon, left on the porch. Kyle's doing? Or his father's? Rose had been receiving strange phone calls too.

He offered to make coffee but she declined. "Better get to work," she said quickly. "I've held you up long enough."

He reached over, gave her shoulder a reassuring squeeze and told Rose how important she was to 3F House, that she was like a second mom to many of the kids.

"They're special to me, all of them," Rose admitted, pushing up from the sofa. "I worry about them. Some more than others, of course."

"You mean Lily."

"Yes. And Chad Malvern. Something's off about him. But as you've told me a few times, I'm not a counselor."

Joshua nodded guiltily and stood as well. "Something you should know, Rose. Yoshi's missing."

"Not that quiet boy I met the other night? What happened?"

Joshua was bringing Rose up to speed, just as he planned to do with the others later, when Rose went to the window.

"What in God's name? I thought he left at least ten minutes ago."

Joshua followed her and looked out in time to see Kyle Pezeshki hurrying down the sidewalk like a man pursued by hounds. Joshua glanced along the street but saw no one else.

They watched as Kyle disappeared around the corner at the top of the street, Rose rubbing the tops of her arms to quell a shudder. Despite Rose's protests, Joshua made tea anyway and poured them both a cup before retreating upstairs to check his messages. Perhaps Carolyn had called while he had been taking lunch to Paige. Or maybe Ishiguro had heard from Yoshi.

Joshua's wishful thinking didn't pay off. The only message was from Faye Gillespie saying she was sick and that Robb would be taking her three-to-ten shift. He was about to check his e-mail when he heard a faint, high-pitched cry. "Rose?"

He pushed back his chair and hurried to the window but again saw nothing below on the street. He ran into the hallway and leaned over the banister, calling Rose's name down the stairwell. Had she fallen? The cry sounded far away. Was she in the basement?

Joshua remembered Rose saying she was going out to the shed to get an ant trap. She had spotted a fresh colony under the kitchen sink. Joshua moved toward the rear of the house and entered Robb Northrup's office. The room was cool. Robb liked fresh air and always kept his window cracked open. When Joshua looked through it, he saw Rose Pezeshki in the back yard. She was standing on the lawn facing the garden shed and backing away from it, her hands pressed to her mouth. “Rose!” Joshua called through the window. “Rose, what is it?”

Her answer was a shrill, keening scream.

CHAPTER 44

He was naked, suspended from a ceiling hook, his green swamp jacket a makeshift noose. Bare purple-stained feet dangled above the ground, a pair of dirty Nikes and a three-step stool positioned below ten hypnotically swaying toes.

Joshua squeezed his eyes shut. Couldn't look at the face. Refused to believe.

He willed his eyes open, shallow-breathed through his mouth, drew an arm across his face and buried his nose in the soft flesh inside his elbow. Still the foul stench of excrement and rot seeped past, found every crevice, wafted toward his nostrils and into his body like some malevolent microbe. He swallowed bitter saliva.

A short ladder leaned against the shed wall. A pair of garden shears hung from a nail just inside the door. Would they cut through the tough vinyl of Yoshi's jacket?

He rushed toward Yoshi. He could try to lift him up, free him from the hook. The boy's feet were stone cold.

Sparks of thought flashed through him, jumping synapses.

The Japanese typically remove their shoes before they kill themselves.

I have to call Carolyn. And Ishiguro. And Paige.

I have to look after Rose. She's hysterical.

I have to get Yoshi down from there. Why won't Rose stop screaming? Even for a second?

"What's going on over there?" A shaky voice.

Joshua turned away from the horror and rushed to the shed door. A neighbor, older than Moses, craned her neck, trying to see over the privacy fence. He caught a glimpse of cottony hair.

"I heard screams."

"911," Joshua managed to say. "Please hurry."

It was then he realized the yard had grown too quiet. His plans to tend to the dead were intercepted by the need to care for the living. Rose had stopped screaming. Her body crumpled to the ground and she stared straight ahead. By the time Joshua reached her, she was mumbling incoherently, her English mixed with Polish, sobs punctuated with the repeated calling of her dead daughter's name.

Lori. Lori. Lori.

Joshua crouched, cradled the woman's head against his chest, crooning platitudes and promises until the sirens wailed.

The first officer on the scene was Carson Sterne, just days back on the job after recuperating from a car accident in which a drunk T-boned him at an intersection. Carolyn found him hovering in the doorway to the shed, nostrils gleaming with mentholatum, shining a flashlight beam into dark corners. "Looks like we've got a scarfer, C.L. Least he's not wearing bondage gear or women's clothing. Not a sight I'd want to be dreaming about tonight."

Tonight's dreams would be bad enough. Yoshi's face was paper white, his tongue lolling out like a piece of burnt steak. Death by hanging, from such a low height, would have been slow.

Sterne shone the light onto a magazine lying open beside the Nikes. Carolyn knew it was typical for victims of autoerotic asphyxia to be found nude, often with copies of porn nearby. They usually gave themselves some kind of exit strategy from their dangerous game to keep themselves from dying. Carolyn looked at the overturned stepstool. If Yoshi intended the stool to be his safety valve, he was horribly misguided. Stools wobble. Stools tip over. And when people panic, their limbs flail.

"Poor kinky bastard. Why here?"

Carolyn breathed through her mouth, tasting death. She shook her head. "Why anywhere?"

Privately, Carolyn knew Sterne had a point. Why here indeed? Cypress Village was attracting the suicidal like lemmings racing for the ocean. Now the town had claimed Yoshi. Right here in Joshua's back yard.

It seemed unlikely that Yoshi would have chosen this spot after having written the note to Joshua. If Yoshi intended for Joshua to discover his body, then his dying here was a final act of cruelty. Did Yoshi have such meanness in him? Joshua admitted he didn't know the boy very well. Maybe the kid was as cruel as they come, and punishing Joshua was part of the ultimate sign-off. I'll kill myself, right in your face. You couldn't help me, so fuck you.

It didn't feel right.

"Borrow the flashlight?" Carolyn held out her hand.

She trained the beam along the floor, shone it behind the lawn mower, the buckets of fertilizer, the recycling bin for garden waste.

"You didn't go in here?" she asked Sterne.

"Not me. Figured you'd want to check it out, what with all those others that offed themselves."

Offed themselves. Such a neat, simple way to look at suicide. One minute you're there, then nothing. Click. Like a light switch. She was sure the bus riders saw it that way. Pain. Click. No pain.

When the patrol officers arrived with their forensics kit, Carolyn instructed them to take thorough photos of the knot that had choked off Yoshi's final breath. The precise angle of the stepstool. The position of his pile of clothing. She wanted every piece of lint bagged, every footprint dusted. If Yoshi had been lured here, the creep would surely have the decency to leave her a clue.

As if any of this was about decency.

CHAPTER 45

Auntie Rose refused to go to the hospital. She was given a sedative and driven to her sister's place in Manzanita. Family was what she needed now, she'd said, not a bunch of strangers in pastel smocks whispering about the poor woman and what she'd seen. She promised Joshua she would see her doctor tomorrow. She wasn't sure when she would return to 3F House. If ever.

"Take all the time you need," he said.

Joshua watched from the kitchen window as they removed Yoshi's body from the shed. Seventeen years old. Nearly five thousand miles from home. Yoshi, who sought the safety of a one-room sanctuary, was now encased in a zipped-up, black cocoon.

I needed more time, Yoshi. What could I have said to make this not happen?

He remembered mumbling to Carolyn that he would track down Ken Ishiguro at Willamette, but Carolyn insisted on making the call herself. She had a few questions for the professor, whom she summoned from his late afternoon lecture.

It was nearly six when Carolyn came inside hurling a spate of uncharitable adjectives about Ishiguro. He wanted to know where Yoshi's body was, how he was to proceed, how much time he would need to take off work. "So damnably practical," Carolyn muttered. "Know what he said when I told him Yoshi was dead? 'That is very unfortunate. His mother will be very sad.'"

Joshua was on his fourth cup of coffee and had already called the other counselors to tell them about Yoshi. They in turn would make calls to the teens, telling them tonight's session was cancelled. For good measure, Joshua also posted a note on the front door. *Due to an emergency, 3F House will be closed this evening. Thank you for your understanding. J. Latham, Executive Director, Friends of Families.*

An emergency. How vague. How watered down. For a moment, Joshua poised his pen over the phrase, ready to cross it out and rewrite: *due to a tragedy* then he decided not to set unnecessary speculation and gossip in motion. The nature of the emergency would reveal itself soon enough.

"It's no good," Carolyn said, stooping to brush dirt from the hem of her slacks. "We can't find it."

Her words barely registered, sounding more like a bad radio broadcast, the meaning lost in static.

"Find what?"

"The knapsack. Remember Ishiguro told us Yoshi's knapsack wasn't in his room? Plus, some jeans were missing, money, that book you bought him ..."

He tried to concentrate, saw visions instead. An olive drab jacket. An overturned stepstool. Ten dangling toes.

"Point is, if they're not in Yoshi's room and they're not in that shed, then where?" Carolyn paced the length of the kitchen, spied the coffee maker and found herself a mug in the cupboard. "Could Yoshi have gotten into the house, Joshua? Have stashed his knapsack in here for some reason?"

He shook his head, a tortoise motion. "Doors were locked when I got here. No windows broken."

"Who has keys to this place?"

"Wes, Faye, Robb."

"What about that lady who was with you?" Carolyn consulted her notepad. "Rose Pezeshki. Does she have a key?"

"No. Just the four of us." Words crawled over his thick tongue. How long did it take for caffeine to kick in? He held out his empty mug for a refill. "Hope Rose'll be okay. She found her daughter ... like Yoshi. Six years ago."

Carolyn poured the dregs of the carafe into Joshua's mug and sat down at the table. "How awful. Don't worry, Josh. She seemed to be bucking up by the time we got through to her sister."

"I know."

"And I'll get you through this, too. I know how much you cared about Yoshi. But right now I've got to be a cop. Can you stand a few more questions?"

He nodded.

"The porn, Joshua. We both saw the magazines in Yoshi's room. He accessed plenty of x-rated stuff on his computer, too."

"*Seijin manga.*"

"Whatever. I know teenage boys and porn are as common a pairing as mice and cheese, but Yoshi was into some pretty sick stuff—"

"No he wasn't. He liked to talk a good game but his tastes were fairly mild, considering what's out there."

"Joshua, the magazine we found in the shed was full of cartoons depicting lone females being preyed upon—that's an understatement—by a host of males. Light on the consensual, heavy on the humiliation."

"*Bukkake.* Yoshi wasn't into that. The magazines in his room were mostly *ecchi*—soft-core. Nudity, partial nudity, provocative clothing. And *bakunyuu.* Large breasted women."

The caffeine surged through his veins. Joshua felt his mind clear. To his surprise, he was even remembering the Japanese words he'd learned from Yoshi.

"I need to get a handle on this kid," Carolyn said. "You're telling me one thing, I'm seeing another. The magazine in the shed was open to a page showing a nude woman being savaged by some gigantic octopus-creature."

"Tentacle rape," Joshua told her. "One of the fetishes catered to in some *seijin.* Again, definitely not Yoshi's thing."

Carolyn frowned. "You'd swear to it?"

"I'd swear that's what Yoshi told me. Compare what you found out there to the *manga* in Yoshi's room. Or what he explored on the Net."

"I will. Something else, Joshua. When you looked into the shed, do you remember seeing—"

"I remember Yoshi," he cut in. "And I remember wanting more than anything to get him down."

"But you didn't. Why?"

"Because Yoshi was ... beyond help. And I heard the neighbor calling out. Then Rose collapsed. She needed me."

Carolyn stretched out her hand, grasped him firmly on the arm. "Right now I need you. To look in the shed again. Tell me if there's anything unusual."

He must have flinched. Carolyn gripped harder.

"It'll be okay. Yoshi's gone. We'll just stand in the doorway."

He pushed his chair away from the table, stood up and went through the back door. On the porch steps, he felt his legs wobble but continued on, Carolyn keeping pace beside him.

It was a sturdy garden shed, an eight-by-ten-foot structure built by the previous owner to mimic the Victorian architecture of the house. Crossbeams ran beneath the peaked roof; these had been outfitted with hooks and brackets to store the owner's considerable outdoor gear and rid the floor of clutter. The former owner had been an avid outdoorsman and had managed to store his bicycle, kayak, skis and fishing rods above ground and away from moisture.

When Joshua reached the doorway, he forced himself to ignore the chill that prickled the length of his spine. He swallowed hard and said, "The ladder."

He motioned to where a six-foot ladder rested on the floor, leaning against the wall to his left.

"It usually hangs from those hooks." He pointed. "That one, and the one where Yoshi—"

"Okay," Carolyn said gently. "Anything else?"

"The stepstool. It goes there. See those two big nails sticking out of that 2x4 on the wall?"

Carolyn looked. "It hung from there?" She didn't need an answer. She could see exactly where the stool would go. The shed, save for the ladder and stool, was well organized and neat. Typical Joshua. And Yoshi's footprints led to and from both spaces.

"Otherwise, everything's the same."

Carolyn tugged on his arm and started to close the shed door. "Ever lock this thing?"

"Yes. Not that there's anything to steal in here. Everything's second-hand, even the lawn mower. But the fertilizers, some of the chemicals ... we don't want any kids getting into that stuff. But Robb came out the other day and mentioned that the lock was gone. I hadn't gotten around to replacing it. Shit."

"The other counselors ever come out here, use the shed?"

"Sure. We take turns mowing the lawn, raking, doing all the outdoor maintenance. Cheaper than hiring a service."

"And when you brought Yoshi to 3F House, did he see the shed?"

Joshua thought back to that night. Only nine days ago. Yoshi had balked at going, needed reassurance, wanted to be safe. Fat lot of good Joshua had been. He had promised Yoshi safety, coaxed him from his comfort zone. Now he was dead. Joshua felt his throat close.

"It's possible, I guess, but I don't know when he'd have had the opportunity. We drove here, went upstairs to the discussion circle, and I don't think Yoshi left his chair until the session was over. After that, we went straight to the car. By then it was dark. And the shed is directly behind the house. It isn't visible from the street." He heard the tremor in his voice, cleared his throat, and hoped there weren't too many more questions.

Carolyn pointed to the narrow walkway between the houses. "Red Cannondale mountain bike leaning against the side of the house. Ever seen it before?"

Joshua shook his head. "Robb bikes to work sometimes, but he owns a Trek. And it's white. Wonder if it belongs to Ishiguro ..."

"I'll check." Carolyn led him back toward the house and into the kitchen. She shut off the coffee maker, rinsed their mugs in the sink and locked the back door while Joshua slouched in a chair and waited for profound grief to wrap around him. Instead he felt curiously numb, enshrouded by a thick layer of impenetrable muck.

"Something wrong here, Carl," he said. He felt his sister's hand on his shoulder. "Yoshi's gone. He died horribly and I couldn't reach him. Yet I don't seem to be able to ... feel anything."

"It'll come, Josh. All the sorrow and the anger and the guilt, though you've got nothing to feel guilty about. And when those feelings come, you've got Paige, and me, and your fellow counselors to talk to. Right now, let's get you home. Older sister's orders."

"Older by ten whole minutes," he said, rising. "Big deal."

"Still counts. Come on. Don't make me use my stick."

They walked toward the front of the house, the old jokes between them sounding sad and stale.

The evening *Examiner* rested on the stoop.

"Good," Joshua said. He picked up the paper and locked the door. "Maybe I should check the want ads. Think about a career change."

"You didn't fail Yoshi, Josh."

"How can you say that?"

"Because I'm your sister and I love you. I know you sweat blood for that boy."

"And it wasn't enough."

"Go home, Joshua," she said again and led him to his car.

Carolyn watched as he drove off, knowing that Joshua shared her trait of wanting to save the world, and that both of them, with the passing of years, realized the impossibility of that goal. Now it seemed neither of them could even save a small piece of it.

CHAPTER 46

SOMEONE HAD AFFIXED RED AND green bows to all the computer monitors at the police station. A retro artificial Christmas tree with flea market decorations and strands of mangled tinsel stood in the corner, looking pathetic.

"The elves have been busy, I see," Carolyn said to Ziggy.

"Doesn't feel much like Christmas, does it." Ziggy glanced at the droopy ribbon on his screen, then at the newspaper photo of Yoshi on his desk. "Another dead teenager. Has the world gone mad?"

"Seems that way."

Carolyn assigned Ziggy the task of checking out Yoshi's virtual girlfriends on the Net and looking through the boy's *seijin manga*. "Poor men. We always get the dirty work," he said, "but I suppose I can rise to the job."

Carolyn rolled her eyes. "You could have gone all day without saying that."

For her part, Carolyn had already spoken to Ken Ishiguro who greeted her at his apartment with icy reserve. It was Saturday morning, and Ishiguro had been hoping to sleep in. He had been up all night talking with relatives from Japan. Grudgingly, he offered Carolyn a cup of coffee and she accepted, noting that Ishiguro still seemed more inconvenienced than sorrowful about his nephew's death. People grieve differently, Carolyn reminded herself, but that didn't erase the irritation she felt toward the man.

From him she learned much of what Joshua had told her previously—that Yoshi loved his gadgets, that he had been despondent over a break-up with a girlfriend, and that he'd been so determined to never leave the apartment again, he had threatened both Ishiguro and Joshua with a knife. But Ishiguro provided one crucial bit of information that set Carolyn's brain in rapid motion.

Yoshi was a southpaw.

The knot around Yoshi's neck had, according to investigators, been tied by a left-handed person. Beneath the knot was an inverted, V-shaped bruise. The only fingerprints they found on the swamp coat and the porn magazine belonged to Yoshi. The overturned stepstool was in a position consistent with where it would have fallen had Yoshi kicked it out from under him. They had searched the shed and surrounding yard carefully but had found no ladder symbol like the one discovered at the diner and on the rented Neon. Much of the evidence pointed to suicide. That Yoshi's death did not connect with the others was one obvious conclusion, but Carolyn didn't trust obvious conclusions, especially not where this investigation was concerned.

She thought back to a question posed by Carson Sterne. *Why here?* Why had Yoshi died in a shed behind 3F House when his bedroom closet would have served equally well? To punish Joshua? A viciously cruel act, one Joshua would believe Yoshi incapable of. Perhaps her brother didn't know the real Yoshi as well as he'd thought.

According to Joshua, Yoshi didn't know about the existence of the shed. That being the case, Yoshi wouldn't have known about the ceiling hooks, or the stepstool, or that the shed was custom-made for a hanging. But he could have discovered the shed's existence on one of his after-midnight prowls. It was possible.

Carolyn scrolled through her mental list. She was bothered by the swamp coat. People who experimented with autoeroticism used a variety of ligatures from ropes, chains and telephone cords, to panty hose and silk scarves. But the sleeves of a vinyl swamp coat? If Yoshi's intention had been to satisfy some autoerotic urge, would he not have come equipped with something more appropriate for the occasion? One of Ishiguro's neckties, a belt from his bathrobe, the cord from his computer—any of these would have done the job. Likewise if his intention had been suicide. Something about using the sleeves of the jacket he was wearing struck Carolyn as impromptu, not the act of someone who had carefully planned his own death.

Troubling as well were the footprints. Aside from Yoshi's and Joshua's, another set appeared—three giant steps into the shed, three giant steps out. Someone had stood near Yoshi's pile of clothes. Doc Martens. Size 10.

Carolyn was bothered by the porn as well. *Bukkake*. Joshua had insisted Yoshi didn't get off on it. Ziggy was poring through the boy's *seijin manga* now, a huge stack that Ishiguro had eagerly relinquished to Carolyn. If Ziggy discovered more hard-core porn in Yoshi's collection, it might mean once again that Joshua had merely scratched the surface with the boy. Then Carolyn could indeed be looking at suicide, or at least, an orgasm gone terribly wrong.

That idea was dashed to dirt moments later when Ziggy entered her office and said, "Something's off here, C.L. The magazine you found at the scene isn't anything like the other porn Yoshi bought."

"Zig, are you sure?"

"'Course I'm sure. I've been through that pile and seen breasts the size of dirigibles, but I couldn't find anything that would churn my stomach like the magazine we pulled out of that shed."

Carolyn handed Ziggy another taxing assignment, to find out what stores carried the type of porn they'd found and see whether anyone remembered who had purchased a copy. Odds were great that the *bukkake* had been bought online, but a neighborhood prowl was still worth a shot. Ziggy was given a high school photo of Yoshi to show around, and Carolyn told him to scare up pictures of Ken Ishiguro and Brady Field as well.

The anomalies that had merely niggled at Carolyn before erupted into full-blown, bright red question marks. What was going on here?

She got back in her car and knocked once more on Ken Ishiguro's door. This time Yoshi's uncle was openly hostile. He stood in his doorway, fuming. "What do you want now? Isn't it enough that you woke me this morning? Didn't I give you what you asked for? This is intrusive. Very intrusive. I will complain to your superior."

"Just another few questions, Mr. Ishiguro," Carolyn said, controlling her urge to match him decibel for decibel. "You've been very patient. Very cooperative. And the police certainly do appreciate that. We're just trying to do what's best for your nephew, so his parents in Japan—and you, of course—can rest easier. Tell me Mr. Ishiguro, are you left- or right-handed?"

"This is bullshit. I'm left-handed. What does this have to do with Yoshi?"

"You graciously let me take Yoshi's magazine collection with me earlier," she said, neatly deflecting the man's question. "Have you any magazines similar to Yoshi's?"

"This is bullshit!" he said again, a thick vein throbbing on the side of his neck. "I have a subscription to *Playboy*. What of it?"

"I can be back in an hour with a warrant to seize your magazines, Mr. Ishiguro. Are you sure you haven't got anything more exotic in your collection?"

"Come! Check if you want!" He stepped aside and allowed Carolyn to enter.

She should have asked another officer to accompany her. But they were short-staffed and overworked, and now she was alone in an apartment with a man on the knife-edge of going berserk. She strode into the living room with all the authority she could muster and opened drawers to Ishiguro's coffee table and end tables. A TV Guide. A book of Sudoku puzzles. Matchbooks. Pens.

"In here," he snapped, motioning for her to follow him.

She held back, her gaze attracted to Ishiguro's large-screen television. It sat on top of a contemporary stand, a pair of smoked glass doors revealing an extensive DVD collection. Some English titles were among the collection, but Ishiguro had an equal number of Japanese films. Carolyn asked for them.

Ishiguro flipped an angry hand. "Just return them soon. And in good condition."

In the man's bedroom, Carolyn found *Playboy* issues for November and December. The man even lifted his mattress, flung open his closet door, opened drawers to his dresser. Carolyn conducted her search quickly but thoroughly. If Ishiguro was into *seijin manga*, he wasn't keeping it there. But he might have known where to buy it.

Carolyn flipped open her notebook. "Mr. Ishiguro, what do you know about *bukkake*?"

"I know what it is. That's it. Not my thing."

"Any idea where such a specialized magazine might be bought?"

"If it's not my thing, why would I know? Cypress Village is a pretty small place. A small, *Caucasian* place. I think for *bukkake*, you'd have to go to a bigger city. Why are you asking all these ridiculous questions? Yoshitomo hung himself. Can't the police let me alone?"

"I mean no disrespect, but Yoshi—and his illness—must have been a tremendous burden."

"Yes," he answered quickly then caught himself. "But we cared for him. We wanted him to get better."

"Still, it was difficult."

His lips tightened. "Will there be anything else, Sergeant? I am very tired."

"That will be all for now, Mr. Ishiguro."

She was ushered swiftly to the door and heard the resounding thud behind her.

CHAPTER 47

CAROLYN KNEW SHE NEEDED TO question the 3F counselors, find out where each of them was on Monday night, the night Yoshi disappeared. There was her favorite cardiologist, Brady Field, as well. Carolyn wondered what kind of airtight alibi the good doctor would come up with.

She started with Wes Bertram, who to her delight, was an enthusiastic gossip. He let it slip that Faye Gillespie, though devoted to the 3F kids, had a personal life that was the shits, and occasionally, he'd seen the bruises to prove it. He didn't have much use for Robb Northrup either. Eventually he got around to talking about Yoshi, whom he'd only met once.

"Kid was scared of his own feet," Bertram said. "Damn shame what happened. Given time, we might have got somewhere with him. This has been tough, especially on your brother."

Carolyn agreed that Joshua was taking Yoshi's death hard. Next, she asked Bertram if he thought that Yoshi was suicidal. "I know you hardly knew him," she said. "Just your impression, that's all."

Bertram didn't hesitate. "Yeah, if ever there was a suicidal kid, he was it. Not trying to besmirch Yoshi's memory or anything, but given his illness and how he was allowed to continue like that for so long, I'm amazed he didn't kill himself sooner."

"Pretty rough shape when you saw him?"

"Pitiful. You know, my counselor's ego doesn't like to admit we've lost one. First thing I'd have done is teach the kid how to play football. When the opposing team is rushing you, you use your fancy footwork and just keep on charging. Yoshi needed the confidence and strength to storm the barricades."

That was the thing about today's kids, Bertram said—when a problem came their way, they just didn't know how to dust themselves off and get on with it. Didn't appreciate what they had, either. Always something to complain about, then they fucked things up worse with drugs or gangs, or in an even bigger way, like Yoshi.

"My five-year-old's got more courage than the lot of them put together," he told Carolyn. "Spends half her life in the hospital throwing up, watching clumps of her hair fall out, but does she complain?"

Carolyn interrupted the soliloquy to ask him where he was around the time Yoshi disappeared.

On the night that Yoshi went missing, Wes Bertram was having dinner with his wife and another couple. They occupied the back booth at Marley's and stayed there until the place closed at midnight. That didn't impress Carolyn much; Yoshi could have left the apartment to meet his killer after that. There was no way of knowing for certain.

To Carolyn, Bertram was rigid and judgmental, not the sort she would have pegged for a counselor and not one she would have warmed to if she had been a troubled teen. Yet perhaps it was his take-charge attitude and tough-love approach that got the job done. She tried to keep an open mind, thinking Bertram's stress over his daughter's condition could easily deplete his patience when dealing with the teens and his colleagues.

Carolyn went straight from Bertram's bungalow to pay a visit to Robb Northrup. She found the young counselor at the funeral home his parents owned, clad in a dark suit, his wingtips perfectly shined. He had just finished guiding a clutch of mourners to a room at the end of a wide hall when he spotted her. Carolyn introduced herself.

"No need," Northrup said, still using his soothing funeral parlor voice. "I remember you from Spencer Rowan's funeral. You look so much like Joshua. Is this about that boy Yoshi?"

She nodded and he led her to a meeting room down a small flight of stairs. He offered her coffee, but she declined. The room mimicked the décor of the upstairs parlors—upholstered wing chairs in deep colors, a patterned rug, floral artwork in gold frames, mahogany Queen Anne tables covered with boxes of facial tissues and bowls of mints. Carolyn sat at a round table surrounded by four chairs, her back to an open doorway leading to a room full of caskets. Northrup sat opposite.

"You've worked at 3F House for how long?"

"About two years. A great place. I couldn't ask for a better boss than your brother."

"Yet I understand you're quitting..."

Northrup cast his glance downward. "Burnout, I suppose you'd call it."

"Some of the kids are a challenge, I'll bet."

"They have their moments, sure. But leaving 3F is more about me. Maybe I'm not cut out for being surrounded by walls."

"But you're working in a funeral home ..."

Northrup smiled. "I help out part-time. When it gets busy. But I'm not making this my career."

"Any plans?"

"A little hiking, I guess. Maybe head into Canada to ski. I love Whistler. Great vibe there."

"Ever been to Cascade National Park?"

"In Washington? Sure. Beautiful spot."

"Recently?"

Northrup stroked his chin, a gesture that Carolyn found studied, contrived. "Not in three or four years," he answered, his gaze flickering to somewhere over Carolyn's shoulder. "Anyway, I'm not sure how much good talking to me about Yoshi will help you figure out why he did it. I never met him."

"But you would have liked to?"

"Sure. Yoshi and his illness intrigued me. I'd never heard of hikikomori until Joshua told us about it."

"Mr. Northrup—"

"Robb."

"Robb, Yoshi went missing from his apartment on Monday night. You weren't by any chance at 3F House on Monday, were you?"

"No." He laughed a little, nervous. His neck flushed. "Faye was running the discussion that night. I wanted to go there, meet Yoshi, but Joshua said it wouldn't be a good idea. I stayed in, rented a DVD, ordered a pizza from Pepe's at about 10:00. Anyway, what does it matter? Yoshi killed himself, right?"

"We're just trying to determine if anyone may have seen Yoshi around the place," she said quickly, "or maybe witnessed him going into the shed ..."

"Not me. Like I said, I stayed in. But maybe one of the other kids saw him. Even though it's against the rules, I'm sure a couple of them sneak back there to have a smoke once in awhile."

Carolyn concluded her meeting by telling Northrup to call her if he learned anything new, particularly if he heard scuttlebutt about Yoshi from any of the 3F kids. Perhaps Yoshi had let something slip to one of them. About the way he was feeling. What he might have been planning. Or what he was afraid of.

Carolyn wasn't sure what to make of Northrup and tried to reconcile his yearning for the wide-open spaces with the suited-up, polished and preened person she'd just sat opposite. The two images didn't jibe. The meatball sandwich she grabbed on the way back to her office didn't jibe with her stomach either.

Officer Chloe Grier was at her desk and updated Carolyn on Faye Gillespie. The counselor was barely a shadow over five feet tall, a fragile creature who physically couldn't have managed Yoshi's demise in the shed. Not without some help. The night of Yoshi's death, Faye had been at 3F House until ten o'clock then had gone straight home to bed. She had been fighting a cold, and any of the kids in the discussion group could vouch for the fact that she had sneezed her way through half a box of facial tissue. No proof that she actually went home and stayed there, but Chloe saw no reason to doubt her story.

Carolyn heard from Joshua late in the day. He was adamant—Yoshi did not kill himself. He had no explanation for how or why Yoshi had gone to the shed. He only knew that it wasn't to die.

She found herself agreeing with her brother, if only to temporarily try and untangle the snarl of thoughts plaguing her. Assumption then—Yoshi wasn't suicidal. He'd gone to the shed because ... he had been lured there. By whom? Possibility—the same person responsible for the deaths of the other bus riders. Given that, then the killer brought the *bukkake* to the shed. Somehow, he knew Yoshi dabbled in *seijin manga*. Perhaps Yoshi had bragged about it on the Net. People's tastes in porn could be highly specialized, so Ziggy had said. They like what they like. The killer made a leap—eeny meeny—and bought a magazine thinking that Asian porn is Asian porn, not realizing that Yoshi's tastes didn't run to the exotic or violent. A mistake.

Someone had gone to a lot of trouble to make Yoshi's death look like it wasn't connected to the others, but was instead a case of autoerotic asphyxia. He had stripped off Yoshi's clothes. It would have taken time.

Another assumption—the killer, if there was a killer, knew Yoshi was left-handed. How? Damned if Carolyn could figure it out. And if there was a killer, then he knew about the shed, had been in it before or had come upon it, broken in and decided that, for an apparent suicide, it would do nicely. The killer didn't bring a ligature with him, not wanting any object traced back to him. He would improvise at the scene. Risky, but he had taken risks before.

Another thought nagged at her. If Yoshi's death was in some way connected to the others', why did the killer suddenly change MO? She knew in the case of serial killers, that changing methods was deliberate, a strategy to keep the police guessing, confused, off the scent. But in this case, the killer didn't have time to manipulate Yoshi into doing the deed himself. Yoshi's death had become a hands-on job. Why did Yoshi need to die, and why so quickly?

Yoshi, what did you know?

Carolyn puzzled over the question until darkness outside her office window forced her from her chair. She realized then, with profound regret, that she'd been sitting in the same position for too long. Bursts of pain, like kiln-heated glass, flared through her hip and sent flaming shards down her leg. Sciatica was teaching her an agonizing lesson—she hadn't been taking care of herself. Late nights, lack of exercise, she didn't know what to blame. Perhaps her body was just telling her, *Enough already*. She needed to swallow an anti-inflammatory, walk around until her symptoms eased a little before getting behind the wheel of her car.

She left her office and headed for the vending machine at the end of the hall. The Christmas elf had been at work there too, and had festooned the vending machine with a fake garland and sagging plaid bows. Carolyn shoved coins into the slot and watched her chocolate bar drop into place. Two extra-strength Datril and a Coffee Crisp chaser should fix her. She headed outdoors, remembering what Wes Bertram had said earlier.

Keep on charging.

She fought to ignore the searing pain, even managed to smile at the young lovers walking toward her in Santa hats, arms around each other. It should be that kind of night, she thought. A night for lovers. A night to think about Christmas presents, celebration, the promise of a bright new year. Instead, Carolyn was thinking about death and a killer who stalked the Net, preying on those already teetering on the edge. She wondered for the thousandth time about the killer's motive and kept returning to the same reasons she had ruminated on since she had first been called to Signal Hill.

He kills for power. For thrills. Because he *can*.

Which one? Did the killer even know the reason for his own cunning, his own malevolence? Was it all just some sick game with him emerging victorious every time?

Carolyn forced the thoughts from her mind, knowing that the *why* probably mattered least when it came to apprehending someone.

She approached the downtown shops, each decked out in holiday finery, a Christmas card without the snow. In front of Beale's Bookstore, she noticed Chad Malvern, a junior at the private school where Carolyn had given a keynote address on crime prevention in September. Malvern had been chosen to thank the speaker and Carolyn remembered the boy as being polite and poised, though his thanks had a well rehearsed ring.

Chad was talking to a lanky man with a serious case of the jitters. When the boy spotted Carolyn, he motioned for the man to wait, and he came over to where she'd stopped. "Hi, Sergeant Latham. Remember me?"

"Course I do, Chad. How're things?"

"Great. Last day of school yesterday. We don't go back until the fourteenth."

"Plans for the holidays?"

"Going to Anguilla with my dad and his new girlfriend. It'll be cool. Got PADI certified, so we'll be able to dive together."

"Good for you, Chad. Listen," she inclined her head toward his shaky friend, "everything okay here?"

Chad turned and looked briefly at the man, now staring at a display of children's books in the store window. "Him? He's cool. He used to work for my dad. Are you coming back to speak at our school again? Everybody really enjoyed it."

"Sure, if the school will have me." Her pain had eased but only slightly. She needed to keep moving. "Well, better be off."

"Me too, Sergeant Latham. Nice seeing you again. Merry Christmas."

"Same to you, Chad."

Carolyn made an about-face and headed toward her vehicle, parked in the station's lot. She was about to unlock the door when her cell phone trilled.

It was Joshua. "Carl, I've been a dolt."

"And this is something new?"

"I'm serious. My brain was fried yesterday. Plus I've been busy looking after Paige, calling Ishiguro to see if I could do anything ..."

She disengaged her door lock, climbed into the Explorer and locked the door again. "What is it, Joshua?"

"Yoshi's knapsack," he said. "I know who has it."

CHAPTER 48

By eight o'clock the next morning Carolyn found herself sitting across the table from Kyle Pezeshki. He hadn't been tough to locate. Night patrol had picked up the twenty-six-year-old on the beach, stripped down to his undershorts and slippery with sweat. He might have camped there all night undetected were it not for the passing couple who'd heard a loud and off-key rendition of Nine Inch Nails' "Something I Can Never Have" emanating from the edge of the Pacific. It took two seconds for Carolyn to realize that Pezeshki was in a bad way, his tics, twitches and bursts of agitation revving her own heartbeat.

"Which one of you's gonna play good cop?" he said, his bug-eyed gaze darting from Carolyn to Ziggy, who'd just entered the room.

"Good cop?" Carolyn said as Ziggy pulled up a chair beside her. "There aren't any good cops in this room. What you have here are two *excellent* cops, so why don't you tell Sergeant Takacs and me what brings you to our fair village?"

The words spilled out on a single breath. "My stepmom lives here. No law against a guy visiting his stepmom, is there? Least not last time I looked. Something changed?" He scratched at the dry skin on his arm.

"No, but we're given to understand that your stepmother isn't interested in seeing you. In fact, she pretty much blew you off yesterday. I know if I was rejected like that, I'd be putting plenty of distance between me and whoever shunned me. Yet here you are."

Pezeshki gave a double shoulder-shrug and kept scratching. "Christmas is almost here. Time to get together with family, right?

Besides, this is a nice enough town. Plenty to see and do. Forests, beaches—"

"Not many people hit the beach in December," Ziggy cut in. "Especially not in their underwear."

Pezeshki flashed a rotten smile. "Little wasted last night. Once in a while, I like a good buzz. Nothing serious."

"Once in a while?" Carolyn said. Pezeshki's teeth were poised to fall out of his skull. His skin was covered with sores. "You're twenty-six, but you look more like sixty-six. I'll bet you haven't slept in what, five days?"

"I've been a very bad boy," Pezeshki snarled, amber teeth bared. "Big fucking deal. So I spend a night or two in one of your cages. Then I'll find Jesus, see the error of my ways and repent like a son of a bitch." He leaned toward them, narrowed his gaze. "Let's cut the bullshit. You let me off with a stern warning, I grab the next stagecoach out of this hole, then I won't have to spend Christmas making nice with the old steplady."

"Let you go?" Ziggy said. "Not gonna happen. See, we don't appreciate crankheads running half naked on our beaches disturbing folks. And you'll be depressed wherever you go once the effects of that shit you've snorted or smoked wear off. May as well come down right here where we can keep an eye on you."

Ziggy calling Pezeshki a crankhead earned him another snarl.

Carolyn smiled. "Didn't I tell you he was excellent?"

"Fuck you," Pezeshki shot back. "And you too, asshole." He directed a venomous stare at Ziggy.

Carefully, slowly, Carolyn folded her hands, kept them visible. "Now that you've got that off your chest, Kyle, suppose you tell us what you did with the knapsack?"

"Wha—?" He furrowed his brow.

"Never mind the dumb, confused look," Ziggy said. "It won't wash here. You spoke to your stepmother, Rose, yesterday morning at her place of employment on Sutter Lane. She assumed that after she slammed the door on you that you'd left the premises, but we know that's not how it went."

"Huh?"

"Rhodes scholar," Ziggy muttered.

Carolyn shot him a cautionary look, wanted to nudge his foot under the table but was afraid Pezeshki would pick up on the motion and flip out. Ziggy wasn't sleeping lately either, and his fuse was short. She wondered if she should have him leave, yet she craved the security his six-foot frame provided.

She kept her voice low and hoped Ziggy would take the hint. "You were seen moving in a huge hurry away from the property a good fifteen minutes later. What took you so long to leave the place, Kyle?"

"Can't blame a guy for wanting to stop and smell the roses." Another rancid smile.

"Not convincing," Carolyn said. "Try again."

"You're fucked in the head," he said, switching now to scratch at his other arm. "Do I look like a schoolboy to you? What would I be doing with a knapsack? Anyone who thinks they saw me with one is fucked, too."

"Here's how it went down," Ziggy said. His voice took on an impatient edge. "You were about an hour away from wanting to peel your skin off, so you needed cash. Your stepmother was tapped out, so she sent you away without your lunch money. You swing around behind the house, maybe figuring you'd break in later, maybe catch stepmom alone so you can put the touch on her again, get rough if you have to. Instead, you spot the shed, wonder if there's something inside worth stealing."

Pezeshki's stare was feral now, full of hate. His lip curled. "It's just like I said. You're fucked, man."

"No," Ziggy said, opening an eight by ten envelope he'd had in front of him since entering the room. "You're the one who's fucked. You went into the shed with your size ten Doc Martens." He held up a copy of the footprint. "You glanced at the poor white-faced bastard who was hanging from the rafters, but you were like a vulture picking at a carcass. I'll bet you searched his pockets then you spotted the knapsack. Easier to grab it and run instead of rifling through it in the shed. After all, it didn't smell too pleasant in there."

Pezeshki stopped fidgeting. The air in the small room stilled. The silence stretched for maddening minutes. Carolyn's nerve endings sparked, on high alert for the strung-out man's next move. A tweaking meth user posed a serious threat to anyone within range, mood swings shifting from affable to volatile in the time it took to twitch twice. The only thing worse than a tweaker was a silent tweaker. If Kyle's paranoid delusions took over, Pezeshki could be across the table in seconds, his ragged fingernails at her eyes.

Carolyn was both relieved and disgusted when Pezeshki slouched in his chair, crossed his ankles and said, "Who gives a shit about some knapsack? Dude was already dead."

"I give a shit, Kyle," Carolyn said, her tone gentle. "That knapsack wasn't yours. Neither is that Giants cap you're wearing." It was Pezeshki running down the street, his straggly locks tucked under a baseball cap that twigged Joshua's memory. He hadn't been wearing the cap when he'd argued with Rose.

"On top of locking you up for disturbing the peace and indecent exposure, we can add theft and tampering with evidence at a possible crime scene. I'd prefer to cut you a little slack."

She needed to stand. Her hip was starting to ache again. Alternating heat and cold packs during the night had eased her symptoms, but she was due for another dose of ibuprofen. A slow walk about the room would help some, but she knew she couldn't risk it. Any movement might have appeared suspicious to Pezeshki and caused him to combust. The equilibrium in the room was tenuous enough. She settled for a nearly imperceptible shift in her chair and when Kyle's glance flickered to the ceiling, she shot Ziggy a grimace.

"I believe Sergeant Latham has asked you twice now about the knapsack," Ziggy prompted. "Tell us where it is, and we might be able to let our memories slide about your naked romp on the beach."

What started out as a bored sigh from Pezeshki turned into a sputum-wracked cough. Carolyn half expected to see a tooth fly across the room.

Between spasms, Pezeshki managed to gasp, "There was no fucking knapsack."

"Think, Kyle," Carolyn said. "A navy knapsack. With a book inside. Some designer jeans, a few T-shirts, some cash."

Pezeshki shook his head, face turning red. Eventually, the coughing ceased and he said, "I'm telling you, there wasn't any knapsack. The dude's clothes were in a pile on the floor. I checked his pockets like you said. I sure as hell didn't find any cash."

"No wallet?" Carolyn asked. That couldn't be. Ishiguro said Yoshi likely had several hundred dollars. Plus the boy had a passport and birth certificate, neither of which was found in his bedroom.

"No wallet. Guy didn't have a cent with him. Lissen, I could use a little exercise. And maybe some Gatorade. Been cooped up here a long time." Pezeshki sat up straight and eyed the door, blinking like a man in a sandstorm. His foot tapped a furious beat.

"This look like a health club to you?" Ziggy said. "You trying to tell us you didn't find a passport? A set of keys?"

Another head shake. Ziggy and Carolyn exchanged looks. A pair of Diesel straight-leg jeans was missing from Yoshi's closet, and though Ishiguro couldn't swear to it, he thought a black hoodie and long-sleeved Gap T-shirt were gone as well. The James Dean book hadn't surfaced either.

Because they'd been in the knapsack. Yoshi had packed them because he was running away. To meet his savior. He hadn't been planning to die. But the killer had taken Yoshi's clothes, his wallet, his book. Someone intent on achieving an autoerotic high wouldn't need to tote such things along.

"I scored nothing from the kid," Pezeshki said, and sounded some pissed about it.

"Okay, Kyle. Tell you what. You come downstairs with us. We'll get you a decent meal, make sure you're safe and comfortable. If we—"

Ziggy dragged his chair away from the table and turned toward the door. Too sudden. Too much noise.

Pezeshki was on him like a fired bullet. Carolyn heard an agonizing howl, unsure if it came from Pezeshki or Ziggy. The young man leaped on Ziggy's back, his arms locked across the sergeant's throat. His grip shifted quickly, hands now on either side of Ziggy's head as he tried to wrench his neck. This time she was certain the howl came from Ziggy who kicked back, met air. He bent forward, trying to flip Pezeshki over his head, but Carolyn was there, Taser aimed squarely at Pezeshki's upper thigh.

With a shrill animal scream, he collapsed as the current charged through him. A blur of activity followed, officers rushing with handcuffs, two of them carting Pezeshki to lockdown, his feet dragging like a limp marionette's. Ziggy rubbed his neck, uttering "Fuck me" with every exhaled breath. Between curses, Carolyn asked him if he was okay.

"Gotta tell you, C.L.," Ziggy said when he composed himself and tucked in his shirt, "and hope you don't take this the wrong way, but I kind of like that Rambette part of you."

"Sweet talker," she said.

Carolyn had a pair of officers do Dumpster duty in the commercial area closest to 3F House, but the navy knapsack didn't surface. She insisted Ziggy check in with his doctor to make sure he didn't have whiplash or worse. She planned to throw every charge she could at Kyle Pezeshki but sadly wondered how many of them would stick and for how long. She knew Pezeshki would eventually end up in jail for the long haul and that the prison health-care system would be obligated to provide a set of veneers to replace the eroding dental work inside his meth mouth.

No surprise that Chad Malvern had tried to steer Carolyn clear of Pezeshki on the street the night before, Pezeshki who had supposedly once worked for Chad's father. How easily the lie had been uttered. Carolyn dry-swallowed two ibuprofen, grabbed her jacket and headed out to the parking lot, imagining the verbal whipping she would get when she told Keith Malvern that his son Chad wouldn't be accompanying him on his Christmas trip to Anguilla.

CHAPTER 49

Keith Malvern threatened Carolyn with a lawsuit. He would have her job, he blustered to anyone who would listen. Preventing his son Chad from enjoying his island vacation was a perversion of justice, a vindictive movement on the part of those jealous of the Malverns' good fortune. All this fuss for a trumped-up drug-trafficking charge. Why would a boy who had everything need to sell drugs, the senior Malvern wanted to know. Carolyn suggested that was a question Keith should ask his son. Abandoning the spirit of the holiday season, Carolyn wished she could run over the blowhard with his own Hummer. Glad tidings. And to all a good night.

By the time Malvern father and son were to have boarded their flight, Carolyn had half a dozen witnesses willing to testify that Chad was the key supplier of drugs to The Powell Academy, the private school he attended, and the local high school as well. She was certain there would be more who were eager to topple the privileged kid from his perch, but she would save those connections for another day, if she needed them.

For now, Malvern senior and junior would have to step to the back of the bus.

Back of the bus. Catch the bus. Carolyn was free-associating now, thoughts rapidly rolling forward. To where? She hated that odious CTB euphemism for suicide, as if choosing death could ever be as simple as dropping the correct change into a slot. Choosing death.

A spark there. Why hadn't she thought of it before? Carolyn wheeled her chair closer to her desk, poised her fingers over the keyboard and typed in “Hemlock Society.” Within moments, she learned that the society had changed its name to the more empathetic “Compassion and Choices” and that the group had a chapter in Oregon. She clicked on the link, skimmed the mission statement, and read about the peaceful and humane deaths of its clients. Others received better pain management or were referred to hospice care. During the previous year, the society claimed it had prevented seven violent suicides, those individuals having a change of heart after working with supportive volunteers culled from area physicians, social workers, clergy, attorneys and palliative care workers.

Carolyn scrolled through a few newsletters and read about the annual dinner and fundraiser, but when she scanned the information under the “Services and Volunteer” heading, she stopped short.

Compassion and Choices would provide a qualified person to be present at the time of a person’s death.

A duty tailor-made for the Monitor.

How many volunteers did the organization have?

It was then that Carolyn noticed the darkened sidebar to the right of the screen. A list of the society’s directors and advisors.

Son of a bitch.

She reached for the phone.

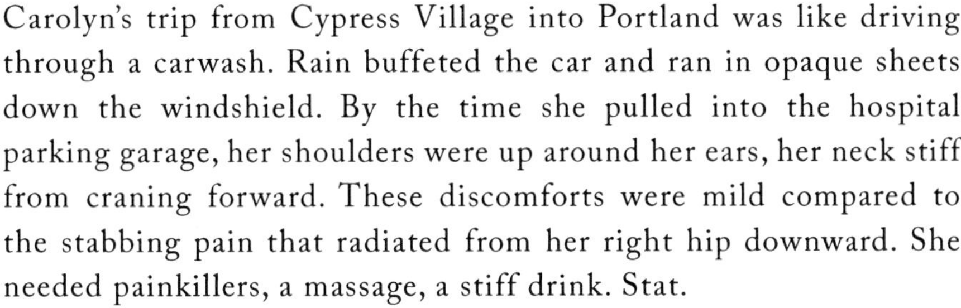

Carolyn’s trip from Cypress Village into Portland was like driving through a carwash. Rain buffeted the car and ran in opaque sheets down the windshield. By the time she pulled into the hospital parking garage, her shoulders were up around her ears, her neck stiff from craning forward. These discomforts were mild compared to the stabbing pain that radiated from her right hip downward. She needed painkillers, a massage, a stiff drink. Stat.

Brady Field was waiting in his office, a small square room that was the antithesis of his home surroundings. The space was replete with clutter. In/Out trays on his desk and credenza were stacked with files. Various diplomas, certificates and framed awards highlighting Field’s charity work formed rectangular mosaics along one wall. Medical texts filled two floor-to-ceiling shelves on either side of his window. Still for all the paraphernalia, the room was organized. Carolyn had no doubt that Field could put his hands on a particular file or journal in moments.

"Must be something incredibly important to bring you out on such a wretched night, Sergeant Latham," Field said, glancing through horizontal blinds before offering Carolyn a seat.

She settled carefully into an upholstered tub chair, adjusted her position to relieve pressure on her hip. She shrugged her jacket from her shoulders and said, "Yes. There's been another death."

Field, still in scrubs and looking exhausted, sat as well. "Someone from the website? Not another suicide ..."

"We're not sure." She removed an envelope from her jacket pocket and slid a photograph of Yoshi across the desk. "Recognize him?"

Field examined the picture and frowned. "Never seen him before."

"His name is Yoshitomo Tagawa. You might know him better as Jim Stark."

The doctor's eyes widened.

"I see the name is familiar to you."

"Of course. Stark was one of the forum's regular posters. Very depressed, from what I recall. And a social isolate. I think I first spotted Stark's messages some time in August."

"That would be right. He moved here from Japan with his uncle in the middle of the summer."

"He seemed to form a bond with some of the others, especially someone named Nightshade. Stark wrote a lot about dying, about how he was ready to go, but some members had their doubts and thought he was just posturing for attention. At other times he wrote about his broken heart, the things that made him saddest. Sergeant, how did Stark die?"

Carolyn looked hard at Field, searching his tired face for some hint that he was toying with her, that he knew full well how Yoshi died because he'd been there. His expression revealed nothing except fatigue.

"He was found hanging in a garden shed. On Friday."

Field squinted in concentration then cocked an eyebrow. "The eighteenth. I was in surgery that day. Quadruple by-pass. Then I had a late dinner with a colleague."

Carolyn made note of the doctor's zealous rush to alibi himself. She also recorded the name of his dinner companion and shifted uncomfortably in her chair. "Actually, Dr. Field, although we found Yoshi on Friday, we know he disappeared from his uncle's apartment much earlier in the week. We suspect that he died on Monday. Do you remember where you were that night?"

Field opened the centre desk drawer and pulled out a day planner. He flipped several pages then traced his finger along, saying, "Monday the fourteenth? I was home."

"Make any phone calls? Have company?"

"If you're asking if anyone can verify that I was in my living room reading, the answer is no. Unless you're willing to consider Jezebel a credible witness." He smiled.

Was he trying to charm her?

She smiled back. "Unfortunately, law enforcement holds the view that a person's cat is highly biased in its owner's favor. It would be more helpful to have a verbal acknowledgement of your whereabouts."

"A pawprint won't do?"

"Afraid not."

Field stood and walked around behind Carolyn. She turned to look as he opened a small fridge that nested in a recessed alcove. "Soft drink? Juice?"

She accepted a bottle of orange juice and was surprised when Field brought not only that but an ice pack as well.

"This may help," he said. "How long have you had sciatica?"

"Three years."

"How are you managing the pain?"

"Anti-inflammatories. Cold packs. Hot packs. Massage. Yoga. Screaming fits."

"They're doing marvelous work with endoscopic discectomies now. Local anesthetic, no stitches—you're in and out in about an hour with nothing more than a tiny bandage. Much less invasive than surgery, and at a fraction of the cost." Field returned to his chair and spoke at length about the latest updates in spinal decompression therapy as well. He gave a detailed discourse about the time commitment, the success rate, the price tag. "You could feel like a new person within days. I can put you in touch with a specialist if you like."

"Thanks. I'll let you know."

Carolyn tucked the cold pack under her thigh, wondering about Field's sudden concern for her health and why he was running off at the mouth.

"I wish I could be of more help, Sergeant, but everything I know about Jim Stark I learned from my computer screen. You've got access to the same information. Stark stopped posting to the forum over a week ago, but I got no indication that he was planning anything so drastic. He just said goodbye and made some cryptic comment warning the others about Samaritans. I didn't really understand what he was getting at."

"We believe now that the person you knew as Jim Stark was lured from his apartment to meet someone. There are some inconsistencies at the site where he was found, inconsistencies that lead us to believe Stark ... Yoshitomo Tagawa may have been murdered."

Field hung his head. Sorrow? Or was he trying to prevent her from seeing him smirk? He covered his face with his hands. Beautifully formed hands, Carolyn noted. Hands that had just saved a life in the OR. Hands that also belonged to Yoshi's savior?

He looked up again and met Carolyn's gaze. "You think one of the other correspondents is a killer?"

"Let's just say we're open to the possibility."

"I need to shut that message board down."

"There will be time for that—"

"No, Sergeant," he said firmly, "I have to shut it down. Don't you see? If someone is using those people as ... prey, then we have to keep the others safe. Make no mistake, I still believe in a person's right to choose when he wants to die and how, but all that is secondary now. A murderer trolling the site looking for victims is as horrible as it gets."

Field interlaced his fingers over his mouth and closed his eyes. A gesture of genuine pity? Or was Field feeling the walls closing in around him, planning his next move?

At once his eyes snapped open. "Is it possible someone's trying to set me up, make it appear that I'm using the site to kill people?"

"Who for instance?"

"You spoke to her yourself, Sergeant. My ex-wife wouldn't be above exacting revenge. The news of my affair with Stacey circulated through every bistro and charity event in the South. Rebecca claimed she couldn't hold her head up anywhere for months afterward. Just because we're divorced doesn't mean Rebecca has swept those memories away."

"To be honest, Dr. Field, Rebecca Holland didn't strike me as the type to be so conniving. Manipulating all those people across the country into killing themselves, then murdering Yoshi, just to get even with you? It might play on a movie-of-the-week, but in real life? I can't see it. It's too elaborate."

"But you can see me in the role of murderer, am I right, Sergeant?"

"You're closer to the front of the line, yes."

Especially since Ziggy had located a store in downtown Portland that sold *bukkake*. The owner had been shown Ishiguro's photo and was adamant he'd never seen the man before. He lingered longer over Field's picture, unable to confirm or deny that Field had been in his store to purchase porn. It was possible that he'd seen him before, but he couldn't swear to it.

"No one can fault you for your lack of candor," Field said. "Now let me tell you something about my ex-wife, Sergeant Latham. Maybe six to eight months after she hit it big with her event-planning business, another woman came to Atlanta to give Rebecca some competition. Nothing wrong with a little healthy competition, right? And there was plenty of business in the area for both companies to make a nice living."

Carolyn already saw where this was headed. Making a nice living wouldn't be enough for Rebecca Holland. She was the local star, and she intended to remain a star. Much easier to do if no one else was twinkling.

"So both companies bid on the same event. It was an AIDS benefit. Huge. Some Hollywood celebrities were planning to attend ... anyway, Rebecca didn't win the bid. Then what do you suppose happens? The limo that was to transport the keynote speaker got a flat tire, making him an hour late. About half the guests developed raging cases of salmonella. Before the meal even began, the wine ran out. Someone had phoned the liquor store and changed the amount of the order."

"Are you saying your ex-wife sabotaged the event?"

"I wouldn't be able to prove it if you asked me to, but Rebecca's response to the fiasco was a philosophical 'well, if they'd picked me in the first place, none of this would have happened.'"

"That doesn't mean she was responsible."

"It doesn't mean she wasn't, either. You had to have been there, Sergeant. She gloated over the collapse of the other woman's business. Let's just say my ardor toward Rebecca cooled after that. Nothing dampens one's desire more than a woman who'll smile sweetly while she's feasting on someone's carcass."

"Yet you stayed."

Field nodded. "Rebecca was pregnant. Regardless of what Rebecca told you, my relationship with Stacey didn't doom our marriage. It was dead in the water long before we lost Kara."

Carolyn directed a sympathetic nod at the doctor. Then she asked, "What can you tell me about Lyndon Kerr?"

For a split second Field's eyes widened. Just as quickly he answered, "He's dedicated. A hard worker. He'll be a fine doctor."

"Heavy work loads, these interns?"

Field smiled. "Brutal. I'm glad those days are behind me."

"Not much sleep. Lots of studying. Plays hell with a young doctor's love life, I would imagine."

"The focus is on the work. It has to be."

"So where would Lyndon Kerr find time to act as an advisor to Compassion and Choices?"

Field shrugged. "Community service. It's an admirable quality. We all make the time for causes we believe in."

"Apparently Kerr admires you very much," Carolyn told him. "Idolizes you, even."

Another smile, this one an attempt at bashful modesty.

"Do you know whether Lyndon Kerr has been present for anyone's final exit?"

"To my knowledge, he hasn't, but then, you'd have to ask him. I wouldn't think he'd necessarily confide in me about that."

"Funny, I think he would. You're his mentor, his Svengali. I should think he'd come to you immediately if he attended someone's ... deliverance."

"He's said nothing to me." Field paused, his studious gaze penetrating. "You've already asked him about it, haven't you, Sergeant?"

Carolyn nodded. "He denied participating in any of Compassion's deaths."

"But you don't believe him."

"I don't believe anybody. Tell me, Dr. Field, why didn't you tell me that you were one of the organization's directors?"

The cardiologist's smug reply came as no surprise. "You didn't ask me."

By the time Carolyn left the hospital her mind was reeling. Brady Field had tried to deflect her suspicions not once, but twice; first, by bringing her an ice pack and talking about her condition, an act of consideration she hadn't been prepared for; and second, when he'd thrown Carolyn that bone about Rebecca Holland. Was the media-savvy event planner as calculating as Field had portrayed her? Did her pride run so deep that she would stop at nothing to destroy whomever tried to topple her from her pedestal?

On the phone, Holland had seemed likeable, and definitely not a fan of her former husband. But murder? No. Carolyn didn't see a woman's hand in this. It would have taken strength to hoist Yoshi up in that shed, and someone with a much more sinister agenda than merely exacting revenge on a cheating spouse. Unless Rebecca Holland was completely unglued ...

My wife gets what she wants, Sergeant. Brady Field's parting words.

Worth a look to see whether Rebecca Holland, or someone resembling her, had boarded a flight for the west coast in the past week. Neither Robb Northrup nor Wes Bertram had solid alibis for the night that Yoshi died. Neither did millions of others in the Pacific Northwest, Brady Field and Lyndon Kerr among them. Fine job she was doing narrowing the list of suspects. Another cheery thought—Christmas Eve was quickly approaching, and Carolyn still hadn't bought a single gift.

She steered the Explorer for Cypress Village, only to have her gray mood turn solid black by the sight of Nadia Willes, her ex-husband's lover, emerging from a boutique and looking radiant, her swollen belly beautifully rounding the front of her bright red coat.

CHAPTER 50

THE CHOIR AT ST. BRIGID'S ended midnight Mass with an exuberant "Hark the Herald Angels Sing" complete with trumpet accompaniment. It was impossible not to be swept away in the gloriousness of it all—the birth of a savior and hope for the future.

A savior of another kind crouched in wait, crooning promises of eternal peace and salvation. Even on Christmas Eve, the Monitor wasn't far from Carolyn's thoughts.

Back at the cabin with Paige and Joshua, Carolyn felt reality close in once more, and the future bore down with all the bleakness of the immediate past. The three drank a toast to the memory of Spencer Rowan, another to Yoshi. Then they just drank, period. The new year would be better. It had to be.

By the time they finished opening their presents, it was two thirty. Paige offered Carolyn the guest room, but she declined. "I'll be getting up early tomorrow, and besides, I need a change of clothes. Can't go to work in a skirt. I'll never live it down."

The day shift was supposed to belong to Ziggy, but Carolyn insisted on taking it. Amanda was still grieving deeply for Melissa Waller and needed both parents near her.

"We'll save you some turkey," Paige said. "Get back here when you can."

Parker seemed to agree with Paige and planted a doggy-breath lick on Carolyn's chin in appreciation for his Christmas treats, a soft chew toy and a tube of canine toothpaste.

Joshua walked her to the door. "I always figured Chad Malvern was a little too good to be true, but when I read Fallon's article about his arrest, I was blind-sided. His father must be furious."

"He is, but not at his son."

Carolyn noticed Joshua's words starting to slur. His eyes looked hollowed out; they were heavy-lidded and ringed with dark circles.

"I'm sure Keith Malvern will be playing the 'not my kid' card," he said. "His time would be better spent trying to really get to know his son instead of jetting all over the place."

"If he heard you say that, he'd accuse you of jealousy."

"Small wonder that Gavin Polley hated Chad, what with his sister OD'ing last year. Yoshi wasn't impressed with Chad, either." The mention of Yoshi's name deepened Joshua's frown.

"Hurts like hell, doesn't it?" Carolyn said, touching her brother on the shoulder. "This whole thing with Yoshi."

"I still don't get it, Carl." He reached into the closet for her coat. "That kid was determined not to leave Ishiguro's apartment. I've been wracking my brain to figure out what could have changed his mind."

She slipped her arms into the sleeves. "Maybe he didn't leave. Maybe he wasn't lured at all and his uncle is dirty up to his Ph.D. in this. His resentment of the kid was pretty clear. Maybe he found a way to incapacitate Yoshi somehow, get him to that shed to throw suspicion away from him and onto you."

"You believe that?"

"I don't know what I believe anymore, Josh. It's late, and my brain feels like pudding."

"You okay to drive?"

She nodded and buttoned her coat, slipped on gloves. "At this hour, I'll probably be the only car on the road."

Joshua reached for the doorknob then stopped. "I keep thinking about Yoshi's letter to me. How he said he'd found his savior."

"Don't torment yourself, Josh."

"I'm not. No matter which way I look at it, I keep coming back to the girlfriend."

"Who? Ishiguro's mystery date?"

"No. Yoshi's. He worshipped Aoki, was devastated by their break-up. The end of their relationship is what drove Yoshi into his hikikomori prison. But if Aoki reappeared suddenly, promising to reconnect with him ... I can see Yoshi leaving the apartment to meet her. His savior."

"No," Carolyn said, suddenly wide awake. She slapped a gloved hand against the wall. "Not Aoki. Someone pretending to be Aoki. Of course. That's how it was done."

"How—? Oh God, you mean online." Joshua rubbed his forehead, as if the action might erase the lines of worry that had etched there. "You're telling me that by confiding in his cyber friends, Yoshi opened the door to a killer?"

"That sick son of a bitch," was all Carolyn would say. She hurried to the Explorer before Joshua could ask any more questions.

At home Carolyn was wired. She peeled off dark tights and changed from her knit skirt and sweater ensemble into pajamas. Instead of heading for bed, she brewed some tea and booted up her computer. Yoshi had told someone about Aoki. In the next day or so, Ziggy and his hacker friend would discover she was right. If the offshore ISP continued to ignore the subpoena, there were other ways to gain information. One way or another, Carolyn intended to get the bus riders' pseudonyms. Then the Monitor, or whatever he was calling himself this week, would be flushed from his hole.

The cyberworld didn't take a night off, not even on Christmas Eve. Carolyn checked her personal e-mail first, opening a greeting card from Ted Tarrant in Marblehead. The chorus line of high-kicking Santas raised a smile, one of the few she'd been able to summon in days. Gregg's "Best of the Season" card had gone straight into her recycling bin a week ago, the cheesy dime-store sparkles leaving a glittery trail on her dark shirt. She deleted a message from Betty F. who promised unlimited sexual rapture and another from wpzqthrbv, whose special interest was penile enhancement. Comfort and joy, indeed.

She clicked on Favorites and the busriders.com forum appeared. The posters were out in full force. Several of the regulars wondered about Killcrazy from Belgium. He had been absent from the message board since December 12th, so speculation was rampant that he may have succeeded in his plan to have someone murder him. Someone else provided the web address for the *De Standaard*, one of Brussels' newspapers and suggested looking in the December 16th archives, in which a first-page article cited the tragic death of a young man who'd been run over by a taxi on *rue Montagnes aux Herbes Potagères*, near the Grand Place. A witness to the horrible accident claimed he'd seen the victim, 29-year-old Jan Veldhoen, not fifteen minutes earlier in one of the city's most popular beer cafés. The name of the café—*La Mort Subite*. Sudden Death. The witness also claimed it appeared the victim had been pushed. No one else could corroborate the story.

The forum was rife with messages from those ready to end it all. Carolyn typed her own message.

Hello Everyone,

So it's Christmas Eve. I spent the evening with my brother. Not exactly my pick for a hot date, but then again, I haven't had a hot date in so long I wouldn't recognize one. Who wants to be with someone who's in constant agony? My entire body has turned against me, pain shooting down my legs so often now I can't remember what it's like to be normal. What's worse is knowing that my ex is celebrating the holidays with his new family—his younger lover and a precious baby girl. Did I mention there's another child on the way? And did I mention how badly I wanted a child and how he refused to give me one? In short, my life sucks and I'm just sick, sick, sick of it.

It's over for me. No hesitation. No turning back.

I need your help, riders. I'm ready to go.

Fading Away, Fading to Black.

It was settled then. Carolyn was going to catch the bus.

CHAPTER 51

JUST BEFORE NOON ON CHRISTMAS Day, Sergeant Zygmunt Takacs appeared in the doorway of Carolyn's office. His crimson necktie, upon closer inspection, was decorated with miniature reindeer.

"Very festive indeed," Carolyn said as Ziggy wrapped her in a hug. "Merry Christmas, Zig."

"You too, C.L. Brought you something." From the inside of his topcoat he removed a silver flask. "One look at you tells me it's a brandy kind of day. Be my guest."

The thought of drinking more alcohol after last night's bottles of wine didn't hold tremendous appeal, but then Carolyn reasoned that most people's teeth were furry around the holidays. She uncapped the flask and poured a mouthful into the silver shot glass. "To the good guys," she said and knocked the brandy back. The liquor burned all the way down and nearly back up again. She wondered how people could drink the stuff and how they distinguished between brandy and paint thinner.

"To the good guys," Ziggy repeated and drank from the flask. "Can't stay long," he told her. "Ilona and Amanda are waiting in the car. Off to the outlaws for lunch and to unwrap more useless gifts like this tie they got me last year. Now do you see why I carry the booze?"

"You love Ilona's parents. Regardless of their taste in neckties."

"They're good people," he admitted. "Now quick. Fill me in on what's going on around here."

She thought of her conversations with Northrup, Bertram and Field, and her more recent web plea for help. Would the Monitor be fooled? Had she sounded desperate enough to convince the madman to hatch another mass suicide plan?

"Nothing that can't wait until tomorrow," she told Ziggy. "It's Christmas, for crying out loud. Your family's waiting."

"I hate the thought of you being here," Ziggy said, enveloping her in another hug. "You're family too, you know."

Reluctantly she gave him a gentle shove, feeling her mouth tremble, her body's signal that a good cry wasn't far off. "That's the nicest thing anybody's said to me in a long time." She cleared her throat and added, "Wish Ilona and Amanda a Merry Christmas for me."

"Will do. You okay?"

"Yes. Now go. That's an order."

"Want me to leave the magic elixir with you?" He held up the flask.

"I wouldn't dream of depriving you. Have a great day, Zig. See you in the a.m."

"You could come by our place after you're finished for the day," he offered. "We should be home around seven."

"Thanks, but I'll probably go over to Joshua's." Or straight to bed with a thick book and Pookie Bear.

"You know where we are if you change your mind."

"Will you get out of here already?" She shooed him to the door and this time, he went.

She turned quickly away from his retreating back, feeling rotten that he was leaving, ashamed that she resented his family for tearing him away, and miserable that she couldn't remember the last time anyone had held her, really held her. She swiped angrily at a tear that had the audacity to escape.

Nose to the grindstone, she told herself. She had work to do, so the self pity would have to wait. Or be buried altogether, if she could manage it.

She reread the files they'd amassed on the victims, both at the Aerie and the diner, and the five who had died in Washington State. She wasn't sure what she expected to leap out at her, but was disappointed when nothing did. Hours later, her vision starting to blur, Carolyn stopped for a coffee break and a few trips up and down the stairs to loosen her aching body.

At four o'clock she punched in the cell phone number that Ishiguro had given to her and connected instantly with Aoki Noda. It was now morning in Japan, the day after Christmas. Carolyn explained who she was and that she needed to ask some questions about Yoshitomo Tagawa.

"Yoshi?" the quiet voice at the other end said.

Carolyn detected a sour note at the mention of Yoshi's name.

"I have not seen him in over a year," Aoki said. "He is hikkii. I even heard a rumor he's not in the country anymore."

"That's right. Yoshi is in America. He's been living with his uncle."

"Well. He always wanted to go to the States. He said we would go together someday. But of course, Yoshi was always saying things like that. Everything was 'someday.'"

"You didn't believe him?"

A bored sigh crossed the ocean. "Yoshi made many promises."

Promises that were only good if they took effect immediately. Carolyn suspected Aoki wasn't the patient type.

"You are a police woman?" the girl said. "Is Yoshi in trouble with the law?"

"No, Yoshi's done nothing wrong. You said you hadn't seen him in some time. What about phone calls? E-mails? Text messages? Anything like that?"

"No." Aoki laughed as if talking to Yoshi was beneath her. "Yoshi still wanted to be friends, but such things are ... difficult. And I'm seeing someone else now."

"Someone older, more sophisticated, I bet," Carolyn said, woman to woman.

"Yes. He bought me diamond earrings for Christmas. Two carats." As an afterthought, she said, "We're in love."

"Congratulations." An idea struck. "Tell me, Aoki, did Yoshi ever buy you gifts? Jewelry?"

Another derisive laugh. "Once. A ring. A silly silver band with a cheap red stone. Red like blood, he said. Because I was in his heart."

"That seems like a nice thought. It sounds like Yoshi cared for you very much."

"So he always said."

"Do you still have the ring?"

"Of course not. I gave it back to Yoshi when we broke up. Sergeant, I'm confused. Why are you calling me?"

"Just wanted to know whether you'd heard from Yoshi recently. And I appreciate you telling me about the ring. It's very helpful."

"Helpful? How? You told me Yoshi has done nothing wrong."

"He hasn't. Aoki, Yoshi is dead."

There was a brief pause then the girl said, "Oh. That is too bad."

For all the emotion the phrase carried, Aoki may as well have uttered, "The time in Japan is eight a.m." Once more, Carolyn felt overcome by sadness. Yoshi, even at his moodiest and surliest, didn't deserve a girl like this. And his heart hadn't been broken; it had been sliced, diced, and fricasseed.

As soon as Carolyn hung up, she was on the phone to Ken Ishiguro, asking him whether he had ever seen a silver ring with a red stone among Yoshi's possessions.

His response was a curt negative.

Carolyn bit her lip. Flies with honey, she told herself. "Mr. Ishiguro, I know this is a difficult time for you, but the police really need your help. If you could search Yoshi's room, turn it upside down if you have to. We have to locate that ring."

"I have already cleaned the room. The clothes are in boxes to be donated to the poor. Also the video games, the CDs. Someone is picking up these things tomorrow. I saw no ring."

Ishiguro was nothing if not efficient and certainly eager to reclaim his apartment. They weren't even Yoshi's clothes any longer, but *the* clothes. *The* video games. *The* CDs.

Carolyn squinted through Venetian blinds to the large room beyond her office. Chloe Grier, newly split from her realtor boyfriend, was soloing this Christmas, too. "Better still, Mr. Ishiguro, to save you from further unpleasantness, I'll send one of my officers over. Sometimes teenagers have very good hiding places for things they value." Carolyn surmised that once Ishiguro saw the leggy blonde, his disposition would mellow. "You can be expecting Officer Grier within the hour," she told him and for emphasis added, "You'll like her."

She didn't give him a chance to protest.

After describing Yoshi's friendship ring to Chloe, she said, "Go through every one of the boy's pockets, flip the mattress, upend his dresser. Pretend you're looking for a grain of sand."

Finding the ring among the packaged possessions was slim, Carolyn thought. She didn't think Yoshi would have thrown it out. He was sentimental, a romantic. The ring had been precious to him, a reminder of what he'd shared with Aoki. He would have brought it to the States. And if he believed he was going to meet Aoki the night he died, he would have taken the ring with him. The importance of sending Chloe on the wild goose chase was not in hopes that she would find the ring, but that she wouldn't find it.

Carolyn descended the steps to the basement where Kyle Pezeshki was in lockup and surveying his diseased gums in an aluminum mirror. Carolyn grilled him. He denied knowing anything about a ring. She grilled him some more. There was no goddamned ring and no goddamned knapsack, he hollered.

She thought as much. Because the Monitor had taken it. Along with Yoshi's wallet and other possessions. Autoerotic thrill seekers didn't bring such things along for the ride.

Ziggy phoned late in the day from his in-laws' place. "Big trouble here, C.L. Karaoke machine's come out. Can you hear it?"

"'Jingle Bell Rock,'" she said. "Not bad. But it sounds like they could use a tenor. How come you're not joining in on the fun?"

"They wore me out with 'The Twelve Days of Christmas.' I got my pipers and drummers all screwed up, so I thought I'd sit this one out. How's it going?"

"Checking up on me?"

"If I don't, who will?"

He had a point there. "I'm fine," she insisted. "All's quiet here, just the way we like it."

When he pressed her, she filled him in on her conversation with Aoki Noda and told him that Chloe Grier was tossing Ishiguro's apartment looking for the missing ring.

"She won't find it," Ziggy said.

"I know."

"What are the odds it was in the backpack and that creep Pezeshki hocked it for his dope?"

"Been there, covered it. No ring."

"There's something you're not telling me."

"What? I already wished you Merry Christmas. Get back to your party, Zig."

"I haven't worked with a stranger for five years. I know when you're withholding. Give it to me straight, C.L."

Today, tomorrow, what difference did it make? "Yours truly, Fading Away, is feeling quite despondent, it being Christmas and everything. She's put out the all-call for some help catching the bus."

Ziggy groaned. "Ah, Mother of God, you didn't. We don't have time to set this up."

"We're running out of time, period. This guy may have become hands-on. You think he's going to stop? The new year's coming, Zig. I won't start it off with another stack of bodies. I can't."

"Jesus, Mary and Joseph."

"I'm calling a meeting for first thing tomorrow. We organize then we wait. My guess is that it won't take the Monitor long to bite."

"Question is, who gets thrown out as bait?"

"Up for discussion in the a.m. Right now, try to forget you're a cop and go enjoy what's left of today."

Advice Carolyn couldn't follow herself. Chloe Grier returned from Ishiguro's as Carolyn was locking her office. The ring was nowhere, and if anyone knew how to toss an apartment, it was Grier. She looked everywhere but up Ishiguro's ass, she said, though she suspected the professor might have been open to the idea. Ishiguro was one horny toad. Any sign of grief for his nephew? Carolyn asked her. Not so's you'd notice, Chloe said.

That Ishiguro was one horny toad was supported further by his DVD collection. Carolyn had spent a few hours watching segments from the man's Japanese films. She expected there would be porn among the stack, and Ishiguro didn't disappoint. But one film, "Jisastsu Sakuru," made the brandy Carolyn had swallowed much earlier in the day return sour to the back of her throat. Filmed in 2002, the movie opened with a graphic scene of fifty-four teenage girls throwing themselves on the subway tracks at Tokyo's Shinjuku station. Blood and gore spattered everywhere, on the tile walls, on the bystanders' faces. A victim's leg became a horrific projectile through the train's windshield. When Carolyn Googled the title on the Net, she found its translation: "Suicide Club." It was a cult classic. And Ishiguro found it entertaining. Otherwise, why keep it?

When Carolyn first met Ishiguro, she had been annoyed by him. Then angered. Now she found him disturbing. Dark. Complex. And Chloe Grier, who'd met all kinds, didn't have much use for him either.

Exhausted and sickened, Carolyn called Joshua from her car, said that it had been a long day and that she was going straight home. She'd have a turkey sandwich with them in a day or two. Love to Paige and Parker.

Pulling into her driveway, Carolyn wished she'd left some lights on as she usually did. She knew better. Her place had that "come rob me" look about it, but when she'd left for work, her personal safety hadn't been in her mind. Now it was.

Fear coiled around her, and she welcomed its embrace. Fear was a good teacher. It made her wary, every reflex poised. She would savor her fear, keep it tightrope taut. With any luck, it would keep her alive.

Living alone, she sometimes worried about a stranger launching at her from the shadowy shrubs, felt nervous as she imagined a gloved hand clamping across her mouth when she entered her condo. Now she was more afraid of what was to come, knowing that soon she would revisit that dizzying precipice where a false baby step would lead to pain, to blackness, to nothing. She had taken a bullet once. To catch the Monitor, what would it cost her this time?

No one's in the bushes, she told herself, but still her skin prickled as she made her way up the sidewalk as if anticipating a blitzkrieg attack. None came. She turned her key in the lock. Her fingers trembled as she groped for the light switch, half expecting the cool caress of a silky scarf across her hand, one that would in seconds tighten around her neck. Instead, her living room was bathed in soft light. No masked intruder waited.

In the corner, the frail evergreen put on a brave face. She turned on her Christmas lights and found herself saying, "Congratulations. You made it." The tree had hung in there, most of its needles intact. A trooper.

Carolyn checked her voice mail, heard a whispered "Merry Christmas" from Gregg while young Gillian cooed for her daddy in the background. She erased the message and reached under the tree for one of her gifts from Joshua and Paige, a dog encyclopedia. She would thumb through it in bed, read about the various breeds and zero in on which would become her new companion. She would experience motherhood, one way or another.

Before she clicked off the living room light she checked the busriders.com web board again. Nothing new. Even the suicidal crowd was spending Christmas with someone. She was about to log off when she decided to check her e-mail. What she read on the screen made her breath catch in her throat.

I'm here for you, dear, as I always told you I would be. Within a week, your suffering will be at an end, and you will make your peaceful journey. Until you hear from me again, strength and patience,

The Monitor.

CHAPTER 52

THE SCREECHING OF BRAKES.

Severed limbs. Pandemonium. Geysers of blood.

A glorious spectacle of gore.

It would be quick, painless, certain. He had assured the riders of that. And the fools bought it.

A small group would be boarding this time, three newcomers to the website. Someone calling himself Dementia XXIV was driving up from Chula Vista and would arrive in Cypress Village later. He planned to check into a lovely seaside motel and spend the next few days watching videos, ordering take-out, practicing knots and writing letters. To family and friends, he had already apologized, saying the business trip that was calling him north during the holidays was unfortunately unavoidable. To his boss and co-workers, he spoke affectionately about a favorite cousin who had finally lost his war against cancer. He had driven away from his suburban storey-and-a-half the morning before with everyone's sympathy and/or wishes for a speedy return. He packed the necessities for a business trip/funeral—a dark suit, black shoes, his toiletries, a pair of pajamas. He threw his attaché case in the trunk, the large coil of baling wire tucked under a manila folder filled with blank paper. The bus riders were nothing if not thorough. There were two tense moments, Dementia had written on his last private message to the Monitor—the first when his wife handed him a half dozen of his favorite peanut butter cookies for the road, and the second when his daughter asked if Daddy was going to bring her any seashells from the ocean. When words wouldn't come, a hug would do, he'd written.

Dark Victory was going out as the last of the big spenders. He had already caught a plane to London and was staying at the Dorchester. From there he would jet to Paris for spa treatments followed by dinner at L'Atelier de Joël Robuchon. A Broadway show in New York was booked for the 29th, leaving him plenty of time to fly to the West coast and rendezvous with his fellow riders.

Fading Away, her physical agony unbearable now, had no such grand ambitions. She just wanted it over.

The continental United States has one hundred and forty thousand miles of rail line, and just as many railway crossings, making suicide by train difficult to prevent. While rare, the Monitor had read that commuter train engineers might see anywhere from three to twenty suicides during their careers. Death was not always instantaneous—he had lied about that. Nor was it always inevitable. Ten percent of those attempting to die on train tracks survived, often with horrific injuries. That would not be the case this time.

The possibility always existed that someone would change his mind. A case in the papers described a distraught man who had already stabbed himself before parking his vehicle on the tracks. As the train approached, the man bolted from his SUV. When the train struck his vehicle, it derailed, killing several passengers. The suicidal man survived to face ten charges of murder. A monumental screw-up.

Changing one's mind was against the rules. That was what baling wire was for.

As always, the instructions were clear. Memorize the directions to the final location. Wear black clothing. Dispose of all cell phones, erase e-mail, attract no unnecessary attention during your final hours. Make peace however you choose.

When the locomotive rounded the bend, it would be traveling at 15 mph, a far cry from the rocketing velocity of France's TGV or the Tokaido Shinkansen, but still fast enough to crush, to decapitate. He wondered if the passengers aboard the Scenic Coastal Dinner Train would appreciate ushering in their new year with a bang.

CHAPTER 53

IT RAINED FOR FOUR DAYS straight. The roads along the coast were black satin ribbons that made driving treacherous during the day, suicidal once darkness fell. The police scrambled to scenes of fender-benders and van rollovers, mostly teenagers coming home from parties. Though there were no fatalities, a considerable cross-section of lacerations, bruises and concussions kept hospital emergency rooms humming. Other than the party-hearty young, most were choosing to stay home, and retailers cursed the weather, complaining about the drastic slump in after-Christmas sales. On the positive side, Carolyn knew that when the weather was lousy, most criminals stayed inside too.

With one exception.

Carolyn felt deep in her bones that rain or shine, the Monitor would be anticipating New Year's Eve with the exhilaration of an adolescent embarking on a first sexual experience. She imagined him savoring every detail, priding himself on his meticulous planning, anticipating the horror that would result from a scheme so diabolical only a madman could conceive it. She wondered if he fantasized in color, if his senses went into overdrive. She wondered what he was thinking right now.

The plan was that Dementia XXIV, Dark Victory, and Fading Away would bind themselves to the tracks just beyond the curve south of the village, making sure to position their necks directly on the rails. Their dark clothing would render them nearly invisible. The conductor wouldn't see them in time to apply the emergency brake. Somewhere, off among the detritus of the adjacent wrecking yard, the Monitor would be lurking, listening to the clackety-clack of the approaching train, building to that moment when one of the trio might struggle against his bonds, scream at the inevitability of his fate—was that the drama racing inside the Monitor's head?

It wouldn't go that far. Long before Dementia produced the baling wire, the police would spot the Monitor's arrival, take him down. The police had driven by the death spot several times over the past days, changing vehicles, taking photographs, plotting strategy. They had sought and received permission from Hank Baylis, owner of Hank's Wreckers to conduct their surveillance on his property. The business was shutting down early on the 31st. The stake-out would be as smoothly choreographed as a ballroom dance, with everyone in place under cover of darkness well before the trio's scheduled rendezvous. Dirt bikes would be hidden under grease-stained tarps; an unmarked vehicle would be muddied up and driven into position alongside Baylis's shredder. A single road ran alongside the tracks—one way in, one way out. The Monitor could not escape.

On the morning of the 31st, Carolyn showered, cooked a full breakfast, listened to the news on the radio. Another normal working day. This time, though, when she went to her closet, she reached for a black turtleneck, black leggings, black shoes. A black jacket. To the mirror as she was leaving she said, "You look like a cat burglar."

The chief was allowing her six bodies—five from the High Risk Response Team plus Ziggy—and those bodies had been gearing up for what they were calling a slam dunk operation. During the earlier meeting, Carolyn quickly dispelled that notion. She reminded them of stake-outs that had gone wrong, of civilians needlessly injured by over-zealous cops. She trotted out newspaper headlines to drive her point home.

"Hey, C.L., what're you trying to do? Scare us?"

Carolyn directed her gaze to Bob "Toby" Tobias. "Yes. That's exactly what I'm trying to do. Let me remind you—there's no such thing as a slam dunk."

She remembered reading about a stake-out in Nebraska, another supposed slam dunk, one that had dragged on into the small hours of morning. A rookie had lasted for eight hours before nature called. Refusing her partner's suggestion to pee into the container he had brought along for such purposes, she exited the car and was slammed by a bullet that sheared off part of her kneecap. The modest cop still walked with a limp.

"Our Monitor is smart," Carolyn told the officers. "He's been preparing for this. So we have to be smarter, better prepared." She encouraged them to get plenty of rest, to eat properly. One of the enemies of any surveillance was lethargy. A stomach full of carbohydrates combined with hours of sitting in the dark dulled the senses and could put people in danger.

No more victims, she vowed.

As she locked her front door and prepared to join her team, she repeated the vow aloud.

CHAPTER 54

Hank Baylis's wrecking yard was a monster—forty acres of rusted, twisted, crushed metal and hollowed-out, burned-out vehicles. Carolyn and the crew she'd assembled had already spent days on the property, arriving separately in unmarked cars, donning safety glasses and hard hats provided by Baylis, who uttered cautionary words of wisdom. *Eyes in the back of your head aren't enough.* During both the day and night shift, the yard pulsed with danger—forklifts moving flattened stacks of vehicles, dump trunks carrying loads of pulverized metal, the front-end loader creeping forward on army tank wheels, its four-pronged claw swinging out and down to grab yet another mangled parcel to feed to the shredder. And always, the noise—a continuous, deafening chorus of pounding, screeching, and grinding, accompanied by a pervasive storm of dust and grit that peppered the air gray. Peril lurked underfoot as well in the form of decimated steel and aluminum. Baylis was right. Eyes in the back of your head weren't enough. Not by a long shot.

The Monitor had chosen his site well, Carolyn thought bitterly. The wrecking yard was a logistical nightmare. As if the vastness of the property wasn't enough, hiding places on the yard were also plentiful. A dozen corrugated buildings were scattered about. Colorful heaps of automobiles, flattened like playing cards, formed gigantic towers; between these, a labyrinth of walkways snaked in random patterns like bad pop art. Along the front of the property, railway tracks ran parallel to the road; on the other side of the tracks was a thickly wooded area. Tobias and Heath had spent the better part of the day before searching the woods, keeping Carolyn's pep talk as their mantra.

Think like the Monitor. Where would he hide? What would afford him the best view of his kill?

Most of the trees were mature pines, their lower branches spindly and bare, but there were a few sturdy maples that could be climbed, making it possible for the Monitor to watch the tragedy unfold from on high. Another clear vantage point on this side of the tracks was atop a small knoll. Tobias and his partner would wait nearby, their dirt bikes hidden under trees.

At noon, Hank Baylis loaded his two slavering German Shepherds into his pick-up. Weapons of mass destruction, he called them. Take your arm off just for sport. He returned twenty minutes later to supervise the last few hours of the afternoon shift and wish his workers a Happy New Year. As Baylis's last man punched out, two of Carolyn's team arrived with T-Rex, the force's formidable canine. If anyone was still lurking on the property, T-Rex would find him.

The rest of the police arrived at nightfall, headlight beams cutting through gray plumes of fog. Tobias and Heath made their way into the woods, equipped with thermoses, binoculars, rain suits, and sheets of plastic to sit on. They intended another sweep through the area before settling down in the hollow.

Directly behind the security hut which guarded the entrance to the yard was the largest building on the property. Carolyn and the others headed for it. Inside was the workers' lunchroom, handsomely decorated with a forklift, an array of lethal-looking cutters, some crowbars, hammers and industrial-sized magnets. The building also housed Baylis's small office which consisted of a battered oak desk and a wall of mismatched cabinets. Scraps of paper were thumb-tacked to the walls—phone numbers, business cards, a faded photograph of Baylis with his dogs. Adjoining the office was a grungy two-piece bathroom which Carolyn hurried toward. It would be a long night.

Two cops, Rossi and Kozell, would remain in the building with T-Rex. The Monitor might make an appearance here, hunker down out of the weather, intending to watch from a window while his trio of despondent puppets gathered by the tracks for their swan song.

From inside the building, the officers had the best view of any cars approaching the yard from the road. Another cop, nicknamed Sniper Joe, had already climbed a set of iron stairs and was in position high atop Baylis's shredder. Patrol officers in the area were on stand-by; if by some fluke the Monitor managed to flee the scene, they were prepared to pursue.

"Showtime, C.L.," Ziggy said when Carolyn emerged from the bathroom.

Carolyn swiped imaginary insects from her clothes. "I feel like you should hose me down. I know I wasn't the only living thing in there."

Ziggy hazarded a cautious smile then gave a slight nod. Time to boogie.

In stealthy silence, they crept across the yard, glancing forward, backward, sideways through the mist, alert for any movement, anything not quite right. It would be hours before Dementia and Dark Victory appeared, but the Monitor's schedule was less predictable. Carolyn suspected he would arrive in plenty of time to get into position, drink a toast, immerse himself in the delicious build-up before the grand finale. Before slipping into the car, Carolyn stole a glance at the place where chaos would be unleashed. The tracks lay barely two hundred feet ahead, a good ten-to fifteen-second sprint away, Ziggy had said. A decent shot with a wedge. Still, it looked so isolated, so ... unprotected. And suffocated by a layer of dense fog. She reminded herself that nothing would happen, that she wouldn't be tied up, that the Monitor would be in cuffs well before midnight.

She had already disengaged the car's dome light. They entered, with Ziggy sliding into the driver's seat. They left the doors partially open.

Tobias and Heath were in place, Toby complaining about the cold and that the misty conditions were making his hair frizz. "You two kids behave yourselves," Toby whispered into his radio. "And Happy New Year."

Ziggy was already unscrewing the top off a thermos of coffee.

"Not the kind of New Year's Eve you pictured, I'll bet," Carolyn whispered, settling in for a long wait.

He shrugged. "Could be worse. I could be stuck in that hollow with Toby. Did you smell the garlic on him? Gotta make a rule, C.L. No Caesar salad before a stake-out."

"Good to know I smell better than Toby." She feigned an annoyed sidelong glance. "Ilona must be ready to brain you for becoming a cop. Did you two have plans for tonight?"

"We're not much for the razzamatazz of New Year's Eve. When I left the house earlier, she and Amanda were spreading out jigsaw-puzzle pieces on the dining-room table. They'll be fine. And so will I. You look better than Toby, too." He passed the thermos over.

"Thanks. I think."

"How about you, C.L.? Any plans for tonight?"

"George Clooney called, but I turned him down flat."

"You did, huh?"

"You know, Zig, once you've been to one of those villas on Lake Como, you've been to 'em all."

"Did you tell him that?"

"Gently."

"Atta girl."

They were quiet for a while, listening to the night's stillness. Even the crickets and rats had abandoned this place, the silence broken only by Ziggy's occasional gulps of coffee. Then Rossi's voice came over the radio, signaling that all was quiet in the building, too. It was ten o'clock.

"Least there's some starlight," Ziggy said, looking up.

Carolyn craned her neck to look beyond the behemoth shredder that dwarfed their car on her side, but Ziggy seemed to have a better seat for stargazing. She saw only black sky, with a few violet clouds tracing narrow fingers across a gibbous moon.

"Look over there." Ziggy pointed to a derelict vehicle off to his left. Its chassis was intact, an orangey-brown sculpture of what was once someone's prized muscle car. "Barracuda. My dad had one. Felt like hot shit when he let me drive it."

"I can picture you now, cruising the streets on a summer night, scouting for chicks."

Ziggy smiled, lost for the moment in a memory then he said, "Ever done it in a car, C.L.?"

"Beg pardon?"

"You can tell me. It's just us here."

"No, Zig, I've never done it in a car." But as a police officer, she'd surprised a few couples who had.

"Not a lot of room to maneuver and it's pretty frantic, what with always thinking that someone's going to catch you at it, but I tell you, I have some good memories of those teenage years."

"Ever tell Ilona about your backseat conquests?"

"Are you kidding? Ilona was my Barracuda girl." He smiled again.

Carolyn sighed, envying Ziggy his memories and that he was still with the person who shared those memories. She wondered how often he and Ilona reminisced about their dating years and whether the sight of that rusty Barracuda would bring the same goofy smile to Ilona's face.

After a time, Ziggy said, "It's too quiet in here. Everything okay?"

Carolyn nodded. "Why do you ask?"

"You don't seem yourself lately. Kind of ... withdrawn. Maybe a little sad. Wondered if you were becoming a little too much like Fading Away."

"Well, let me see. It's New Year's Eve. We've got a killer preying on the vulnerable. My ex is about to have another kid he doesn't want, a kid I would kill to have, and me—instead of going home to a nice warm family when this is over—"

Ziggy cut in. "What about adopting?"

"I'm kind of old-fashioned, Zig. I'd like the husband to go along with the kid. Can't take the Catholic out of the girl, I guess."

"It'll all work out, C.L.," he said and reached for her hand. "You deserve the best."

Carolyn felt a squeeze before Ziggy released her hand. She wondered where he had gathered the data to form his conclusion. Maybe she deserved exactly what she got.

More minutes passed, with Carolyn trying not to project into the coming year and what it would or would not bring. She tried not to look at the decrepit Barracuda, and she avoided looking at

Ziggy, too. Instead, her mind raced through countless scenarios of what might occur within the next hour. The arrival of Dementia and Dark Victory. The Monitor's appearance. The Monitor being apprehended in the woods, at the tracks, or on the road into the wrecking yard. Perhaps a chase, sirens wailing, dirt bikes kicking up gravel. The reaction of the bus riders when they learned they would not be dying. Disappointment? Anger?

At once, Rossi's voice crackled over the radio. "We've got something here!"

The Monitor? One of the others? Carolyn strained to hear an approaching car.

"Guy coming on foot," Rossi whispered. "Looks like he may have parked his car just off the road. He's heading your way."

Carolyn and Ziggy raised binoculars. Minutes later a stocky, mid-forties man entered their field of vision. He wore a black toque and parka and was making deliberate strides toward the rendezvous point. At the tracks he removed a flask from an inner pocket and raised it to his lips. Looped around his shoulder was a large coil of baling wire. Dementia XXIV was ready for his midnight appointment with death.

Carolyn would wait before making her appearance as Fading Away. It was barely eleven and neither Dark Victory nor the Monitor had arrived. The less time Carolyn spent in conversation with the man at the tracks, the less opportunity there was for her to slip up, reveal her true identity, cause the man to cut and run. The scene needed to play itself out. The Monitor expected three victims.

At the tracks, Dementia paced. Dementia drank. He would be thinking about his recent visit to his doctor, the result of his annual check-up and the test his family, friends and colleagues knew nothing about. He would be thinking about the television ads—*ALS takes your body first*. He would be thinking about his disease and how that progressive, agonizing descent into hell on earth wouldn't catch him. Perhaps he was thinking about none of that, rather simply counting the minutes until it would all be over.

At half past, Carolyn finally looked over at Ziggy.

"You ready?" he asked her.

She nodded and reached for the door handle.

"C.L?"

She paused.

"Tonight's the night. We're gonna get the bastard."

"I know," she said, though suddenly she felt less sure.

"Remember, you don't let that guy tie you up."

"I know," she said again.

"And C.L., in case it gets hairy after," he clamped a firm hand on her shoulder and turned her toward him, "Happy New Year."

A split second longer and she would have hugged him. Maybe even kissed him. Instead she gave him a brief nod and smile and quickly stepped from the car.

CHAPTER 55

DEMENTIA XXIV'S REAL NAME WAS Dan Fleming. When Carolyn drew closer to him, she saw a robust man with perfect skin and dark brown eyes framed by heavy brows. He had a wide smile and a warm, firm handshake. This could not be a man who wanted to die. He stood square-shouldered, with no sign of the characteristic stooped, sagging posture of a depressive. Within minutes of their meeting, Carolyn decided she liked him, enough to want to pack him up and send him home to his wife and child and enough to know that she wanted better for him than to be in this place, on this night.

After some awkward small talk, they strolled along the tracks. "Great night," Fleming said. "Cool, refreshing mist. Nice to see a few stars out, too."

Carolyn couldn't be bothered with checking out the stars, nor was she paying much attention to the crisp, clean smell in the air or the way the wind was riffling through the uppermost tree branches. Fleming was absorbing it all, right down to the tentacles of fog caressing the tracks.

"Quite a world we live in, isn't it?" he said, drawing an appreciative breath.

"Not the attitude I'd expect from someone who's so eager to leave it."

"Don't you see? This is how I want to leave it. Remembering the greatness of it. The beauty. Not wasting away in a broken shell of a body."

"I'm sorry about your ALS. Any symptoms yet?"

"I trip over my feet sometimes. A few twitches. Nothing anyone would notice and worry about."

"That's what this is all about for you, isn't it? Not worrying your family. Not wanting to be a burden."

Fleming nodded. "My wife's parents both died of cancer. She nursed them through their final agonizing months. I saw what that did to her. Sleepless nights turning into sleepless weeks. Guilt over not spending enough time with her own daughter. Guilt over ordering too many take-out meals. Guilt over our shrinking sex life. It took her nearly two years for her to get back to being the type of woman she could face in the mirror. I won't be responsible for that happening to her again."

"You've left her a note? Explaining?"

"Yes. She'll probably find it tomorrow."

They turned. Retraced their steps. Talked some more. "Your wife sounds like a strong woman," Carolyn said. "Maybe your illness would give her a chance to love you in a different way. Your daughter, too."

"By watching me suffer? Seeing me lose my body a little every day, and me depending on them for everything? No offense, but I prefer to wipe my own ass." He stopped for a moment, gazed upward and seemed to consider the harshness of his statement. "Plus, I'm basically a coward. This decision, it's easy. Me living with ALS—I don't have the guts."

"Maybe you'd surprise yourself."

He shot her a cross look. "And maybe you should just support me. I thought that's what we were supposed to do. Be there for each other. I don't see you changing your mind and running home."

"I have no one to run home to," Carolyn said, the words slipping out easily.

"From your last posts, it sounds like you've been in a lot of pain."

She nodded. No problem admitting that.

Fleming checked his watch. "I hope Dark Victory gets here soon. It'll take me a while to get us tied together." He proudly recited a boy scout's list of the loops, hitches and bends he planned to use to anchor them to each other and the tracks. Nice and tight. It would take a master magician to escape. “You want to be in the middle?”

“Sure,” Carolyn said quickly before she could think about it too much. “A rose between two thorns, as they say.”

The two continued to pace a length of the track, with Fleming talking lovingly about his wife and daughter while Carolyn’s gaze darted from the wrecking yard to the building to the fog-enshrouded woods opposite. She was conscious of eyes upon her—Ziggy’s, from the darkness of the car; Sniper Joe, from on top of the shredder; more eyes surveying the scene from the building and the trees.

Monitor, where are you?

Why had no one spotted him? It was 11:30. He was here somewhere. She knew it.

Fleming was no great fan of silence and he did his best to fill it. “It’ll be really quick,” he said, his tone crooning, reassuring. “Especially the way we’re going to do it. Neck on the rail. You won’t have to hurt anymore.”

Carolyn felt her stomach lurch. “Can we change the subject? Just because I want it over with doesn’t mean I need a play-by-play.”

“Sorry. I just sense that you’re nervous. And afraid.”

Afraid? Carolyn had already graduated from afraid and was now majoring in scared shitless. More minutes ticked away.

Come on, Monitor. Show your sorry ass.

She imagined the others, binoculars sweeping the yard, the tracks, the woods. Synapses firing, senses on orange alert. Ready for action. The take-down. Carolyn strained, hoping that through the darkness she could hear the faint clicking of handcuffs.

“I am afraid,” she admitted, forcing herself to focus on Fleming and not to appear like a hypervigilant cop. “But not enough to change my mind.”

“Maybe I should start tying us together. We haven’t got much time.” Fleming slid the loop of wire from his shoulder and began searching for the free end.

“Let’s give it a few more minutes,” Carolyn told him.

Then Fleming looked over Carolyn’s shoulder and smiled. “Ah, here we are.”

In the distance, a dark figure approached from the entrance to the yard, his head bent, his face shielded by the upturned collar of a leather bomber jacket. His hands were jammed into the pockets. As he drew closer, Carolyn felt her hackles rise.

When the man reached them Fleming spoke again. "Dark Victory, I presume?"

The man raised his head. "Good evening, Sergeant Latham. And Happy New Year."

Carolyn's body was ice. "My God, so it is you."

CHAPTER 56

Fleming's face blanched. "Sergeant? You're a cop?"

"Easy, Dan." Carolyn kept her voice low. "Yes, I'm a cop. And this thing the Monitor had planned for tonight isn't going to happen. Is it, Dr. Field?"

Brady Field smiled but didn't answer. He looked at Fleming the way a scientist would study a lab rat. "I take it you're Dementia XXIV?"

Fleming could only nod. Carolyn steadied him by the elbow. The man looked ready to faint.

"Take your hands out of your pockets, Dr. Field," Carolyn said.

The doctor did as he was told. The right pocket still bulged.

"What have you got there?"

"A little present for the Monitor. I'm surprised to see you here tonight, Sergeant. I had no idea you were Fading Away."

"What's going on?" Fleming's voice rose half an octave. "Why are you talking about the Monitor? She was only trying to help us."

"No, Dan," Carolyn said firmly, still holding the man's arm, her gaze trained on Field. "The Monitor is not helping you. And the Monitor isn't a 'she.' The Monitor sets up these scenarios then gets himself a front row seat to a group suicide. It's how he gets off. I'm here to stop him."

Fleming blanched, looked ready to vomit. "You're telling me this is all some sort of—game? And the Monitor is coming here tonight? To watch?" Fleming was hysterical, his head jerking spasmodically in all directions for some sign of the Monitor. For months he had believed in the myth of a grandmotherly Samaritan, with her endless litany of 'dears' and 'I'm there for you's'. The myth had just been shattered. "I don't understand any of this. It can't be true. It's not possible. No-no-no."

"The sergeant is right—Dan, is it? The Monitor enjoys death. Gleans energy from it. He'll be here. In fact, he's already arrived." Field smiled at Carolyn.

"Yes. He has." Carolyn released her hold of Dan Fleming's arm, her stare flitting from Field's smiling face to the bulge in his jacket.

Off in the distance, Carolyn heard the rumbling of a train. Dance music. The sounds of celebration.

"What happens to me now?" Fleming cried. "I can't just go home! It can't end like this!"

"Calm down, Mr. Fleming," Carolyn said, her stare at Field never wavering. "Everything will be all right. We'll see that you get the help you need. I won't let the Monitor hurt you. And you'll cooperate fully, won't you, Dr. Field."

Brady Field's eyes widened. "Cooperate? You think I'm the Monitor?"

"It's over, Dr. Field." She reached into her own pocket for handcuffs.

"You've got it all wrong, Sergeant. I'm here to catch the son of a bitch. Nobody fucks around with my message board and gets away with it."

The Coastal Dinner Train rumbled closer. Over Field's shoulder, Carolyn could see the single beam headlight moving relentlessly toward them.

"Give it up, Dr. Field," she said, her voice raised above the clatter and clack of wheels against rails.

"I'm telling you, I'm not the guy!" Field shouted. "He's the bastard you're looking for!" With electric speed, Brady Field reached into his pocket and pointed a gun square between Fleming's eyes.

Dementia XXIV, pale before, went ghost-white.

"Oh God, Field! Drop the gun! Drop the—"

A shot rang out.

And still the train came.

Field collapsed. Carolyn sunk to her knees at his side. Ziggy raced across the yard. Rossi and Kozell sprinted from the building.

Someone shouted, "Ambulance on its way!" Toby and Heath scrambled out of the woods and crossed the tracks, heading toward the rest.

Sniper Joe was there too, shouting. "I had to do it, C.L.! He could have killed you!"

Everybody screaming at once, surrounding Field, searching for a pulse that wasn't there.

"You okay, C.L.?"

"What was the bastard thinking?"

"Was he the Monitor?"

"He's gone!"

"Ah, fuck me!"

Followed by a louder, full-of-panic "No!"

Carolyn leaped from her crouch, her hands closing on air as Dementia XXIV bolted for the tracks. The train roared. Carolyn lunged forward and slammed hard onto the ground. She managed to grab Fleming by the ankles, but the man fell across the rails. There was an awful falsetto screeching of brakes but too late. The train barreled over him, leaving Carolyn grasping a pair of hiking boots attached to nothing.

CHAPTER 57

THERE SHOULD HAVE BEEN THREE.

What had taken place instead was unacceptable. Unthinkable. Unforgiveable.

The Monitor had arrived at ten o'clock. He had driven his Vespa up a gravel road, passing only two houses, one belonging to a cheese farmer, the other to a retired florist. Both places were in lights-out mode, their occupants either out for the evening or not interested in staying awake to watch the ball drop in Times Square.

He parked his scooter off the shoulder behind the dense cover of a copse of evergreens. From here, it was a short journey through a woodsy patch of land then across the paved road that ran parallel to the route he'd taken. Like his protégés, he had clad himself entirely in black, a fitting, funereal uniform. He moved, hushed as a lover's whisper, through the trees, drawing closer to the location he had surveyed and deemed most suitable weeks ago.

He was traveling light, carrying only a flat artist's brush and a tube of fluorescent paint in his jacket pocket, a Swiss Army knife for emergencies, and of course, his night vision binoculars. No accident that his Night Scouts were called "Smart" binoculars—they did everything but lasso prey. His had a feature that would allow him to lock onto a subject then zoom in for a better view. The lenses were fully multi-coated for optimum light transmission. And if there was no light to amplify, an infrared illuminator would cut through the darkness. Expensive options. Worth every cent. He didn't want to miss a thing. From where he intended to sit, he should be able to see blood spatter.

He reached the main road and hurried across, minutes away from his destination, a large Oregon white oak, one of the few deciduous species in these woods. And got his first sense that something was amiss.

Ahead, in the hollow—*his* hollow—he caught a glimmer of something. A flicker. The merest dot of orange. He stopped cold. Froze. Fumbled for the carrying case that contained his binoculars and undid the snap, keenly conscious of how the click amplified in the night silence.

There were two of them. Sitting close together on a blanket or tarp. Gay lovers, was his initial thought, the one on the right lighting up a cigarette. He was being careful to shield the flame in his cupped hands, to inhale with his head bent. Why so wary?

Cops.

The one on the left was speaking into a transmitter.

Run. *Run-run-run*, his body was telling him. There could be more behind him, coming from the road, closing in.

Yet he stayed. He hid. He watched.

He took shallow breaths, waited until the non-smoking cop spoke into the transmitter again before daring to move to one side and sink to his knees behind a tree. He swore he could almost smell the tobacco smoke as the other cop exhaled then he realized his senses couldn't be that acute. Or perhaps they were.

That being true, he should have been able to determine where he had gone wrong, how he had been discovered, and what it was that had drawn the police to this place. Had one of the bus riders changed his mind? Developed an attack of conscience, chosen to hope for better things in the coming year? Had one of them decided to save the others by calling the police, aborting the mission?

And such a good mission it was. Now it would be a debacle of a different sort, but one from which he was determined to emerge unscathed. Whatever would transpire between now and midnight would take place ahead of him, at the tracks. He could still watch, still learn, still revise and improve. Still leave his mark. He simply had to remain undiscovered for the next hour. And hope that whoever else was part of this surveillance wasn't behind him, with cuffs waiting.

His thighs cramped and his knees were soaked. He silently cursed whoever had ruined this night for him, but he kept his anger in check. He needed to think clearly, to observe with the canny shrewdness of a nocturnal predator.

Time passed and the smoking cop squirmed in place, rose to a crouch. Then a cautious stand. He peered about, alert, then he walked over to a clearing and relieved himself against the exact tree that the Monitor intended to climb. The Monitor inhaled, wondering if the soft breeze would send a whiff of urine through the trees. He used the faint sound of the cop's peeing to shift his own position. He sat, heels tucked close to his body, elbows resting on his sodden knees, binoculars still raised.

It had to be one of the newcomers, he decided, thinking of who could have betrayed him. Dark Victory and Dementia XXIV were recent posters; Fading Away had introduced herself to the site on December third. A mental note—neophytes would no longer be allowed to catch the bus, not until they'd been members for at least six months. He had been too eager. His fault. Never again.

What happened after that was a horrendous blur, horrendous because it lacked detail, it lacked nuance, it lacked art. It was nothing more than a chaotic flurry, a movie clip that failed to titillate, failed to intrigue.

Over by the tracks, a man appeared. Then, from somewhere in the wrecking yard, a woman emerged. Fading Away. Finally the third. A commotion. A shot. A minuscule figure in a frantic race toward the train. The squealing of brakes, so much more subdued than he had imagined. The two cops running from the hollow.

From where the Monitor hid, he hadn't even managed to catch a glimpse of the accident. He was too low to the ground, and too far away. He may as well have been at home, watching the news on television.

The night would not be a complete loss. He had learned something useful. Fading Away's demeanor said it all. The way she interacted with the others and took charge of the scene. She was a cop.

For some minutes, The Monitor took advantage of the frenzy near the tracks to walk calmly over to the tree the mongrel cop had pissed on and remove his paint brush from his pocket.

CHAPTER 58

Carolyn felt that a sadist with a scalpel had scraped her insides raw. The churning, burning feeling she had felt for most of the night eventually subsided. There was nothing more to come up. Her throat felt scoured raw as well, hoarse from repeating her witness statements to the chief, the Internal Affairs rep, the High Risk Response Team sergeant. Her jaw, which had been clenched for hours, was slack now, but the palms of her hands, her fingertips, still tingled and ached with the tactile memory of grabbing onto Fleming and pulling, pulling.

She remembered Ziggy's voice. "Let 'im go, C.L.," and his hands gently prying hers away from Fleming's bloody ankles. She remembered screams. And crying. And the sounds of people in the distance retching on the ground. There were sirens. Ambulances taking away passengers suffering from shock, the train's conductor among them.

"Interruption on the rails," he gasped, clutching Carolyn's hand. "We always look for it. Depend on those two silver lines gleaming. When there's a break in the shine, we know there's trouble."

Days before, Carolyn had called the company that ran the dinner train. Warned them of a possible calamity. Told them they would need to slow their speed when they reached Cypress Village, to be vigilant.

The conductor swallowed hard. "Goddamn fog. Visibility was shit. And the curve. Couldn't stop in time. Felt the bump under the wheels. Heard the crunch. I—"

He tottered then, his face turning as gray as the fog. A stretcher scooped him into an ambulance. Ziggy and the rest moved down the tracks to where the train eventually stopped. They kept the passengers well away from the terrible sight of the mutilated body on the tracks, herded them further from where the severed head lay. Carolyn remembered retreating briefly to Hank Baylis's grotty sink to clean the blood that had soaked her hands, splashed across her face, streaked through her hair. The walk to the building and back on her own felt like the longest she'd ever taken.

By the time she returned to the tracks, more police had arrived, along with the chief who was separating the officers at the scene. Sniper Joe was made to surrender his weapon, his union rep at his side for support. The fire department was there as well, setting up their generator and flood lights. Hours of work stretched out ahead of them.

Brady Field's body went straight to the morgue. Fleming's too, except that his was in six pieces.

Fallon McBride pressed through the throng of hysterical passengers, looking for passengers' reactions to the disaster that had ushered in the new year.

The sun was up now but hidden behind a blanket of charcoal clouds. In the chief's office, Carolyn refused coffee and balked at her superior's advice that she should eat something. A few sticky pastries sat untouched in a cardboard box on his desk. "Hopefully, McBride will put a positive spin on this," the chief said. He was no fan of the *Examiner's* reporter.

"How can she, Chief? Two men are dead, and we were right there. You know there's nothing Fallon loves more than a good police barbecue, with our flesh sizzling on the grill."

"You're forgetting, we got the web freak. Field is dead. The case is closed."

"But Fleming ... I had him, Chief." She held up her hands. "And I let him go."

"To tend to an injured man. A natural reaction. And when Fleming started to run, what choice did you have? To stop him, you'd have had to shoot him. Either way, he was going down. You're not responsible for his death. Not for a millisecond."

But she was. In Chula Vista, a wife and daughter would greet the coming year wearing black. Because Carolyn hadn't planned for every eventuality. She had been so intent on capturing the Monitor, she hadn't allowed for the simple reality that another player in the scenario might still be determined to make his date with a train.

"Last chance on the danish," the chief said, nudging the box in her direction.

She shook her head.

"Then go home, clean yourself up, get some rest. Matter of fact, you've got some days coming. Why not take 'em? First, get somebody to check out that chin of yours. Looks like hamburg."

Carolyn left the chief's office, knowing her scraped chin was the absolute least of her problems. Her clothes were still covered in Fleming's blood. As she made her way down the corridor to her own office, a chorus of voices sang out. "You did great out there, C.L. The bastard's dead." Applause. Pats on the back. A few more "way to go's."

Yet even as she listened to the congratulations of her peers, Carolyn could still hear Field's voice resounding in her ears, overriding the others.

I'm telling you, I'm not the guy.

CHAPTER 59

By noon on New Year's Day, Sergeant Carolyn Latham's face and name had gone national. After posing as the suicidal Fading Away, the sergeant had lured an Internet killer into a trap, one from which he did not escape. To the profound sadness and regret of the police department, there was an additional casualty, the victim's name being withheld until next-of-kin had been notified. On CNN, a reporter described the tragedy of the victim's death as being an unfortunate product of a much greater war and that his escape from the sergeant's grasp was a sad commentary on the man's determination to hasten his death. In Atlanta, Rebecca Holland, the Internet killer's widow, was unavailable for comment.

The Monitor clicked off his television.

For the next few days, he would be unavailable as well. He had matters to attend to. It would have been simpler to disappear—the police thought they'd killed their man, after all. Easy enough for the Monitor to resurface elsewhere using a different online nick. But like the ever intrusive, oh-so-clever Sergeant Latham, the Monitor didn't intend to fade away.

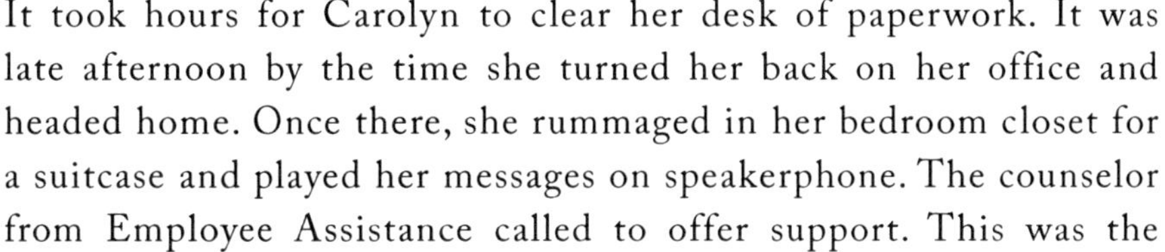

It took hours for Carolyn to clear her desk of paperwork. It was late afternoon by the time she turned her back on her office and headed home. Once there, she rummaged in her bedroom closet for a suitcase and played her messages on speakerphone. The counselor from Employee Assistance called to offer support. This was the second major traumatic incident Carolyn had endured on the job within the period of a year. It certainly couldn't hurt to come in and talk things out.

She imagined how that would go. How am I coping? For starters, my body is turning against me. I've been dumped by my husband. I've been shot. I'm having impossible fantasies about Sergeant Takacs, and I want a baby. And last night I held onto a man while he got sliced like deli meat. All things considered, I'm coping pretty well.

Carolyn erased the message.

Joshua called as well. "I can be there in ten minutes, Carl," he said.

She flew to the phone. "Josh, don't come. I mean it." It took every ounce of her energy to deliver her wishes emphatically enough so that Joshua wouldn't decide to show up on her doorstep anyway. "I don't feel like talking, not even to you."

He protested.

She cut him off. "I'm going away for a few days. I'll call you when I get to wherever it is."

"Promise?"

"I promise."

A minor problem. She had no idea where to go. She reached for heavy sweaters, jeans, thick socks.

North. She would go north. With any luck, she'd find a Bed and Breakfast somewhere in British Columbia where they didn't care much for watching the news. Or she could dye her hair black and stuff those thick socks into her bra, keep driving incognito all the way to Alaska.

She was frantic to be out of Cypress Village, even out of her condo, where suddenly she felt overcome by an inexplicable sense of dread. Nothing was amiss, and yet—post-traumatic stress, she reasoned. And fatigue. A night filled with a horror above all horrors. If anyone had reason to be jumpy …

She found her warmest pajamas, shoved them into the suitcase and zipped it shut. Her stomach growled but the thought of food, any food, made her queasy. She would grab something along the road later. When she stopped hearing the shriek of locomotor brakes.

When she stopped feeling the warm spray of Fleming's blood upon her face.

Her phone, speakerphone button still activated, rang again. She nearly shed her skin.

"C.L? If you're there, pick up."

Ziggy's voice. Calling to see how she was. She couldn't deal with it. She left the receiver on the cradle, and lugged her suitcase from the bedroom to the front door and dropped it beside the hallway closet. Hesitated. Felt a seismic jolt of fear. Tried to trace it. Couldn't.

The voice followed her. "You're not going to like this, C.L." A pause. "We found a symbol. Fluorescent yellow paint on one of the trees in the woods, right where Toby and Heath were sitting. It's a ladder."

Carolyn froze.

"With a broken rung. The same symbol we found at the Aerie and the diner. And Field couldn't have painted it. It wasn't there before the train accident. Toby'll swear to it."

Carolyn stifled a full body shudder, felt her jaw tighten. She hurried toward the phone.

"Bastard stood right behind them the whole time. Right fucking behind them. C.L? Field wasn't the doer. He's not the Monitor."

Carolyn stretched her arm toward the telephone, the movement instantly aborted by the electrified piercing of a thousand jackhammers. She was dimly aware of a scream, her own, as her legs gave way. She dropped to the carpet and stayed there.

CHAPTER 60

"IT DOESN'T FEEL RIGHT, JOSHUA."

Paige had been silent throughout most of their meal. Her words startled Joshua from his own reverie.

"What doesn't feel right?"

"Your sister, at her place. By herself. After the night she's had. At least we can go over, help her pack."

"She was adamant about being left alone."

"Joshua," Paige leveled a gaze at him that he had come to call her men-can-be-so-thick look, "sometimes when a woman says 'leave me alone,' she really means the exact opposite."

He gave his head a resounding, open-palmed smack. "Will I ever figure women out?" He pushed his chair from the table and began gathering plates and cutlery. "So I should ignore what my sister said and go over there?"

"Not quite." Paige stood. "*We'll* go over there."

"I don't know, Paige. At least let's call first."

"I tried her number just before supper. There's no answer."

"That settles it then. Carolyn's already left."

"Or she's just not picking up the phone. Come on, Joshua. Just a quick check. Please. I've got a funny feeling."

Paige directed her best beseeching look at him and he couldn't resist. Besides, he knew better than to question one of Paige's funny feelings. She'd had a funny feeling the night her uncle Spence had died, another many years earlier when her parents' car flipped end over end, killing them instantly. Now her intuition had her spooked again. Paige wouldn't sleep until she'd spoken to Carolyn and had made sure she was really okay. In minutes they were in the Jeep, with

Joshua glad he listened to Paige. He didn't care for the thought of Carolyn being on her own either.

Belmor Terrace was a series of grey-washed, board-and-batten townhouses set into the hillside at the south end of the village. Units higher up commanded higher dollars. Carolyn had considered herself lucky to snag an end unit in the complex even though she was at street level and her view of the ocean was blocked by a shoe repair shop, a dry cleaning establishment, and a pharmacy. Joshua remembered moving his sister in, just about a year ago, waxing eloquent about the spacious closets and the flagstone patio so Carolyn wouldn't focus on what a far cry the condo was from the home she had once shared with Gregg Holt. Now as he and Paige turned into the entrance, he could see that the space allotted to Carolyn's Explorer was empty.

"Look," Paige pointed toward #8, "the table lamp in the window isn't on."

Joshua nodded. Carolyn was a creature of habit. Whenever she left the house, she always turned on the same lamp, even during the daytime. She was never sure when she would return; she only knew she didn't like entering a dark house and fumbling for a light switch. Seeing that lamp burning in the window made her feel she was truly home. And safe.

Joshua looked over at Paige, her brow settling into a worried furrow. Without a word he pulled into Carolyn's parking space and killed the engine. They climbed from the Jeep and hurried up the front walkway.

It was only a lamp, he told himself. An inconsequential detail. Nothing more. Carolyn had been distraught when he'd spoken to her. Not herself. Not thinking clearly. It wouldn't be too much of a stretch to imagine her leaving her home in haste without clicking on the lamp.

"I don't know why we're doing this," Paige said as she knocked on the door. "I know she's already left, but still ..."

She knocked again. "Carolyn?" She hollered through the heavy front door. Then louder, "Carolyn?"

Joshua put his ear to the door and listened, suddenly conscious that perhaps a nosy neighbor might be watching them and deciding that they looked suspicious indeed. Quickly he glanced around and concluded that this was exactly the kind of people-keep-to-themselves complex Carolyn had described when she'd purchased it. He stepped through a low planting of euonymus and peered through his sister's front window. The glow of the lamps from the parking area cast an eerie pall over Carolyn's living room. The corners remained in darkness. Still, from what he could make out, Joshua didn't see anything out of the ordinary. It was a neat room, in keeping with the tidying up Carolyn would do before going away. Speculating about the table lamp not being turned on was senseless. Carolyn had just forgotten, that's all. Paige peered through the window, too.

"She's not here," he said, tugging at Paige's sleeve. "We should get home. Maybe Carolyn's trying to call us. She could be in Seattle by now."

"You think she's heading north?"

"You know Carolyn. She's always said that in her next life, she's coming back as a Canadian. She'll go north, all right."

They stepped away from the door, Joshua with some reluctance, as if Paige's funny feelings were rubbing off on him. He didn't like the idea of Carolyn motoring solo to God-knew-where, on a highway populated with hung-over drivers, and her preoccupied with … well, everything. Perhaps by the time he and Paige got home, a message would be waiting. Joshua was relieved Carolyn was getting away. The last thing she needed to see would be tomorrow's edition of the paper with one of Fallon McBride's lurid headlines screaming at her. Horror on the Tracks. No, Carolyn was better off out of here.

In the Jeep, Paige still looked uneasy. "Joshua, how did Carolyn sound on the phone?"

"Exhausted. Like someone had sucked every bit of energy from her."

"Can you imagine the guilt? She couldn't save that guy Fleming. She couldn't save Yoshi. And all the others."

"But she caught the Internet killer. That's got to tip the scales, at least a little. Carolyn's got some pretty significant hooks to hang her hat on."

"If you were Carolyn at those tracks last night, what detail would loom foremost in your mind? Catching the killer? Or hearing that man's screams?"

Joshua knew the answer to that. Bad news always trumped good. "No matter how many medals they pin on her, those deaths will haunt her for a long time. Maybe she's doing exactly what she needs to do now, getting away by herself."

"This is hard, Joshua, and don't be angry when I ask you this, but you don't think Carolyn would ever do anything to ... well—"

"Harm herself?" He was aghast. "Never. That's my twin, Paige. You might as well ask the question about me."

"Okay. You're right. Let's hurry home. She's probably trying to phone us."

By midnight, the telephone still hadn't rung. Paige took Parker for a brief walk down the gravel driveway. When she reentered the cabin her expression was expectant. "Anything?"

Joshua shook his head.

She sat beside him on the sofa, poured them both a glass of wine and said, "We're being silly. So many awful things have happened in the village lately, and we just can't shake the cycle. Carolyn is fine, Joshua. She *is*."

"I don't feel silly somehow, worrying about her," he muttered into his glass.

"I know, but she's a cop, after all. And a damn good one. She's okay."

They spoke about other things, tried to pretend they weren't waiting by the phone. Joshua glanced at his watch. One a.m. Yoshi's body was on a plane back to Japan, he told Paige. Not suicide, but murder, was the ME's ruling. Another victim of Brady Field, the Internet Killer.

"Is Yoshi's uncle going to Japan too?"

Joshua huffed. "Too busy. That was his excuse. 'Much to do here,' were his exact words."

"That's awful. Yoshi lived with him. Now that poor kid has to make the final trip home alone? It's so sad."

It was. In the silence that followed, Joshua wondered what Ken Ishiguro could possibly have to do here that would take precedence over attending his only nephew's funeral. He speculated bitterly that a blonde or brunette might be involved and privately berated himself for being unkind, yet continued to think it anyway.

By 2:00 a.m. Paige had given up the idea of sleep. She sat up in bed, and it wasn't long before Joshua sat up, too. Paige's funny feeling had returned, she said. Something was wrong and though she wracked her brain, she couldn't think why she knew it to be so.

By 3:00 a.m. Carolyn still hadn't called.

CHAPTER 61

She was dimly aware of knocking, but it was somewhere off in a fuzzy, distant place that she eventually determined wasn't a real place at all, only a small part of her imagination where all manner of trickery was afoot. She thought she had heard someone calling her name as well. An impossibility. Deep, wishful thinking.

A cloth blindfold pressed against her eyes. Another length of cotton sheeting parted her lips in a paralyzed grin. She felt cold against her cheek, along the right side of her body. Ceramic tile. Her hands were bound behind her. She tugged. Plastic restraints, she guessed. Pulled tightly overtop of the sleeves of her sweater. Less chance of abrasion. She tugged again. Heard the chink of metal against the floor. What? A chain. Her restraints were linked through a chain.

She tested her surroundings, kicked out with her bound feet, moving like a beached walrus. She made contact with something. Kicked again. Wood? A cabinet? She kicked backward. Solid again, but not the same noise. More metal. A baseboard heater.

Once more she yanked at her arms, felt pain shoot from her wrist to her shoulder. Heard the chain hit the tiles and something else. A slightly different pitch to the chinking sound.

She willed her mind to clear. Too soon. Layers of murky haze floated through her brain, clouding, fogging.

More exploration, more kicking, her body snaking within a wedge-shaped space, toes meeting with the cabinets again. Another yank on the chain. A minor triumph as her mind connected. The chain was wrapped around a toilet.

She was in her own bathroom.

Carolyn kicked furiously, hoping the building was shoddy, hoping the walls were thin, hoping that someone would hear the thumping and knock on her door to complain. Failing to get an answer, then what? Call someone on the condo board? Call the police?

There's a helluva lotta noise coming from number eight, but no one's answering the door.

She kicked at the baseboard heater until sweat and exhaustion overcame her. She cursed at her neighbors who weren't home, or couldn't hear her, or didn't give a damn. She cursed herself for not getting to know them better, for not devising a system to indicate trouble. *If you don't see me open my bedroom blinds in the morning, call the cops.*

Carolyn abandoned the fight with her bonds, slowed her breathing, forced her thoughts back. She had been packing. Her suitcase had been at the door. She had turned toward the telephone and then ... excruciating pain, an agonizing lightning bolt that flared and flamed against her hip and took the legs from under her.

Tasered.

He had been hiding in her front closet. She remembered being uneasy, unable to trace the source of her wariness, learning only too late that the door had been ajar though she had closed it that morning. Just like always.

She recalled playing her messages, hearing that Ziggy had found the symbol on a tree in the woods. Brady Field's voice whispered through the clearing fog. *I'm telling you, I'm not the guy.*

Now the real guy had her. The Monitor. Where was he now? She heard nothing but her own breath, her heart beating wildly in her ears.

Her body ached everywhere. Aftereffects of the Taser. She remembered smelling fruit—very strong, very sweet. Chloroform. How long had she been unconscious? And why hadn't he used the Taser earlier? He could have zapped her as soon as she'd come in the door, gone for a carotid shot. Or aimed straight for her groin. Why wait until she had her suitcase packed, was ready to leave?

Because it was more fun that way.

And in time, the Monitor would return. For more fun.

CHAPTER 62

Sergeant Carolyn Latham's Explorer was resting comfortably in a remote corner of a long-term parking lot near Portland International. Inside the trunk was the suitcase she had packed for her urgent escape from the hell her life had become. Days from now she would be found right under everyone's noses and the questions would begin.

Why did she drive her car to the airport?

So others would see her vacant parking space and believe she'd really gone away.

Why pack a bag?

Perhaps at first she had really intended to take a holiday then changed her mind, decided to make her getaway permanent. So she returned by bus or taxi to the comfort of her home where she could die in peace. Who really knew why desperate people did such things? Speculation would be rampant for awhile, then friends and colleagues would shake their heads and sigh. *Sad about Carolyn, but we've got to move on.*

The Monitor boarded the complimentary shuttle to PDX then hailed a cab for the return trip to Cypress Village.

"Any New Year's resolutions?" the cabbie said over his shoulder.

The Monitor emitted a casual laugh. "If it ain't broke, why fix it?"

"I like your attitude, my friend."

Of course he did. Everybody did. The Monitor was a friendly sort. Warm. Understanding. People trusted him, confided in him.

"Everyone I talk to has promised to lose weight, quit smoking, do more charity work. By February, all that talk has turned to shit, you know?"

"I do."

"Guess you heard about what happened at Baylis's wrecking yard last night?"

"No," the Monitor said, patting a leather overnighter on the seat beside him. "I've been out of town."

He made the cabbie tell him the whole story and sat calmly drinking a cup of take-out coffee as the gruesome details flew from the driver's mouth.

No, the Monitor couldn't imagine being a passenger on that train, feeling the wheels thump over that body. How awful.

Yes, the poor conductor. How would he ever be the same after something like that?

And what about the lady police officer, clutching that poor bastard's severed feet?

What about her indeed. A thing like that could unhinge the strongest person. What on earth would it do to someone who was already in chronic pain, had been dumped by her husband and wanted a child? Her suicide would surprise no one.

The Monitor guessed that much of Fading Away's story had been true. Sergeant Latham had seduced him with the truth. He just hadn't seen her coming. Then again, she hadn't seen him coming either. He smiled.

"It was all over the television today," the cabbie continued. "An Internet killer. At least the police caught the son of a bitch. The one that made all those people die."

The Monitor forced a solemn expression and met the driver's gaze in the rear-view mirror. "Must have taken some doing."

"How do you figure he went about it? Got them all to kill themselves?"

It was easy to heave a sigh. The man was becoming tiresome. "We'll never know now, I suppose."

He had the cabbie drop him off at the We-Never-Close pharmacy where his Vespa was parked, told the driver he needed to pick up a few things and could walk home from there. He gestured across the street to Belmor Terrace. He pressed an appropriate tip into the driver's hand and wished him a prosperous and healthy New Year.

"Careful crossing the street," the driver told him. "Plenty of liquored-up sonsabitches out late at night."

As soon as the taxi disappeared over the dark horizon, the Monitor climbed on his scooter, hefted the leather bag over his shoulder and drove across to the visitor's parking lot. He angled the Vespa between two vans. On foot, he circled around behind the first tier of units and let himself into number eight using the sergeant's back door key. Briefly he was tempted to call out, "Hey baby, miss me?" but he caught himself. It wouldn't do to succumb to arrogance or theatrics. He must keep a level head. Steady on.

Soon, he would have his own suitcases packed and be back at the airport. Nothing would prevent that, especially not Sergeant Carolyn Latham. He checked his watch. The chloroform should have worn off by now.

She was supine on the tiles and facing up, her blindfold and gag still snugly in place. Hearing him in the house made her tilt her head toward the bathroom door. She let out a strangled gurgle, the best she could manage, considering.

"I beg your pardon?" he said. "I can't quite make out what you're saying."

She gurgled again. Cocked an ear in the direction of his voice. Desperate, she squinted against the blindfold, trying in vain to budge the material. He could see her tongue working behind the gag, too. Feisty little thing.

Her efforts to coax him into the open, to lure him to certain iron-barred doom, had been valiant. Borderline clever. Yet in the end, unsuccessful. And the end game was what counted, after all.

He derived a ripple of pleasure from seeing her helpless, this woman whose greatest sin was wanting him caught. Yet he placed himself in a distant realm from the garden-variety serial killer. He had no telltale hard-on straining the tangs on his zipper. He did not possess the desire to mutilate, though the sergeant was now a scant machete's length away from him.

He was, for wont of a better word, a voyeur. An aficionado of the macabre, the grisly, the darkly unique.

He bore no ill will toward his captive. If anything, he admired her pluck. But she, along with the young Yoshitomo Tagawa, was a very dangerous loose end, and that he could not afford. He stood maddeningly still, his breathing quiet.

Was he still in the doorway, she had to be wondering. Did he have a weapon? What was coming next?

Carefully, silently, he grabbed both sides of the door frame and leaned into the room toward her. He detected a faint trace of floral-scented shampoo. She had probably lathered twice, to rid her hair of the coppery scent of Fleming's blood.

He examined her face—what he could see of it—for signs of an adverse drug reaction. She didn't appear agitated, nor was she having difficulty breathing. No spasmodic movement of her limbs. Indeed, she was sparing him the dramatic flailing about that he'd expected from someone in captivity.

Her medicine cabinet held a pharmacopoeia of painkillers and muscle relaxants, and if she'd taken any of these recently, the drug he'd given her would exacerbate their effects. She seemed fine. For now.

Poor Fading Away. Short hours from now she would do exactly that—fade away. He would allow enough time for the Compazine to kick in and prevent her from vomiting the rest of the suicide cocktail that he had ready for her. What other avenue did she have, really? Misery upon misery had been heaped upon the woman's shoulders—broken heart, broken body, broken spirit. A new year was a time for looking forward, for affecting change. Yet she would know that some things never changed. Some things never got better. Family and colleagues would sigh. They should have seen it coming.

Could she sense him now, hovering so near? Could she feel his warm breath on her upturned cheek?

He leaned closer still and cleared his throat. Watched her flinch. Smiled.

"Sorry," he said gently near her ear. "Did I startle you?"

From behind the tightly bound gag, he heard a slight whimper.

"You're curious, I suppose. Despite your fear, you're curious. Am I right?"

She nodded.

"Of course you'd agree. You're not in a position to do much else, are you?"

An almost imperceptible head shake. Ear straining toward him, just for a moment. Trying to identify his voice.

"I'd be willing to satisfy your curiosity somewhat. Remove your gag. Have a civilized conversation. That would be nice, wouldn't it?"

Another nod.

He reached out, stroked her jawline with a feathery caress. Again, close to her ear, he whispered, "Or I can just slit your throat."

She recoiled sharply, her head slamming into the unforgiving porcelain of the toilet.

"That's exactly what will happen if you scream. Understand? Now, will you agree to be civilized? No screaming?"

A rapid succession of frantic nods.

He stepped into the room and reached behind her, feeling her withdraw from his touch before surrendering to his dexterous fingers as they untied the tightly knotted fabric. What would her first words to him be? A contrite thank you for releasing the gag? Perhaps a bargain—*I haven't seen your face. Let me go.* Or the more predictable and tedious, *Why*?

When the material fell away, he watched her exercise her jaw for a moment, then saw the red welts across her cheeks slowly fade, revealing smooth alabaster skin. She had a lovely complexion, and beautifully formed lips. They parted slightly and she said, "You've shown us all, haven't you?"

Flattery. He should have expected it, should have known she wouldn't resort to histrionics and risk incurring his anger. She was a cop. She would try what she thought would work, what would buy her time, soften him up.

"Not my goal, I assure you."

"Really? You're saying you get no satisfaction from duping the police, from showing us just how intelligent you are?"

He sat down on the tiles, drew a bent knee to his body and rested his folded arms on it. "I don't have to prove anything to anyone. I'm not trying to rise above a troubled childhood. There was no uncle who tried to diddle me under the bedclothes, no mother who made me wear dresses, no alcoholic father who beat me with a cane. I was a happy, normal boy, and I'm basically a happy, normal man ..."

"But—"

"But there's just something powerful about watching people die. It's more explosive than any orgasm. Besides, the people whose deaths I've monitored really want to die. I've seen it in their faces. So that's what I do. I help them die. And I don't intend to stop."

He watched her tiny bosom expand with a sharp intake of breath. She gnawed nervously on her lower lip, thinking, puzzling. She was a marvelous creature. Truly. One hundred and twenty pounds of taut muscle condensed into a shapely five-foot-five-inch frame. And she was displaying more grit under duress than he would have predicted.

"Tell me, Sergeant, what was it like by those tracks? When Dementia died? Your vantage point was much better than mine."

She swallowed. Bit down harder on her lip. Stayed quiet.

"No details? How selfish of you. You had the best seat, after all. You must remember something. How those flange wheels sounded as they sliced across his body. Perhaps the spray of his blood on your face. Was it warm? Did you taste it?"

For what seemed minutes she remained mute, her chin raised in his direction, her eyes blinking rhythmically behind the blindfold. Then she said, "That's a very nasty demon you've got perched on your shoulder."

How intriguing. She was interested in him. Perhaps even a little sympathetic. "Meaning?"

She allowed the question to remain unanswered. Toying with him. Was that what was going on here? Playing the cat instead of the mouse?

Eventually she shifted her position and rolled onto her back, bound hands beneath her buttocks. It had to be uncomfortable. There wasn't enough chain to allow her to sit up. Soon she would negotiate to have the restraints removed. She would promise not to run away.

"The five in Washington State," she said. "You observed their deaths from a distance. You got closer at the Aerie, closer still at the diner. Your demons are pulling you apart. You're taking more chances. You'll get caught."

"You think so?"

"Soon you won't be satisfied being just a puppeteer."

He laughed. Loud and long. He studied her face, waited for what he knew would be that magical moment of realization. "I appreciate your concern," he said, observing the controlled rise and fall of her chest. She was willing herself calm. Remarkable. "But you're miles off on your profile, Sergeant. I'm not degenerating into becoming a disorganized killer, one of those feeble-minded, slap-dash crazies who resorts to savagery and leaves a thousand clues at the scene. Everything I do requires care. I just happen to excel at thinking on my feet."

He leaned forward again, just enough for her to notice the air stir. "It worked with Yoshi, didn't it?"

She didn't recoil from him this time. "You killed him."

"Well done, Sergeant."

"You put the noose around his neck, lifted him onto the stepstool ..."

"And let him drop. And I'll just bet your crack forensics team can't find one speck of physical evidence."

"We'll get something. You've already made mistakes. Yoshi's porn. You left a magazine at the scene that Yoshi would never have bought. And his knapsack. It's missing. His book on James Dean. A friendship ring. *You* took them."

"Oddities. Nothing more. No one will be able to prove that Yoshi didn't pitch those things himself. Even if the scene in the shed looks suspiciously like murder, a jury will want physical evidence. Surely you've heard about the CSI factor?"

She had. Hollywood was to blame for the new jury experts who watched too much television and insisted on a full catalogue of hair, fiber and prints. "Yoshi was just a kid. A mixed-up, sad kid. Why did he have to die?"

He removed the hypodermic from his inside pocket and tapped it near her ear. "Because he wanted to. The arrangements had been made, but Yoshi was late for his appointment."

"He was *seventeen*. And Melissa Waller was only—wait. You didn't say Yoshi missed his appointment. You said he was late. *Late*?"

The Monitor imagined a flicker of comprehension in the sergeant's blindfolded eyes.

"Oh, God, he saw it all, didn't he. Yoshi watched everyone die at that diner. And he saw you."

Could she sense his smile?

It was almost a shame, the fate that would befall the officer. In the few minutes that they had been talking, the Monitor had developed a grudging fondness for the woman. She was a brave soul in so many ways. Though he suspected her heart hammered wildly beneath the rhythmic rise and fall of her breasts, he felt too, that she was meeting her fate with more fortitude than an army of trained soldiers. Perhaps she had really grown tired of living, grown tired of her myriad problems and was resigned to ending it all. In essence then, he was doing her a favor.

Magnanimity. His middle name.

"Something else—" Her mouth pressed into a puzzled frown. "You said you'd seen it in their faces. That the people really wanted to die and you'd *seen it in their faces*. But it can't be. You met them on the Net. Those people in Washington were miles away from you when they jumped..."

"I was speaking generally, of course," he said. "I didn't really mean *all* their faces. But I have met many of my ... clients, seen that look in their eyes, right up close."

He gave her moments to process what he was saying.

"How?" she said again.

"Tell you a secret, Sergeant. Just because you've been so cooperative. Those five in Washington ...?" He paused, tried to surmise what she was thinking, how she would complete his sentence.

He watched her heartbeat pulse at the hollow of her throat. *Lub-dub, lubdub, lubdub-lubdub*. Quicker now. Quicker still.

With the deep, suggestive moan of an aroused lover, he said, "They weren't the first."

CHAPTER 63

THE SCRAMBLED EGGS JOSHUA FORCED himself to eat at Marley's lodged in the pit of his stomach like a sack of ball bearings. He'd been distracted, a poor breakfast companion, his preoccupation concerning Carolyn's whereabouts following him to 3F House where he intended to clean his office. Robb Northrup's red compact was already parked along the curb. He found the counselor in the kitchen rinsing out his coffee mug and staring through the window at the garden shed. After mumbling a New Year's greeting in Robb's direction, Joshua headed upstairs to his office and reached for his phone. No messages. Carolyn hadn't tried to call him here or on his cell. Quickly he flipped through his Rolodex and punched in a number.

"Sergeant Takacs? It's Joshua Latham. Wonder if you could give me a call at 3F House." He recited the number to Ziggy's voice mail.

Joshua wasn't certain about the wisdom in calling Takacs or in adding anything else to the sergeant's already overloaded baggage but then again, Joshua wasn't thinking too clearly. He and Paige had slept little, their anxiety about Carolyn growing as dawn approached, and they still hadn't heard from her. Ziggy might accuse him of being a worrywart, privately call him a pest or worse, but Joshua could live with that. When the phone rang minutes later, he apologized in earnest.

"Look, Zig, I'm sorry if I'm being a pain, but—"

"What's up, Josh?"

"It's Carolyn. You don't by any chance have a clue where she's gone, do you?"

"Gone? What do you mean, gone?"

"Told us she had to get away, but we can't reach her on her cell. Said she didn't feel like talking to anyone but—"

"That doesn't sound like her."

"And she didn't leave her lamp on. It's like she left in a hurry."

"Well, given the night she had, none of us can blame her for wanting to hightail it out of Dodge, maybe find a nice hotel with a swimming pool and hot- and cold-running Chardonnay. Could be just like she said. She needs some space. She probably drove until she couldn't see straight then hit the first clean mattress she could find. Give her a chance to grab a little breakfast and I'm sure she'll call you later this morning."

Joshua appreciated the reassurance. He'd uttered a similar message to Paige, and she to him, as they seesawed between worrying and comforting each other during the night. Yet Joshua detected something in Ziggy's tone—a tentativeness, a hesitation—as though he didn't quite believe his own script. He was worried, too.

"I know my sister," Joshua insisted. "She promised to call. And she always keeps her promises."

"Tell you what," Ziggy said. "Either one of us hears from her, we call the other one. Deal?"

They exchanged home and cell phone numbers and Ziggy signed off with, "She's a smart woman, your sister. I'm sure everything's fine."

Again, Joshua heard doubt creep into Ziggy's voice but the dial tone cut off his next question. *Is there something you're not telling me?*

Joshua replaced the receiver, wishing there was something more he could do. He had called Ziggy. What else was there? Perhaps the sergeant was right. Carolyn would call once she'd settled in somewhere, grabbed something to eat. Next best scenario—she had met up with a handsome stranger, decided to ring in the New Year the old-fashioned way and wouldn't call until later in the afternoon. Picking up a stranger for anonymous sex didn't sound like his twin, but then, Carolyn wasn't acting like Carolyn. Why hadn't she called? He refused to think of more terrible possibilities, even when those threatened to overtake his already whacked out brain.

Across the hall, Robb was scrambling to clear out his desk. His replacement had been hired and would be starting in another week to the delight of Wes Bertram, who had run out of patience and was ready to personally boot Robb to the curb. Even Auntie Rose approved of the new counselor. Joshua crossed to Robb's office.

"This should be all of it," Robb said, folding the flaps on the single box he would be taking away with him.

Joshua looked at the walls of Robb's office, at the gray marks that showed where his diploma had hung for just over two years. He had packed his personalized coffee mugs, his desk calendar, an electric pencil sharpener and a small cactus he had nicknamed Prickly Pete.

"It'll be strange to look across the hall and not see you at your desk ..." Joshua said wistfully. "...Hear you calling 'hey ho, let's go.'" Despite the change in Robb that had taken place over the past few months, Joshua still waxed nostalgic for the days when Robb had been a dedicated counselor, devoted to the kids.

From the look on Northrup's face, Joshua doubted Robb was feeling nostalgic about anything. Rather, he was in a mad rush to clear out his things and leave.

Robb tapped the lid of the box. "I like to travel light. It's a new year, right? New horizons. New adventures. I'm really jazzed."

Joshua asked Robb about his plans, but he merely shrugged, gave Joshua's hand two brief pumps and wished him and Paige all the best. He had scarcely put the period on the end of his sentence before he was racing down the stairs toward his car. Joshua followed, nearly running to keep pace, but Robb slammed the door on his Focus before Joshua could even wish him well. With a perfunctory beep of the horn, Robb was gone.

Definitely a man on a mission. Joshua turned and went back inside, uneasy with Robb's haste, his secrecy, Joshua's sense now that Robb wasn't rushing off to a new life as much as he was escaping an old one.

I don't want to talk to anyone, Joshua. Not even you.

The first words Carolyn remembered upon awakening, words she regretted with every breath she took.

While her brother might stew about her and wonder why she hadn't called, especially when she had given her promise, eventually he would conclude that she just needed a breather. He and Paige would decide she was a big girl who could look after herself. They wouldn't think anything suspicious of the number of hours or days that passed without a word from her.

And what about Ziggy? Neither he nor any of the other officers would sound an alarm about her disappearance. Not until next Monday, when she didn't return to work. By then it would be too late. The Monitor hadn't wasted any time in killing Yoshi, his first loose end. He wouldn't hesitate with her either.

She sensed the Monitor had left the house. She listened for his stealthy footfall but heard nothing but the rhythmic ticking of her hallway clock. Seconds passing. Minutes. The sound was a welcome lullaby because she was still alive to hear it; it was also terrifying, because she wasn't sure how much time she had left.

He had replaced her gag, tying it extra tight though she pleaded with him to leave it off. She wouldn't scream, she promised. She didn't want to aspirate her own vomit. That wouldn't be a problem, he had told her.

Carolyn yanked hard at her restraints, reasoning that if she died, investigators would find evidence of abrasion on her wrists, even through her thick sweater. She continued to kick out at her baseboard heater. Surely the metallic rattle would bring someone to her door. Where were the goddamned neighbors anyway?

She tried to kick back toward the toilet. How much punishment could porcelain take? Would repeated kicks shatter the bowl and allow her to slip the chain overtop? Her efforts were as effective as smashing a rock with a feather, leaving her exhausted, sore, and as imprisoned as ever.

Which prompted another thought. Why the restraints in the first place? Why bother with all this? The Monitor could have killed her instantly. Shot her. Stabbed her. Beat her with any number of heavy objects she kept around the house. What did he have planned?

He had told her she wouldn't choke on her own vomit. Why? She recalled the Monitor tapping something near her ear after she'd roused from the chloroform. Minutes later, a pinprick. He'd given her something to knock her out. And an anti-emetic. Yes. To prevent her from spewing up what would come next. More drugs. To mimic a suicide. Of course.

During her few restful moments, she conjured the Monitor's voice, willed each inflection, each hateful phrase to her forebrain. Once more she allowed his words to crawl ominously close to her ear and surround her with their crooning evil. She tried to imagine what his voice would sound like in regular conversation, minus the throaty seductive quality he was deliberately injecting into it to terrify her. She had heard the voice before. Recently? Months ago? She couldn't be sure. She memorized faces, not voices. Fatal flaw.

Pointless to denigrate herself. It didn't matter who the Monitor was, nor why he wanted her dead. She was here, with no way out. Here was where she would die. Bitterly, she imagined Fallon McBride bringing the sordid elements of the story to the pages of the *Examiner*, certain the toilet would receive a mention. No one would know that at the end, she had tried, really tried to be strong, to suck it up and be the kind of cop ... the kind of *person*, that would make someone proud.

She struggled to recall the last time someone had told her they were proud of her. It was Ziggy, holding her hand in the ambulance after she'd been shot. *Ya done us all proud, C.L.*, he'd said, in his best palooka voice. During her months of recovery, she had tried complaining about her sore shoulder, the physical therapy she had to endure, the ugly scar left by the bullet. Ziggy didn't let her away with it. His response: *Quit your bitchin'. You've still got your arm, haven't you? Plenty worse off than you.*

She needed some of Ziggy's no-nonsense, quit-yer-whining talk now. *Sure, your situation looks bad now, C.L. What are you gonna do about it?* And his favorite credo: *We outsmart the bastards then we catch 'em.*

Could she do it? Outsmart the Monitor? Shackled, gagged and blindfolded as she was?

You don't know what you're asking, Zig.

What did she really know about the Monitor? What had he told her? He had said there were others. Before the group had died in Washington. But Carolyn had searched the crime databases, had discovered no modus operandi similar to the mass suicides anywhere in the States. What had she missed?

In the corridor, the clock's pendulum continued to sway, ticking off more minutes. The wedding gift her parents had bought for her and Gregg had a lovely chime which Carolyn no longer wound because it kept her awake. Another regret. Impossible to tell the time, impossible to determine how long she would be given to struggle for freedom, to give up the struggle; to have hope, to lose hope.

Too soon, Carolyn heard the dreadful snick of the lock to her back door. The Monitor had returned. Carolyn's throat went dry. Her jaw clenched. Muscles tensed. She willed herself to deep breathe, as if any amount of forced relaxation would help now.

He entered the room. "I'll just sit with you awhile," he said softly. "I've always tried to be present … near the end."

She could feel him settling in on the floor, his voice, agonizingly familiar now, wafting across the narrow space. She could smell spearmint. He had just brushed his teeth, used mouthwash, chewed a Clorets. The Monitor had Tasered her late last night, given her some kind of knock-out drug. It was morning now. And The Monitor had eaten breakfast.

"I've just spoken with your brother, Sergeant."

Joshua? The Monitor knew Joshua? A ruse. It had to be. Part of his game.

"He's looking tired."

Worried about her. That was why. He knew she always kept her promises. If she hadn't phoned him, it was because she *couldn't* phone him. Bless you, Joshua.

"Losing Yoshi, hearing about the arrest of that Malvern boy … at least you'll be relieved to know that he's not worried about you. In fact, he never even mentioned you."

Oh God. What could she count on now? Who?

"So perhaps we should just get on with things."

She shook her head furiously. Began to kick in the direction of the voice. She sensed the Monitor rising, backing away, though none of her kicks landed.

Eventually she grew weary. And she heard him laugh.

"Enough hysteria? Yes. I can see you've discovered the futility of such flailing about. Face it, Sergeant. You are going to fade away. Your husband has left you for another woman. You are childless. Your body is a scarred and degenerating piece of wreckage. What is there left for you? More painkillers? More days spent wondering whether anyone will love you again? More nights cuddling up to a stuffed animal instead of a child?"

She cringed. He had been in her bedroom. Seen Pookie Bear nestled among her pillows, drawn his own conclusion. The right conclusion.

"Admit it, Sergeant. It's been no life at all this past year, has it? Oh, how thoughtless of me. You can't admit anything with that gag on, can you?"

He was close again, and working the knot at the back of her head.

When the gag was removed, she said, "Others. You told me there were others. Before the people in Washington jumped. Who? Tell me what I missed."

"I'll do better than that."

He reached behind her again and slid the blindfold upward.

Carolyn blinked once, let her eyes adjust to the light then she blinked again. And suddenly wished she couldn't see. The pieces of the Monitor's puzzle that had eluded her for weeks suddenly fell into a hideous collage of horror, an unimaginable annihilation of human life. For moments, she refused to believe. She gazed into the eyes of the Monitor and waited. He would deny. Refute. Be aghast.

He stared back, the corners of his mouth upturned. Enough for her to know what he had done. To know that he was proud of it. That he had enjoyed it. That he had gotten away with it and would again soon.

CHAPTER 64

May 2005
Murnei Camp, West Darfur

He arrived at the camp by plane during the height of the rainy season. He thought he had been well briefed for the atrocities he would face, the gut-wrenching plight of eighty thousand displaced Darfuris who had fled their burning villages in the midst of a campaign of looting, rape and murder that had begun two years earlier. He knew that the camp was surrounded by the same janjawid militia who had targeted the villages, keeping the refugees trapped within the camp, too afraid to venture beyond its perimeters for firewood and food. He had been told about the hospital cots with giant holes cut in their centers to accommodate the large volumes of diarrhea. Latrines were rare; the rain would carry human excrement in filthy rivulets throughout the camp. Stagnant water begat anopheles mosquitoes which begat malaria.

Less than half the required amount of food made it to Murnei. Stealing rations was a lucrative living for the government-armed militia. The minimum standard supply of water, twenty liters per person, was a joke. On a good day, each person received seven.

During a typical month, up to two hundred people would die in the camp, killed by disease, starvation, violence. And still the politicians and ambassadors would come, viewing elaborately staged presentations that showcased Murnei as a model of effective aid response. Existing in a situation of omnipresent intimidation and constant fear for their lives, these refugees were considered the lucky ones.

His role was to set up a program of psychosocial rehabilitation for traumatized victims of violence. He would be dealing with panic attacks, anxiety, sleep disorders and depression. Many of the refugees had witnessed the slaughter of family members, neighbors, friends. Many still screamed in the night. In his first week alone, he met with three hundred people. Only five women admitted to being raped. He suspected the number was much higher. Fear of being ostracized kept the rape victims silent.

Yet amid the stench, the filth, and the relentless suffering, he discovered people of formidable courage. A man who collected spent bullets, saving the metal to start a blacksmithing business. A young girl who acted as surrogate mother to her murdered neighbor's orphaned children. Others who volunteered to teach. Within this garrison of despair, blinked the faintest glimmer of humanity.

Short weeks after his arrival at Murnei, he looked up to find a frail dark woman standing in the doorway of the clinic. Acai had been referred to him by one of the doctors. Her matchstick arms hung limply amid the folds of her brightly colored garment, her swollen belly just starting to protrude. Acai had been giving her food supplements to the children in a nearby tent, her water as well, the interpreter explained. She had no interest in nourishment, no interest in the prenatal information the nurses were providing. One of the nurses had discovered her drinking from the contaminated water that flowed along the ground. Acai had heard about Hepatitis E, discovered that it could be fatal to pregnant women.

He sat across from her, the interpreter a discreet distance away, and waited. Eventually the horror of her story emerged. He learned that Acai had been forced to watch while her husband was beaten to death with an axe. For days afterwards, alongside her husband's brutalized corpse, she was whipped, gang-raped, urinated on. Often during the assaults, her attackers sang. They broke her legs so she couldn't escape.

She begged the janjawid to kill her. They refused. She must live, they told her, to give birth to an Arab child.

Now she cushioned the offspring of one of the monsters in her womb. She would be shunned, the child as well. What loomed ahead for her? To raise a child of the enemy in this fetid, open-air prison?

Rumors were rampant throughout the camp that the refugees would be displaced again, that the armed bandits would come soon and set fire to the tents, the hospital. That they would kill more men, rape more women.

Death was better.

Acai had already been caught trying to steal a knife from one of the men in the camp. She had also entered the clinic late last night, looking for a weapon, drugs, anything to end her suffering.

You are still trying to kill yourself, he said. The interpreter translated. *By starving yourself. By drinking water mixed with human filth.*

She nodded. *It is taking too long*, she told him.

In the few moments that followed, he and Acai exchanged an electric look, one that transcended culture, language, borders.

He offered her words of comfort, praised her strength, her compassion, and urged her to be strong for yet another day. By the time Acai had left the clinic, he was exhausted. He turned to face the interpreter. "I don't know if I reached her. She wants so much to die."

"We do what we can. And most times, it never seems like enough."

During the blackest hour of that same night, he donned a slicker and crept to the tent where Acai slept shoulder to shoulder with dozens of refugees. He placed his finger gently over her lips and beckoned her to follow him so they wouldn't disturb the others. They tried to hurry through the torrential rain, but Acai's crippled legs had not fully healed. She hobbled, limped, moved ever forward, following him, trusting him. They stepped over puddles and streams rife with human waste. Eventually he was half-carrying her until they reached a spot behind the hospital. They wedged themselves between the building and a row of storage containers, the relentless rain beating down upon them. Amid the misery, Acai's brown eyes glinted with hope. With anticipation.

He slid his hand inside the slicker and produced a scalpel, then held it on his open palm. Her eyes flashed their understanding. A sacred offering.

In those final brief moments, he recalled stroking her cheek. She returned the gesture then placed her tiny, rough hand in his. With her other hand, Acai plunged the blade deep into her heart.

Behind his eyes, a kaleidoscope of color exploded in a cataclysmic head rush. A current passed along his arm, her vitality leaving her, flowing into him. He was floating, flying, his pulse surging hot blood through every vein.

In Murnei camp, the security of the displaced persons can never be guaranteed once they leave the hospital. Many are beaten, raped, killed, the population in a near constant state of flux. People disappear on almost a daily basis, their whereabouts unknown.

The Monitor was in Murnei camp for six months.

CHAPTER 65

"My brother has told me so much about you, Dr. Risk."

Dr. Samuel Risk bowed his head like a true gentleman. "Joshua is a fine man. Very noble. With a good heart."

"Which is why you broke it by killing someone he cared about . . . ?"

Risk dismissed the murder of Yoshi with a flip of his gloved hand. "The boy wanted to die. He said so daily in his postings on busriders.com. 'My girlfriend left me. There's so much pressure.' Wah-wah-wah. Yoshi was just an overgrown baby who hid in his room so he wouldn't have to step up to the fucking plate."

"Joshua was trying to help him do that."

"Yes, he was, and it was your brother who led me right to Yoshi's door."

"What? He wouldn't have. He—"

"He most certainly did. Joshua confided in me about Yoshi's condition, told me of his fascination with James Dean and his identification with the movie character Jim Stark. Voilà. Couldn't be a coincidence that there was a different Jim Stark posting from Oregon on busriders.com. I knew Joshua was taking Yoshi to a discussion group at 3F House. It was easy to follow him, just as easy to e-mail him and pretend to be his beloved Japanese girlfriend. I didn't know Aoki's name until Joshua revealed it. So you see, in essence, Yoshi died because of Joshua."

Her brother had confided in his mentor, sought his advice, and Risk used the information to his own wicked end. She hoped Joshua never learned how Yoshi was lured to his death. "Joshua cares about people," Carolyn said bitterly, "and he thought you did, too. You're a psychiatrist, Dr. Risk. When did you lose your empathy?"

She saw the doctor's mouth harden. She half expected him to coil up then strike. Instead, through his set frown he said, "When I saw how readily, how cavalierly some were willing to relinquish their lives, and for the most mundane reasons. 'I lost my job,'" he mimicked, "'I think I'm gay. I'm addicted to gambling. My parents never read me bedtime stories.' It's enough to make you lose your lunch. A country of such opportunity and privilege, and it's populated with whiners. There is no greater sin. If people like Yoshi and ... Nightshade want to die, then ..."

"But you didn't just let them slip quietly away. You watched Melissa convulse from strychnine. You lured Yoshi to a shed and hung him where my brother would surely find him. You enjoyed mentally torturing me, keeping me blindfolded, whispering close to my ear. Face it, Doctor. Orchestrating the end of those people's lives has nothing to do with their wishes, nor is it about some twisted philosophy you have about thinning the herd. You've seen death, you relish it, you get off on it. What you're doing is all about you."

She noticed the faint trace of a smile quiver at the corner of his mouth. "Perhaps you're right," he answered. "Maybe we all have a little of the devil in us. But it didn't start out that way. And I can assure you, I haven't lost my empathy. I simply choose not to waste it on those who don't deserve it."

He told her a story about a Sudanese girl named Acai. Another named Dalila. And Jaha. Men, too. Monyyak. And Poni. He knew all their names. Remembered each detail of how he had aided in their deaths, how grateful they had been, what a powerful bond had existed between them. He waxed eloquent about Oregon's Death with Dignity Act, needlessly reminding Carolyn that the terminally ill in the state, since 1979, were legally able to hasten their own deaths with the aid of physician-prescribed drugs. The people Risk had met in Darfur were terminally ill, too, he claimed. What hope was there for them, their bodies battered, their spirits dashed, waking each day only to greet more struggle, more violence, more hell. Carolyn, sickened by what she was hearing, expected to feel her gorge rise. Her stomach remained surprisingly calm.

"Enough now," he said suddenly. He shifted onto his knees and reached into his pants pocket. "It's time for Fading Away to live up to her online nick. This won't hurt a bit."

In the palm of the Monitor's hand were several capsules. She was certain he had told the others at the diner that they wouldn't feel pain either. But there had been pain. Excruciating, endless, wish-for-death pain.

Carolyn shook her head, felt her voice shake as well. "You've got it all wrong this time, Dr. Risk. I'm not like the others. I don't want to die."

"Don't you? Are you quite sure?"

"I've had some black moments this past year, and yes, I drew upon those to create Fading Away. But I'm not her. I'm not that person."

"Take the pills, Sergeant," he whispered. "You'll fall asleep well before your heart stops."

"I was going on vacation," she said stupidly, her stall tactic obvious. "Why couldn't you have just let me go? We weren't even close to sniffing you out. Why all this?"

"I suppose it's because you were absolutely right earlier." He paused, flashed an engaging, best-friends smile then added, "It *is* all about me."

Carolyn's mouth went dry. Once more she pulled futilely at her wrist restraints, felt nothing give way, only more searing pain against her abraded skin.

"Tell me about the symbol. The ladder."

"*Owuo atwedee*," he said. "Translated, it means 'the ladder of death.' A reminder to live a good life so one can be worthy of the afterlife."

"And you showed the top rung broken because you saw your victims as unworthy ..."

"Judge. Jury. Executioner."

She had told Ziggy as much weeks ago.

"A dirty job, but—"

"You're insane."

He smiled. "We all go a little mad sometimes."

Carolyn fought the chill that shook her core. "The rental car on Signal Hill. You scratched your ladder symbol into the paint ..."

"As the four pathetic little mongrels died. I even gave them a friendly wave through the windshield as they gasped their final breaths. Delicious entertainment, with me sitting front and center."

He emitted a chuckle, a self-congratulatory, amused chuckle. This time Carolyn could not suppress the tremor that rocked her entire body. A thought came unbidden, that madness must be contagious, as she felt her own reason slip away.

"Now be a good sport. Once you're asleep, I'll untie you, lay you nicely on your bed. You'll be at peace. Take the pills, Sergeant," Risk said again. "It's better than the alternative."

"I won't," she replied through clenched teeth. "I don't want to die. I won't help you."

"Consider what will happen when your brother finds you. Or perhaps your partner, Sergeant Takacs. Would you rather they discover a peaceful, sleeping angel in her own bed, or a pathetic wretch with her brains and bone strewn across the ceramic tile."

He reached behind and from the waistband of his pants produced a Glock. It was hers. He shoved the muzzle beneath her chin and forced her head back. "Plenty of distraught police officers have swallowed their guns, Sergeant. It won't be a stretch for your loved ones to think your black moments, as you call them, got the better of you."

"You'll never convince anyone that I killed myself," she gasped, feeling the insistent pressure of cold steel against her throat. "You Tasered me. The barb is still under my skin ..."

"Not anymore. I removed it. A simple matter of spreading the surrounding skin and tugging sharply. The puncture wound on that lovely backside of yours is minuscule."

Carolyn gagged, the butt of the gun pressing against her hyoid. He'd had his hands on her. Probed her naked flesh. She forced the thought away. There were worse things. Much worse.

"Your plan won't work," she told him, slowing her words, buying every precious second she could. "No one gets the angle of the gun right when they try to make murder look like suicide."

"Now that's the funny part," the Monitor said. "The suicide versus murder thing? You see, Sergeant, I don't care. By the time someone finds you, I'll be back in Africa, working with more Darfuri refugees who've crossed into Chad. So if someone should conclude that you've fallen victim to an intruder, it makes no difference to me. And if by some remote chance the police discover that I'm the person who has caused this ... devastation, well—I can't be extradited from Chad. So, what'll it be, Sergeant Latham? A nice peaceful nap?" He gave her chin another nudge with the gun. "Or brains and bone."

She choked back a sob. Swallowed hard, her saliva long gone. She thought of Joshua. Of Paige. Of Ziggy. "Put the gun away, Dr. Risk."

He stood up, tucked the weapon into the back of his waistband once more then ran water from the tap into a glass. How long would it take before she fell asleep? And would her death really be painless? Would she rouse from a drug-induced stupor, struggle for breath as her heart slowed? None of the people she had met on busriders.com had reported trying to kill themselves by overdosing on a cocktail of drugs. Too risky, others had warned. If someone saved you, you could live for years with brain damage.

Soon, too soon, the Monitor was stooping before her, water glass in one hand, capsules in the other. She fought him, spat out the pills, gargled, spat water. Then he held her nose, tipped her head back and poured. She was choking, drowning. She bit down on the pills, crazily hoping that in doing so, she was somehow reducing what would surely go down her throat. In the end, sputtering and exhausted, she swallowed.

The Monitor grabbed a towel and roughly wiped away granules from her lips and chin. He made her drink more water to wash the last traces of powder from her tongue.

Still time for a plan, Carolyn thought, her mind racing. "You'll lay me on my bed?"

"I promise," the Monitor said.

That was it then. She would pretend to go to sleep. Then when he untied her wrists, she would fight, kick, use whatever strength she still had. Perhaps she could grab for her gun—

Carolyn closed her eyes. And pretended to sleep.

CHAPTER 66

Where could Carolyn have gone? And why hadn't she called?

Joshua checked his watch, unable to shake the sensation that something was terribly wrong. From an early age, he and Carolyn had that special connection that twins shared, a bond of intense empathy for each other. When Joshua got pneumonia at age four, Carolyn cried for days, wondering why she didn't feel sick too.

He had read stories of twins, living on opposite sides of the country—when one burned her hand, the other developed an unexplained blister in exactly the same spot. He and Carolyn had no such telepathic experience in their history, but now he fervently wished for even a trace of twintuition, some sign to tell him where his sister was. In the quiet of his office, he stared at his hands as if some stigmata would appear to show him the way.

Carolyn, if you're hurting, why can't I feel it?

He'd rushed out of the house earlier, Paige chasing him down the driveway with a brown oxford when she realized he'd left wearing two odd shoes. She had tried to allay his fears though Joshua saw the worried lines that had etched around her frown. Yes, Paige admitted, woozy from lack of sleep, her funny feeling was still with her.

He removed his gaze from his hands and fixated on his telephone, willing it to ring. Let it be Carolyn. Or Ziggy. Was it asking too much, to just have a damn phone ring?

In his mind, Joshua retraced his steps from the night before. Carolyn's parking spot had been vacant, the lamp in the window off. He and Paige had looked in the front window. There had been enough illumination from the parking lot for him to see that Carolyn had left the place tidy. An afghan was neatly folded at one end of the sofa. A few magazines were stacked symmetrically on the coffee table. Beyond the living room, he remembered seeing an orderly kitchen. No mess on the counter, no coffee in the coffee maker. Yet he was missing *something*. He knew it.

His thoughts were interrupted by Faye Gillespie announcing her usual hello-it's-me from the foyer below. Joshua hollered a greeting in the direction of the open doorway then focused his attention on his DayTimer. An appointment in two hours with a newly divorced mom who was having trouble controlling her rebellious daughter. He had the woman's business card in his wallet.

He turned to see Faye coming up the stairs, a travel mug in one hand, her oversized purse slung over her shoulder.

Oh shit.

He sprung from his chair and bolted into the hallway, nearly toppling the petite Faye as he barrelled down the stairs. "Hey, what the—?" Faye cried out.

"Cover my meeting with Mrs. Daniels," he called back, picking up speed. "And phone Paige. Tell her to get to Carolyn's. Quick." Then he was out the front door, racing for his Jeep and punching in Ziggy's number on his cell.

Carolyn lugged the same purse everywhere, a huge black leather bag that she carried half her house in. Joshua called it her other twin, convinced that Carolyn and her purse had once been conjoined. The purse, Joshua remembered now, the one his sister had paid too much for and rarely left her sight, was resting on her kitchen floor beside the island.

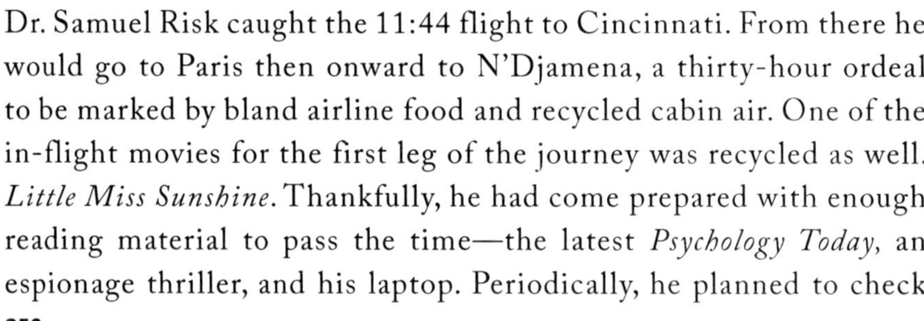

Dr. Samuel Risk caught the 11:44 flight to Cincinnati. From there he would go to Paris then onward to N'Djamena, a thirty-hour ordeal to be marked by bland airline food and recycled cabin air. One of the in-flight movies for the first leg of the journey was recycled as well. *Little Miss Sunshine*. Thankfully, he had come prepared with enough reading material to pass the time—the latest *Psychology Today*, an espionage thriller, and his laptop. Periodically, he planned to check on the news, see what was happening in his home state of Oregon. He wondered how long the good sergeant would lie tucked in her bed before someone found her. She had been going on holiday. Six days then. He had at least until next Monday before someone would miss her.

He checked his watch. 1:20. He smiled. It didn't matter when they found her. She was dead already.

CHAPTER 67

"SHE DIDN'T DO THIS TO herself, Zig," Joshua said. "You know that."

In the lounge reserved for emergency patients Joshua and Paige sat close together, their arms around each other. Ziggy paced, his face white. They had found Carolyn lying in her bed, her stuffed bear nestled in the crook of her arm. She was unconscious, her breathing slow, her heartbeat irregular. EMTs had responded within minutes, minutes none of them were certain Carolyn had.

The doctor emerged from the emergency wing's double doors, his expression grim. He told them he had inserted a feeding tube into Carolyn's trachea to minimize choking. He had administered activated charcoal. Now he would wait, watch for signs of nausea, vomiting, abdominal pain, and determine whether to give more charcoal or put Carolyn on dialysis.

"Has she come to?" Joshua asked.

"Has she said anything?" Ziggy asked at the same time.

The doctor shook his head then returned inside.

"She's got to be all right," Paige sobbed. "She's ... *family*."

Ziggy joined them on the vinyl banquette. "She's gonna come out of this. And she'll kick all our asses for doubting it, even for a second." Then he added, "She's special to me too, you know."

Paige closed a hand over his. "Anyone can see that."

Ziggy had reached the condo first. When Paige arrived, he had already punched in 911 and was cradling Carolyn in his arms. "Come on, C.L.," Paige had heard him whisper. "Just hang on a little longer. Do it for your partner." She had seen tears.

"I should have thought of it," Paige said. "That damned purse. Why didn't I put it together? It was right in front of me."

"But thank God for your funny feelings," Joshua said, omitting what they were all thinking. *I just hope we were in time.*

"She's been through so much. We should have insisted on going over. We should have—"

"I'm telling you," Joshua said, his raised voice reverberating on the cold tiles, the block walls, "Carolyn didn't do this."

Paige looked at Joshua, then at Ziggy who stopped pacing.

"When C.L. wakes up," Ziggy said, "she'll tell us everything."

CHAPTER 68

"IT'S NOT POSSIBLE."

"You were in the room with her, Joshua," Ziggy said. "You heard her as clearly as I did."

It had taken hours for Carolyn to regain consciousness. The first word she uttered when her eyes opened was "risk." No one made the connection. It was interminable minutes longer before she could gather enough strength to form a coherent sentence and tell them that it was Dr. Samuel Risk who had forced her to ingest a lethal drug cocktail and that it was Risk who had scouted out the shed behind 3F House and decided it was the perfect place for Yoshi to die.

"The entire time I was having breakfast with that son of a bitch, he had my sister trussed up like some piece of meat ..."

"He wanted her dead. He'd failed on New Year's Eve and was determined to succeed this time. He would have gotten away with it, too, if you hadn't remembered seeing her purse."

The activated charcoal had soaked up most of the toxins. The doctor didn't feel dialysis would be necessary. Everyone was taking normal breaths now.

Joshua and Ziggy needed a break from the hushed silence of the hospital room and were walking the length of the corridor, their voices low after being cautioned by one of the nurses.

"What do you mean, 'he would have gotten away with it?' He still might. We haven't found him yet."

Ziggy nodded. "I know. But the net is cast. We'll get the son of a bitch."

A Samuel Risk had boarded a Delta flight for Cincinnati shortly before noon. Joshua remembered Risk had said he was going to Chad for another tour with DOM so with additional checking, police learned that the connecting flight for N'Djamena went through Paris. The Monitor would be escorted from the plane as soon as it hit the tarmac at Roissy/Charles deGaulle.

Prior to landing in Cincinnati, the Monitor checked the news on his laptop. It was a small article, scant paragraphs, but it chilled his core. The item mentioned a Cypress Village police officer, Sergeant Carolyn Latham, lucky to have survived a potentially fatal drug overdose. The reporter, Fallon McBride, wrote that this incident was the second close call the sergeant had recently, having endured months of physical therapy following being shot last year.

Risk tasted bile at the back of his throat. Quickly, before passengers would be instructed to disengage all electronic devices, he keyed in furiously, finding a flight to Frankfurt that would suit his purposes nicely. That was the beauty of plans—they could change. By the time he boarded the Lufthansa flight, he was no longer Samuel Risk. His passport, one of a collection he had for just such an emergency, was issued for Dr. Drew Murray. His dark beard was gone and he'd shaved his head. He looked very Bruce Willis-like, a little sexy, a little dangerous, a look he'd been toying with trying out anyway. The results pleased him.

What did not please him was the notion that he could never return to his Portland apartment. He had some lovely antiques there, a few precious *objets d'arts* and a nice collection of first edition books and rare wines. Now the police would swoop in, maul his treasures, and conclude that the doctor who professed to being changed by the poverty and suffering he'd seen, wasn't living so simply himself.

Unmasked. By Sergeant Carolyn Latham. Who should have died.

The woman was invincible. But that couldn't be. She was only thirty-six years old. In time she would heal from this near-miss as well. In time she would grow tired of looking over her shoulder.

Meanwhile, he would recover from tragedy too. He would rebuild. And emerge better than ever.

CHAPTER 69

THE MONITOR WAS GRUDGINGLY SETTLED in his new apartment, a drab one-bedroom on Kwangbok Street in Pyongyang, the high-rise blocking the view of the shabby cottages that lurked behind. The job he landed, working with one of the few humanitarian organizations willing to stay on in North Korea, involved distributing medical kits to clinics and hospitals. He took home a paltry paycheck which mattered little, since there was almost nothing to spend his money on.

For two months he busied himself with the task of setting up his apartment, such as it was, but now his life had settled into a tedious routine that made him ache for the next flight to anywhere. He was weary of a steady diet of rice and soup, weary of the propaganda that permeated the airwaves from six until eleven each night, weary of walking from place to place and being stared at, informants around every corner eager to report on anyone who was dressed inappropriately or sported the wrong haircut.

When he needed a break from vacuum-packed food and state-controlled television, Risk took occasional dips in the pool at the Koryo Hotel. Wilder nights were spent listening to karaoke Celine Dion in the bar at the end of the block. Most evenings, he wandered the streets close to his apartment, his eyes never quite growing accustomed to the pitch dark. Street lights lined some of the main thoroughfares, but electricity was unaffordable. If there were no dignitaries visiting, the lights remained off. To Samuel Risk, Pyongyang was a ghost town.

Thank you for all this, Sergeant Latham.

In the villages outside the capital city, people were starving. Reports of cannibalism were rampant. Last weekend, the rural poor received a visit from a benevolent stranger, one who listened to their tales of how last summer's flood destroyed their crops. He heard about children who had sustained themselves by eating grass. He watched as they walked over frozen earth for miles to chip away at ice to get at the water that flowed beneath. He helped carry the water, Samaritan that he was, and delivered the most destitute from their suffering.

In this godforsaken place, it was the only diversion he had and a rare one at that, his movements severely curtailed by the oppressive regime.

He was no stranger to primitive conditions, but now things were different—he had no freedom here, and he could never go home.

He logged onto his laptop, hoping this wouldn't be another night of power outages. He had installed some sophisticated circumvention software so the government could neither discover what websites he accessed nor pinpoint his physical location.

Though web master Brady Field had died, there was always a niche market for the suicidal and several new sites had sprung up. How interesting. Many of the bus riders were still active and had shifted allegiance to endoftheline.com.

Most of the posters were new, but their complaints were the same old. They were friendless, penniless, childless. They were hooked on drugs, on booze, on sex, on being miserable. They were fat, bored, despised, ugly, preyed upon, and sick to death of everything. Then he discovered a new wrinkle.

He read from the screen.

endoftheline.com
March 1, 2010 15:21
Join Date: June 8, 2009
Location: Bangkok
Posts: 95
Monitor
The Journey Home

```
Swansong, you sound desperate and ready to
CTB. Death Maiden is looking for a partner
to ride with. I'll PM you; peace is closer
than you think. For all of us.
```

Risk stared at the posting until the letters blurred. Then he blinked. A fan? Was he supposed to feel flattered? He searched the archives and found several postings from the new Monitor. In places, the imposter was a reasonable mimic, though a little shy on the grandmotherly attributes that had made Risk such a trustworthy Samaritan. Within a few of the longer entries, Risk noticed the language style slipping. An occasional spelling mistake, an error in diction.

Sloppy.

And no longer posting from the Pacific Northwest, but from Thailand.

Inexcusable. An abomination. Did this disciple, this *poseur* really think he could fill Risk's shoes?

He keyed in a message and wondered which of his alter egos should make an appearance. Shooter? In the end he signed it: Strait Razr.

The new Monitor was skeptical. Strait Razr had always talked a good game. He didn't suffer the whiners and didn't shed a tear over a single suicide. So why now, Strait Razr? the message came back. Why are you ready to take that final step?

My anger, my sarcasm, my bitterness ... are just masking the hurt. I want to stop the pain. Once and for all.

It took more convincing. Three weeks' worth. He logged on every night but was informed that sadly, this bus might have to leave without him. Risk was in a panic. As the Monitor, he'd never turned anyone down. What kind of bullshit was this? A suicide audition?

I just want you to be sure, the new Monitor said.

I'm very sure.

More stalling. More questions. These decisions were not to be made lightly.

Eventually the location was disclosed to him, a beautiful Thai beach. A picturesque plan, he hated to admit. The group—there would be four—would take a boat to the limestone cliffs and enter one of the caves. They would celebrate with a Nembutal picnic and fall into a deep sleep before the tide came in. A peaceful place. A peaceful death.

The date was chosen. Risk booked his flight and after much red tape, cleared his exit plans with the government.

For a solid week, he barely slept. He imagined the unmasking, the imposter's surprise when he came face to face with the real Monitor. The one and only. The original.

Was there room for more than one? Risk had never been a team player.

The five-hour flight seemed endless. Risk closed his eyes and pushed the bleakness of Pyongyang to the back of his mind and envisioned palm trees, pinkish white sand, turquoise water. He hadn't had a vacation in years. North Korea had been a colossal mistake, a decision made in haste. But it had one advantage—who would dream of looking for him there? It was a wasteland.

He pondered new horizons. Where next? Vanuatu? Vietnam? Perhaps the Maldives. Yes. Some beautiful luxury resorts there. It was definitely time for some luxury.

Once inside Suvarnabhumi terminal, he was astonished to hear someone call out. "Dr. Murray? Dr. Drew Murray?"

He turned. And felt cold metal encircle his wrist. Heard a click then another as his other wrist was pulled behind his back. It took ten seconds.

He was flanked by two police officers in snug brownish gray uniforms. The one on his right spoke.

"Sergeant Latham says hello."

Then he looked behind him.

Carolyn smiled.

During the long flight home, Carolyn conjured up monstrous acts of revenge. Her bad-ass, Rambette side wanted to chain Risk to a toilet, croon every cruelty she could think of into his ear as he struggled, blindfolded and helpless. She wanted to force-feed him a Darvon cocktail and watch as he heaved up half his stomach. Her mind filled with wild, dark imaginings—Risk plummeting from the aircraft, his screams at thirty thousand feet the sweetest music she could hear. For the briefest moment she allowed herself a vision of him tied to railway tracks, straining against the bonds that held him to the rails while his legion of victims cheered from the sidelines. Each scenario was no more than a split-second vignette that flickered in her mind, but none quite as satisfying as the sight before her—Dr. Samuel J. Risk, shackled and led off the plane on his home soil. He hadn't had time to perfect his prisoner's shuffle and stumbled a few times, though Carolyn suspected that was contrived. Bruises from a fall might be interpreted as having come from unnecessary force. The Monitor would not slip through any loopholes. Not now. The marshal who had accompanied Carolyn overseas kept a firm hold on Risk's upper arm, a formidable escort.

Setting the trap had been painstaking work, a task that had tested every last grain of her patience, but Carolyn had learned from the best, the Monitor himself—for those who wait, the rewards are great.

She wondered about getting the handcuffs bronzed.

Risk had spoken only once upon seeing her. "You should take better care of yourself, Sergeant Latham. You've lost weight."

He expected Carolyn to react. To be enraged. To call him a depraved, sick son of a bitch.

She said nothing.

Carolyn was at the shooting range. She always doubled up, wearing liquid-filled earmuff protectors over custom-fitted earplugs. She had no idea Ziggy had entered until he stood right beside her in the cubicle. She removed her ear protection in time for Ziggy to plant a sloppy loud kiss on her cheek.

"I could shoot you dead, you know," she told him.

"Yeah, but you won't. Congratulations, C.L. You beat the Monitor at his own game. Your money's no good at Marley's tonight. It's gonna be a shit-face extravaganza."

"Maybe just one beer," she replied. Too many lives had been lost to warrant a shit-face night. She would toast to the Monitor's capture then go home early to privately mourn the loss of Yoshi, Brenda Koch, and the others. And she would hope that those on the brink of despair would choose to get up and fight another day.

"These guys with the egos," Ziggy said. "It'll bite them in the ass every time."

Carolyn nodded. "And by the way? A handshake would have been fine. A punch in the arm even. You didn't have to kiss me."

But she smiled anyway, slid on her earmuffs and faced the target. Then she executed a perfect trinity of bullet holes, two for the eyes and the last in the center of the forehead.

THE END

ABOUT THE AUTHOR

After teaching elementary school for several years, Cathy Vasas-Brown's thoughts drifted to murder, and in 2001, her first novel, *Every Wickedness* was published by Doubleday Canada. It was nominated for an Arthur Ellis Award for best first crime novel. Cathy's second thriller, *Some Reason in Madness*, was published in 2004. *Safe as Churches*, the first in a series of books set in the fictional town of Cypress Village, Oregon, was released in 2013.

Though Cathy has been described as a writer who "shows a talent for great gore," she has a very soft spot for animals (and she likes people, too). Cathy spends quality time with her two cats, Spike and Arthur, and she misses the company of the four felines no longer with her—Sherlock, Watson, Moriarty and Holmes.

When not writing, she enjoys traveling, skiing, in-line skating, playing cards, cooking and going to concerts. She has been known to dance as if no one is watching. Cathy credits her late father with giving her a love of music and puzzles; her late mother blessed her with an appreciation for nature and the gift of storytelling. Cathy's husband, Al, gets an A-plus for simply being the best partner on life's exciting journey.

Visit: www.cathyvasasbrown.com and connect with the author on Facebook.

OTHER TITLES BY THE AUTHOR

Every Wickedness
Some Reason in Madness
Safe as Churches

PRAISE FOR THE NOVELS OF CATHY VASAS-BROWN

SAFE AS CHURCHES

"Right from the get-go, Vasas-Brown's storytelling seizes you like a compulsion." —Rick Mofina

"Vasas-Brown brings us an outstanding baddie—the True Gentleman is narcissistic, psychotic, and bone-chillingly evil. *Safe as Churches* is compellingly alive and Vasas-Brown builds the tension to a stunning climax." —Tammy Dewhirst, thriller reviewer

SOME REASON IN MADNESS

"This clenching crime thriller doesn't let you go. The book grips you so tightly that your fingernails will leave indentations in the pages. Before opening this book, lock the door and keep the lights on." —*Hamilton Magazine*

"Vasas-Brown has pulled out all the stops in *Some Reason in Madness* ... there are enough creepy details to satisfy anyone who wants a good case of the willies." —*Winnipeg Free Press*

EVERY WICKEDNESS

"In the tradition of James Patterson and John Sandford ... there is no shortage of books dealing with serial killers on the loose, but *Every Wickedness* rises above the rest, with first-rate characterization and action. Her style is impeccable, and plot twists and turns mark the signs of a great author." —*Shelf Life*

"The sinuous plot has readers looking out for the protagonist every step of the way and guessing at the outcome as the story gallops to a climax. A very satisfying read." —*The Chronicle-Herald*, Halifax

CPSIA information can be obtained at www.ICGtesting.com
Printed in the USA
LVOW13s1647210414

382584LV00002B/675/P